L&L Investigates
Book 1
–

The Mystery of Priory Mansion

Nathalie M.L. Römer

Emerentsia Publications, Sweden

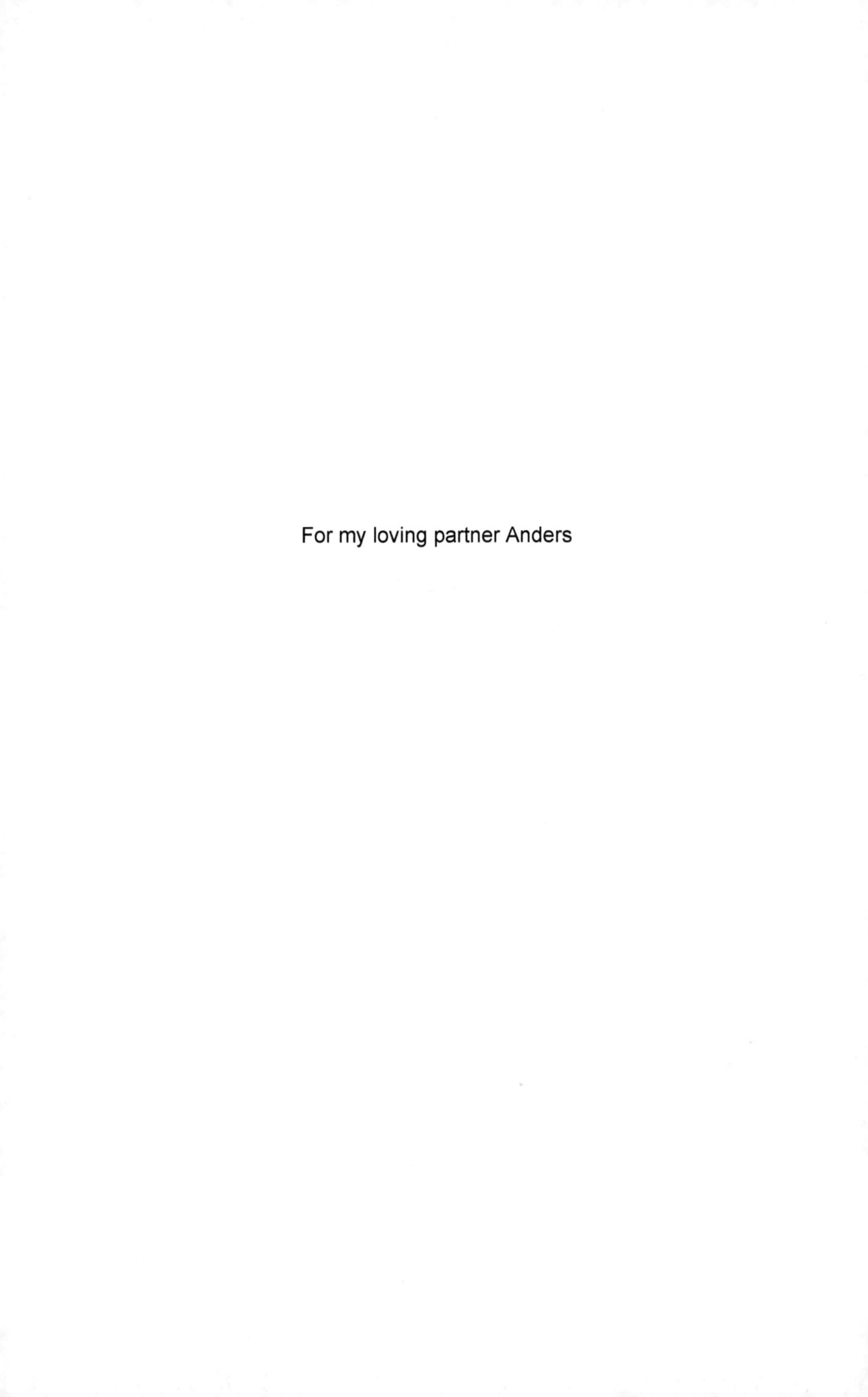

For my loving partner Anders

Part One

CHAPTER ONE

A FLURRY OF PAWS, RUSHING over the wooden floor and then the tiles of the hallway, announces a small, happily wagging dog, and it was the rather pleasant start of a routine that Lucas Cayton had settled into for the past few weeks. The dog, listening to the name Tucker, stood at the man's feet, looking up with obvious expectation and an expression of excitement on his face, then was gone again a moment later when it seems he needed to tease the man as he tried to fasten the dog lead to a collar…

"Tucker, come here, buddy," Lucas calls out, repeating the earlier command of a few minutes ago.

A second, fast flurry and an excited dog sits wagging at the man's feet, this time he stays put as Lucas had attached the dog lead, then the man gets a few licks over his hand as a gesture of companionship towards the human, who glances down for a moment then asks excitedly, "You want to go for walks—do you then?" Lucas smiles when the dog's tail wags faster at the recognition of the words. There was something about how the dog stared back at him that would cause Lucas to smile a lot more. Lucas appreciated the dog could cheer up his mood so often. Even with *that* annoying neighbour…

Both of them, but especially Tucker, was looking forward to the walks. Tonight wasn't dissimilar to any other. He puts on his coat, check he has his keys, a bag of dog treat for Tucker and a can of cola for himself.

He loves walking through the quiet streets of the sleepy village where he'd moved to only a few months earlier. A village with a curious past if he could believe the neighbour. She was useful for certain things. Such as finding out the history of the village, though more often it involved her divulging what he considered being gossip. She'd tittle-tattle on other neighbours, individuals further afield, even certain individuals from the past of the village. She was incessant with her behaviour so much so that Lucas tried to avoid encounters with her.

Even despite the chances of an encounter with her, Lucas enjoyed his walks through the village and in his mind, he was comparing the things she had told him with what he saw in the village. The staple of her gossip was the house central in the centre of the village. A house, he found out, named Priory Mansion. It dated from around 1830, or so *she* had said. They established the village around the house and the family that lived there. Well, until the war, as she had stated…

Contemplating over the things, Lucas walks from the house, glancing sidelong to check on her presence in the garden. He didn't see her so he shrugs and locks the front door, then glances over his shoulder when he's certain he heard a noise from the neighbouring garden. A singular thud, and nothing more. He waits for her to begin her jabbering on about the latest gossip she wants to convey to her relatively new neighbour. It was at these moments he regretted moving to this house.

Then he'd remember that he didn't choose 'moving here' based on whatever neighbours he might have but because he had spotted an advert for a beautiful turn of the century cottage. He'd gone to see it and promptly planned to purchase the dwelling. Even when he'd smirked at the estate agent, rolling her eyes when that neighbour began her yapping. He'd smirked at the way it looked, ignoring that him moving in meant he would be at the receiving end of this behaviour. He decided it was the sort of house he could live in for a long time…

* * *

The dog, Tucker, had come a few weeks after he'd moved in and only by chance. In the window of the local newsagent, Lucas had spotted an advert for someone to take a dog. A further explanation, from the woman answering the phone, explained the dog was previously owned by his elderly owner who was going into a retirement home, and they didn't allow dogs there. He said he would think it over, but only a day later he called the number again and said he wanted to adopt the dog. Tucker was coming home with him a week later, being led to his car, enthusiastically wagging.

Tucker walks beside Lucas, wagging his tail constantly and looking up at him with an expression Lucas only can describe as a 'dog's cheerful smile.' The dog was a worthy companion who was giving the man a chance to explore the village and surrounding fields and not get all this information from a nosey neighbour. This had become a routine pretty soon after the dog arrived. Lucas would arrive home from something, then he'd take the dog for walks. Initially, they were quick walks just to get them done. However, as time passes, and he gets more curious about the village, the walks became longer. Especially after he quit the job. While he was still working, Lucas would come home from work then walk the dog…

The commute had been boring him after a while. He felt guilty for leaving the dog at home, and it made him think more about what he might want from the future. Each day, whenever Lucas came home from work, he would make the routine a bit more extensive. As he walks the garden path, he goes over the daily routine in his mind. *So, I commute to work by driving to the nearest town with a train station, then I need to travel on the train to work*, Lucas thinks pensively, *and then, after a day of work, I'd do the journey in reverse…*

On arrival at home, since getting Tucker as a companion, this attitude had shifted drastically. Recently he'd gone home earlier, and then would take the dog for an hour-long walk, which was extending almost daily now, especially because of the extensive source of information he gained from his neighbour, even if she was annoying.

Because of this longer walk, Lucas now always seemed to walk first past a particular house at the end of the street - not that a small village, such as this one, had many streets.

As he walks briskly, Lucas glances down towards the dog. Tucker wags his tail because he notices the attention being given to him. In response to his actions, Lucas smiles. Then he smiles even broader when he realises that, in a few weeks from now, he could go for walks with the dog all day long. So a few days ago he'd altered his life and handed in his notice. He was going to chance it to get himself a job locally. Then a day ago, he saw an advert for a suitable job in a nearby town, though he'd also been trying to find a suitable job in this sleepy village with its beautiful name - Mellowstone Greene - but he hadn't succeeded in the endeavour.

Not yet, at least…

So, now Lucas has been trying in the nearby towns, and then

finally found a job just a day ago, which he could start next month.

Just three weeks to go until I start the job really, Lucas thinks. *Life goes by so fast really…*

Lucas glances around for a moment and smiles. The landscape, quiet streets and silence made him realise that giving up on the city life felt good. He reaffirmed the feelings by breathing in deeply for a moment. The village, its peaceful surroundings, and most of the people Lucas had already met all seemed nice. *Okay, maybe not her.* He had met his neighbour on the day he was moving in. He noted her to be annoying in a charming sort of way. Reminding him of a past landlord in some ways. Her charm came from her bringing over biscuits and cakes, or a casserole on two occasions; the annoyance came from her doing it *too* often when Lucas was still sleeping. She did it most times on a Sunday - so far - and never seemed to grasp the concept of a lie-in on a Sunday.

Dammit, the worst of all is that she's my neighbour…

* * *

Lucas stands at his gate for several minutes, listening to determine if she'd deserted the neighbouring garden. Would eye roll yet again whenever she'd appear with her latest cooking endeavour…?

He walks towards his house, and after another moment of listening, he shrugs a moment. He guesses it would be at his next outing with the dog she might make an appearance again…

* * *

Dusk is descending over the village when Lucas takes Tucker for his final outing for the day. The routine was so familiar that he realises that both he and the dog are standing at the front door in a matter of minutes. Lucas opens the front door and steps outside, followed by Tucker.

He steps into the brisk breeze of the evening, smiling because he assumes that the less friendly weather would keep her inside.

"Good evening…!"

Lucas cringes visibly, then he hopes she didn't see his gestures. His neighbour, Peg Whitwell, is tending to her roses in the middle of her front garden.

"Good evening, Mrs Whitwell," Lucas says, trying to make his voice neutral in how he sounds. For once.

"Call me Peg," she chides immediately in a mock-sincere voice, "and how many times am I going to tell *you* to call me Peg, young man?"

Lucas smiles for a moment, then sets his gaze neutrally as he thinks, I *guess I could do it if I'm going to have her as a neighbour for god knows how long…*

"Good evening, Peg."

"Cheerio," she replies. "See—That wasn't so difficult."

Lucas sighs and when the neighbour glances down he rolls his eyes then glances down at the dog who wags when the man glances at him. He smiles weakly towards the dog.

How can she make something as simple as a greeting sound so excruciatingly painful?

"I need to go," Lucas blurts out after a minute of standing there indecisively. "The dog needs walking…"

"Sure, sure, isn't that old Dorrie's old dog?" she quips loudly with an annoying cheeriness in her voice.

She gets no answer. Lucas turns on his heels and walk fast from the garden, and is walking on the street only seconds later. He can pretend to not have heard her. "Old…?" he mutters in a hushed voice under his breath. "How can *she* call someone else old when she's an old wrinkled bag of gossip?"

Lucas feels angry at himself for thinking in this way about his neighbour. She'd been nice to him, perhaps a bit *too* nice but still nice, mostly.

Lucas walks silently along the street, thoughts drawn inward, now contemplating over decisions made in recent months. One such decision would become the reason he ends up curious the village in other ways than he's been up to now. It distracts him from the dog. Tucker notices his companion is less playful today compared to other days, so he yips a soft bark at the man. He does it one more time when he doesn't catch his owner's attention immediately. Lucas glances towards the dog. "I'm sorry, Tucker," he says, trying to sound cheerful. He bends over and strokes the dog's head. "You want to go for a run?" Lucas takes off the lead. "Go on, Tucker," Lucas says quietly, pointing ahead when the dog walks for an additional few minutes.

"Go on then, go run." Lucas motions ahead once more with added urgency. The dog hesitates only for a minute, then he rushes forward fast, with his tail wagging fast. He halts when a smell catches his attention, and circles in place for a few moments, then he lifts his left hind leg, and lets go of the content of his bladder. Once completed with this task, he rushes back to Lucas, tail wagging in happy delight and showing off a massive dog grin with the tongue flapping out. Lucas kneels and embraces the excited dog, scratching him over the ears and under his chin. Lucas gets several licks of a wet tongue on his face and hands in return…

Lucas gets up after a few moments, and walks again with Tuckers rushing away once again, sniffing about in places, then rushing back to the man, circling around him with the tail flapping against the man's legs, and moments after repeating the process, except for the occasional times when he'd roll over the ground; obviously to relieve an itch or two. The dog's behaviour brings repeated grins to Lucas's face.

I should brush him over tomorrow, Lucas thinks. *He'd enjoy that…*

* * *

Twenty minutes into the walk, Lucas is approaching the centre of the village and he's in the central road through the village after he turns a corner…

He spots the owner of the newsagent's store about to cross the street, and waves when the old man waves at him. Mr Howey, as Lucas always preferred to call him, and he decided the man was rather nice. Even if the man himself would insist repeatedly on being called Dick, even if his proper name was in fact Derrick Howey. Lucas repeatedly would insist privately in his mind that he might call the older man by a first name whenever he'd lived in the village for longer time. And maybe much later by the name the man seemed to prefer…

In that moment, on seeing the other man, Lucas decides he could call him Derrick. He was now hoping that Mr Howey would let him.

He watches as Mr Howey slowly disappears into the distance, walking like he hasn't a care in the world. He smiles when he realises that the same now applied to him too; specifically in the last few weeks for certain.

Maybe not yet but once my notice time is up, Lucas thinks, *and I can come home on the train from a job for the last time it will like that for me…*

"Hmm, two weeks' holiday until I start the new job," he mumbles under his breath. The new job was as a trainee dog-carer for a veterinary practice a few miles from Mellowstone Greene where he'd registered with Tucker by chance. The explanation of his skills had been simple. He'd been studying biology and animal anatomy at a university and earned a degree. *Well, I can finish that now because I have the time*, he thinks. He hadn't finished it but wanted to convince himself he had, then realised that he wanted to have such an achievement. Instead of the degree he'd worked at the American firm which is how he got his savings and then the windfall for affording the house now…

The new job came with a bonus. They'd allowed to bring his dog with him to work. The job was a three-times-a-week position, and although the pay was *half* of what he'd earned in the city, the costs of living in the village and having no commute had reduced his costs significantly. With the cottage fully paid for the asking price from his savings and the windfall, Lucas discovered, when he took time to calculate all the finances, he was several hundreds better off each month now with the new job and from living here over living in the city. It was a good start for a new life. *Except for my neighbour*, he bemoans silently.

His thoughts turn to a person he'd not considered in everything that had recently been happening. Louellen who'd been his on-and-off girlfriend for almost a decade. Maybe he could persuade her to come visit him at his new home in this village, and if he could do that, then perhaps he could also persuade her to move in later. *Yes, if I can get her to do these things everything would be perfect. I wonder what old Mrs Peg will make of Louellen*, he thinks, chuckling somewhat at the idea of them 'meeting.'

* * *

Lucas has walked on and now turns into the alleyway that serves as a shortcut to his street which exits twenty meters from his front gate and the furthest from his neighbour at a slight curve so she may not see him arrive home. It's a long alleyway, flanked on both sides by gardens. Noticing the contrast between the two gardens was the first evidence of his increased curiosity and he still found the contrast between the two gardens striking.

To his right, Lucas observed beautifully trimmed rosebushes and privet bushes. To his left, he would see an overgrown mass of hedges, trees and vines, intertwined with nettles, and a variety of wild flowers which attract a constant stream of bees, flies, and other insects that Lucas can't identify, and a variety of different butterflies, who attract Tucker's attention as he would run after one, and snap at one indulging itself on the nectar on offer within the wide variety of flowers, which causes the butterfly to fly off.

As he smiles at the dog's antics, Lucas contemplates over whether a butterfly could feel anger, but decides the behaviour is probably just the instinct of scurrying off when it has a large animal near it. His mind turns to the neighbour also scurrying off whenever things don't seem to go her way.

He gives the overgrown garden a few glances as he walks it by. As previously, he wonders who might live there, and why they let their garden go to such a disarray.

Maybe Mrs Whitwell might know something about this house and garden, Lucas ponders. *When I'm finally free from the burden of a job in the city, after the notice period, I can walk here more often, to the end of this street and check out what's here—*

A nudge against his leg distracts him from his thoughts. He finds Tucker sitting at his feet with his tail wagging wildly. "Seems you're getting to know the routine too well—" Lucas states softly to the dog. Tucker wags his tail faster when the man speaks. He bends over and fastens the lead in place, then he puts his hand through the loop and winds the lead around his hand a few times. He straightens up and walks on, and the dog enthusiastically walks on beside him, with his tail wagging constantly.

A brisk walk got them home in record time, and as he rushes from the front gate to his front door, Lucas sighs relief when he notices that Mrs Whitwell had gone inside her house, and there wasn't any sound to show her leaving her house as earlier. *The way she does that feels so creepy really,* Lucas thinks, then shrugs at the idea of him having a weird sort of neighbour. *It hasn't been the first time I had an oddball of a neighbour...*

Lucas stares confused for a moment as he steps onto his entrance porch, and sees an unfamiliar cooking pot sitting there. He touches it, and it's still reasonably hot to the touch still. *It hasn't been here for that long,* he thinks, frowning deeper. *She saw me coming home, and rushed to get it from her oven, carried it through the street and garden to place this on my porch, then rushed home before I saw her...*

"Thank you, Mrs Whitwell—" Lucas says loudly, and he's so pretty certain his neighbour is near enough to know he'd arrived home and found the food. He forces himself to ignore how weird the behaviour really is as he lifts the pot in his arms while he struggles with his keys as the same time...

Lucas opens his door and lets go of the lead. Tucker rushes inside, followed quickly by Lucas who glances from the dog to the pot in his arms for a moment, smirking at the thought of just feeding it to the dog. He places the pot down on a small dresser near the front door, shuts and locks the door quickly, and takes off his coat. He doesn't want Mrs Whitwell to walk in unannounced like she'd done a few days after he'd moved in when he stood painting the living room, wearing only some shorts.

He hangs up the coat on the coat hook next to the front door, then he picks up the pot. Then he smirks with delight. *I could just thrown all its content into the bin...*

He's pretty certain that Mrs Whitwell *would* notice that he hadn't eaten the food... somehow.

I'm not entirely sure how she would know, but she would know. Maybe she's a secret cousin of Mrs Marple...

Lucas chuckles at the idea of his favourite detective somehow being related with a busy-body such as Mrs Whitwell. He stands with the pot in his hands for a few more minutes, then he realises it's actually still too hot to hold, and then realises that he might drop it then and she might hear the crash. He rushes into the kitchen and places it on the kitchen table.

Then his stomach plays right in the hands of his neighbour by announcing his hunger with a loud rumble. He sighs and goes to the sink for a plate and fork, which he washes quickly. He carries both to the table. It causes him to realise that he should really unpack all his possessions. *Especially if I want Louellen to visit,* he thinks as he readies his table for being able to eat, *even more so if I want her to stay for a longer time… or forever.*

Realising moments after sitting down that he has nothing to spoon the contents of the pot onto his plate with, Lucas gets up and rummages through several of the boxes strewn around on the floor of the kitchen. In the third box opened hastily he finds a large serving spoon. He stares at it for a moment, then he frowns at its size as it would make eating an almost hazardous endeavour. It could spill over his shirt…

Shrugging his shoulders at the thought that he could end up having to walk shirtless into the garden the next day, Lucas sits down and after a final evaluation of the spoon brought with him, he pulls the pot of food towards him with an audible scrape over the kitchen table causing him to cringe for a few moments. Then when the moment comes to eat the food, he hesitated as he'd never bothered eating Peg Whitwell's food before today, but then a rumble from his stomach—a rather audible rumble—tells him to shut up and eat. He's rather surprised when he puts the first mouthful in his mouth…

This is delicious.

The food turns out much better than the planned toast with a sprinkling of old Parmesan cheese he'd planned; his usual meal since moving to Mellowstone Greene. He decides on being nicer to the neighbour because of this meal, especially now he knows how well she can cook. If he couldn't persuade Louellen to move in with him he had someone around to take care of meals for him in the most ironic sort of way…

CHAPTER TWO

AS HE PICKS FROM THE meal, savouring every bite, Lucas grins momentarily at the thought of him dictating to the neighbour what his next meal should be. He isn't entirely certain she'd appreciate such behaviour from him, but it would a rather hilarious and good way of rewarding her for being a nosey, interfering busybody that she always is.

But she's not really that interfering. Maybe she's just lonely, and she wants someone to talk to occasionally. She seems to like Tucker too, so perhaps I can use him to get her to open up to me more.

After he's filled his belly adequately, Lucas glances at Tucker, who lies a few feet away from him, gnawing on a doggy bone that Lucas had given him a few days ago. The dog had been grunting as he chewed at the bone. When Lucas looks at the dog, Tucker stops the chewing motion and looks up at him, tilting his head sideways as if he's asking, "What's the matter?"

Often the dog knows before Lucas does what is on the man's mind and tonight it's no different. Obviously something about how the man had been grumbling under his breath, and how he'd been frowning, had amused the dog, so he stares at the man with a dog grin. Lucas smiles at seeing the dog's behaviour…

Tucker yips at him, then when Lucas grumbles more and frowns, the dog repeats his yip, and a bit more whenever the man glances in his direction. It amuses Lucas too, so he makes a game of it. Then, after a while, Lucas looks at his plate as the dog does a low-pitched whine. Then Lucas glances at the dog, and the dog gives a high-squeal bark. The man repeats the process a few more times. Each time Lucas glances at the dog and makes faces at his companion, the dog gets more excited. The dog yips again…

Lucas glances at his plate, then the dog does a low-pitched whine again. He sits upright a moment later, and he gives a high-squeal bark. Their actions repeat a few times likes a game, and each time Lucas makes it a bit more obvious that he's teasing his companion about being allowed to clean off his plate. Once the dog is so excited that his tail sweeps over the floor, he inches forward towards Lucas.

After a final hesitation, Lucas changes his mind about whether to feed the leftovers of his meal to the dog, the grabs hold of his plate and places it on the floor beside Tucker, doing this despite his own earlier assumptions about whether a dog should even eat human food. He straightens up and shrugs.

I've eaten most of it, so a few leftovers won't harm the animal—hopefully…

Lucas waits until the dog finishes with cleaning out the dish, and he picks it up and then rises to his feet and places the dish in the sink, pouring scalding tap water into the sink to soak the remnants still present on the plate, then he realises he got no washing-up liquid at home. He shrugs his shoulders as he makes a mental note of yet another item to purchase. After turning off the tap, he walks back to the door. He'd let the dog out one more time before it was time for bed.

Lucas opens the front door, and he motions at the dog to go into the front garden. He stares around and suddenly the darkness of the area around him feels somewhat unsettling. He glances left and notices that Mrs Whitwell's house is all dark. There's a stillness in the air that he hadn't noticed previously, and for an unknown reason, it causes his hairs on his arms and neck to stand up. Usually, Lucas has trouble getting Tucker to come back into the house, but tonight the dog rushes past him to the front porch, and he stands at the front door, whining to be let in.

Lucas stares at the dog, finding his behaviour unusual, but at that moment he's more concerned about the odd feelings he's getting himself. He opens the door and lets both of them in the house, then he locks the front door, and once they're inside, the feeling of his own hairs standing up disappears, and the dog seems to behave normally again once more. The feeling of his own hairs standing up has now disappeared…

I guess I'm not used to a quiet, tiny village with no night-life yet—

He readies himself for bed and, about fifteen minutes later, his house, too, is in darkness, and the only sounds left are that of a softly yipping dog and the sounds coming from six hundred feet away, which might have been interesting to Lucas if he wasn't so tired or on edge…

* * *

The following morning, sun light woke Lucas, glaring into his bedroom through the curtainless windows. The man rubs his face. He glances sidelong at his companion lying sprawled over the bed. He whimpers like he always would do whenever Lucas wakes up. Lucas realises he's groggy, and for unknown reasons these days he woke up again with a sour taste in his mouth, but guesses this morning it was being caused by him eating the freshly cooked meals that Mrs Whitwell had been making.

After looking out of the window, Lucas glances again at the dog beside him. Usually the dog didn't want to sleep on the mattress with him, but today Tucker seemed unnaturally nervous. He seemed to act almost like he didn't want to be in the house anymore…

"Do you want to go for a train ride with *me* today?" Lucas knows the dog can only understand the tone in his voice, but not the words spoken, so he adds, more for his own benefit than for the dog. "Perhaps a day away from Mrs Whitwell's nosey busy body nonsense will do you good too. You'll get to meet Louellen then. She'll adore you…"

Tucker wags like it's supposedly showing that he likes the idea. Like he'd understood everything Lucas was saying.

After lying on the bed for a while longer, Lucas shrugs then he gets up and walks to the bathroom. Tucker jumps from the bed and follows him closely. "Hey, hey, hold on. You wait out here," Lucas grumbles under his breath, then pushes the dog from the bathroom and quickly shuts the door. "It's bad enough being spied on by Mrs Whitwell," Lucas mumbles under his breath, "and I don't need my dog to be watching me showering or whatever."

He brushes his teeth and relieved himself. He takes a quick shower. Standing at the tiny mirror, and realising he needs a larger mirror instead, he stood drying himself and contemplating over the feelings he'd experienced the previous day and weighing up life from this point onward. As he busied himself with getting ready, Lucas keeps glancing towards the bathroom window.

That window needs an extra blind or curtain on it, he thinks. *Even though it's thick matted glass on the bathroom windows, I feel exposed. Like it's a plain pane of glass, and it almost feels like everyone in the street can see me. I'll buy me a curtain for that window, and net curtains for all the rest of the windows as well while I'm at it...*

After finishing in the bathroom, Lucas opens the bathroom door to find Tucker sitting outside the door. The dog wags his tail immediately. Lucas smiles at the dog...

Yes, I think I have to take you with me. If Louellen comes shopping with me, one of either can hold your leash if a shop doesn't allow dogs in—and that's most of them. If I treat Louellen to some shopping for shoes or clothing, I am sure she won't mind holding your leash while I buy my curtains and such—

Lucas walks back to his bedroom, glances around the room at the many boxes lying all over the floor. He walks to the nearest box, and looks inside it, realising it has paperwork inside. He walks to another box and looks in it. Over the next fifteen minutes, Lucas looks through the boxes spread around the bedroom to find some clothing that isn't creased all over.

In the end, a thin woollen jumper seems the best choice, even though it might turn out too warm in the early spring weather outside.

* * *

Lucas spends most of the next hour measuring the many windows of the house, the doors and also the sizes of the rooms. Not doing anything to get his house decorated was one of those things related to 'being single' that was now bothering him as he grumbles under his breath, "I wish Louellen was here to write stuff so this would go so much faster..."

After measuring all the rooms downstairs, Lucas rushes up the stairs, then repeats his actions for the rooms there, and each time he passes it he stares up at the outline in the ceiling, wondering each time if it was just an outline, evidence of 'bad decorations,' or that his earlier assumptions about it being an old entry are correct.

"I guess I'll have to investigate it once he gets home—*after* the curtains are up so that Mrs Whitwell cannot stick her nosey curiosity into what I'm doing in my home," Lucas mumbles. "Though I'm certain she'd hear any hammering will alert her that something is going on here…"

Best to lock all doors downstairs if I'm going to busy up here with that ceiling, Lucas ponders, *and I wonder what might be up there, and why someone had plastered it over like that…*

Lucas looks over the list he made as he worked through the house, measuring everything, then he shrugs his shoulders. Though he realises, it will be trial and error to get the right curtains matching each room as he realises that the list hasn't got the location of each room listed beside it.

"It will have to do," Lucas mumbles. "I will not measure everything all over again…"

Lucas sighs, then he glances around one more time. It escapes his mind at that moment that it was the same lack of checking things properly that had resulted in him having too short-sized curtains in the old apartment back in the city. He was at risk of repeating the same situation as had happened at the old apartment, during his life in the city, and that two tea towels fastened onto the bottom with few safety pins had become the reason Louellen had always refused to move in with him in those days…

Lucas looks around the room. Suddenly, the room feels way too sparse, and that it needed more furniture, a television and pictures for the walls, and to feel lived in. It needed to be like home…

I definitely got room for spreading out. Maybe this room could be a proper living room, next door the dining room, and that other room an office for something.

He was uncertain right now what the something would be - either just a room for storing junk or for it to be used in another better way - but Lucas is uncertain about what he should do in this moment. However, he knows with some certainty he wants that 'something' to include Louellen, and he sighs loudly. He also realises that this future shouldn't include the annoyance of a nosey neighbour. He feels alone suddenly. The village isn't the best place for socialising, and although he'd got acquainted with quite a few of the people of the village, he couldn't yet call any of them a friend.

Lucas grunts loudly, then he turns and walks downstairs. He stops here too, to look around to contemplate over his situation, to figure out whether he'd been making the correct decisions. *I need more furniture here too to make the place homely. More homely…*

"I wonder what Louellen likes as colours," he mumbles loudly. "Not blue. She complained about my blue curtains in my last home. Well, in one of the last places I lived in…"

The best way to get her to be convinced might be by getting her to look at stuff and decide for herself what she likes or what she doesn't like, he ponders. *Hmm, moving seven times in four years hasn't helped the matter either. Not in the slightest.* He shrugs once more. *I hope I can persuade her to move in with me, and this is my 'forever' home regardless of how weird the neighbours or the people in the village might be…*

Lucas puts his coat on, and looks around one last time, almost feeling fatalistic about his loneliness, then he picks up the dog's lead, fastens it onto the dog collar, then he walks outside, followed by Tucker who's wagging his tail. Lucas glances at the dog and smiles. He hopes sincerely that the dog will be the key factor in persuading Louellen…

* * *

Lucas and Tucker walk to Dick Howey's newsagent store to buy a magazine, and he also buys a few small bottles of cola, chocolate and biscuits to consume while he's travelling on the train.

The elderly owner of the shop had been a bit puzzled to find Lucas turning up in his store during the week, but Lucas doesn't tell him about his current plans, which leaves Mr Howey playing a game with his eyebrows going up and down and Lucas doing his best effort so not to laugh. Lucas convinces himself that the entire village would know of his visit before the day was over, and if he told the man any of the plans they'd be gossiping about that too, and specifically he didn't want Mrs Whitwell to find out *why* he'd gone out. It felt like he was lying about something, but so to avoid problems with the neighbour; he wanted to be silent about it all…

It will all work out, Lucas thinks as he leaves the shop, then at seeing Gylda Simones at her house, he waves at her. After talking with her a few days before adopting Tucker, Lucas knew she's a woman in her forties, and the granddaughter of Dorrie Michaels, who was Tucker's previous owner. He had found out so much more about her and her grandmother that it felt like she was warning him about something that he couldn't ignore after his earlier unsettling feelings he had felt. He didn't want to alarm Gylda and let her pet the dog, and as she busies herself with the dog, she's overly apologetic about why she couldn't take in the dog.

"It's my husband, Roger. He's been allergic to dogs and cats all his life, since he was a child," she quips somewhat nervously. "I'd have a half dozen cats, and at least two or three dogs as well, if it were up to me. Also, can you keep Tucker away from—" Gylda stops speaking abruptly. *It's like with one of Louellen's friends who discovered she's allergic to cats, so I understand about the situation she mentioned*, Lucas thinks. "I understand about your husband," Lucas says. "It's the same with a friend. You could come visit *me* to see the dog if you like," he suggests gently. "I'm okay with it..."

Gylda glances up at him and smiles appreciatively at him, then she nods affirmatively. "I'll remember your offer," she whispers in a quivering voice. "Thank you..."

Lucas realises that he might have made his first real friend in the village, so he speaks once again. "I'm visiting my friend Louellen in the city," he announces to Gylda. "We're on our way to the station..."

"Oh, I have an old friend who lives there. Her name is Lynn Standage," Gylda says. "If I'm correct in my memory, she has a job in a library there."

"Do you know where the library is located?" he asks.

"If my memory serves me, it's somewhere in the north part of the city," she answers, "but I'm uncertain of the address at the moment. I would need to ask Roger..."

"Okay," Lucas remarks, then after another ten minutes of inconsequential talking, he excuses himself and rushes towards the station. That's fifteen minutes of brisk walking from their location. As he walks, Lucas glances back and fights the feeling of foreboding he'd felt earlier. Now, after her so quietly spoken response, he was curious why she almost sounded scared.

Lucas speeds up his pace as he doesn't want to miss the train on *this* day of all days. At the station he discovers a queue for tickets, which seemed odd to him, then he realises that the people waiting were likely from various local villages, on their way to the city for potential events happening there.

When he gets on the train, he looks behind him in annoyance. He couldn't blame the people around him, really. He'd opted to leave his car at a parking lot a little way from the station, as getting out of the station car park could be problematic as it was likely too overcrowded, and as he stared at the people, he was glad of the decision. It had caused a longer walk to the station, but leaving to go home later would be easier…

The doors slam shut abruptly behind Lucas a moment later. He curses loudly and a rather posh-looking woman walking past him glances at him with anger. Glancing after her, Lucas smirks somewhat. *She's way too posh for being on the train, really. She really gave me an evil eye for cursing…*

Lucas looks after the woman with some curiosity. She seems to walk the entire length of the train for the furthest end of the last coach car where she sits down while talking with someone in a rather animated manner. He turns into the direction she'd come from until he finds his reserved seat and sits down with the dog on his lap. He'd let Tucker look out of the window as they travelled, so to keep the dog from getting bored and doing something annoying. Tucker stands with his front paws on the man's arm, and his tail wags constantly as it's obvious that the people walking by are catching the dog's attention. For most of the next five minutes, the platform is busy, then suddenly it's empty and a moment later the train pulls out of the station. A moment after the train sets off, Tucker settles in the man's lap. Lucas grins at the dog when it's obvious that he'd decided that being on a train equalled nap time, and it shows in his behaviour that he'd been on a train before…

I guess you went on the train with Gylda before. I guess she took you on trips. No wonder you wagged seeing her.

Lucas looks at the landscape flashing by at an increasingly faster speed. It's sunny, though in the distance he can see dark clouds.

I hope it won't rain today.

* * *

"Tickets—Tickets, please!"

Lucas searches for his ticket, then gives it to the ticket collector, who gives Tucker a scratch behind his ears before moving on to the next person sitting ready with their tickets. Tucker is still wagging enthusiastically long after the man walked away from them. Lucas smiles at the dog, then also scratches the dog's ears and Tucker's tail moves faster once more…

"Louellen will adore you, Tucker," Lucas whispers to the dog. The mention of his name causes the dog to wag some more, then he licks the man's chin with his raspy tongue. "Stop it," Lucas says sternly. "Lie down." He taps on the seat beside him. Tucker sniffs his hand for a moment, then climbs off his lap, and after a few moments of turning in circles, he lies down and curls himself into a firm ball next to him. Lucas glances down and smiles broadly at the dog, then he looks up out of the window as the train is setting off again, but the speed seems slower than before for a time…

Then, slowly, the speed of the train increases in speed, and after a few minutes, everything outside is a blur. Lucas looks at the fields, trees and houses only for a few minutes, then he opens the bag lying beside him on the other side from where the dog is now yipping softly in his sleep, and from the front pocket he retrieves one magazine. He raises his eyebrows when he notices that it's a scientific magazine he had chosen in Mr Howey's shop for all the magazines that had been on offer. He wasn't certain why he chose this specific magazine and assumes that something among the listings on the first page of the magazine…

I guess Mr Howey annoyed me with his monologue when I was in his shop. That's why I grabbed the first magazine I saw…

Lucas opens the magazine at a random page. At first he's frowning because he doesn't understand what he's looking at, but after a few minutes of staring, he realises what he's looking at is some sort of new form of psychological test done to determine whether people have lied about their own past.

I wonder if I could try any of these techniques out on Louellen. Lucas smirks for a moment. *But if she realises I did this, then she'll never trust me again. Maybe she and I could team up and play tricks on friends if she's okay with that idea.* Lucas knows he has other things to sort out before that could happen. Then he sets aside his mindset to read the article thoroughly and wonders why the article was referring to several criminal cases of more than a hundred years ago: the scientist being interviewed for the article had figured out that it was that long ago the beginning of the psychological test originated from. Even if they didn't call it in that way, as was stated in the article…

"Hmm, if it can be determined that someone lied a hundred years ago with *this* test I wonder if it could solve crimes that are even older than that," Lucas mumbles, "I guess they make advances in the skills used to catch the criminals all the time."

Lucas turns to the next page of the magazine, then he raises an eyebrow when he sees the article isn't simply and only about criminals but also about the individuals who were and still tasked to catch, find the evidence needed to convict them and then get them to a trial…

For example, take the case of 1857, when an inspector by the name of Charles Fairey was investing in the case. It was not until 1897 that they discovered that he had botched up the investigation, and by then it was too late to do anything to find out what happened to the young female who disappeared from the lord's house.

Lucas frowns. He glances over the article a few times more, then leans back. The article didn't say where the case had taken place, but he's certain he'd heard the name mentioned in the past. Somewhere else. In something. However, right now he wasn't certain *where* he'd heard the name…

CHAPTER THREE

"HMM, CHARLES FAIREY… WHERE DID I see the name…?" Lucas whispers under his breath after searching his mind for several minutes while he stares from the window. *Perhaps Louellen will have her laptop with her. She could look up this name for me to help me. Maybe I should purchase a laptop for myself soon, like she's been telling me to do for a few years now…*

Lucas leans forward and reads the paragraph for a fourth time.

Why hasn't anyone bothered to check what this Charles Fairey did—or didn't—do? If it was me who'd found out about him first, I'd investigate him—not this apparently cold case from the mid-1800s.

The thought had warranted for him to give more urgency to finding out about the name that the article had mentioned. "I must talk about this with Louellen," he mumbles. "She might have her own thoughts about the information…"

Lucas goes back to staring out of the window at the fast-moving landscape, allowing this to put him in a pensive mood, though his mind is already going into overdrive without him trying, also unnoticed by his pensive mood. There are layers to his thinking processes whenever he's in this mood.

Something new to do in my life is what I want. I've fully quit the old job, which has only been possible because of the windfall, he thinks. *I guess I'm a bit like Sherlock Holmes in a way if I was going to investigate the things this article mentions.*

Lucas smirks at the idea of him running around asking questions and then solving a case. He glances one more time at the article and wonders where the 'house' that was mentioned in the article might be. *Which part of the country? It mentions my county, so that's a small clue, but it doesn't mention where in his county it is.*

If I'm going to do this new 'hobby,' then I need to first be able to find this piece of information. I guess I'll get onto that if I cannot persuade Louellen in any way…

He glances up again when he feels the train slow down and looks out of the window to check in which town he might be now. It seems the train has arrived in a small village, so he glances left and right to check for a name. He feels annoyed when he realises that he'd taken the slow train into the city.

I hope I'll get there on time. I cannot be late, today of all days, and cannot have Louellen waiting at the station, Lucas thinks, a*nd it's something I absolutely don't want to happen. Not today of all days, and especially if I want to have a little hope in persuading her…*

The train stays put in the station, and Lucas uses the waiting time to think more about how to do the investigation he wants to do so urgently. He realises he had to be careful or some people around him would think he was being too curious about certain details.

I've noticed how everyone tries to keep from talking about the village like it will cause problems for them. Seems to me that something is going on in Mellowstone Greene that everyone has an opinion about, but that they don't discuss with others.

"Hmm, my neighbour is dodgy to be honest," Lucas wonders softly, "as she has such a nosey attitude and it was already obvious when I was viewing the house…"

Maybe the behaviour is some sort of defence mechanism to make sure her new neighbour - him, of all people - wouldn't discover 'stuff' that happened in the village years ago. In preparing himself for a visit to Louellen, he'd found what she doesn't want found.

What she doesn't want found, Lucas thinks. *What the fuck does that even show? Now it seems the village is news in a science magazine and that makes her behaviour suspicious…*

Lucas is certain now she's behaving in this way because of something that happened. They wrote a magazine article because of something that happened.

What if I find out more…?

Suddenly, now that he'd read the article, all the behaviour of his neighbour but also of others in the village seems less of a laughing matter. In fact, now he thought it over more thoroughly, while away from the environment, the behaviour worries him…

If the village in this article is Mellowstone Greene, then I have to find out more for certain. Because it's a village with a mansion, and almost all the details listed, fits the bill. I wonder about this Charles Fairey. He seems like one of those corrupt cops in a television series these days. If he really did such a bad job back then, no wonder the villagers want to keep quiet about what happened there.

"Hmm, the house. I *did* 'pledge' to go check it out," Lucas mumbles. "Hmm, I wonder now if I made a right choice…"

So the previous evening that had begun as every other became the evening where he went to find out more. Dozens of times of passing the house and suddenly he'd felt the urge to look at it. However, he couldn't ignore the way he'd felt every time he walked past. How a chill went down his spine as he walked past the undergrowth, blocking the view of the house.

The abandoned house… according to Mrs Whitwell…

Lucas glances up, somewhat surprised, when the train moves again. He puts everything to do with the house and the village out of his mind for now. He smiles when the intercom announces there are no more stops between this village and his ultimate destination.

Lucas settles back in his seat, but only for a moment. The sound of other people catches his attention. He glances over his shoulder and notices that the sounds come from a noisy group of people has entered the compartment he'd been sitting in alone in up to now. The people alert Tucker and he raises his head, and he has his ears pricked up in the air, sniffing the air, and he yips once. Lucas turns back looking forward then places a finger over the dog's nose bridge to stop him from barking.

"Is this the train to London…?"

Lucas finds a woman standing beside him and her words were spoken in an obvious, heavy accent.

"Yes, it is," he answers.

"Okay, thanks…" She turns and walks back to the group of the other people who'd been noisy constantly up to now. Lucas glances at them for a moment to listen carefully so to work out what language she is speaking to them. He guesses she's telling them what he had said to her. He was guessing she was telling them about this being the train to London…

Lucas glances at the dog, then strokes him for being obedient. The dog looks around a few more moments, then lowers his head, and as Lucas scratches over his head, he settles back into sleep. Lucas goes back to looking from the window absentmindedly. The train is going slower than before. It causes the landscape to feel almost hypnotic. It allows Lucas to get caught up in the thoughts forming in his mind.

Someone wants the past of the village hushed, Lucas thinks, *and there I come in swooping and wanting to know more about what had happened in Mellowstone Greene. Why is the past being hidden? What has happened…?*

The article gives Lucas the idea that a new purpose in his life could be possible. "I could do a job as an investigator," he mumbles. "I wonder what it takes to be one?"

Now his mind is racing instead of the matter of what skills to know to be an investigator. It would differ drastically from a desk job in the city.

Or any other job I've ever done…

Lucas smiles when he realises that he's rather lucky in regards to his work history. He'd started his final job before quitting to move to a small village six years earlier. Literally had landed in the job by chance and by accident the day after he'd left college with his diploma for business studies.

Paid for with all the jobs as a teen from when I was eleven, he thinks.

When the job came after he was finished with college he studied also for a degree for a few years but he quit the studies before completing it, even if he couldn't remember currently why not. He got into a good job with many perks, and then the windfall had come. That had happened because the company had won several lucrative contracts when most companies were feeling the effects of the ongoing recession, which had started during his days in college.

From that moment, he'd become better off financially. However, he realised fast that the money wouldn't last long if he stayed in London. So he looked about where to live. The small apartment he bought five earlier was a stopgap until he found a forever home. When he spotted the cottage in an advert, he put the apartment up for sale, sold it relatively quickly, then could buy the cottage as a cash purchase.

For profit no less…

To save money, he lived in a tiny two-room apartment a few miles north of his job, which he found accidentally. One room for his bed, and the other was a living room, dining room, and kitchen. Louellen pulled her nose up when she saw it. She visited little because the way the rooms looked put her off.

Especially as it had possessed possibly the smallest bathroom on record…

The rent had included the electricity, water and the council tax. The cost was half of what it had been in the previous apartment he'd owned. Louellen avoiding this apartment was ironic.

"Yep, that was the apartment that caused us to drift apart," Lucas whispers under his breath, folding his arms over his chest resolutely.

But it allowed me to save up enough, together with the windfall, to get this cottage, he thinks, *and also, got funds for four years to live from even with the money set aside for the improvements I want to get done...*

"... And then granddad died," Lucas mumbles with a lump in his throat. "He left me all that money in the inheritance..."

Lucas glances around to make certain no one had heard him talking though it could be interpreted as him talking on a phone.

"Thanks, granddad," Lucas whispers. "I had enough money to buy the cottage with cash and not get any mortgage. I wish you could have seen the cottage in Mellowstone Greene. You would have loved it there..."

The advert for the cottage had been in some sort of women's magazine, left behind on the table of a café where he'd been eating lunch. It was more curiosity than wanting to read such a magazine that got him grabbing for the magazine, and he'd skimped through it until arriving at the pages with adverts. In the centre of the page was a photo of a beautiful cottage with information about it listed beside it.

The cottage caught his attention immediately. It looked a bit dated, like the previous owners hadn't maintained it well for a decade or more. However, the cottage had caught his attention immediately because of its rustic beauty. He'd called the real estate agency listed immediately while he was still in the coffee shop. He spotted the details at the bottom of the advert, and the viewing was arranged for an afternoon two weeks later.

When he'd arrived at the cottage, the charm of it literally had melted his heart. Normally Lucas feels reserved with his emotions, but when he saw the cottage, he just *had* to have it, and did *not* lessen his enthusiasm: he signed the papers and exchanged a week later.

Then Mrs Whitwell inserted herself into my conversation with the estate agent, Lucas thinks. *I was the beginning of my misery in Mellowstone Greene. The more I think about it now, the more that I'm convinced she isn't a good person in the slightest. I have to watch my back...*

Despite all the misgivings about the neighbour, Lucas was glad about his decision to purchase the house. From the original windfall - as Lucas liked to call the money sitting in the bank account - he had perhaps two-thirds of the original money, received from work, inheritance and savings, left over. When he was thorough with calculating the running costs of the cottage, and occasionally travelling to the city, it became clear quite fast that it would cost him considerably less than the last rented accommodation he'd lived in while he still lived in the city. He'd handed in the month's notice for the apartment, and was moved to the cottage only a week later, though it had meant him living from boxes for the foreseeable future but that was a choice he'd made willingly.

I think the new purpose in life really started when I found the cottage.

Now his mind turns to the reason he'd been analysing how he ended up living in a small village his mind, and he realises that he desperately wants to share *that* life with the *one* person he cares the most for in his life, and that would be Louellen, who he was going to visit today. He realises then she'd been having reservations about all his previous choices of accommodation.

Will she be charmed by the cottage as much as I was…? Lucas wonders. *Or will Mrs Whitwell drive her off forever with her nosey behaviour? First get her over for a visit, then see how things go after that…*

When Lucas had told Louellen of the changes in his life and had opted for accommodation in the countryside, buying the cottage, she'd laughed about it. But he noticed how interested she was when he showed her the advertisement that had made Mellowstone Greene his new home. She studied the advert for a while, silently, then leafed through the magazine, then after she'd pushed it back to him and seemed quiet, somewhat reserved, and to him it had felt that she didn't want to admit that she had found the cottage pretty, interesting and maybe more…

That meeting was months ago. Then, over the weeks that followed, their meet-ups became fewer because he had to commute into London to see her.

That's one reason I'm seeing her today. It actually feels like a last-ditch attempt to persuade her that the new life in the countryside would do her a world of good too, and that she'd enjoy it there.

Lucas knows that the dilemma in the matter was being caused by how Louellen's friends would hold sway over his girlfriend, often innocently, but it caused *him* to be eye-rolling at seeing their behaviour. So often, in fact, that he was left shrugging at the behaviour. They had also told her that living in the countryside would be boring. That she would be bored within weeks. *That was why I started paying more attention to my neighbour,* Lucas thinks. *Louellen hates people who behave entitled, and Mrs Whitwell does that so often, really. Though she certainly makes it less boring than they might assume the village to be. Something is up with her for certain…*

Lucas is certain that the friends were looking at *him* as boring and because of it were always hammering on at Louellen not to fully commit to a relationship with him.

I'll prove them wrong, Lucas thinks angrily, *and show them all how exciting it can be to live in the village...*

Louellen had been an on-and-off girlfriend for the longest time, ever since they had met eight years ago. They'd been part of each other's lives. It had come to a halt with a whiplash because he moved. Even while he did his business studies and she'd done her art studies, they maintained the relationship. However, now this situation of them being in a relationship on and off had ended.

No, I'm not accepting it has ended between us, Lucas thinks, then he mumbles, "I'm going to convince her to visit, then convince her that the neighbour is normal, and get our relationship going with a do-over..."

When the dog beside him grunts loudly, Lucas glances at Tucker, then he scratches the dog's ear. In response, the dog wags his tail. Lucas smirks at the dog, even if the animal couldn't understand its meaning, then whispers, "I guess you're my ace card to persuade her, to get Louellen to want to give my suggest some amount of consideration," he says. "I hope I'm right with that assumption..."

All Lucas gets as a response is more wagging. The dog looks at him with his head pressed between his paws, with his eyes glancing up, and this is a sort of behaviour from the dog that makes him the happiest and which lets him forget some of his pessimistic thoughts for a while. "You look like a puppy, you know," Lucas whispers, grinning.

"What is the dog's name?"

Lucas glances to his left and sees the foreign-sounding woman from earlier standing beside his seat. She glances past him at the dog with a broad smile, making it clear she's here about the dog and not the man.

"His name is Tucker," Lucas answers, smiling at the woman politely.

"Can I pat dog? Please?"

Lucas nods. "Of course," he replies. "He likes it here, behind his ears..." He shows where she should scratch the dog's ear and it causes the dog to wag some more. She kneels and crawls her hand towards the dog to let the animal sniff it first. She crawls her hand towards the dog's ear like she expects the dog to snap at her hand at any moment, and when she reaches his ear, she rests her hand there for a moment, and Lucas notices she glances at him for approval, so he nods slightly. The woman moved her hand over his head.

"He is nice." The woman smiles at Lucas as she speaks.

"He's friendly with people," Lucas responds.

She nods at his comment, but a momentary frown shows she's not entirely certain about the English language. She glances behind her and says something in an unfamiliar language to the group sitting there. Lucas glances in the same direction, realising they're speaking the language he'd wondered about earlier. Two of the people nod at her comment to them, then they walk towards where Lucas is sitting. He nods a greeting at the man and woman who stand beside the first woman who says something to them. Her hand motions show to Lucas what she might have said. Silently, he watches on. From the actions of the two other individuals, it's clear that she's showing, in her native language, the instructions that Lucas had given to her…

The foreign man holds out his hand and lets Tucker sniff it for several minutes. He's copied by the two other individuals. It's clear she's telling them instructions similar to what Lucas had explained to her, and she's being copied into action after action. First, they both let the dog smell their hands, and at first Tucker was hesitant and backing off somewhat, and Lucas rubs his hand over the length of the dog's back, after which the dog is more inquisitive about the strangers interacting with him. After a few minutes of letting the dog sniff their hands, they move their hands to the dog's head, letting it rest there for a minute before each of the scratches; one hand on the left side, the other hand on the right side. The dog seems pleased by the new attention and wags vigorously…

* * *

After perhaps ten minutes of patting and cooing the dog, the trio gets upright, then they all say bye to Lucas. After one final scratch over Tucker's head they go back to their own seats located behind Lucas who glances back at them a final time, noting that the others in the group had gone closer to the exit and making clear they were getting off the train soon. Whether it was the upcoming stop or the final stop they were preparing for, which was where he'd disembark as well, wasn't certain from their actions…

Once he sits looking ahead again, it occurs to Lucas that he'd never found out any of the names of the people in the group, and not even the individuals who interacted with Tucker. He shrugs then, as they didn't know his name either. Glancing at the dog, he thinks, Only yours though…

He listens again to the melodic sound of their language and realises, once more, that it's an unfamiliar language and likely would remain unknown, so he turns his mind inward once again.

Hmm, I guess I'll be discussion for the longest time, Lucas thinks, *and they'll talk about Tucker whenever they're with other friends of theirs…*

But he pricks up his ears, listening discretely, and trying to pick up individual words that might be easy to remember, which could give him a clue of where the people are from. *I could ask around if anyone would know the language.* But they speak too fast for him to pick up individual words. *Dammit, but I could still try to repeat some of their words if I remember it*, Lucas thought. *There might be a clue in how sing-song it sounds, especially when any of the women are speaking.* He recalls from his former work that he'd noted the same sort of lilt present in the voices of overseas representatives of other branches of the company. *Especially among people in south-European branches. They could be from Spain or Italy, I guess…*

He concludes that they're from somewhere in the southern parts of Europe, based mostly on their sun-tanned skin tones and them all having somewhat darker hair than most.

Lucas smirks for the briefest moment, but feels uncomfortable for paying so much attention to the strangers behind him. Someone is having a private discussion. He realises then that in reality he's already applying parts of the knowledge gained from the article in the magazine to his surroundings. He grabs the magazine and slides it into his bag.

When the first woman uses the dog's name in her answer to someone's question, at least he's certain she was asked something, he becomes more self-conscious that he'd been listening to them purposely. He glances from the window, fighting the urge to want to blush, but realises there's no need for such behaviour as he didn't know what was talked about other than the mention of the name Tucker.

The dog tilts his head when his name gets mentioned. He's listening to people he might consider his 'new friends' but after a short time his head drops back down on the man's lap. Lucas places a hand

instinctively on his head, stroking him mechanically. The few thumps
of the dog's tail show he knows Lucas is giving him attention, and it
causes the man to stop thinking negatively for the rest of the
journey…

CHAPTER FOUR

AFTER PASSING A FEW MORE stations, Lucas glances up when the last station - his stop - gets announced over the intercom. He packs up and reflects on a few of his previous train journey, with his mind turning to one particular journey undertaken as a child with his parents…

In some ways, this journey into London was almost like the time when he was going there with his parents when he was eleven when the dog, that he ironically called Max, which was quite to his mother's annoyance, had been alive still.

She was quite old, Lucas thinks wistfully. The dog had been a Labrador, and he recalls the dog would settle down beside him as he'd sit opposite his parents, who'd busy themselves with chatter between themselves, leaving their son to entertain himself with the dog or by looking from the window. *She was eleven when she finally passed away.* He thinks with some sadness and realises that he still missed her. *She would lie beside like Tucker is doing right now…*

He sighs, feeling sadness for a moment, remembering now when he'd come home one afternoon, only to be told by his mother that, earlier, late in the morning, the dog had collapsed and died without never getting up…

"She could have lived years longer," Lucas whispers angrily. "I'm going to do everything possible to give *you* the longest life possible, Tucker."

That stupid driver shouldn't have driven his car so fast. For several moments, Lucas feels bitter because after that day his parents, still together for a few more months, refused to let him have any other dog. *Max was special to me,* he thinks, *and he had his life taken from him at a too young age. Max was only three when it happened…*

Lucas guesses that this was the reason he was being so protective of Tucker, who was also three. *I want nothing bad to happen to Tucker,* he thinks, *and I want him in my life for at least the next half a decade or longer. Maybe I should get another dog, so he's got a friend to play with. But what kind of dog? If I'm going to persuade Louellen to come live with me, she should have a say in that too. I don't even know yet if she'll like Tucker.*

Lucas glances at his watch. It's almost coming towards the agreed time that he'd arranged over the phone with Louellen. A last glance, and he sees the train was going faster now, and that it was approaching the station, but from previous journeys he knows it would slow down soon. He was getting nervous now as he imagined that he'd be at the station much too late, and therefore miss the opportunity to meet with Louellen. He assumes she'd go back to work or go home if he didn't turn up…

Glancing up at the display towards the end of the carriage and then a few back-and-forth glances at his watch and back up at the display and Lucas has figured out the train arrives in sixteen minutes, that he was due to meet up with Louellen in twenty minutes and he curses under his breath for how much longer a 'slow' train takes to get into the city and then in his next breath counts his blessings for not having to go to a job anymore…

It worries him to be late. He knows Louellen is a stickler for being punctual, and he's tempted to assume she wouldn't be there when the train arrives finally.

I guess I can't assume anything.

Lucas gets distracted when he notices someone standing at his side. The woman from earlier, who'd asked him about Tucker, was standing at his side, smiling at him. No, she's grinning in almost a teasing way. He hears the group of other foreigners laughing for a few moments. They speak for a few moments, then they laugh once more. Suddenly, he is wondering if they were actually laughing at him, at his reactions towards the woman standing by his side. He assumes for a moment she said goodbye to Tucker. However, he remembers from the article that people always make up assumptions about the motives of others around them, and apparently a rather human thing to do, and his own thought patterns betray he's making assumption in this way. It causes him to jump almost a moment later when she speaks in the now familiar foreign voice.

"My friend, she wants *your* name," she exclaims.

"Huh, what?" Lucas blurts out, glancing behind him and blushing brightly. He frowns when their laughter resumes.

The woman at his side points to the group, then she speaks again. "She ask your name."

Lucas glances longer over his shoulders, and sees now that a woman among the group has reddish-brown hair and not the dark as with the others; something he hadn't noticed until now. He blushes when she waves at him. "She ask your name," the woman next to him repeats, and the other woman giggles and he feels like his face is burning from the blushing.

"Errr—Lucas!"

He quickly turns to glance out of the window.

This isn't what I had in mind. To be chatted up by some foreign woman on my way to see Louellen. Today of all days, that's what I didn't want to happen… or to be honest…

Lucas can already picture in his mind what Louellen's reaction was going to be on seeing him with these women, with them chatting him up, and that she'd be stomping off in anger. After a minute of staring out of the window, he glances sidelong rather inconspicuously and realises the woman had walked off without him noticing. Giggling from behind him gave him more answers about why he was now alone.

However, it seems I have a problem now, Lucas thinks, *and they know my first name and they know Tucker's name, but I don't know any of their names.* He grins for a moment at his stupidity when he realises he could easily find out more about the foreigners. *If I approached it in the same way that someone like Sherlock Holmes or perhaps Miss Marple might have found out such information. There might be a way to do this, even with the risk of anyone noticing what I'm doing, and without Louellen thinking I'm chatting them up…*

Lucas gets up, signals to the dog to get down to the floor, and then walks to the other end of the compartment, past from the group of foreigners, and as he passes the group, he eyes them sidelong to check their belongings for evidence of *where* they might be from, glancing at their belongings lying on the table between them. He quickly walks on and at the end of the compartment he stops a moment, then he waits until the incessant giggle between the four women in the group has died down, then sits down on the seating closest to the exit. After he has sat down, he glances one more time towards the group, staring them down…

I guess they're from Italy if I understood the words displayed in the book correctly.

Lucas lifts Tucker onto the seat beside him, and the dog stretches his head in the air to sniff the air, wagging momentarily when one person makes clicking sounds with his fingers at the dog. Lucas sits down beside the dog. After a moment, the dog turns his attention to Lucas and then the man plays with the dog when it's obvious he wants to look at the fast-moving world outside. Until the dog bores of this activity, lies down, and curls into a tight ball against the man's thigh. He's a bundle of grunts and sniffles for the rest of the journey…

I hope they think I moved because Tucker needed to stretch his legs, Lucas thinks, *and not because I was being nosey about them…*

∗ ∗ ∗

An announcement comes over the intercom. Lucas listens to the lengthy explanation, which concludes with telling the passengers the train will arrive in five minutes. It leaves him eye-rolling…

He gets up, straightens his t-shirt somewhat, then he pulls his bag and coat from the opposite seat and places the bag beside Tucker where he'd been sitting, and pushes the dog back down. He lowers the coat beside the bag, and grabs the pile of belongings and magazine from where he'd dropped them opposite of him. First, he places the magazines into the side pocket of his bag. When the dog tries to sniff inside the bag, he pushes Tucker's nose away. He picks up his coat once again, and he puts on his coat, facing towards the door to the exit so he couldn't see the foreign woman likely looking his way, then he glances from the window for a moment.

After a few minutes, he sits down again, pushing the bag to his left, and out of the way of the curious dog. When the dog tries to reach for the bag, Lucas taps Tucker's nose gently to tell the dog to behave, then looks up as the ticket collector arrives back in the compartment once more. The man nods at him and reaches to Tucker's head and scratches the dog behind the ear.

His ears prick up when he hears the ticket collector speak to the group, and from the few words he spoke it seems he understands what their language is, but then as he walks past Lucas again he grumbles under his breath, "Bloody foreigners—they had to have the wrong tickets." The ticket collector walks through the doorway, then is back with a device to allow for credit card payments to be done which

Lucas recognises from a previous train journey when he'd ended up almost too late on the train…

They're paying a hefty price if they're only now paying for their tickets, Lucas thinks, remembering his grumbling at the price being almost twice as much as the normal price. Lucas didn't dare to glance back at the group, so he just listens to the discussion between the group and the ticket collector, who sounded more and more annoyed as time went by. Then it's all done and the ticket collector walks back past Lucas…

"The girls in *that* lot seem to fancy you," the conductor hisses under his breath as he walks past Lucas again, then he winks at him with a knowing smile. Lucas shrugs at the comment but turns to stare from the window with a resolute 'I'm going to ignore everything, especially them' look on his face.

A minute later, the train slows, and Lucas now glances intently from the window to find Louellen in the crowd.

I'm certain I just saw her. Where is she…?

Lucas moves closer to the window with the dog on his lap and pulls his bag closer at the same time. He glances left and sees a woman with light-brown hair and perfectly sculpted face covered with immaculate make-up covering her face, wearing a dark-blue parka, tight jeans and high heels and she's running in his direction for a few minutes, and as the train stops so does she. She walks a few more meters, and then she stands opposite of where he sits in the train staring out. He waves so she notices he knows she's on the platform…

"I wonder how she can run in them," Lucas wonders for a moment, then he shrugs off the thought that he had just voiced aloud.

Lucas waves at a familiar woman standing on the platform, who'd been waiting there for who knows how long. She waves back when she spots Lucas behind the window of the train, then she grins broadly when she notices Tucker leaning against the windowpane. He hadn't told her he wasn't turning up alone…

Tucker wags excitedly when he realises there's someone outside the train waving at 'him' and he assumes she's trying to grab his attention. She waves even more enthusiastically at the sight of the dog noticing her. Lucas smiles and waves more at Louellen. The dog had done the work to get her appeased…

After he's certain that Louellen has arrived to meet him, Lucas feels more confident of himself so he gets up once more, picks up his bag which he places over his left shoulder, tugs at the lead to get

Tucker to jump to the floor, then he walks to the exit that's in the opposite direction of the group of foreigners to exit the train. It only takes him a few minutes to get to the door, to leave the train and then to stand on the platform waiting for Louellen.

It takes a few moments for Louellen to see where he is, then she's at his side a moment later…

* * *

Glancing over Louellen's shoulder, Lucas feels relief when he notices the foreigners had left the train before him, and are walking towards a stairway which he knows will take them to another platform from which a train would travel west. He could only guess where they'd travel after that. He was certain he'd never see them again. In a few hours, they'd be on their way home; possibly Italy…

If I was right about them being from Italy, they'll be there tonight.

Turning his attention back to the person he saw, Lucas stepping away somewhat from the woman and he looks down at Louellen. She's still petting and scratching the dog's back, and Tucker is wagging so hard that the back half of his body is swinging from side to side. Louellen coos at the dog to encourage more excitement and wags. Then the dog licks over Louellen's face, and for a moment Lucas worries that she'd push the dog away and straighten up, but he raises an eyebrow when she keeps encouraging the dog for more playful behaviour and then points at her face like the dog might understand she wants more dog kisses…

After a few more minutes of this interaction, Louellen straightens up, and she stares at Lucas, studying him for a moment. She looks down, then back up at him. Lucas is quite used to this scrutiny she'd shown every time they had met up in the recent couple of years. He waits for her rebuke that would come: he's late, or he hadn't called her, or perhaps he's living too far - but no rebukes come. After several minutes of awkward silence between them, she speaks, and her comment causes him to raise an eyebrow. "You've put on weight. Someone's been feeding you decent food…?"
Lucas grins immediately upon hearing her comment.
"What's funny?" Louellen asks.

"Actually—t's correct for you to assume it." Lucas grins even broader when her face shows more dismay at hearing his words, but he adds quickly the reason, "and don't worry about it. It's the old lady who lives next to me with her overeagerness for making me meals who is responsible for me being fattened up…"

"Ohhh…"

Lucas frowns momentarily when he notices how uncertain Louellen sounds, and there's a quiver present he has never really heard before in her voice. "Want to go shopping…?" he asks.

She glances up at him, smiling weakly for a moment, then she answers, "Yeah, sure. Where did *you* have in mind…?"

Lucas thinks for a moment. "Well, I thought I should treat you to some new clothing," he suggests cautiously, "and I want to buy a few things for the cottage…"

She smiles for a moment, then states plainly, "Okay, but I get to hold the lead," Louellen quips. "What's the dog's name…?"

"He's called Tucker."

"Where did you get him from…?" she asks.

"There's an old lady who had to go into an old people's home. She went there a few months before I bought the house. The advert appeared a few months later. Someone looked after the dog for a short while and I was told the dog couldn't go into the home with her, and the person looking after him was moving abroad for a job," Lucas explains. "I saw the notice, and called the number asking to see him, and I liked him so much he came home with me that day, just one hour after meeting him…"

"I find him adorable," Louellen says quietly. "Perhaps—errr—perhaps you can come visit me *more* and bring him every time…"

Lucas smiles inwardly, then chances his luck. "Or *you* can come visit me to see him…" he suggests. "Then we could go for walks in the countryside and we can let him off the lead…"

Louellen is silent for a moment, then she says, "Perhaps." She stops speaking abruptly and changes discussion. "Can we go shopping now? We talk about this later, okay?"

Lucas nods silently.

* * *

The initial twenty minutes of them walking side by side is done silently; except for the occasional grunts coming from Tucker. They left the train station, then turn left, walking towards the nearest street with rows of shops.

"Perhaps…" Louellen whispers as she stares intentionally at the clothing on display in the shop window they were just passing. The word spoken is a likely response to the suggestion he'd made earlier about visiting him. Lucas guesses she was thinking things over, and this was an interim answer rather than a 'yes' or a 'no.'

"Do you want to buy anything in this shop?"

Lucas uses the question to distract Louellen from the potential discomfort she was likely feeling from the conversation happening.

"Errr—the clothes are rather expensive…"

"I don't mind," Lucas states, "perhaps a splurge is good…"

"I'll ask inside if they mind the dog…"

Louellen walks inside, and Lucas observes her speaking to the woman at the till, and then Louellen points in his direction. She speaks a little longer, then a moment later she motions at him, looking towards him with a big smile plastered over her face. He walks to the door hesitantly, and as Louellen approaches him, she explains her conversation with the shop assistant.

"You can be inside but only if you carry the dog in your arms," Louellen explains, "and *only* if you stand near the till area where there are no clothing to get dog hair on…" Lucas nods once, then bends over and lifts Tucker into his arms tightly. The dog leans his head onto the man's arm.

He grins at the dog's actions, and Louellen giggles when a moment later he wraps his coat around the dog. "No dog hairs for certain this way…" He walks to the till area and even the shop assistant is smiling at the dog being held inside the coat. She walks around the till area to where the man stands. She lets the dog sniff her fingers, then gives the dog a quick scratch on his head, then walks back to where she'd been standing before the pair had arrived in the shop…

Louellen walks around the shop looking at clothes, and Lucas sees she *had* to pick two blouses, a skirt, a pair of trousers and a dress to try on. That Lucas assumes she wants to try on the clothing in her arms. She goes to the changing rooms, is busy there for a time, then walks out to show Lucas the blouse and skirt she's wearing. She swirls around for a moment, then walks back to the changing rooms, and after a while she's back wearing another blouse and a pair of trousers.

Lucas smiles at her as he thinks the clothing compliments her hair colour.

Finally, she walks from the changing rooms wearing the dress and Lucas draws in his breath…

* * *

After another ten minutes, Louellen is back from the changing rooms in her own clothing, carrying the pile of clothing she places on the counter, then she selects the second blouse, the trousers and the dress to buy. He makes sure he doesn't flinch when he hears the price. It's over four hundred pounds for these three items of clothing alone.

He duly places his credit card in the machine on the counter to pay for them…

A few minutes later they're standing in the street once more, and Lucas lowers the dog to the pavement, then he hands the lead to Louellen, smiling at her and holds out a hand to accept the bags from her to carry. When he takes the bag, she reaches up and kisses him on his lips, surprising him somewhat with this gesture.

They walk along the pavement in a slow, relaxed pace, with some of the tension between them gone now.

For now at least, Lucas thinks, and he hopes that the gift of clothing could end up being the start of him being able to persuade her. He feels annoyed - somewhat - at her pulling her phone out repeatedly to answer yet another text message sent to her. There were so many, it seemed to him…

I had promised myself before arriving in London, Lucas thinks bitterly as he glances towards her phone again, *that I would not say or do anything to upset the chance of success. I wish she'd just turn off that damned phone for a while though…*

He wanted to have a chance of having her with him in Mellowstone Greene no matter what.

* * *

They've walked on for another half hour when they stop at a vendor selling ice cream, and both select a double scoop of vanilla ice cream in a tub to eat on the go. Feeling playful, Lucas grins as he places a bit of the ice cream on Louellen's nose, and she pushes her portion of ice cream against his chin in response. She giggles loudly when he protests visibly at her actions.

After spending a few more minutes eating their ice creams, they walk on and stop at a nearby park to allow Tucker a bit of time to run around off the lead.

While they watched the dog, it felt to Lucas that the day was turning into a nice, relaxing day of fun.

"It's my turn to throw it," Louellen says, grabbing the thick, smooth dog toy that he'd retrieved from his bag, and she throws it as far as she can.

"You haven't lost the strength in your arms," Lucas says, smiling at Louellen when she glances at him as he makes the comment.

"I still occasionally go practise my ball throwing skill," she says, "and I may not play baseball like I did at school but I *do* still practise the skills…"

Lucas looks at Louellen, surprised. "When did you stop playing?" he asks.

"A few years ago," she answers.

"Why?"

Louellen is silent at first, plucking at a few grass blades near her foot, then she speaks. "I got bored with it," she says softly. "I started a new job so I didn't have as much time—and you didn't even notice that I had stopped playing…"

Louellen laughs, but nervously according to Lucas, then he stares at her perplexed, causing her to laugh even louder before adding, "… and also I got myself a proper boyfriend. That's why…"

CHAPTER FIVE

LUCAS STARES AT LOUELLEN WITH even more confusion. "Errr—what?" he asks sheepishly.

"You—silly," she quips.

"Ohhh, right—" Lucas fights off the need to blush and he looks away, with some annoyance, going through his emotions whirling through his mind. He shrugs off his thoughts a moment later.

"… But I do still come here occasionally with Kayla," Louellen continues, "and we throw balls to each other to keep our skill good."

"How is she?"

"She's doing fine," Louellen answers, "and she's sitting her exams this year. She wants to be a nurse…"

"That's a worthwhile job to do," Lucas comments. "And what sort of job are *you* doing these days? I'm losing track of them."

"I work now in an art gallery—" Louellen glances at Lucas and grins deviantly, knowing his opinion of her choice of art-related career choices. "—and I'm actually the art buyer So much for studying art being a silly thing to do, huh—"

"I never said that…!"

"But you did laugh when I said I studied that—"

"Okay, maybe, well, I'm sorry I did," Lucas says apologetically.

Louellen is silent for a moment, looking away and watching the dog for a while, then she speaks again. "Okay, I'll accept your apology, but only if you do something for *me*," she whispers. Louellen's smiles broadens to a mischievous grin.

"Errr—what?"

"I'll accept it, if you go clean *that* pile of shit that Tucker left there on the footpath, and do it before the park warden sees it."

"Oh, fuck…!"

Lucas scrambles onto his feet. He rushes to the bins where he retrieves a bag and a scoop, then rushes to the culprit of his dismay, cursing under his breath while also having the listen to Louellen's hysterical laughter as she holds onto Tucker's collar to keep the dog by her side and he glances their way a few times, seeing how the dog looks from him to Louellen confused, wagging because of her giggles and get to him whenever he looks at the dog and not capable of doing this because of Louellen's grip on his collar. He tidies the mess the dog left in the middle of the footpath as fast as possible, then throws the full bag into the bin, and pulls up his nose at the smell from the bin which was causing more laughter from Louellen.

After a few minutes, Lucas arrives back at Louellen's side and drops on the ground beside, glancing at her, annoyed. Each time she looks at him, she falls backwards in the grass, laughing while he keeps cursing under his breath because of her behaviour.

Lucas stares in the other direction of where Louellen sits, feeling annoyed at her for having to have fun at his expense. He's certain she's staring at him when she finally falls silent, and he assumes she's grinning still for having fun and causing his outburst.

"We could visit a tearoom I know about from a friend," Louellen suggests softly, touching Lucas on his lower arm cautiously and sounding somewhat uncertain for a moment. "They serve nice sandwiches there—I'm hungry…"

Lucas sighs visibly.

Louellen pivots her head so Lucas won't see that she'd been staring at him. To make out she hadn't heard his grumbling. She feels annoyed at herself for almost ruining their happy, carefree day that the day had been so far. She glances back, and she sees that he still sits staring away from here, though he's silent now.

Something must bother him, she thinks.

After a minute of silence, Lucas speaks suddenly. "Okay, let's go," he says, and he sounds despondent to her. He gets up a moment later, and he reaches out to her with a hand, then he pulls Louellen up onto her feet. For a moment, their gaze locks, then both look away; neither wants to admit to the sudden flash of feelings that well up for each individual.

"Tucker, come here, boy," Lucas calls out as he pats against his leg. "Tucker, come…"

The dog rushes to him, and the man puts the lead back on his collar, then he straightens again, then helps Louellen with her coat. After standing in the same spot for a few minutes, Lucas points towards the middle of the park. Lucas picks up his coat, puts it on, then lifts the bag strap over his head so the strap is across his chest.

They walk again, now at a leisurely slow pace, and their route was now through the park towards the tearoom that Louellen had chosen as their next destination. After about fifteen minutes, they reach the exit and there they turn left. After another fifteen minutes, they're waiting at the zebra crossing. Louellen pushes on the button so they could cross over, and it takes several minutes before the light turns green. They cross the road, then turn left again. As they pass a garden, they both nod at a man standing there who leans on his garden wall, waiting for someone, and they both notice the man stares at the street ahead of them. A busy street with many people and cars travelling along it…

Lucas realises he was already being more observant of his surroundings because of reading the article, so decides that he needs to speak to Louellen about what he'd read.

At the next street, where they turn right, Lucas uses the opportunity to look back towards the man they'd greeted only minutes earlier, and sees him staring rather intently at someone, and on scanning the street it seems the individual is a woman who is walking on the other side of the road, and who, in Lucas's opinion, is struggling with the bags being carried. He glances back at the man to see if he'd walk out to help her, but a nudge from Louellen in his ribs interrupts his efforts and he stares ahead again…

I'll never know more about them, he thinks, then he shrugs somewhat, *and I have to assume that it was just a normal day for the two people I saw in the street just now…*

Lucas stops thinking about the previous street when the tearoom comes into view. A few minutes later, they're standing at the front of a rather pretty building - according to Lucas - which is a well-visited tearoom by the number of visitors both inside and out. Lucas opens the door and waits for Louellen to step inside. He stays outside with Tucker, waiting as she asks about whether they would allow Tucker inside. When she gets permission, he walks inside and then they choose a table near the windows. Lucas motions the dog to lie down under the table, and he fastens the lead to the chair beside his own. They walk to the counter together and quickly order food and drink from the shop assistant. Ten minutes later, they sit quietly eating the food.

"In fact, I have to agree with your suggestion about this place," Lucas says. "This food tastes good."

"I told you so." Louellen smirks at Lucas.

"When did you find this place?"

"I came here occasionally with Emlyn. She actually found it first."

"Ah, I see. Well, tell *her* I give this place a definite thumbs up."

"I will if ever I see her…"

Louellen smiles at hearing him speak positively about *her* friends. They both knew it was likely the first time he'd been positive in this way about her friends in the longest time, ever since they'd known each other initially, and he can guess without her needing to speak what she might think: *I guess it's because he moved to that village, perhaps.*

"What are the people like in Mellowstone Greene?" she asks, almost like she's giving voice to her thoughts.

To Lucas, it seems now that Louellen has showed some interest in his new life after Lucas had been so nice for most of the morning and early afternoon so far.

"I'd say it's a mixed bag."

"What do you mean?"

"There are a few people in the village I already get on well with," Lucas answers. "Such as the daughter of the former owner of Tucker. A rather gracious lady in her forties, if I may say so… But there are others though. Well, all I can say of them is that they're too nosy for their own good, or too reserved, but of the latter I should add they might need time to get used to someone new moving to the village—"

"That's likely true of whatever town or village any person moves to in their life," Louellen says plainly. "You're new there. They've probably lived there all their lives, or most of it, and most of them were likely born there too. Their families probably come from there too. At least two or three generations worth…"

"I guess so," Lucas admits, realising how right Louellen is with her assessment of the situation. He's silent for a while then he adds, "… my neighbour is Peg Whitwell. She's odd, but I think she means well. She's retired, though I'm uncertain what sort of job she did before."

"And she's the one fattening you up?" Louellen asks teasingly, grinning broadly as she speaks. "She could be like the wicked witch in the Hansel and Gretel story for all you know—and that will mean that she'll want to cook you up for a meal once you're fat enough…"

They both laugh at the idea of a fairytale being true somehow.

"I'll make sure I lock my doors," Lucas quips, "so she can't do any of that stuff to me, alright?"

"Okay, but I think it's quite a nice thing that someone is looking out for your well-being," Louellen says softly, then she ignores the next words Lucas mumbles under his breath by glancing down at her phone for a few minutes.

"I rather it is you—" Lucas mumbles under his breath.

For a while, they sit eating there, slowly picking through their food and savouring every bite, each caught up in their own thoughts, or distracted by other things, which with Louellen means two phone calls from friends, which she answers but deals with outside the tearoom. She takes Tucker with her and pulls a couple of bags from Lucas's bag - obviously to clean up any poop by the dog. Lucas glances from the window and sees a bin for such use about five minutes of walking from the tearoom. As she talks on the phone, Louellen is walking slowly towards the building. Halfway to the bin, Tucker does his business, and with her nose pulled up in disgust, which is rather comical to Lucas, she clears up the mess on the pavement.

"Ha, now we're even about earlier," Lucas grunts under his breath, then he leans back in his chair to wait for her return with the dog. It doesn't take long before she's back, and Lucas guesses she used the dog's presence as a plausible excuse to cut short the call. She sits down in the middle of her second call. He observes her from the corner of his eye, trying to make it not-so-obvious he's listening. She hands him the lead.

Lucas stares after her, and rather surprised, when she got up again, and was outside a moment later, and seemed to find the need to pace back and forth on the pavement, almost appearing impatient with whoever she was talking to…

Best that I don't ask her for details of the phone call when she comes back inside, Lucas thinks while he continues eating small morsels of his food.

"Bloody hell…!"

Lucas jerks upright when Louellen unexpectedly arrives back at the table. She sits down again, but now she sits next to him, then pulls her plate and drinks towards herself but doesn't eat or drink for now. She stays silent and not explains why she's so angry about whoever she'd talked with on the phone.

If she wants to tell, she will do it later when she's ready…

After a few minutes, Lucas cannot keep silent anymore and he makes a suggestion to distract Louellen from whatever annoyance she still was harbouring from the call of just minutes earlier.

"I thought we should go to *one* other store so I can get all the curtains for the cottage," Lucas comments diplomatically, "and maybe you can choose the fabric for the curtains for me as you have a better eye for colour than I as it always seems…"

"Oooh, can I…?" Louellen implores, and she already sounds much happier than just minutes ago.

Lucas nods once, smiling at her.

"Sure—I'll make sure you'll have the *best* looking curtains of the village," she states plainly.

Lucas feels confident that he'd said the correct thing, and keeps smiling inward when she's looking on her phone now for potential shops to visit. He knows she has the skills for home decorating from her art degree. *I hope this attempt to include her will show her now that I appreciate her choice of study and career,* he thinks, *and the enthusiasm in her voice seems genuine enough…*

"Shall we go to the shops?" Lucas asks.

"Sure," she answers.

They get up and Lucas grabs Louellen's coat from the other side of the chair, then he helps her with putting on her coat. He receives a cheerful smile as a reward. When Lucas untangles Tucker's lead, she insists on holding the dog's lead, which Lucas lets her do. They leave the tearoom, turn right and return to the busier high street where they turn right again, and start their walk along the road in a relaxed, unhurried pace. Lucas puts his arm around Louellen's shoulders and feels surprise when she doesn't automatically push herself away from him for once…

Lucas smiles, feeling happy now with their situation, and he wishes that the day would go on longer. All the misgivings of the past five days were now set aside for now.

They arrive at the bus stop, wait only minutes for the bus to arrive, then board the next bus that will head to the shops where Louellen would select the fabrics for the curtains and other things for the house. Their destination was the busy shopping centre where, according to Louellen, they would find the best curtain shop in all of North London…

I hope she's right, but I'm not about to say it to her.

"Here it is—"

Lucas looks through the window when Louellen speaks. They get off the bus, then walk towards the shop that Louellen points out to Lucas. On their arrival, Lucas looks through the window at the curtains that Louellen is pointing out to him. *Hmm, these curtains look good. I like what I see here,* Lucas thinks. *The colours are pleasing to the eye, and the pricing isn't too expensive…*

"You like them?" Louellen asks, and when Lucas glances at her for a moment, she stares at him with an expectant grin on her face.
"Yes, I do…" he answers, smiling.
"Good, let's get your curtains sorted," she continues. "You brought measurements, right…?"
"I did…"

They walk to the entrance door, then spot the sign about 'no dogs' on the door, and they fasten Tucker onto a hook near the door, then they walk into the shop single file. Lucas signals for the dog to lie down and he ignores the desperate whimpering of the dog.
Lucas is curious about the choices that Louellen would make to determine which would be suitable curtains for each room. Lucas feels impressed at her choices and decides the colour choices look great.

After they've finished in the shop, they exit quickly and Louellen kneels beside the dog then she unwinds the lead from the hook on the wall, while Lucas sorts the bags so he can carry a few of each in each hand with them evenly balanced in terms weight. They discuss their next destination and settled in a pub for a drink, and a bit of last discussions, before it was time for Lucas to go home…

"What would you like to drink?" Lucas asks. "It's my treat…"

Louellen sits down in a chair outside the pub and thinks for a moment. "A cola for me, please, with ice only," she answers, smiling at Lucas. He nods, smiles back for a moment, then turns and walks into the pub to order the drinks for both of them; a large glass of orange juice for him and cola with ice for her. After five minutes, he sits down in the chair left of her so they got Tucker between them. Now that the man is back, the dog settles down, in a ball, at his feet.

"I was just checking for news about train travel times," Louellen says absentmindedly. "It states here that there's a delay on two routes, and there's also a cancellation. You'd better take the seven o'clock train home as it's the fast service…"

Immediately, Lucas feels annoyed at the comment and all the earlier misgivings come flooding back.

"Errr… okay," he grunts. He doesn't like the news conveyed, as it causes there to be a time limit on how long he could still visit Louellen. *An hour until I go home and now all the earlier misgivings are back with a vengeance. Still no answer about whether we got a future…*

"Maybe you can come visit me, and see how these curtains look once they're hanging at the windows," he says sheepishly, and for a moment, he feels stupid for the suggestion. *I know already that she said she isn't interested in visiting or even moving in, so why do I keep pressing the matter…?*

"We've been over this before," Louellen snaps at him. "I don't want to visit some stupid, tiny village with nothing to do there…"

Lucas feels deflated suddenly. "I just wanted—" he grunts.

"Was all *this* just to get me to agree to a visit…? Or were *you* hoping to bribe me with gifts into changing my mind?" Louellen says coldly.

Lucas stares angrily at the woman, but he keeps most of his emotions in check. "Okay, I get it. If you don't want to visit, I won't ask anymore." He looks away, then glances at her again, and sees she's staring back at him.

"So, you wanted me to move in with you?" she asks. "Is that what this is all about…?"

"Yeah, kind of…" he says defensively.

Louellen silently glares at Lucas, with a stare that could melt ice, but as quickly as she stared she glances away. He guesses she doesn't want to tell him any genuine feelings as this makes her feel vulnerable and he knows this and had glanced away a moment later and felt sorrow about their situation. He doesn't dare glance back at her. They're silent for the next fifteen minutes…

Both are acutely aware that this argument is the first time in over four years that they'd argued about anything…

After a little more time has elapsed, Louellen speaks once more. "Perhaps," she says softly, "but I won't promise anything. However, maybe tell me what fascinated you about the village causing you to decide to live there. Because every time you've moved somewhere before this move you grew bored so fast you could just pick up still packed-up boxes from four moves earlier…"

Lucas glances at her because of her comment, feeling surprised. *Is she saying this to be diplomatic?* he thinks, but he sees insecurity in her eyes, and from past situations he realises she's not admitting to her feelings.

"There's a house in the village that has been abandoned for the longest time," Lucas says. "I've heard strange stuff about it and want to investigate it…"

"Why…?"

"Because it's so interesting," he answers. "They've told me stuff about house and the village. The people in the village who I've met so far… and I'm curious why…"

"Is that *why* you're still living there? Months later…"

"I guess so," he answers. "There's something—not sure what— but there's something mysterious about the entire village. It's like they're hiding something—and some of what they told me seems to match up with something I was reading on the train on my way here…"

"What did you read?"

Lucas picks up his bag and opens it. He retrieves the science magazine from its side-pocket and then hands it to Louellen. She accepts it and momentarily pulls her nose up at the subject of the magazine, then she studies it with a more neutral stance on her face.

"It's on page thirty," he says plainly, pretending he never saw her facial expression.

Louellen opens up the magazine to the suggested page. She reads through the article, then she glances up at Lucas. "You think *this* article is about Mellowstone Greene…?"

"Yes, I'm quite certain of it," Lucas answers. "There are details in the article that match some of the information I've been told about the village by people who live there… People I've met so far and who I've spoken with. Such as the woman I spoke about earlier who'd put the advert up for Tucker. She was the first individual to tell me certain stuff about the village and said that, as a newcomer, I needed to know about it…"

"Oh right," Louellen remarks, frowning then for a moment before she adds, "… but there's one thing that's rather unclear in what this article states…"

"What part of it?" Lucas asks.

"It mentioned an individual in the article. A man named Charles Fairey," she answers. "I'm uncertain of it, but I'm certain I may have heard the name before somewhere, but right now I cannot figure out where from…"

"And *why* don't you understand it?"

"Well, because it mentions he was an investigator based in Central London. Why would an investigator from the middle of the city be so interested in a tiny Norfolk village?"

"I don't know, to be honest," Lucas answers. "That's why I want to investigate the house."

Louellen laughs, then says, "Are you planning on being Sherlock Holmes…?" she asks. "I know your ongoing obsession as well with the Miss Marple stories…"

Lucas blushes. "I guess so," he replies after a few minutes.

"And how are you going to find out what's going on with the house if a trained investigator such as Charles Fairey sold a darn thing related to the house? Whatever that something might be…"

"I guess the best place to start is at a library," Lucas says, smirking and therefore causing Louellen to roll her eyes in response.

"Well, let me do some digging for you the modern way," she comments.

She places the magazine on the table in front of her, and from her bag pulls her phone, then leaning forward taps in on the phone's keyboard the name 'Charles Fairey' and clicks on the search button.

"Well, I'll be damned," she mutters loudly.

"What?"

"Err—it gives zero results."

Now Lucas is laughing loudly and he comments, "… And you said 'modern way'—so how can it give zero results? Explain that, please…?"

CHAPTER SIX

AFTER ANOTHER MOMENT OF EYE rolling one more time, Louellen feels a need to glare at Lucas for a moment, then she looks at the article again. "It mentions a few other names here. I'll try them…"

Lucas watches on as Louellen busies herself with her phone. She taps in the name of the village, then she glances up. "I get a wiki page for the village, and mention nothing about Priory Mansion at all. The three other names give a bit of information, but all of it is quite outdated."

"So much for modern technology," Lucas quips, and when Louellen glares at him again, he adds, "… you had said it, not me…"

"I said that *when*…?"

"Just a few moments ago… When you were swearing at the lack of information on that wiki page. I could hear you saying: '… and they should bloody well update things so I can find information when I want it. So much for modern technology,' and then you swore again."

"Errr okay—" Louellen says softly as she blushes brightly.

"If there's *no* information on the internet, then I wonder how the hell I'd find out more about what happened in the village."

"There's another thing to consider—"

"What?" Lucas asks.

"Who's trying to hide the things that have happened in that house? I've re-read the text several times. Someone doesn't want the world to know that something had happened in this house—It's called Priory Mansion, right?"

"Yes, it is…" Lucas says, and he frowns for a moment.

"There's a name in the credits for the article, here at the end…"

"Oh, I must have missed it… I looked and thought there wasn't anything of the sort in the article," Lucas admits. "Ah yes, it was probably the foreigners on the train when they came to pet the dog. They distracted me that way, and then I just stopped reading the rest of the article…"

"The names I've tried to find are *all* listed in this section."

"Maybe I should ask about them when I next see Gylda."

"Who is she?"

Lucas notes a defensive edge to her voice.

"She's the daughter of Tucker's previous owner. The one who put—" he explains plainly.

"Oh right. Okay, yeah, maybe ask her."

"I will."

They're silent again for a time, then Louellen asks a question. "Have you visited the house…?"

"Visited what?"

"Priory Mansion. You said that you live near it. So, have you been to see it…?"

"I walk past its garden every time I'm walking Tucker—"

"But you've not been inside it?"

"No, I don't think it's a place you can visit. It's not like they have tourist signs outside it—"

"But why don't you check it out tomorrow or something?"

"I can't just start poking around there. Someone would see me and—" Lucas protests.

"Do it when everyone sleeps." Louellen curls her lips at the memory it invokes.

"Hmm, perhaps…"

Louellen has made a good point. Just sitting back and waiting won't help him find out more about the house. He needs to visit the house to check inside it for potential clues. Especially clues that might match parts of the article…

"Maybe I need to do such investigating," he says after a long pause in their conversation.

"Is it something *you* want to do?" Louellen asks. "To find out the stuff this article talks about…?"

"I guess so… I don't have a job yet. I got time right now. However, I was considering applying for the job in one of the nearby small towns that I had spotted in an advert, but now I'd rather do this stuff instead… With the windfall I have in the bank, it's not like I really need a job urgently…"

"That's quite true," Louellen quips, laughing a bit.

"It isn't like I've decided yet about it."

"To me it sounds that you have—" Louellen chuckles again softly.

"Oh, really? And why do *you* say that?"

"Because you've actually not stopped talking about the house since arriving."

"Errr—have I…?" Lucas asked.

"Yes—but I think the house is interesting—I don't know why I'm so interested."

"So, that's why *you* don't stop asking me about it."

Louellen glares at Lucas, and she tries to glower at him. Lucas stares back at her with a mischievous grin on his face. A moment later, she bursts out in laughter.

"Oh my god, Lucas," she snorts as she speaks. "You always do this."

"Do what?" Lucas leans forward and grins broader at her.

"This…!"

"This what?" Lucas asks.

"You…!" Louellen shrieks loudly. "You're teasing me when I'm trying to have a serious discussion."

"Ahh, okay—and there I thought *we* were discussing my career choices—"

"Were we?"

"I think we were," Lucas replies, "and to me, it seemed you were disagreeing with my career choice."

"No, I wasn't."

"Hmm," Lucas grunts under his breath, looking away.

* * *

Silent now, and unable to think of anything to say, Louellen frowns, then she looks down, and moves her almost-empty glass aimlessly for a few minutes. She frowns inwardly at the realisation of what's happening between them. They were arguing so much, and something about it was also bothering her at the same time. She glances towards Lucas from the corner of her eye and sees he's leaning away from her and she notices then acutely that a distance between them had grown a lot more in the preceding months than she'd realised up to now..

It's not like we see each other almost every day nowadays, she thinks bitterly, *like it was when Lucas still lived here in London and I could just hop on a bus and be at his apartment within ten or twenty minutes. Now it would take me an hour or more to go see him…*

Louellen sighs, feeling uncertain about her feelings now. She cares for Lucas, and they'd been in their relationship since they were both fourteen. It had begun as a friendship, but slowly, over the following three years, a friendship grew into a deep-rooted love. But their relationship came with a snag. Louellen knows she loves Lucas, but she'd never stated it ever. In all the time they'd known one another, out loud…

Hmm, now I'm thinking about it. I realise that neither of us has ever said it out loud, Louellen thinks pensively, *but I know we're in love and we got something going on between us that will last for the longest time…*

Louellen sighs for a moment, hoping Lucas doesn't notice it. She needs to address this dilemma she finds herself in and to allow her to get things sorted out with life to benefit her and *not* leave Lucas out in the cold. *I have a job I love and that's now getting in between whatever Lucas wants and whatever expectations he has for us, and what I want from life,* she thinks pensively, *and I know that most of the complications come from the way all my friends are telling me he's the wrong guy but I don't think he is…*

All of Louellen's friends had been saying that they thought Lucas wasn't the right guy and to find someone who'd appreciate her for her artistic skills, and perhaps even for all her other skills.

But that's not really true, she thinks, *and it was never true. He's allowed to have his own interests, and he's said nothing that says that he disregards any of mine…*

She glances again towards Lucas, who was turning out to be so different from she'd given him credit for. He'd grown appreciative of her artistic skill, and today proved it.

He also seems interested in my job…

She notices Lucas is staring towards the people walking past on the street and has his face set in a stiff posture.

He's angry, Louellen thinks with a bit of sadness welling up. *It's rare he gets angry… and especially not this angry…*

She knows why he may behave in this way. To this day, Lucas had reeled from what had happened a few years before they had met. She knows why. He'd told her his life story often enough for her to recall it word for word.

It's probably when 'his' father had moved to America when he distrusted most people and ended up with the idea of only having a few friends, Louellen thinks as she glances at the man. And he had left him and his mother behind. *His mother arrived at the school. I had only just started there. I heard them talking, and I didn't know him yet. It explains why he's angry right now. He wants me in his life, but I can't pack up and leave my life behind like it doesn't matter…*

Louellen lifts the magazine somewhat and reads some of the article again. *She had left her life behind if what it lists here is true*, she thinks. *I'm not like that, and Lucas knows it. He was joking before, but I know it's a defence mechanism in his demeanour. He always does this when stuff doesn't go his way. It's a consequence of him losing his father for no reason…*

Louellen gently reaches out to Lucas, touching his arm gently, then she pulls her hand back, but a moment later she changes her mind and places her hand firmly over his arm. Lucas turns to look at her, and she sees sadness in his eyes, and not the anger she'd expected to find there. He turns away once more, and for a moment Louellen expects him to pull his arm away, but it never happens.

He speaks a moment later.

"Maybe I should get going. I can then be home early enough to do a few bits of decorating."

Louellen stares at the man for a moment longer, then she sighs, feeling deflated and also kind of defeated. His suggestion would cause them to part ways more than half an hour earlier than the time she'd suggested.

"Okay," she whispers.

"I'll let you know what I find out about Priory Mansion if you want to know more about the house," Lucas says softly, sounding subdued. "Yes, I'd want to know more too," she comments hastily, and she feels surprised at how enthusiastically she answers the question.

Lucas picks up his glass and gulps down the last few mouthfuls of his juice, then he gets to his feet. He unwinds the lead from the chair beside him, where Tucker had been fastened to stop the dog from moving around, then he straightens. The dog wags for a few moments, but then sits. When he receives no attention, he sits down on his hind legs. In response to the actions by Lucas, Louellen also gets up and puts on her coat before Lucas can offer to help her with it. She doesn't ask for the dog's lead and therefore she adds to the feeling of finality she feels now about the situation.

They stroll silently along the road to the nearest bus stop. They wait for the bus without speaking, and sixteen minutes later sit silently, side by side, in a noisy bus filled with many passengers. Each person looks through a different window, avoiding to talk about the apparent rift that's growing being between them. It could easily be their last time seeing one another.

A similar rift had happened before, but had they'd talked, each individual would have realised that today's situation was so much different in so many ways. They both felt the schism, and neither could reach out and overcome it with a kind word, a gesture, a glance…

Not immediately at least, but then Lucas says just a few words. "I'll call you," he whispers.

* * *

At the train station, Lucas glances down at Louellen and weighs up whether to say more, especially whether to try one more attempt to persuade her. He realises things might be better if he can leave her behind, feeling happier at a minimum, so he takes hold of her hands and pulls her closer. He embraces her and notices that she copies him. They hug, though to Lucas it doesn't feel as intimate as previous times they had hugged before parting ways, and he's certain the earlier argument was impeding their moment of affection.

Lucas leans in and kisses Louellen's forehead, which he usually would do in moments such as this, then he notices that her response was to pull herself even closer, even tighter against his chest, and he guesses from this that this was *her* way of saying sorry for the argument.

"So, you're certain you don't even want to visit tonight?" he whispers as a last-ditch attempt to persuade as he pushes away from the woman and steps partly into the train coach. Louellen shakes her head, looking down somewhat, and Lucas ignores the apparent attempt to bite her lip.

"No—perhaps another day," she whispers, but to Lucas it's obvious she's quite uncommitted to the idea, so he sets the idea aside for an undetermined time.

"I can call you if I find more information about the house, the village, and so on," he suggests softly.

"Yeah, do that, please," she says, "but only if it's really important."

Lucas nods.

"Are you working tomorrow?" he asks.

"Yes," she answers, "and also most of next week."

"Maybe—errr—maybe you can ask for a holiday," he suggests,

"and come visit me in Mellowstone Greene at least once, for a brief holiday…?"

He looks at Louellen with a hopeful stare.

"I will see," she answers. "I won't be able to promise it…"

Lucas nods again. He leans forward and gives her a last kiss on her forehead, then he boards the train after picking up Tucker to carry him on board. He waves and smiles for when Louellen scratches Tucker's head, causing a few wags of his tail.

He turns and enters the train, then turns right and walks through the compartment to a seat about halfway in the carriage and he glances out of the window and notices that Louellen has walked alongside the train over the platform, and in how she stares at the train, like she's searching him out now that the inevitable departure was happening. He knocks on the window, and a moment later she stands close to the window, waving frantically at both of them, and Lucas thinks it's mostly so she can grab the dog's attention. Tucker quickly realises what's going on and he wags for a moment. Louellen taps on the window several times and then the dog wags his tail fast and causes her to grin at the dog. Lucas watches them interact through the window. He notices a sadness on her face despite her grin, so when she catches his gaze, he smiles at her to cheer her up. She glances down at the dog instead, avoiding his gaze until the train finally leaves…

A few minutes later, the train comes into motion, and now Louellen looks up and waves at him frantically, and then at the dog and then again at the man. Lucas reciprocates the emotions on display. After a minute Lucas sits down beside the dog, holding onto the dog.

"I guess it's just you and me for now," Lucas whispers towards the dog, hiding his face behind the dog so Louellen wouldn't notice him speaking to the dog, and he glances up on hearing Louellen's next words.

"Call me," she calls out.

"I *will*," Lucas calls out as loudly as he dares, then glances to check for others in the carriage.

Lucas waves through the window until he can't see Louellen anymore, then he waits a moment before he turns and leans back. He feels emotionally drained, and suddenly he feels exhausted. He sighs deeply, then glances at the dog when he whimpers softly. The dog has its head strokes thoroughly.

"You had fun today, didn't you…?" he whispers to Tucker, who licks his chin in response, and when Lucas scratches his head more thoroughly, the dog wags several times. "Did you *like* Louellen? Did you…?" Lucas asks, and he gets a soft yip from the dog.

They distract Lucas from playing with the dog when the ticket collector arrives. She smiles when she notices the dog beside Lucas, and pauses in her tasks to tickle the dog's head for a moment. She checks his ticket, then after a final scratch over Tucker's ear, she's gone.

He feels a need to glance each way in the compartment when memories flood in of the other time he'd interacted with a ticket collector. He glances to make certain that the annoying group of foreigners isn't present anywhere nearby…

Bleh—I'm getting paranoid…

Lucas leans back, and closes his eyes for a moment, then opens them again and stares out of the window at the darkening landscape beyond. The sad feelings overwhelming him in this moment weren't quite that unfamiliar to him. He had felt this way pretty much since the first time that Louellen had rejected his feelings for her in recent months…

This time it feels so different…

* * *

The first time Lucas had laid eyes on Louellen was from across the courtyard of the school he was attending when he was thirteen. It was her laughter that caught his attention, and he glanced up. He recalls then that she'd been sitting beside Anna, someone she was already close friends with back then. Immediately, he took a liking to her.

She only really noticed me six months later when we were in our next grade, and we were both fourteen, he recalls pensively, *and then also only by accident as well, to be honest…*

When he'd met her in person for the first it was when she was just leaving the school library and he recalls she was carrying the largest possible pile of books he'd ever seen. He'd stared, and smiled for a moment as he'd realised she was similar in one hobby at least; she enjoyed reading many books like him.

A boy, and Lucas realises he couldn't recall his name, was running along the corridor past the library, and rather than slow down or even stop he had sped past the library door, and had slammed the door against the pile of books in her arms. They all fell on the floor.

He was nearby, heard crashing books, and had been walking in the other direction, and then had to sidestep as the boy had rushed past him, and glancing back had seen all the books lying on the floor. Louellen, he didn't know her name yet, was picking them up, and she was loudly grumbling swear words…

For the briefest moment, he'd been hesitant about whether she'd appreciate any help, but his mother had taught him to be mindful of others, so he helped her. She'd brought him up that way, always saying, "You're not like your father, who is unmannered, sullen and worthless, and who upped and left me alone with a newborn baby while he had to go trek around the wild west…"

So, Lucas had walked gingerly towards the girl who he recognised from six months earlier, and quickly had picked up all the books behind her. When she turned, thinking she had more books to collect still, she saw him standing there with them in his arms, broadly smiling at her.

Not a teasing smile, Lucas thinks and inadvertently smiles at the memory, *but a smile that was warm, inviting and told the girl that he'd helped her because he cared about her. She was hesitant at first, then accepted the books from him and thanked him.*

"My name is Lucas," he'd said.
"Louellen—but my friends call me Lou."
"I like your name. I'll call *you* Louellen if you're okay with that," he had said. "My full name is Lucas Cayton—"
"Louellen Herbert."

He recalls how he'd stared at her. That she'd stared back at him with her deep blue-green eyes. He liked her appearance immediately. He'd always liked her short coppery-red hair too, though nowadays it was more shoulder length. She'd dyed her hair since a long time before them, meeting with blue and green shades. *She wore her beret that had been altered to make it unique that day*, Lucas thinks, *and she wore it again today…*

Louellen still used the beret, and had done so in all the time they'd known each other. Because it was so unique, he stared at it and this was when she spoke for the first time.

"What are you looking at…?"

"I like your beret," he'd answered sheepishly.

"What about it?"

"It's pretty…"

"I did it myself. I plan to study art and stuff," she'd stated, "so I'm practising with craft stuff."

"You're good."

"Thanks…"

They stayed silent from shyness for several minutes, both looking in every direction than at one another. When he'd glanced back he'd realised he was alone, and when he looked for Louellen, it seemed she'd rushed away with haste in her step to wherever she'd been heading originally.

He realises that he'd shrugged at that moment, then continued his own trek through the extensive school building until reaching his destination. *It had been lessons about communication science;* he recalled.

Also, as he realises *now,* he was constantly thinking about this past encounter, and he'd forced himself not to get obsessive about her. It was about a month later when he had another chance encounter with the girl, with Louellen, but this time it was a more emotional situation.

She was sitting on the stairs in the west block of the school, and when he got closer, he saw her wipe away tears from her face.

"Are you okay?" he'd asked as he approached her. At first, she didn't hear him.

"Louellen, what's the matter?"

She'd looked up, and from her puzzled expression for several minutes, she didn't comprehend why he'd be asking her. It even seemed to him she didn't remember who he was.

"Have we met?"

"I helped pick up those books when a boy knocked them out of your arms."

"Ooh yeah, right, now I remember. Thanks for that, by the way."

"Did something happen? You seem upset."

"It's just that today would have been my mother's birthday."

"How come?"

"She died when I was just seven years old."

"That sounds sad."

"I was sad. Still feel sad every day."

"How did she die?"

"She had—an illness." the answer came hesitantly.

"If you don't want to talk about it, that's okay. Want me sitting with you?"

"Sure, if you want to…"

Lucas had sat down beside the girl, and at first Louellen had sat beside him in a rigid posture, though the occasional hiccups he heard coming from her showed to him she was still upset and crying. He sat there silently, letting his presence be soothing to her, never offering his hand or hugging her, and he was certain that she had noticed that he was letting her just be caught up in whatever was upsetting her.

Then, after about twenty minutes, he'd smiled at her indiscreetly when she slumped against his shoulder.

CHAPTER SEVEN

After a brief jolt from the train's motion as it sped up had pulled Lucas from his thoughts, he goes back to contemplating over the past, over how he'd been with Louellen in the earliest days…

Lucas smiles when he remembers that they'd sat there silently for an hour. He had just sat beside her without putting an arm around her or anything. They also never talked. As the hour passed, her sobbing had become quieter, then had stopped apart from an occasional hiccup. Then, after a while longer, even that had stopped. She'd got up a little while after that, and silently had walked off, leaving him there on his own, with his own thoughts racing through his mind because of what she'd said about her mother. It had caused him to think about when his father had left…

"Hmm, I still haven't seen him," Lucas mumbles. "It would take a miracle for me to see him. I don't even know if he's still alive…"

He recalls he saw Louellen again a few days later. She was with her friends. They were sitting in the school canteen, and she was sitting there with four girls; three of about the same age and one girl was younger than the others. He'd been heading towards the other end of the canteen when a voice had called out his name and he altered his plans.

"Lucas!"

He had turned as he recognised the voice who'd called out, and on turning around, he saw Louellen beckoning him over to her table. Feeling self-conscious and hesitant, he'd walked to the group. She'd tapped on the seat beside her. He had sat down, then glanced around the table.

"This is Lucas," Louellen had explained. "He's the boy who was so nice to me after that other boy had knocked those books out of my hands—and so you know, Lucas, this is Anna, and this is Kayla who is my niece—and this is Emlyn and her sister Sylvia."

"Hi," he'd said, addressing no one at the table in particular.
"Hiiii," the girls had all echoed.

Lucas had cringed somewhat when all the girls crumpled in a heap of giggles, causing him to blush. He felt a need to glance sidelong at Louellen. He saw then that she was *also* blushing a deep shade of red. Then, Emlyn had commented, and it had him wishing that he could just sink into a hole in the ground. "So, is this your new boyfriend then, Lou…?" Emlyn had then giggled even louder, and he glared angrily at her.

"Shut up, Em," Louellen had grunted.

Lucas had glanced back at Louellen again, noticing how angry she had sounded, and saw that she was also glaring at Emlyn. In fact, her stare had a venom in it that made it clear this wasn't the first time she'd reacted this way to the other girl. When the other girls had also chanted: "Lou got a boyfriend…" she finally got up from her chair and rushed out of the canteen. He was sitting there only for a minute before he also got up and left the building through another exit. Once outside, he had glanced around. Louellen wasn't anywhere to be seen…

Later in the day, Lucas had spotted Louellen as she had walked along the street outside the school, about a half hour after school had ended for the day, and he rushed to her side.
"Go away," she had snapped at him.
Lucas had ignored her outburst. He hesitates only a moment before he had said, "I just thought we could go to the library together, and there's a small office where they let you do homework," he'd suggested, "but I can go away. If you want this."
He'd stopped walking, waited a moment, then simply walked off. Lucas always had been the sort of person to allow people to make up their minds about what to do next…

"Wait!"

Lucas had stopped walking and turned and waited. Louellen had quickly rushed at him, stopping a couple of meters from him, having caught up with him quicker than expected.

"I like to go there!"

She had panted as she spoke. He had nodded plainly.

"We need to take a bus then," he had said. "The bus stop is in the next street if we walk to the end of this street and turn right."

They had walked side by side silently through the streets until they reached the bus stop. Lucas checked the time table fastened on the pole, then just stated plainly to Louellen: "Soon."

She nodded once.

They'd sat down on the nearby bench side by side and didn't need to wait long for the bus to arrive. When the bus had arrived, they boarded it, and Lucas had paid for her ticket as well, which had brought a smile to her face. They had walked through the busy bus until though found two seats where they could side by side. Louellen had sat beside the window, glancing at the traffic and people outside.

After a few minutes, she had turned to him, asking, "How many stops is it to the library…?"

"Six," he'd replied, "and then we need to walk for about *five* minutes."

"Would you mind helping me with some of my homework?" Louellen asks. "I don't really like some of it, and I struggle to understand it."

"I'll try," he replied, "and if I don't know, we can look for books to help us—"

He'd stopped speaking when he glanced at her and she'd showed a glorious smile towards him and had clarified that he was correct without needing to say so…

About twenty minutes later, they'd been walking side by side towards a large grey building. They had stopped when Louellen wanted to stare up at the building for a moment, then they had walked on. "This is the library," Lucas had said, "and my mother works here, which is why I come here after school every day."

"She's a librarian…?"

"No, she works in the department where they keep the old archives—newspapers, old magazines, information about dead people… that sort of stuff," he had explained.

"Ewww…"

"Errr—I'm not sure exactly what the skill is called," he'd said. "It's more about history stuff about parents, grandparents and so on…"

"Ooh right, I think it's called genealogy."

"I didn't know that."

"You didn't know that, and your mother works there."

Louellen had giggled loudly.

"I guess I didn't pay enough attention when she told me," he'd said defensively. "We don't really talk much. Not since my father left to go to America. All she does is moan about it all day long…"

"You just live with your mother, then?"

"Yes."

"I live with my father. He brought me up after my mother died."

"Where do you live?"

"We live in North London. He owns a house there."

"My mother and I live just west of here." Lucas had pointed towards the west at the sun that was already getting low in the sky, then he'd hesitantly added. "Maybe you'd like to come visit. I'd like that."

"If I come to visit you, then you must visit me. Dad will want to meet *any* new school friend that I get." The comment had somewhat deflated the way Lucas had been feeling about this girl, but he went along with her comment.

"Sure," he'd said, trying to sound enthusiastic.

"But are we ever going inside? I'm actually getting cold."

"Okay."

✳ ✳ ✳

A few meters from the desk was the escalator that would take them to the floor where his mother had worked. He'd walked towards it, followed closely by Louellen.

She had felt in awe of the library once we walked inside, Lucas thinks, *and hadn't known the library existed…*

"This place is amazing," she had whispered. "I could come here often."

"We could come here together to study," Lucas had suggested.

"I would love that."

Lucas had smiled at her, then he'd chanced his luck. "Then it's a date…"

He hadn't looked at Louellen for a while after he'd said stated these words, and her being silent hadn't made it easy for him to determine whether it was shyness, anger or shock that was causing her silence, then had walked past a few desks, followed by Louellen. He waved at a woman sitting nearby, which Louellen noticed, and she glanced in the direction where he'd waved. A woman with a striking resemblance sat there, and she waved back.

"Is that your mother?" she'd asked softly.

"Yes."

* * *

As she'd settled herself beside Lucas at the table he chose, she glanced towards the woman who was in her mid-thirties, with her blond hair streaked with brown, red, and purple. She saw two massive, colourful earrings and a matching necklace. But mostly, she appeared to be dressed as a smartly dressed office worker, with the rest of her appearance. Later, Louellen had whispered to Lucas she liked his mother…

As they sat at the table, his mother had walked into the room.

"How was school?" she'd asked, adding, "and I see you made a friend…"

"School was fine," Lucas had answered, then had introduced her. "This is Louellen. She goes to school with me. I'm going to help her with her homework."

"Ah, right, would you *both* like a chocolate drink?"

They both had nodded…

Normally, Lucas would have protested whenever his mother came over to where he sat and suggested a drink, but then he'd seen Louellen nodding, so he nodded too. His mother had turned, and a few minutes later she was back with the drink, then left again and shut the door of the room behind her.

"She's nice."

"I guess so," Lucas had said reluctantly, which caused her to frown at the lack of his enthusiasm. Then she'd shrugged like she figured out he was probably embarrassed.

They'd got to work on their homework, each sipping the drink slowly, which was still almost *too* hot to drink. After a while, they'd taken a break and had wandered around the library, before finally ending up in the aisle with science fiction books on one side and detective stories and mysteries on the other side…

Lucas glances momentarily from the window while thinking over the happier memories. *I always loved going back to that aisle*, Lucas thinks as he smiles at the memories of the first few times they'd met up.

The next time they had met up, he'd walked the few steps outside the library, and he'd pulled the heavy entrance door open, and nodded at Louellen for her to walk inside. The library had been warm, and they took off their coats at the same time and hung them on coat hooks near the entrance among the mass of other coats.

"Seems busy here."

"It always is, but the room I was talking about is actually for staff, so it will be quiet in there."

"Oh, right?"

They'd picked up their bags and had walked past the desk with the librarians, some of whom had recognised Lucas and had greeted him…

* * *

Lucas glances out of the window as the train comes to a gentle stop. *Four more stops before I'm home. Unfortunately, I'm going home on my own…*

As he sat there waiting, he recalled when Louellen had told bits and pieces about herself. She'd told him more about her mother's passing when she was seven. He'd told her about when his father had left, which had happened three years before he met Louellen.

"He just packed up and walked out, got on a plane to America," he'd said, "and I've not seen him since. My mother was so angry at him. I hate him for doing that to her."

"I hated my mother for leaving me, but she was ill with a terminal disease—it wasn't cancer… It was something else," she'd said, "and Dad doesn't want to talk about, and he actually never told me what she died of…"

"It sounds like her dying made her very sad," he'd responded.

"I think so too," Louellen had said. "He never goes out. He has a few female friends who come over for a meal from time to time, but always says he's too old for a new girlfriend and all that."

"My mother is the *same*, but the bad thing for her is that, technically, she's still married to my father," he'd continued. "She doesn't know where he is, so cannot do anything about it."

"How horrible…" Louellen had said softly, looking genuinely shocked.

"I've vowed never to be like him," he'd said, then he'd smiled at her and she'd blushed in response and glanced down. He'd grinned at her display of emotions.

Their visits became a nice routine of going to the library, and they'd ended doing this for a better part of the next six months, but then summer was approaching and brought with it the dilemma of them not seeing one another for several months, so he broached this subject.

"Lou," he'd whispered. "In the summer, would you want to go to an activity camp with me…?"

"An activity camp? What happens there?" She'd sounded curious but also had sounded sceptical about the suggested 'activities.'

"It's a camp that runs for two months in the summer. There are places where the boys sleep, and the girls have their own huts," he'd explained. "It's a place where you can learn things. Last summer, I learnt archery there, and the reason I'm so interested in business studies is because I helped in their supermarket. It's totally run by the kids who go to the camp… and there's other stuff. I've seen you draw. They got art classes for drawing, painting, stuff with clay, even making clothes—and if I remember right, the people who make them organise a fashion show event to show it off."

Lucas saw a smile appear on Louellen's face, which went from indifferent to a broad smile.

"Oh, I love designing clothes," she'd shrieked, then had cringed, expecting the librarians to come over and tell her off for being too noisy.

"So, you'd want to go?"

"Sure—but I've to ask dad if it's okay," she'd answered. "He probably would want information about the place."

"Errr—I came prepared. My mother is on their mailing list. I can ask her to get an extra brochure for you," he'd suggested, but then he'd reached into his bag and had pulled out a large A4-size brochure and handed it to Louellen.

Louellen had taken the brochure and pulled it in front of her. She'd turned to the first page and ran her finger through the list of activities, then glanced up, grinning. Then she'd reached up and hugged him tightly, much to his shock and surprise in equal measures, and had planted a kiss squarely on his lips before realising what she was doing, then had quickly pulled away from him blushing brightly. He'd also blushed as brightly. They each had looked in every direction than towards each other…

***

It had taken them both a while to get over their shared, earliest initial embarrassment of what had occurred between them, but some thirty minutes later, they'd sat smiling at one another knowingly. Then, a little while later, Lucas had put his hand over hers. Rather than pulling her hand away, she'd looked up at him into his eyes. They'd known immediately that something was now between them. They both sensed it from the other individual and themselves. It was obvious this might be a beginning of something new between them…

They'd hugged when they were ready to go home. Lucas had glanced over his shoulder often at her fast-disappearing figure of Louellen, who'd rushed to the nearest Underground Station.

Obviously to take the Tube home, he'd thought.

It wasn't until two weeks later when he'd seen Louellen again. She'd apologised for being absent, saying that her father had organised a trip to France for them. It had been so brief notice that she only had enough time to get home and get packed up, and they'd been off to the airport in under an hour. Lucas had got to see the photos she'd taken…

"That's my dad," Louellen had said, and pointed at a tall man in one photo. Lucas had looked at the photo and had felt envy all the sudden, wishing he had a father to go on trips with him.

***

"You *still* hang out with him, Lou…!"

Emlyn had stood in front of Louellen and Lucas. She had been sneering at them, especially at Lucas. Behind her stood Anna. He'd looked up at them both. There was something about how Emlyn had said the words that he didn't like, and on glancing sideways at Louellen, he'd noticed she didn't like it either.

"He's my friend, Emlyn Singley," Louellen had snapped.

Lucas had raised an eyebrow. It was the first time he'd heard Louellen speak in such an angry to Emlyn in all the months that he'd been friends with her. He was actually wondering why Emlyn could be so rude to him.

"He's a loser," Emlyn had jeered.

"I think YOU are," Louellen had responded coldly. "If *you* don't like my friends, you might as well go away because I don't want you as my friend."

Lucas had glanced at every girl. It felt like he'd landed in the middle of something that had been ongoing for quite some time. Whatever it was made him feel uncomfortable, and he'd shifted his position, had looked down at his bag, and considered walking off and leaving Louellen alone with her friends. Leaving her would allow her to mend whatever the damage was in her friendship with Emlyn, which might be better for her…

Lucas had just taken hold of the handle of his bag, but Louellen held her arm in front of his chest that was preventing him from getting up. He'd glanced at her questioningly.

"You don't need to go," she'd said forcefully. "Emlyn needs to go. I don't want her here."

To put emphasis on the words, Louellen had stared coldly at the tall girl in front of them, who still stared at him. After a few moments, Emlyn had realised that Louellen had stopped talking and was just staring at her.

"So, I guess *you* like losers better," Emlyn had spat out. "You coming, Anna…?"

Anna had jerked into the realisation that the girl next to her was now making *her* choice between two friends. She'd glanced from girl to girl, then had pleaded with her eyes with Lucas, hoping he could help her get out of this cat-and-mouse situation. He'd mouthed 'sorry' at her, then had looked away. He was in no position to her choose sides; it had felt so similar to when his parents had argued long before his father had left.

He'd glanced back towards the girls when two people giggled loudly. Louellen was sitting beside him with Anna beside her, and when he searched out the surroundings, he saw Emlyn stomping off and pushing people out of the way as she rushed away.

"Anna has been friends with me a *lot* longer than Em might

realise," Louellen had explained. "She's like you in some ways. She doesn't like conflict either…"

Lucas and Anna had stared at one another past Louellen, who'd leaned back.

"Are you *really* friends with Lou?" Anna had asked with an obvious curious tone in her voice, rather than the malice with which Emlyn had spoken with.

"Yes, I am," he'd replied. "We've been friends for a few months now."

"Good! Lou has *too* few good friends," Anna had said. "If you're her friend, then you're my friend as well."

Lucas had smiled and had said, "I'd like that…" then he'd glanced at Louellen and he saw her bite her lip for a moment and she appears hesitant.

"He's my boyfriend," she'd blurted out, going bright red at the same time. Lucas and Anna both stared at her, and Anna had her mouth open in disbelief. "Since when, Lou…?" she'd asked.

"Errr—since—errr… a few weeks ago, when we were in the library together."

Lucas had stared at Louellen, realising that 'a few weeks ago' was when the accidental kiss had happened. She'd never told him how she felt about it happening, nor had he said anything about his feelings…

But was she just teasing him now, Lucas thought, *or am I really her boyfriend as she just said to Anna?* Lucas had paid little attention to the conversation between the girls afterwards. He listened discretely and realised that Anna was right about them being long-time friends. *I should ask Louellen later about how they met…*

But he'd stayed sitting there and felt a need to get to know her better, to get her to be a friend.

It's all worth it… She's the sort of person I've always imagined as a girlfriend as I was growing up…

* * *

An hour later, on their way to their next lessons, he'd broached the topic. "Lou—you'd said I'm—errr… your boyfriend?" he'd asked. "Did you mean that…?"

Louellen had stopped walking and glanced at him before answering. "Yes, I meant it," she'd said. "I like you a lot, and I want us to be more than just friends."

"I want it too," he'd replied.

"By the way, I showed dad the brochure, and he said I can go."

"Really?"

"Yes," she answered, beaming a smile at him.

Lucas glanced around for a moment, then saw the corridor was empty now, and he leaned forward and quickly kissed Louellen's lips. When he pulled back, he saw her staring, perplexed, almost dazed.

"What was that for?" she'd asked after a moment of silence.

"To return the kiss in the library."

"Ohhh…!"

Now she'd glanced around as well, then she grabbed Lucas by the collar and dragged him to a short side-corridor, and only grinned at him for a moment…

Lucas had felt her arms slide around his neck and she stood closer than ever before. They looked one another in the eyes for a moment, then they kissed. Not a quick kiss this time, nor was it hesitant. After a few minutes, they stopped kissing and pulled away only slightly, and her arms were still around his neck.

"Now we're a proper girlfriend and boyfriend…!"

"Ah, so it takes a kiss for that to be true?" he'd asked.

"Yep—In my rule book, it does."

"Any rules in the book about telling someone you love them?" he'd asked.

"Errr—" Louellen had stopped speaking and glanced past him to think.

"I'm going to count to ten and if you have no answer, the rule exists," he'd said.

"Errr—errr—umm," she'd stuttered.

"Ten—nine—eight…" he'd counted down.

"Hang on—you're counting too fast."

"Seven—six—five…"

"Okay, I give up. I can't think of any good rule."

Lucas had stared at her for just a few moments, then plainly stated, "I think I love you, Lou…"

Louellen had just stared at him, but she was biting her lip again, and he could see some uncertainty in her eyes. He'd wondered then if he'd said the wrong thing, and that she'd walk away any moment now; and that he'd never see her again. She'd answered with her next action.

Lucas was taken aback when Louellen had kissed him, but with more passion than a moment earlier…

CHAPTER EIGHT

With the memory of a nicer day on his mind, Lucas watches for the evidence of him arriving at the station because the train had slowed, then goes back to his reminiscing about Louellen…

He'd kissed her passionately on that day, much to his surprise, and as he kissed her, she pushed closer to him and he'd tightened his arms around her slender waist. The kissing had lasted longer. It had almost been like she was avoiding his question by kissing more. But then she'd stopped and pulled back slowly, looking him in the eyes.

"I love you as well," she'd whispered.

They'd just stared at one another for the longest time. When Louellen had said these words, he felt like his heart almost exploded from his chest. He'd recalled then when he'd heard her for the first time across the school courtyard and that his feelings for her had started that day.

"You still want to go to the activity camp?" he'd asked.

"Yes—if we go together, it'll be so much fun," she'd answered.

"I'm glad your father said yes," he'd continued, "because if I had to go on my own this time, I would have been so lonely."

As he spoke, he'd reached up and brushed some of Louellen's hair from her face, and she rewarded him with another smile…

* * *

That summer had been a roller coaster of emotions, and about learning what it was like to have a girlfriend. He could still smile about it all, even with the events of the day clouding it with other emotions. Lucas smiled as the landscape outside the train window started fading from view in the early evening hours. Lucas sighs…

I guess I'm missing Lou's presence, he thinks, *and I wonder now if moving to Mellowstone Greene has been such a good idea, but over there I can live for a substantial time from the inheritance and the windfall money from my last job in London. In London, the money would have been gone in a matter of three or four*

Lucas notices now that he was approaching the station where he'd depart the train, so he gets up and put on his coat. He puts all the bags in a row on one seat and glances out of the window if he could see his car.

Hmm, it's too dark to see anything outside now, he thinks.

He feels a gentle jolt as the train comes to a halt, and he picks up all the bags in one hand and scoops up the dog with his other arm, then rushes to the nearest exit and steps from the train. He glances each way to realise he's alone on the entire platform except for Tucker, who he lowers to the ground.

He strolls through the spacious interior of the train station to the exit and is standing on the pavement a minute later. After readjusting the bags, they walk towards his car, and once he's by its side, he places the bags and dog all in the boot with the back seating lowered so the dog would have space to move around.

Before he gets into the car, Lucas glances at the restaurant where he'd hoped to take Louellen *if* she'd agreed to visit Mellowstone Greene.

Another sigh…

Lucas gets into his car, pauses a moment before turning on the engine and leans back to think about what he could do now. An option was to just sell the cottage and move back to London.

But that might be costly…

The other option was to persuade Louellen that 'life in the countryside' wasn't as horrid as she seemed to make it out to be.

Either way, I want to have a life that includes her, he thinks, *and that's what I wanted back then and it's still the case now. I told her as much when we'd just started being together all those years ago…*

Lucas turns the key in the ignition and starts the car engine, then he slowly reverses out the parking slot he'd used and then drives slowly to the car park exit. He glances a few times each way for oncoming traffic, and when he sees none, he turns right and begins the lonely journey home…

* * *

"Well, hello, I saw you've been busy shopping…"

Lucas curses under his breath when a familiar, annoying voice rings out from the neighbouring garden only a minute after he'd parked up and exited the car with most of the bags. His second haul of bags since he'd left them under the blanket in the car the previous evening. Because of Louellen's rejection, the neighbour's jolliness was most annoying today, and it acutely reminded him of asking Louellen to move in with him…

Lucas rolls his eyes and suddenly wishes that Mrs Peg Whitwell would just get swallowed up by a deep hole. He was already feeling miserable, and her comment and her overly cheery voice made it worse.

"Good morning, Mrs Whitwell."

"Now, now, what did *we* agree on? You were to call *me* Peg."

Lucas now just ignores her comment, and walks back into his house, then shuts and locks his front door. He rolled his eyes again when he hears her bemoan his apparent rudeness. "Well, I never…" from outside, and suddenly he feels a need to grin broadly at causing such a disarray in her oh-so-orderly world.

Suddenly, his mood had lightened somewhat, even though he'd slept poorly and tossed a lot, and got up twice during the night, but after that little happen-stance, he felt a lot cheerier than before. Suddenly, he felt energised to do stuff, so he glances around the hallway.
Maybe I can get cracking and get a lot of stuff done everywhere in the house.

Now that he'd brought all remaining decoration bits and pieces inside, he'd left 'procrastinating' in the car into the house. When he arrived home from London the previous day, he had no excuses to do nothing around the house anymore. He should get on and make the house nice. When he realises this was how he'd described the lack of him decorating the cottage to Louellen, he smiles for a moment. Suddenly, the terms were very hilarious, and he wasn't certain why…
"Right then, Lou, they're *no* longer procrastinating in the back of my car. I can get the house *all* sorted, I guess," Lucas says loudly, adding the thought afterwards: *Maybe I can actually have a 'home' to live in*

Lucas picks up the bags of curtains—and the other items he'd bought for the house, and which he'd dumped near the front door when he got home—and he carries them to the living room, placing them on the floor there.

He opens each bag to be reminded of what it might contain, then lifts two of the bags from the floor and places them on the other side of the room. He walks back to the hallway, grabs his coat that's draped over the handrail, and carries it to a chair in the kitchen. After about half an hour of this back and forth, he has cleared everything from the hallway, the stairs and the landing upstairs. He picks up the wallpaper stripper from the floor in the living room, where he'd left it a few days earlier, and carries it upstairs and sets to removing the old wallpaper off the walls…

After completing to remove wallpaper, Lucas climbs from the ladder, then he walks downstairs and retrieves his broom from the kitchen cabinet, then walks back upstairs and vigorously sweeps the floor, and allows as much of the wallpaper to fall down the stairs.

Slowly, a large heap of old wallpaper gathers at the bottom of the stairway, and to get downstairs Lucas has to climb over it awkwardly. He walks back to the kitchen, and searches for the roll of bin liners he knows he saw only a day earlier, and once he finds it, he glances around and grumbles about being so lazy and why hadn't he done more tidying up around the house sooner than on *this* day.

"If Lou was here now, she would have grumbled about the state of the house," Lucas mumbles angrily.

The collecting of all the bits of wallpaper almost became a game of sorts, and Lucas smirks at the thought of 'accidentally' dumping the contents of this bin liner onto Mrs Whitwell's well-maintained lawn, and then to just claim to her: "It must have been some animal that opened the bag, and then the wind might have blown it everywhere…"

But I cannot do that if I want to live here in peace, Lucas chides himself, *and she might claim it was Tucker, then they might take him away from me…*

Like he sensed Lucas was thinking about him, Tucker came running from the kitchen and stopped at the man's feet, wagging his tail.

"Are you asking *me* to take you for a walk?" Lucas gets a fast, wagging tail in response. "Walkies…? You want walkies…?" Lucas says to the dog, grinning broadly. He lifts the dog half off the floor, and walks with him to near the front door where he lowers Tucker, who sits down and waits, wagging constantly. Lucas grabs the dog's lead from the chair just inside the living room where he'd dropped it the previous evening and fastens it to the loop on the dog's collar. He clambers over the wallpaper heaps to grab his coat from the kitchen.

He holds the doorknob for a moment before opening the front door and vows to ignore his neighbour if she's busy in her garden…

* * *

Lucas walks from the house with the dog by his side. He shuts and locks the front door, then paces quickly down his garden path to the street, and quickly turns right to start his routine walk with the dog. He wants the walk to feel like routine, but deep down the feelings of worry had started once he was passing the hedge beside the unkempt gardens next to Priory Mansion. His pace increases. This time, the walk with Tucker would not last that long, and Lucas just wanted to go home to get on with decorating his house.

I want to show Louellen that there is something here for her, he thinks. *Maybe I can persuade her to visit with a beautifully decorated house rather than a dump that it is right now…*

On the completion of his outing with the dog, Lucas rushed to his front door and cursed loudly after closing and locking the door. "Fuck, she's making me paranoid now," he mumbles. "Fuck this. I'm just going to do things my way and totally ignore her reactions…"

He removes the lead and collar from the dog, deciding that Tucker can have a bit of time unencumbered by a collar. He places the lead collar and his coat on the chair in the living room. Next, he takes off his jumper and places it also on the chair.

Lucas picks up the tin with white wood paint, and the brush beside it, and then grabs the bottle of cleaning fluid and carries all of it upstairs where he places the items on the floor at the top of the stairs, then turns on the light…

… and the light switch won't turn on the light, and Lucas frown for a moment, feeling annoyed.

He grumbles under his breath, turns and goes back down the stairs, and he walks down the stairs and goes to the area below the stairs where the electrics box is located. He opens up the box and counts the fuses and then runs his finger along the row of switches to check whether one has tripped. Now that he's actually paying attention to the electrical box, it's clear someone had messed with it. Or at least, that's his impressions of what he sees…

He tries a switch, and scrambles for his flash-light the next moment when every other light in the house also turns off. It's only early in the evening, but Lucas was in a darker part of the house.

I guess I need to put a window on the wall beside this electric box.

Then his flash light flickers for a moment and turns off as well.

"Argh, I guess I need to get new batteries for this," he grunts loudly.

Lucas fumbles around until he finds the reset button, and a moment later both the kitchen light and hallway light turn back on. He peers up the stairs to see that the light at the top of the landing is still off.

I guess something is wrong with that switch or that bulb doesn't work.

Before going upstairs to check if either theory is correct, Lucas first checks all the light switches in all rooms downstairs and confirms they all work properly. He climbs the stairs and momentarily stops at the small window halfway up, and stares at the neighbour's house.

Her lights are all on, he thinks.

Lucas arrives back at the offending light switch, and he glances down at the downstairs lights. "Here goes nothing," he mumbles. He flips the switch, and… nothing happens with the lights. "What the hell," he mumbles louder. He looks closely at the switch again. When he tries the switch once more, all lights turn off again. He goes back downstairs, repeats resetting the lights, then he searches for his copy of the Yellow Pages, which he'd put somewhere in the house. On finding it, he checks his watch and realises it's *too* late for an electrician.

I guess I'll call for one to come over tomorrow and leave that switch alone for today.

Lucas goes back upstairs and tries to paint the wood there by the light of his flash-light. It wasn't easy, but slowly and steadily he makes progress.

Maybe not going to be the neatest job ever, but it will have to do. Besides, if I'm doing that rebuilding later, which I'd drawn in my notebook, then this wall will be gone, and all this side of the house will be a large master bedroom with an en-suite bathroom.

Lucas looks out of the window for a minute.

Maybe I should add one more room to the plans.

He smiles now.

I should get a good-sized studio added. Maybe I can persuade Lou that way…

Lucas stares at the other end of the landing, and he wonders for a moment what to do about everything he'd been thinking about on the train on his way back home.

Maybe if I can persuade Louellen to visit, she'd feel more comfortable if she's able to have a room of her own. The room at the other end of the landing is right next to the bathroom. It will mean that I'd constantly walk past her door whenever I have to use the bathroom, but it's a bit late to swap stuff over, and I like the room I'm using too much. Besides, it feels uncomfortable to be so close to the window through which Mrs Whitwell can see everything from her house.

Lucas frowns.

I guess the window needs a blind for privacy. Dammit, that's the one thing I forgot to get when I went shopping. Maybe I could put one curtain there for the moment, but it wouldn't give us enough privacy.

He grabs his measuring tape, and walks to the window in question and measures it, then spots the movement of a curtain in the house next door just as he's about to walk away and wonders why Mrs Whitwell keeps looking at his house. So he shrugs and just walks away from the window. He grabs the piece of plywood he'd used for the pots of paint and carries it nonchalantly to the window, then places it against the window at a slight angle, and peeks past it just in time to see the curtain drop in place.

I guess she doesn't like this. I wonder why she keeps looking at the house.

Lucas had convinced himself that she's just a nosey neighbour, but *now*—ever since he'd read the article in the magazine—something nags at his mind about *her* behaviour. It's almost like she's worried that he's going to find out something about the house he's living in…

* * *

Hours later, in the pitch darkness of the night, Lucas got ready to take Tucker out and he sets aside his thoughts about his worries. He has another puzzle to look at, and that's as an old building called Priory Mansion. Lucas wants to see if he can see anything outside it or, if possible, inside it. That's different from the accounts given by the villagers.

Suddenly, he realises that most of the information had come from Mrs Whitwell, and always it was something negative she had said. So negative, in fact, that he'd got the impression she wanted him to think that the village was a terrible place to live in.

Lucas walks into his bedroom and takes off clothing worn since arriving home and doing decorating around the house. He places the clothing on top of one of the unopened boxes in the room. He walks to the bathroom and realises that the neighbour might have seen more than she'd wanted if not for the plywood in front of the window then he grins for a moment but then feels self-conscious and walks to the plywood and adjusts it so she cannot see him however she might try to do this…

He washes quickly, using the wash basin, dries off, then deodorises thoroughly and stares in the mirror for a while to make certain that no pain got smudged on his face. He turns and walks back to the bedroom, where he pulls a shirt and jeans from the wardrobe and dresses himself. After getting dressed, he walks to the windows and looks out at the nearest houses for a moment, then he glances at the science magazine that's on the table beside the window. He picks it up and re-reads part of the article:

> "If you are after answers, especially the most obvious ones, start by inve
> around and investigate the area further afield. By elimination, you can slow
> for such investigations. Such perseverance solved most of the more horrific

Lucas frowns for a moment, realising the scientist conveying information in the article was right. *I can start with my house*, Lucas thinks, *and I could start with my loft.* He glances up at what could be an entry point into the loft space. *It's still too early in the day. Any banging and her next door would definitely complain until she's blue in the face.* He grins at the thought of Mrs Whitwell standing on his doorstep with a blue face…

He shrugs and returns to his original plan of going out with the dog.

Arriving downstairs, he finds Tucker near the front door

obediently and he guesses the dog knows he's going to go for a walk with him. Tucker sits there showing a dog's equivalent of a smiling face and his tail wags every time Lucas glances towards him. "I guess you're ready for your walks…"

He gets a loud, excitable yip, then the dog rushes around in a happy rush.

Lucas puts on his coat, puts the collar on the dog, fastens the lead on the collar, then steps from the house…

* * *

A few minutes later, Lucas was slogging the usual route, but today he walks much slower, and he wanted Tucker to have fun in the fields they usually bypassed. He walks a slow, deliberate pace. It's eight o'clock in the morning and he wants to be out long enough so that when he gets home and starts making the planned noise, there was no way for Mrs Whitwell to complain about any of it…

Lucas frowns and wonders why he's even thinking about his neighbour when he has better things to think about, such as the almost naggingly annoying situation with Louellen.

It's such a simple matter, really, he thinks. *She said no, and that was the end. But was it…?*

Something about why Louellen might have said no was making him more determined to change her mind. He wanted her with him in his new life in Mellowstone Greene, *but only if she knows she can feel happy here…*

Lucas crosses the street towards the path that will get him to the fields outside the village. Another fifteen minutes later, and he stands at the edge of the field watching Tucker running around, even if he was shivering and wondering if perhaps going out for a walk so early was a good idea. He watches as the dog has fun. It gives him time to think over his plans for the next few days, but it would involve leaving the dog home… perhaps.

So, Lucas stays standing there and allows the dog to burn off as much energy as possible, so it's going to be easier for the dog to cope alone at home for the first time since becoming his companion.

After about forty minutes, the chill in the air becomes too much and because Tucker is less active, Lucas decides it's time to go home.

An exhausted dog finally runs to him, with his tongue lolling from his mouth, and drops on the ground at his feet, loudly panting. Lucas places the lead back on the collar, and after a few minutes the dog gets up and they head back home…

* * *

"Good morning, Gylda…!" Lucas calls out and then he waves towards his friend when he sees a familiar woman cross the road ahead of him.

"Ahh, good morning, Lucas," Gylda calls back. "How are you lately?"

"I'm doing well," Lucas calls out, grinning.

Once he catches up with the woman, Lucas lets Gylda do her usual patting and stroking of Tucker.

He broaches the question to his mind. "I'm not sure if you'd be willing to answer my questions," he says, "but I'm very interested in finding out the history of this village."

"Have you been to the library that I mentioned during our last conversation?" she asks.

"No, I'd forgotten about going there," he says. "So sorry…"

Gylda pulls a piece of paper and a pencil from her bag and she writes on the paper. "This is the address of the library," she says. "This library will be the best place for you to get started with your search, but if you come to my cottage at, let's say, three o'clock, I'll sit down with you and tell you as much of what I know."

"I'll come over for a visit," he says, smiling even broader.

"See you this afternoon."

Gylda walks away from Lucas before he can say any more to the woman, and he glances after her for a few minutes, feeling curious and wondering what she might tell him…

Part Two

CHAPTER NINE

AFTER THE CONVERSATION, HIS JOURNEY home took longer him longer that expected overall and it was because he was attempting to find excuses to stay out longer. He used this self-imposed excuse to stay out longer. He used the excuse of refastening his shoe laces to kneel and peer through the undergrowth at the massive mansion that lies hidden in the large, unkempt garden that once would have looked rather beautiful.

Remnants of that old beauty are still visible in a few places. He glances over his right shoulder through the undergrowth to judge the size of the garden and determines that it's possible that the garden once stretched all the way to the field where he'd let his dog play not so long ago. He realised he'd been at the small copse in between the garden and the field and, from what he can determine, the bushes there had just kept growing without being kept under control after the garden stopped being maintained regularly.

Perhaps when the last owner had died, he thought pensively. *If only someone worked on it for a few weeks…*

But the gardens were in such a terrible state that Lucas had the impression immediately that the old building - that's just visible between the many bushes and trees - would be in a similar state.

Lucas straightens up.

For several minutes, he fights off the urge to push his way through the undergrowth lining the path. He'd always walked along the path with Tucker, and he would go there to check the house out from a distance. However, as he stares towards the house, he gets the sensation of 'being watched' from within the house, and the feeling immediately unsettles him. He shakes his head to shake off the feelings, then slowly walks on - looking ahead rigidly to stroll home, then after a few minutes he turns his head and stares towards the house, forcing himself to stare. The feelings from moments before flooded back. He stares ahead again and repeats the actions… and another sensation of 'being watched' happens. He feels physically unsettled now.

He shakes his head, then slowly walks home again—but constantly staring at the house now—and wonders, for a moment, why he always takes this path back home, and why he never simply walked back home along the main road, which was a longer route but wouldn't cause this situation of feeling equally anxious and curious…

Slowly, his pace hastened. He wants to get home as soon as it's possible, even if it's just to get to work on the task he'd set for himself while planning his day during the previous evening. He wanted to work on most of his plans before it was time to visit Gylda. As he walks, he pulls the folded paper from his pocket and stares at the elegant handwriting. She'd only written an address, with 'London' below it. He recognises the street name but cannot recall he'd ever visited this part of North London before…

… and what's so important about this specific library that she wants him to visit…? And why…?

He folds the paper and now puts it in the top pocket of his coat.

First a visit to see Gylda, and hear what she has to tell me, then perhaps a visit to this library, where she says I can learn much more about the village more. But why would some library in North London even have information about a tiny village in the northern part of Norfolk…?

He stops again when Tucker stops to sniff at some bushes, and then the dog decides it's a good place to relief himself. "Okay Tucker, I'd think you drunk a bathtub of water with the way you piss yourself dry," Lucas mumbles.

But he doesn't pull at the lead and just stands there for several minutes; he isn't in any rush yet.

Slowly, he and Tucker wander back to his house. When he sees the neighbour busy in the garden, Lucas feels like slowing down, but then she sees his arriving, and gets up, and she rushes into her house. He frowns at her behaviour. *She's acting so odd*, he thinks, *and to be honest, now I think about it, she's always behaved odd…*

Lucas walks into his garden hastily before Mrs Whitwell would change her mind, shuts his gate, then he let Tucker off the lead, and just casually strolls to his front door. *No pot of freshly cooked food is waiting for me*, he thinks. *How ironic… I guess she fed me enough. Or I'm fattened up enough. Oh, so what next? Is she going to turn out to be an evil witch who wants to cook me, like Hansel and Gretel?*

Lucas glances quickly towards his neighbour's house one more time before he walks inside. She definitely wasn't anywhere in viewing distance. He walks inside, then closes and locks his door. He realised then that the locking part was becoming a necessary habit, as it seemed now. *I wonder if I'd have her knocking on his door if I started doing the more heavy-handed work now. Only one way to find out and that's actually to do it…*

He looks around him, and he wonders what he should do first, but then glances down and realises that it's best to get changed into his old clothing again. He walks upstairs, quickly changes clothing, then he walks back downstairs and wanders from room to room and can't decide where he should begin with his endeavours. Finally, he settles on sorting out the dining room, though at first he's clueless why…

He realises that he'd wallpapered the room over two months earlier. However, most of the items lying on the floor there were various furniture for this room. "Maybe I should actually do something about all of this stuff and put them together," he mutters, and then he grimaced at the thought of having to do decorating as it wasn't really an activity he enjoyed much. "But if I ever want Louellen here I have to get on with this and do stuff, because she definitely wouldn't want to stay in a place which, as she's observed with previous dwellings, as something only a dump…"

… which is what she always had called all my previous abodes, he adds silently.

The dining table was relatively easy to put together, and in under an hour he's pulling it in both directions, trying to decide whether the long way should go parallel with the doors to the gardens, or whether it's better the other way around. He settles on the parallel position, but then he pushes one end against the wall opposite of the kitchen door. As he only possesses five chairs, it's no issue that the table is in this way.

Lucas constructs the three bookcases next so he can put many of his books in it and clear off a few of the boxes in the living room. He curse when he hits his thumbs or fingers more than once, and then one more time when he notices he put on the back cover for one the bookcases wrongly. It puts him off from doing more decorating. *Not that I'll need to do much of it in the future if I stay here and this is my forever home,* he thinks, *but I should hurry otherwise I'll run out of time if I want to*

Lucas turns and rushes up the stairs and stops at the top of the stairs, and stares up at the small, oddly shaped appendix that almost appears to be caused by enlarging the house. The estate agent who'd showed him around the house had stated that the left side of the house was more modern than the right side.

Maybe there was a cupboard there before, Lucas thought, glancing at the appendix. *I could put a bookcase there if I ever get the damned things put together properly.*

He glances up again. First really work out if he could hang up the lampshades, but then he remembers the electrician still needed to fix the electric cabling in the house. He was about to give up trying to find something to do when he spots something odd about the ceiling. He stared closer at the ceiling, and recalls a thought from earlier in the week that he wanted to find out if, in fact, the somewhat uneven square is bad décor or that someone has actually covered up the entry to the loft.

"Damn, I almost forgot I was going to check if it was an opening to the loft," he exclaims, then he checked the time on his watch that was in the bedroom and found there was enough time for an attempt.

From the crate in the kitchen, he grabs a large crowbar. He weighs it in his hand to see if it would have enough weight for his task, to give his swing momentum. He climbed back up the stairs and, glancing at the boarded window, and smirked at the idea of Mrs Whitwell seeing him with the crowbar as he ascended the stairs.

If she's paranoid, she's going to think I'm some sort of murderer and have a victim up here…

He grins for a moment longer at the idea, but then his shoulders slump, realising that it could cause issues if Mrs Whitwell really thought that he was capable of such actions.

What if there's already a dead body lying up there? And what if she murdered that person…

Lucas laughs loudly at this new idea. "That's almost like a plot from a Miss Marple book," he quips softly, "and I'd laugh even more if Miss Marple turns up suddenly after I had opened this ceiling, and I bet she would say that Mrs Whitwell would have been the killer…"

* * *

Lucas positions himself against the wall that is between his bed and the corner of the room, and spreads his feet out evenly. He glances up once, then he swings the crowbar to the right and then to the left, but not all the way to the ceiling. He lets the momentum make it swing back further to his right, then attempts to swing it as fast as possible up towards the ceiling…

The crowbar strikes loudly, with a crashing sound, and for a moment, the crowbar sticks into the ceiling. Then gravity reverses the momentum, and it swings down again, and Lucas puts all effort into the motion to make it swing upwards again and gets to swing up again. There was a large piece of the plaster that then came loose and, almost in slow motion at first, it falls on the floor and shatters in a pile of small chunks.

Lucas pulls at the crowbar. It becomes loose, and he lets it swing down, then right one more time and now puts in even more force into the motion up, at least as much as he can find. This blow had a greater impact than before, and immediately several chunks of ceiling plaster drop. The sounds of these cause the dog to arrive and Tucker stands at the top of the stairs and is barking loudly.

"Shush!" Lucas grunts to Tucker loudly.

The dog stops barking and stares at the man for a few moments, tilting his head from side to side, like he was asking him: "Why?"

Lucas glances back up at the ceiling. He sees he made a large hole in the ceiling with his hammering. Maybe not large enough for him to climb up and get into the loft, but he hammered out a shape that could have been a properly constructed entry way. Lucas positions the crowbar in an upright position in an upright position and lifts it upward to hit the area around the hole to break, but doesn't make the hole any larger.

I go get my step ladder and a hammer.

He goes downstairs and pulls the ladder from the cupboard in the kitchen, then hoists the step ladder up the stairs. He positions the ladder in the appendix area of the landing, then returns downstairs for the largest, heaviest hammer he owns. Before going up, he shuts the door to the kitchen, so the dog cannot impede what he's doing upstairs, or get hit by bits of plaster falling.

Lucas climbs the step ladder and studies the ceiling closely for a few minutes, which now is just slightly less than an arm's length away from him. He pushes at the surface around the hole and then identifies what part of the ceiling is loose enough to come away, and gives several blows with the claw end of the hammer, then he attempts to give several blows with the flat side that are of a sufficient impact to let the plaster come loose and fall down. Lucas curse when Tucker barks in response…

I guess the dog isn't used to noise like this.

Lucas sees he had moderate success after exerting this effort. Then, when a really large part of the plaster falls off, he sees it was covering most of an area that's also covered over with small pieces of timber. He pulls at one piece. When this happens, it snaps off. It allows for more of the ceiling to dislodge. He takes a while before the small impact hole turns into an area that can easily allow him to get up into the loft.

It will make it easier for the electrician as well, because I'm sure some cables are up here.

After he had enlarged the hole enough to it is a size that might allow him to climb up if he wants to, Lucas climbs from the stepladder. He places the hammer on the windowsill and grabs the broom that was left leaning against the wall near the bathroom door, and he brushes all the dust and pieces of plaster down the stairs.

After staring up at the ceilings for a time, Lucas walks into his bedroom, empties an almost-empty box over his bed, and walks back to the landing with the box and sets out to fill it with the larger pieces of plaster and most of the pieces of wood. An hour later, he has tidied the landing reasonably well, and it looks reasonably tidy again, apart from what a good session of hoovering could sort out even better later…

* * *

Lucas stands looking up at the ceiling while he brushes dust off his t-shirt and trousers. It's obvious from the result of his efforts that there had been a hatch to the loft in the past, and that someone had attempted to make sure it wouldn't get found in the future. Any other person might have just plastered over the ugly bit of plastering, but he wasn't this sort of person. He wonders what he could do with the ceiling now it was demolished. It was too messy to leave it as it was now…

Maybe if I remove all the ceiling above all the stairs and then put a window up there, it will also be a lot brighter here. I could put a wall up to close off the loft.

I wonder what's up there.

He had considered putting up a roof window in the bathroom already so he could remove the window there and gain space for more furniture in the bathroom. Now it turns out he could do the same thing in the hallway above the stairs and therefore gain more natural light.

I wonder if the architect could get permission from me to have an entire row of them. One here, one for the bathroom, and if I did the same in all the bedrooms as here, that's two each in the two smaller bedrooms, and three in my one.

He had smiled at the idea of having a view of the sky filled with stars to look at from his bed.

If I do that too in Lou's bedroom, she'll just fall in love with being here. I'll do the bathroom, her room, and in here first.

With a renewed purpose in his mind, Lucas grabs the hammer from the windowsill, climbs the step ladder again, and using the hammer, he removes more of the ceiling. It was now quite obvious to him there was a hatch here that someone had purposefully covered over, but why someone had taken the effort to cover it over wasn't all that clear to him. Also, he realises that from how the plaster was crumbling to dust that this feature had been here for decades…

I have to check how long the old owner lived here before.

After working for about twenty minutes, Lucas takes a break to go get himself a bottle of cola from the fridge. While he drinks from the cola in small sips, he walks to the dining room where the boxes with paperwork are located. After rummaging through two, he found the house's deed. He studies them thoroughly and checks the dates listed, then he also checks the title information to double check he'd remembered to pay for this cost as well. He sighs with relief when this was actually done.

"I hadn't realised this before. Seems the old owner is Elizabeth Michaels, and I wonder if Dorrie is a relation. I have to ask Gylda later," Lucas mumbled, "Okay, it says here she died two decades ago, and that then it became the property of the company that sold it to *me*. It doesn't say *who* sold it to them. Let's see. It says *this* Elizabeth Michaels lived here since 1950, but *no* information of who lived here before that."

Lucas frowns and wonders for a moment whether he should bring the deeds with him for the visit with Gylda to see if she knew more about the previous owners. He brings the paperwork with him so places the bundle of paperwork in his coat pocket, then he returns to the work of removing the rest of the covering placed over the hatch…

* * *

An hour later, Lucas steps from the shower for a second time in the day and pulls his towel around him and looks in the mirror to ensure he's cleanly shaved for his visit to Gylda. He pulls his shaving foam from the shelf next to the mirror and spreads a thick handful of the foam over his face. He holds his razor under hot streaming water for several minutes, then in a few quick strokes he shaves his face, periodically rinsing the razor under the running hot water.

After another few minutes, he's finished with shaving, and while drying off his face, he glances up at the ceiling of the bathroom, and then towards the window. He examines both features carefully, and notices now that the window in the bathroom seems to be newer than most other windows on the upper floor of the house, and that was going on in a part of the house that the estate agent had described as the oldest part of the house.

As he walks past the window, at this end of the landing, he now notes that it too has a more modern feel to it, and he grins suddenly.

If I move the door of the bathroom to here, and put a large a large window in the ceiling up there, then I can make the bathroom bigger, and 'her' next door cannot even look into my house anymore.

Lucas traces his hand along the wall next to the door of what he'd designated as Louellen's bedroom. There is a ceiling in the bathroom. He smirks at the idea and decides it's a good plan. He looks up at the leftovers of the ceiling in the hallway above the stairs.

I should definitely remove all of it and put a window there. It will make the stairway so much brighter. I could remove that damned annoying little window down there too while I'm at it, as that serves no function.

He stares at the ceiling for a few more minutes, then walks back to his bedroom. There he picks up his watch and realises there are still a few more hours to go until he was visiting Gylda. He already had the clothing he was going to wear later when he was going to visit Gylda. He lifts the clothing and looks over instead at his t-shirt and jeans lying on the floor.

Perhaps—

He doesn't finish the thought and just places his good clothing back on the bed, then walks to the t-shirt and jeans and puts them on again. He walks from the bedroom and closes the door behind him. The ceiling above him has a gaping hole. He grabs his flash-light off the floor near the broken light switch and shines at the hole in the ceiling. And moves the step ladder aside a moment and points the light at the roof where he can see a sort of central wooden support beam. He's certain there is another similar support beam below it. He side-eyes the stepladder, and for several minutes he feels uncertain about what to do. Then curiosity takes over…

* * *

Lucas glances at the stepladder, and for several minutes feels uncertain about what to do. But then curiosity takes over…

He places the step ladder back in an unfolded position, and looks up again, then he adjusts its position until he's certain that he can reach the lower wooden beam to lift himself up into the loft area. *So now I guess I'm going to find that dead person there, and then every cop of the county will be in my house pulling it apart. I wonder how her next door would react to that.* Lucas smirks sarcastically for a moment, pausing on the ladder, then he shrugs his shoulders at the thought. *If that's what I'm going to find up there, then I might as well just move back to London again…*
Lucas resumes his climb up the stepladder. He hoists himself into the dusty loft. He curses when he realises he should have done this stuff before taking a shower, but he sets the thought aside when he sees his surroundings. The loft has a lower ceiling than expected, and Lucas uses the flash-light to check what he might see there even if getting around the loft took effort.
I guess I can quickly rinse off any sweat once I get down from there.
He aims the flash-light in every direction, first simply to check what the roof might have been constructed of so he can confirm whether his plan to add roof windows will work as the roof was so much lower than it had appeared compared to looking at it from outside.
The loft is empty; it seems.

But then he spots the wood crates, even if he didn't register immediately after what he'd seen. He shines his flash-light twice toward the boxes, and in the beam of light, also showing small particles of dust drifting through the air, he sees six medium-sized crates that appeared to be rather old… and of course they had to be at the furthest other end of the loft!

CHAPTER TEN

LUCAS POSITIONS THE FLASH-LIGHT ON the thick wood beam beside him, and when it rolls a bit, he mutters, "Stay—stay…!" He clambers further into the loft, then turns so he's on his hands and knees, picks up the flash-light which he positions inside his t-shirt, and slowly crawls closer to the crates in the corner of the loft…

The surfaces inside the loft space are thick with dust, and there are spider webs in several places. Lucas ignores all of this. He wants to get to the crates as quickly as he can.

Someone had placed these boxes near the outer wall of the additional part of the cottage, but why someone would make so much effort to do this, and in that place, too? That's a mystery at the moment. The thick coat of dust on them shows they haven't touched them since being placed there. I wonder if they put them up here when they added the unused part of the cottage. The estate agent claimed they'd added this part of the building in about 1930… and why…?

After about twenty minutes of getting to the crates, Lucas finally is sitting beside them and he brushes off as much of the dust as he can. He tries to open a box but after checking it over; he realises that someone had hammered it shut when he sees many rusty nails lining the edge of the cover. The man grunts loudly. Of the other five boxes, only one can be opened…

On opening the box, he sees it is only part-filled, and on shining his flash-light closer, he sees papers inside the crate. "I guess I can come back for the other crates later, but I can at least take this box with me," Lucas mumbles, "and then figure out how to open them all…"

This plan proved to be an effort, and because of it, Lucas decides also to retrieve all other boxes at the same time. One by one, they get lined up next to the opening in the ceiling. Once he has completed this task and all boxes are within an arm's length of the ceiling opening, then after that he carries the boxes to the room with the only lockable door, where he was storing his more expensive belongings and important paperwork to keep them same. Something compelled him to treat the mysterious boxes similarly…

Lucas ponders for several minutes about whether he should tell anyone about the paper he'd found in the loft and decides that perhaps he could ask Mrs Whitwell about them indirectly.

Perhaps at least, he thinks, realising she'd become more and more standoffish of late. He could at least attempt to find out more information from her. More than once she'd claimed to have lived in the village all her life, so she likely knew who the named individual, Elizabeth Michaels, might have been.

Perhaps she'd been friends with her, he thinks, *though I've noticed a marked hostility on her part regarding Gylda when she's part of any conversation, and now I'm convinced that Gylda might be related to this person because her mother is Dorrie Michaels.*

Lucas locks the door of this room, and places the key in the pocket of his good trousers that he would wear later, when an idea enters his mind. He walks out of the room and peers along the hallway and stares intently at a specific place. He stares at his crowbar…

Maybe I can open the boxes that are hammered shut with that.

He picks up the crowbar, weighs it in his hand, then walks back to the locked door. He leans the crowbar against the wall beside the door as he retrieves the key from the trousers, walks back, then opens the door. As the door creaks loudly, he cringes as he pushes it open. He picks up the crowbar. Then he stands staring at the boxes for a few moments, deciding on which to open. The man walked to the first box in the row. He positions the crowbar between a small opening he finds on the side of the box where the lid isn't as tightly against the base, then with some effort that lasts several minutes, he gets the lid dislodged and it falls off. He proceeds with the next box, and after about fifteen minutes, he has got all the boxes opened.

Lucas puts the crowbar on the floor and sits down in front of the first box. He leans in to study the papers inside it again. He notes there's something specific about the appearance of the papers. Lifting one piece of paper, he now realises it's some sort of newspaper clipping, yellowed from age, and the texture feels delicate, so he handles all papers with care.

Lucas swings around ninety degrees while he remains seated, so the box is on his right, and pulls each newspaper clipping from the box one by one, and places them on the bare wooden floor to his left.

After about ten clippings, he stops with his actions. He picks up the first piece of paper again and glances at it, studying what had attracted his attention to this paper. He frowns when he spots a now-familiar name in the article, printed in tiny letters - Mellowstone Greene - and Lucas wonders what newspaper the article might have appeared in and from the font he assumes it was a broadsheet.

If I'm right, it's going to be one of the London broadsheets, Lucas thinks, because what Anna had said when she was telling me why she's Louellen's best friend is that they weren't common outside London. Also, she had known the information because she'd always said her great-grandfather owned a broadsheet for a while…

Lucas picks up another clipping. He sees the name mentioned in this clipping as well, and on this clipping it mentions the name of a potential writer as well. The name increases his curiosity.

I wonder if this Jeffrey Herbert is maybe Lou's great-grandfather. She says he worked for a newspaper. But she always claims he sold them, not wrote for them.

He puts the piece of paper down and picks up another of the papers. Again, the article mentions the village name. It lists the same Jeffrey Herbert, but now he reads through what the journalist had written. It mentions a few words that catch his attention…

"The girl was last seen by the gardener of the estate and seen running into the woodland in a panic."

He felt compelled to read the words aloud, then Lucas looks up and ponders about what he should do with the paperwork and information discovered in them.

Maybe ask Mrs Whitwell what she knows.

He looks over at each newspaper clipping. There were no dates visible on any of them. Lucas looks at every clipping, then finds a paper with a partial date that's shown as *'ember 1921'* and, although it mentioned no precise date, it did just say: *Previous reported on by Jeffrey Herbert in 1912.'*

"Hmm, Lou says her great-grandfather died in 1914 so I guess they did *this* reprint after he had passed away… *if* it's even the same person…" Lucas mumbles as he was getting more and more curious what the newspaper clipping was about, and even more why these newspapers were in his house of all places, and then there was the curious situation of someone hiding them all in the loft who also attempted to eliminate access to the loft.

"I *have* to ask Mrs Whitwell," Lucas says loudly.

Lucas rises to his feet, then he places the newspaper clippings back in the box, then looks quickly in the other boxes to find more of the same material is inside them. He places every lid back on all boxes and was about to leave the room when he glances towards the built-in cabinet.

So maybe put them in there so there are two doors blocking access to them… but I'll take a couple with me to go see Mrs Whitwell about…

* * *

After ten minutes of hoisting the heavy boxes into the cupboard, Lucas locks the door of the cupboard. He locks the door, then pulls at it to make certain it's firmly locked. He walks from the room, carrying the two newspaper clippings to confront Mrs Whitwell with; the one with the first mention of the village that he'd found, and the other piece that mentions the girl. He exits the room and also locks the bedroom door, checking he firmly locked it, then after retrieving his trousers from his bedroom, he places both keys in the coin pocket in his wallet. He gently folds the newspaper clippings and puts these into the back pocket of his trousers.

Lucas takes off his t-shirt and jeans, grabs the towel, then goes back to the bathroom for a second shower.

Ten minutes later, he's back in the bedroom to get dressed, then walks downstairs. He opens the kitchen door, and his shoulders slump with annoyance when he spots the pool of liquid on the floor.

I guess it's my fault for ignoring you, Lucas thinks as he rubs over Tucker's head. "You cannot come," he says to the dog, "Gylda's husband is allergic to dogs. I'll let you out in the garden for *this* time because I really need to go soon."

Lucas puts the lead on the dog, but before he goes outside with the dog, he grabs the mop and cleaning liquid and spends the next ten minutes hastily cleaning the kitchen. He places the mop against the wall outside the back doors, then he uses tissue to dry the floor off. He washes his hands with some washing-up liquid. After he has dried off his hands, he walks to the back doors once more. "Tucker—Tucker, come here, buddy," he calls out.

Initially, Tucker acts confused, staring at Lucas with a tilting head. Then, after a minute more of this confusion, he runs at the man with a wagging tail. Lucas opens the door, steps outside, and holds the door open for the dog, who stops a meter from the door, inside the kitchen, still wagging but confused again. "Common on, Tucker," Lucas grunts loudly. "I haven't got time for this…"

Tucker stares at the man for a moment, then gingerly steps outside. When Lucas takes off his lead and points at the garden, the dog dashes off, running around the garden excitedly. Lucas sees him sniff at a pile of leaves at the furthest end of the garden, then the dog squats and the man cringes when the dog does a well-placed pile of poop right no top of what he'd intended to become a compost heap…

I guess it will compost better now, Lucas thinks. *I hope…*

He calls the dog back and both go back inside the house, with Lucas giving the neighbour a quick glance. Lucas locks the back doors and checks he had shut all the doors and windows and also locked. He does the same with the rest of the house. He doesn't bother with the locked room as the window there is covered with his old spare wardrobe, and they locked the wardrobe since he took possession of the keys for the house. After he's finished with checking the house, including drawing a few of the curtains so less of the house can be seen from outside, he takes Tucker back to the kitchen.

"You'll have to be in *here*."

Lucas strokes the dog for a while, scratching him over the ears and reassuring him thoroughly, and then he walks from the kitchen and shuts the door behind him again. He cringes again when the dog whimpers audibly, and he hopes the dog *would* stop before he was meeting with Mrs Whitwell, so she wouldn't have something new to complain about…

* * *

Lucas puts his coat on, walks from the house, and locks the front door before he walks over his garden path to the front gate, then steps into the street, turns left and walks to Mrs Whitwell's house. He opens her gate and walks to her front door and rings her doorbell. Several minutes pass before she opens her door, and she stares at him questioningly, without even greeting him…

He feels tongue-tied for a moment, because he isn't sure how to broach the subject of the newspaper clippings for a few moments. Then quickly pulls the papers from his back pocket a moment later.

"I found something in my house I'm curious about."

"I can't really see what it is. Show me in the sunlight," Mrs Whitwell says, but to Lucas her voice doesn't sound pleasant at all for unknown reasons. She walks from her house, closes her front door behind her, then forces them to walk to halfway down her garden path before she stops walking.

"Show me!"

Lucas holds out the papers and sees Mrs Whitwell lean forward to peer at them. She stares for what feels a long time. Never speaking. Her face staying devoid of any emotions or any recognition of any kind.

"Do you know what these are, and why I might have found them in my loft?" Lucas asks when no recognition ever comes. She glances down at the clippings once more, then she shrugs her shoulders dismissively.

"Never seen them," she snaps at him coldly.

Lucas frowns from surprise as all her usual, friendly quip is all but gone from her voice, and he'd noticed it immediately because of his earlier misgivings. "Are you sure?" he presses.

She glares at him instead of offering any answers. Mrs Whitwell stares at him venomously for a minute, then she turns abruptly on her heels. Lucas stares after her as she stomps back to her house. She doesn't appear angry in her demeanour but something is off about her behaviour and it confirms all his misgivings. She just seemed really annoyed about being asked about the newspaper clippings. *All her friendly demeanour seems gone*, Lucas thinks and the whole situation now worries him greatly. He decides not to call after her and press on the matter further because he really needs to get to Gylda's house soon. He turns and walks out of Mrs Whitwell's garden, closing her gate quietly.

Before walking off, he glances up at her house, and wonders why she'd changed her behaviour so quickly…

* * *

Before he got to Gylda's house, Lucas realises he wants to speak about what he'd found with Louellen and does this before he gets to Gylda's house. She might tell him things he could convey to Gylda in case she needed such information. Lucas waits for Louellen to answer her phone, and she answers her phone after just two rings, meaning she was doing things close to her phone and waiting for him to call her. *Either that or was close to her phone by chance*, he thinks and he realises from this he wanted to with her and even more than before.

He told Louellen he'd call her once the visit was finished…

* * *

And so he'd arrived at her house where Gylda had introduced him to Roger, her husband. The men had shook hands. They'd talked extensively over freshly brewed tea. Gylda had told a lot of information about the village, and she'd recognised the clippings - somehow though never explained why or how - and she'd said they were from a newspaper that used to be in circulation in the village up to 1935.

"You should speak with Dick Howey as he can tell you more about the newspaper delivery," Gylda had said, "as his grandfather and father owned the newsagent shop before him."

On the way home, Lucas gone to see him.

"It was a newspaper that would get delivered in the village," Mr Howey had said, "and my father might have been delivered it locally as a boy, but actual newspaper was before my time…" Mr Howey had shrugged for a moment then had added, "I might be old but not that old," he'd said, "and I think it was around the mid-thirties the deliveries stopped, and if I recall from the paperwork it had been around for fifty or sixty years. Old Dorrie can tell you more. She worked for my father in this shop."

As he had left the shop, Lucas had to smirk a moment at the idea of someone calling Dorrie Michaels by the words 'Old Dorrie.'

She's an old lady and, according to Gylda, she's ninety-seven, Lucas thinks. *It means that perhaps she could have worked in the shop and is probably about sixteen years old in 1930.*

He'd walked home hastily, partially because now he was worried that Tucker was okay and also because he wanted to look more at the newspaper clippings again before calling Louellen about his findings to date, and that was something he wanted to do despite the apparent falling out between them. He wanted to find out from her what she might know of her great-grandfather…

* * *

Thirty minutes later, he's home again, and after greeting Tucker who'd skidded from the back door to the kitchen door in seconds, wagging wildly, and then noticing the dog had *not* made more messes in the kitchen, Lucas had let the dog go out in the kitchen and Tucker out for only minutes before sauntering back into the kitchen, again wagging as he passed the man, and Lucas smiled at the dog's playful antics…

Now Lucas stands waiting for Louellen to answer the call, and he reconsiders some things they'd apparently argued about, and weighs up these thoughts against what he'd discovered now.

Maybe she's right with it being a bad idea to move to a small village in the middle of nowhere—

She pulled Lucas from his pensive mood when he hears her voice. "Hey Lucas, I didn't expect a call from you this soon," she says. "How's things…?"

Lucas feels a momentary urge to tell her he's feeling miserable because she never wanted to visit him, but he fights off the urge and changed the topic to the things he'd discovered since arriving home the previous day. "I've found something rather interesting in my loft," he says plainly. "Rather unexpectedly…"

"What did you find?" she asks.

"I noticed that someone had covered over access to the loft. Not immediately, but after checking the ceiling a few times, I realised it," he says. "I have *no* clue when it was done or by who, but it must have been after the date listed in—and before I bought this house. When I went to look in the loft, I found several crates with newspaper clippings, all from the 1920s…"

"What's so special about those papers?" she asks.

"I don't know yet, but when I showed them to Mrs Whitwell—the neighbour I told you about—she reacted odd."

"Odd…? In what way…?"

"She became very dismissive," Lucas answers, "and I'd even say abrasive about how she reacted…"

"From what you've told me about her, that sounds rather odd," Louellen says. "You made her sound like a nice person…"

"I know I did," Lucas grunts. "I felt rather shocked when it happened."

"Did she shout at you or something similar?" Louellen asks. "I know how much you hate conflict…"

"No, I asked about the newspaper clippings, and I noticed she acted like she knew nothing about them," Lucas answers, "and then she said she didn't even know anything about what's written in them. But there's something else, Lou. Some of the newspaper clippings list a name. I'm wondering if he is related to you…"

"He…? Huh, what do you mean?" Louellen asks, now sounding genuinely curious, as Lucas had guessed she would feel.

"There's a name listed at the top of one clipping," Lucas answers. "It says the name 'Jeffrey Herbert, London' at the top of the article."

"My great-grandfather was Jeffrey Herbert, as you know, but it cannot be the same person as him in that newspaper clipping," Louellen protests. "That's *too* much of a coincidence…"

"Maybe you can ask your dad to see if he knows anything other than what you told me about your great-grandfather?" Lucas suggests.

"I can ask him, but I doubt he'll give a different answer to what I just said," Louellen says. "Don't you think it all sounds too fluky for you to find newspaper clipping and that they have the same name on them as my great-grandfather's name? Besides… Dad had told me he sold newspapers *not* wrote for them…" Louellen chuckles for a bit. "But… as you're being so insistent about it all," she continues, "then I should ask *him*…"

"Thank you, Lou…"

Both are quiet for a few moments, then Lucas speaks again. "I'm going to check out the house again. I'm now really curious how it looks inside," he says, "and I'm going to guess it's all just a big dump inside it."

"If it's all messy inside, then you should be careful."

"I'll bring my flash-light."

"How many times do I need to tell you it's called a torch…"

"Okay, okay, I guess I can blame working for an American company for the reason I use the word, okay?" he retorts, then he pauses with speaking before continuing explaining his plans. "I'll make sure Tucker comes with me again, so that way you know I'm safe…"

Louellen laughs, and to Lucas it almost sounds she's laughing at him. Like he'd done something really stupid or something like it. He stares a moment at his phone, then puts it to his ear and asks abruptly, "What's so funny…?"

"Well, if you're so brave, go there tonight on your own," she answers, chuckling somewhat, "and if you're not scared that it might be haunted…"

"I'm going there another day as I still got a lot to do here," Lucas replies. "I had some plans for tomorrow and wanted to go to bed early so I can be early for those plans."

"Okay—see ya!"

Lucas stares at his phone, astonished when Louellen had just hung up before he could say anything more. *I guess she was in a hurry*, Lucas thinks as he realises a moment later that he'd called her while she was still at work, and slaps his head for the stupidity. *I guess she hung up because a client walked in… or perhaps her boss arrived to speak with her…*

Lucas glances at his coat and reaches into the top pocket a moment later and pulls the piece of paper out and he stares at the address for the library to visit written on it. *And yes, maybe I should go tomorrow to visit there…*

"I'm wondering *why* Gylda was so insistent about visiting," Lucas mumbles. "She'd stressed about going there, saying it was important for me to go…" He realises that she'd become even more insistent when he revealed the newspaper clippings when he'd met her in the street, and had been even more insistent during his visit at his house, and so was Roger. Her husband had arrived halfway through the afternoon, and though neither recognised the newspaper clipping, it didn't stop either from being incessant with their demand of him going to the library. "Yeah, yeah, I'll *go*, okay," Lucas blurts out loudly like either of the individuals were somewhere in his house…

CHAPTER ELEVEN

LUCAS CONTEMPLATES OVER THE THINGS that Gylda and Roger had told him during the visit. It had been a lot of information, and fascinating as well. He'd found out so much from them, and especially Roger was an excellent orator so had enlightened him with the things he'd learned as an 'outsider' to the village, though he'd been born maybe two hours' drive west from the village…

"… I didn't even know that she had them," Gylda had said. "So you know… Auntie Liz was actually Grandmother's older sister. Everyone had always called her that, even all my grandmother's children."

"So you've got siblings?" Lucas had asked cautiously.

"Yes, two sisters—but my brother, who would have been three years older than me, passed away a few years ago," Gylda had whispered. "He lived in a cottage a few doors down of Auntie Liz's house—well, *your* house now…"

"I was good friends with Bill… That's her late brother," Roger had added.

"Selling the house was a decision between all of us," Gylda had said. "My grandmother and the four of us sold the house. We sold the house twenty years ago. They sold it at least twice before you bought the house…"

"I saw the evidence of this on the deeds," Lucas had said. "I went to check the paperwork to work out who could have put the crates with these clippings up in the loft."

"You mean there's more of these clippings in other crates?" she'd asked. "It wouldn't have been Auntie Liz. She always had a fear of using ladders. Bill wouldn't have been able to go up there with his bad leg left over from the war. He served in the army in World War Two, and came home lame."

"But it didn't stop him helping around at Auntie Liz's house, don't you remember, Gylda," Roger had pointed out, "but, yes, you're right, he couldn't have gone up there."

"I don't think it would have been them," Lucas had commented.

"According to the estate agent, the company that was selling the house did all last maintenance to the house, and neither of us saw that there was any sort of entrance when we looked before I decided on buying the house, and then forgot all about it after I bought the property until I started decorating the house…"

"Where did you find that entrance?" Roger had asked.

"Above the stairs."

Roger had shaken his head, had looked at Gylda, who also shook her head.

"I don't think either of us ever saw it," she'd said, "and if it was there, the people who could have known are both long dead and buried."

"I showed these papers also to Mrs Whitwell," Lucas had continued. "Her reaction to me showing these clippings to her was odd."

"Oh! Explain in what way odd?" she'd asked.

"She reacted almost angrily."

"Well, perhaps part of the answer to such a question might be because she never got on with Auntie Liz," Gylda had said. "They weren't enemies, but weren't exactly friends either."

"Bill had told me something about her behaving oddly when he'd spoken to me a year before he passed away," Roger had said, "and until Lucas just mentioned it just now I kind of always just dismissed it as him getting old."

"Oh, and you've never bothered telling me, Roger," she'd stated sternly.

"I never saw it as anything important until now," Roger had said defensively.

"What did *he* tell you?" she'd asked.

"He had said that Auntie Liz had mentioned to *him* that there was a secret hiding in the cottage, and that someone was after it," Roger had explained. "She had said—and according to Bill, he thought she was just delirious because of age—that the secret had something to do with—errr… you said that one clipping mentioned a girl, right?"

Lucas had nodded when he'd realised Roger had asked a question.

"Didn't you say you wanted him to go to London to know more about the village, Gylda?" Roger had then asked his wife.

"I did… and are you going there?" she'd answered then had asked Lucas, who'd felt confused.

He'd nodded again.

"I think you should go," Roger had said, "You can then find out the *truth* when all these others in the village believe the LIE they keep spreading about the girl since the end of the 1900s when she'd vanished in thin air—"

"You mean the one in this newspaper clipping...?"

"Yes, that one. From what my father had told me that his father said to him, there was some sort of investigator from London involved. This was just before Scotland Yard got founded, so the investigator didn't do a good job of it, if you get what I mean," Roger had said. "Especially when—at least to my grandfather—it had involved so much more than a girl disappearing."

Roger had leaned forward and had looked at Lucas conspiratorially. "They spread the rumours to make her look bad and made sure the family living in Priory Mansion came to ruin."

* * *

Hours after arriving home from the visit and after the call with Louellen, Lucas is sitting at the back window of the kitchen, staring out pensively without really seeing anything beyond the glass pane. The story he'd been told sounded too fantastical, but it seemed to have an element of truth to it he couldn't easily dismiss...

From how it sounded now, it was almost like there was a two-way split in the village of people who believed the rumour and people who didn't believe this information. It was clear from their comments that Gylda and Roger had never believed the rumour. According to Gylda, Leigh Governor wouldn't believe any of it either. He found out why not when Gylda explained Leigh was a relation, an offspring, from a child who had been left behind when the girl, mentioned in the clippings, had disappeared. According to Gylda—who'd told him she was still close friends with Leigh—and told him she was still suffering from the effects of the rumour-mongering, and she too had mentioned that Peg Whitwell - his neighbour - was supposed to be her godmother but ironically was never treated favourably by her...

Lucas had noticed that Gylda had pulled her nose up in disgust when she had mentioned Peg Whitwell to him so guessed from this there was no friendship between then either, as with her Auntie Liz and got to see a photo of Liz and Dorrie - Gylda's grandmother - next, and he had smiled.

He'd discovered that Dorrie was, in fact, called Dorothea Michaels as a photo listed below the image: 'Elizabeth & Dorothea '67.' He guessed they took the photo in 1976. It showed a woman who seemed around fifty, and one other who was around thirty. He got told that the older of the women was Auntie Liz…

* * *

Lucas glances around the kitchen, now wondering how much of what he'd considered as 'outdated' and 'old-fashioned' when he was viewing the house was stuff that might have been in the cottage when 'Auntie Liz' was still alive over two decades earlier. He decides he's going to make sure - now - to restore the cottage a lot more in keeping with how it might have looked when she had been living in the house.

If she got the cottage as an inheritance and, like Gylda had said, had never really changed anything in the house, Lucas things, *then most of what I can see here is maybe a hundred years old or more. Maybe Bill had added this kitchen. It seems too modern for it to be an original kitchen. Or maybe the company they'd mentioned earlier had it put in…*

Lucas pondered over this information for a while longer and over his original plan for the kitchen. He shakes his head.

"Okay, maybe I can find a new kitchen that looks a lot more historically correct," he mumbles, "I recall Lou saying that she loves kitchens with a lot of light pine wood and white marble worktops in it so I guess I'll go with *her* dream kitchen instead I guess."

Lucas looks at his phone again, half expecting it to ring, because in the past it always did inexplicably whenever he's thinking about Louellen. But this time it stays silent…

He finishes his drink and gets ready for another walk with Tucker, which was becoming his way to think about stuff and it had happened more often lately. He has too much on his mind to pay adequate attention to the dog, who seems to realise this and just walks at a gentle pace by his side, occasionally stopping to sniff at the ground or to do his business.

One thought Lucas cannot shake from his is why, of all places, he'd ended up living in a cottage in the middle of, as Louellen would say, nowhere…

"Well, at least according to Louellen this is the middle of nowhere," Lucas mumbles under his breath as he glances around and tries to convince himself that she's right, "and then I find out something about the house linking it inexplicitly to her…"

Lucas isn't particularly a superstitious guy, but now he feels like he's heading in that direction. First, it had all begun with finding out why Louellen and Anna were friends, and he'd laughed when Louellen had told him, and she'd glared at him and from this he *knew* she was serious. They had met when they were both just six years old, and according to Louellen, it was one of the last times she'd been anywhere with her mother. They'd gone to a shop, and while there her mother suddenly had felt unsteady. It was Anna's mother who'd rushed at her side, and because she'd been a nurse before, she'd suggested to Louellen's mother about going to hospital. According to Louellen, Anna had been there too, and while the ambulance took her mother to the hospital, Anna's mother had taken Louellen home to her father to tell him what had happened. By the time they were at Louellen's house, the girls were best of friends and stayed friends ever since…

It had been later when both girls had discovered a connection between their respective families when it became apparent that their great-grandfathers had been connected to the same newspaper. Anna's great-grandfather was the owner of what Louellen's father knew of the situation; her great-grandfather had been selling the newspaper…

But then how did his name as a clear writer end up inside the newspaper? Louellen laughed when I suggested it, but it's too much of a coincidence to dismiss it so easily, Lucas thinks as he looks at his watch. *Maybe there's time to go to London…*

He dismisses the idea as soon as it popped into his mind, realising it will be after four before he would have arrived in the borough of London where the library is located.

I'll go tomorrow, as early as I can make it. If I hurry I can get to Mr Howey's shop, and use the photocopier there to do copies of some clippings to show the librarian so he or she may recognise what the paper was called.

Lucas increases his pace as he'd almost forgot that he wanted to get home fast, and the increased pace made the dog wag…

They're back on their way to his house only twenty minutes later, and Lucas again gets the sensation that someone is watching him from an apparently abandoned Priory Mansion. As Gylda had revealed to him in their first meet up in the village, and both Gylda and Roger had both mentioned the name during his visit to their house. He'd also seen the name in the newspaper clippings…

Half an hour later, Lucas is rushing towards Mr Howey's store when he notices the man on the pavement at the front of the store. Mr Howey looks up surprised when he realises Lucas was who'd arrived in his store - for a second time in one day - when Lucas only ever visits the store one time every week in most weeks.

"Needed more groceries?" Mr Howey asks, "I was going to close the store soon."

"Actually, I was wondering if I could photocopy something," Lucas answers. "I won't take too long with it…"

* * *

Lucas had gone into London to find out more from the mysterious woman that Gylda had insisted he should visit in the library there and he finds a woman alone in a spacious library and she's working on a computer, and glances towards him when he approaches her desk.

"I'm not entirely certain if you can help me," Lucas asks the woman, glancing back at him questioningly. "I'm looking for information that I was told you have here in the archives."

"What information are you looking for?"

"I'm searching for information about the village I moved to," he answers, "and it's called Mellowstone Greene, and—"

"Oh, I can help with that. I come from there originally. My name is Lynn Standage. I'll help you find the information you need. Anything specific you're after, hmm…?"

Lucas nods to answer part of the implied question, but he feels tongue-tied suddenly. He hadn't expected to walk into the only library he knew in this part of London, and he'd thought it would be a wild goose chase, but then he discovers now that he'd arrived at the very library on the piece of paper. He'd forgot where he'd placed the paper with the address written on it. So he chanced his luck and got to the correct place and then found out that the person was not only willing to help him, but was also the person originally from the village.

Lynn was, in fact, the friend that Gylda had mentioned in her rushed conversation when she gave Lucas the paper with an address listed on it, and he'd forgotten all about her. Rather ironically…

The woman behind the desk seemed friendly enough, though Lucas was uncertain if she really had meant it when she had mentioned she was from Mellowstone Greene, or whether she was as nosey as Mrs Whitwell in some ways. *I'll guess I'll find out soon enough which version she is,* Lucas thinks, *whether she's like Gylda or like Mrs*

"I think someone had told me to come visit your library specifically…"

"Who might that be?" Lynn asks.

"Someone called Gylda," Lucas answers. "I went to visit her and her husband Roger yesterday."

"Ahh, yes, I know about her," Lynn comments. "She's a pleasant person…"

Lucas smiles and guess this was her way of saying that she and Gylda were friends without dropping her professional appearance as a librarian. Gylda had sent him to this library, of all places.

"I never knew about this library when I lived here."

"You lived in London before…?"

"I moved to live more north, but I was living maybe like five miles east of here before," Lucas explains. "My girl—errr—friend lives in North London with her father."

"I see—and how do you like Mellowstone Greene so far? It must differ from being used to a city for you?"

"It's quieter… but I like it. I'm trying to persuade Lou to come live with me."

"And Lou, is that a girlfriend, I presume?"

"Yes, well, actually her name is Louellen, but she prefers Lou most times," Lucas explains.

Lynn just nods at the explanation, then she points towards a seat slightly behind Lucas and he nods and sits down at the table. "So, what exactly do you want to know about the village?" Lynn asks, "I presume you already checked the wiki entry for the village, and therefore you've seen that there's hardly anything listed for it there."

"Errr—yes, I did," Lucas comments. "Gylda said I could find out a lot about the village at this library specifically."

"She's right," Lynn says. "I've been collecting as much information as I can find for the last ten years. I've gained quite an archive I keep in one of the spare rooms upstairs."

"Okay… then maybe see something I found in the loft of my cottage." Lucas pulls the envelope in which he had placed the photocopies from his bag. Lynn sits down beside him and looks intrigued and curious at the same time.

"Show me."

Lucas grabs his bag from the floor and pulls twenty-two sheets from the envelope retrieved from the inside pocket and pushes them towards the woman. She picks them up one by one and studies each paper closely, scrutinising their content.

"Where did you say you found these?"

"In the loft of my cottage."

"I've seen some of these articles before in my own archives, but there are others here that I've never seen before."

"Are they significant?" Lucas asks.

"If you put them in context with all the other news stories written about what went on in the village in the nineteenth century, they are," Lynn explains. "I'd have to get all my archive material down here for you to look at. I'd have to go up a few times to get it all. Maybe if we go through these and find specific things first for me to go collect."

"Yes, that sounds fine to me. I've become increasingly curious about all this."

"Who else has seen these newspaper clippings?" Lynn interjects, and Lucas notes an element of concern in how she speaks, and looking at her, he sees some worry on her face.

"Only Gylda has seen them," he says, and sees her relax, but the worry on her face is back with his next words. "Oh, and I had asked Mrs Whitwell about them, too."

"She knows about them?" Lynn questions.

"I only showed *two* of them to her. These are the ones I showed to Gylda too, and she told me to photocopy them and come here with them to show you."

"It's best you never tell about these *other* papers or anything else you find to Peg," Lynn states. "She doesn't react well to things that upset *her* 'world,' if you know what I mean."

Lucas nods and refrains from asking more questions. He figures who the 'Peg' mentioned is without needing to ask. He notices that he now had met three people who don't seem to like his neighbour. If he went to meet Leigh Governor, that would make it four…

* * *

A group of schoolchildren becomes the first distraction that leaves Lucas alone at the table for a considerable period, and he smiles inwardly at the enthusiasm with which they rush towards the nearest bookcases which reminds him of how he was as enthusiastic at around the same age as the individuals in the group with library visits.

Especially the later ones with Louellen…

Lynn dashes by the table a moment later, saying, "I'll be awhile," she hisses, "but here are a few books to keep you occupied in the meantime…"

Lucas pulls the pile of books towards him, and is surprised to be excepted to read books about doing private investigative work, and not anything related to Mellowstone Greene, Priory Mansion, the newspapers, or even anything closely related to these topics. Out of politeness towards Lynn, he picks up the top book and raises an eyebrow when he sees the name of the author. He's genuinely surprised at finding out this minor detail. *The person who wrote this book wrote the article in the magazine…*

Lucas turns the book over, reads the text on the back cover, then nods approvingly, as the book seems interesting enough from just the description on the cover. The topic was the psychology behind how people guilty of a crime might behave. He opens the book to the first chapter and spends the next fifteen minutes carefully reading its content. It's about how to identify different behaviour patterns in people who *could* commit a crime, and how their behaviour could affect family members living with them. The information in the book lists also, somewhat to Lucas, that often the most unnoticed form of psychology at play would be manipulation that could alter how a person might perceive others…

Lucas stops reading and looks ahead of him.

If the story Gylda told me is correct, then I can understand how all the stories must affect Leigh Governor. Because if—like she said… someone is deliberately still telling the 'same' lies about that woman who went missing who was her four times removed grandmother, then yeah this author is right… I wonder why Lynn wanted me to see 'this' book specifically.

"Is the book interesting?" Lynn asks as she arrives back at the table a moment later, and he answers her question without having to think about it for long, "Yes, it is—but why *this* book…?"

"Because this book would tell you also part of the story of the village… 'back then' in the village," Lynn explains. "They took the article in the magazine from this book. Like a preview of the book, in a way. Before you ask me, it was Gylda who had called me to say she was sending you here for information. She told me you told her about the magazine according to her. It worried her enough to insist you'd come here, and do this before you asked the wrong questions of the less-well-intentioned people in the people… People who don't possess the forgiving nature all of us should have…"

"Like Mrs Whitwell…?"

"She's one person, but there are a few others," Lynn answers. "Be careful who you ask these questions you might have because, as my mother always would say: 'If the bad news starts somewhere the person always seems to be Peg.' There's a lot you don't know about her, and I'm sure that with being new she has filled your head already with all the half-truths she's capable of, and has told you a few blatant lies about the village and everyone who lives there, and *also* about what had happened in the village for the past couple of hundred of years…"

"Actually, I was already growing suspicious of her," Lucas says softly and a bit hesitantly, "and I'm now cautious around her and the way she reacted towards me on seeing the two newspaper clippings was a final confirmation I needed for my misgivings."

"Be careful that she cannot get hold of them," Lynn hisses. "You may have the evidence in your hands that will prove much of what's said about Nelly isn't entirely true…"

"Who is Nelly?"

But Lucas doesn't get an answer as Lynn walks away hurriedly to see the group of schoolchildren off. When she returns, she purposefully changes the subject, much to his annoyance, and so not to annoy her, he decides - for now - not to press the matter…

Lynn sits down at her desk instead of sitting opposite of Lucas as she'd done earlier, and he continues reading silently but he glances occasionally towards her. He notices she busies herself on her computer. Though she doesn't look angry, he wonders if his question had bothered her somehow. She's busy for the longest time, and by the time she finally rises to her feet, he has finished reading one book and is already working his way through the second book…

CHAPTER TWELVE

THE BOOK THAT LUCAS HAD ended up next was discussing the techniques used by crime story authors, and he finds the information fascinating and rather interesting. Even the choice of book on Lynn's part was interesting…

If this is how Agatha Christie ended up writing Miss Marple, no wonder the stories are so good. Hmm, I wonder if I could do such an endeavour myself. Writing stories, that is… but I'd rather wait until I've solved the mystery of what had gone on at Priory Mansion first…

Lucas sat staring into space for a while, contemplating every idea now popping into his head about all the possibilities open to him, but he settles on the idea that had been there first. He was going to investigate to learn more about what had happened in the village, both in the past and current, and to find information for other cases as well.

Perhaps, Lucas thinks, *and I wonder how Lou would react when I tell her my plans…*

He smiles somewhat at the idea of Louellen looking shocked.

* * *

"How's things going over here…?"

Lucas jumps at Lynn's ability to turn up unexpectedly by his side, able to walk through the library silently. She's standing beside him, glancing down at the books scattered on the table, and checking which books had interested him. He stares for a moment and feels relief when she's smiling.

"I've read all these books," Lucas says, pointing at three books, "and now I seem to read a book about writing crime fiction, but I'm at a loss why…"

"There's a reason for it," Lynn says, then she glances around the table to allow herself a few moments to gather her thoughts. "You'll encounter a few things as you learn about the village that easily could sound like they'd be belong in a fiction novel, and these… facts… or lies… could cause you confusion."

Lynn sits down opposite of Lucas, and after a minute of silence she continues speaking. "But you need to understand how a crime writer might try to work out the unravelling of 'who-dunnit' which would be essential for a situation such as this," Lynn explains, "and you need to learn as much knowledge if you're serious about discovering the truth…"

"Oh, I am certainly interested in that," Lucas says. "This isn't simply fascination or curiosity for me, but it's also important for other reasons…"

"In what way…?"

"Because of Lou."

"That's the girlfriend you mentioned before, right? How does she fit in all this?"

Lucas pulls the photocopy with the name of the reporter he'd spotted from the pile of paper beside him and pushes to the woman, who leans forward to look at it. He points at the name.

"I had asked her about her great-grandfather, and she'd claimed that he sold newspapers. But it's too much coincidence that they're mentioning his name in this article. Especially in saying in the article he'd died in 1912, which is the same year her great-grandfather had died. She has a friend called Anna, whose great-grandfather had owned a newspaper. Lou maintains the idea that her great-grandfather sold the newspapers that Anna's great-grandfather was the owner of—"

"Do you know when Anna's great-grandfather owned it?"

"Lou had told me that Anna's family owned it from 1850 to the middle of the 1930s—"

"Really? I don't think it's a coincidence. Well, maybe you finding it is, but *not* the facts you just mentioned. In fact, there's a lot more truth to it than your girlfriend might realise."

"How come?"

"For a start, I recognise some names mentioned here. Can I see the rest of them, please?"

Lucas pulls the pile of photocopies from the table on his right, and pushes them in front of the woman who leans in and studies the pieces of newspaper, and she sets out, reading them each quickly. Once she has done this for all articles, she looks up at Lucas with even more worry on her face.

"You'd want to guard the newspaper clippings carefully. This could be the beginning of something that can tell us not only what had happened to Nelly but also why some things in Mellowstone Greene are so off limits, and also why poor Leigh is being treated like she's some sort of criminal by *some*."

"Let me guess—by Mrs Whitwell," Lucas blurts out. "But why? I thought she's Leigh's godmother…"

"The arrangement is really in name only," Lynn says rather coldly. "I don't think Peg likes anyone, and least of all men—if you get my meaning."

Lucas stares at the woman, confused.

"I best not say things that could cause you to get in any trouble with her," Lynn says. "Maybe later I can tell you more…"

"I'll put the crates in my car and drive to my aunt's house with them," Lucas says hastily. "She won't know what they are, but she'll keep them safe for me if asked…"

"Where does she live…?"

"On the south side of Norwich."

"That would be far enough," Lynn says softly, then she gets up to help an arrival at the desk for a while, leaving Lucas to read more books and also to contemplate further about what he'd learnt from her. "Just keep reading," she says before walking away from the table, so he complies and continues reading as instructed. He skips several pages he deemed as irrelevant. After a while, he puts the book aside. Instead of picking up the next book, he pulls the photocopies towards him, and reads the news articles more thoroughly to check for any details he hadn't noticed up to now. After his conversation with Lynn and reading the books, he was more interested…

Now that he reads the articles with a purpose, he notices now how often Priory Mansion gets mentioned. The house had been a prominent fixture in the region, especially, as it seems, in its earliest existence; hundreds of years before the events that were being discussed in several articles. Several names kept popping up, too. Also kept popping up…

One such name among the others was the name Jeffrey Herbert from London who'd written these articles. The rather noticeable was that someone had meticulously all traces of what newspaper the articles would have come from. Lucas wonders again if he should call Louellen and find out if she had spoken to her father, but decides against it and to just wait for her to call him instead. *I wonder what Lynn meant by keeping the newspaper clippings safe?* Lucas thinks as he looks up to get Lynn's attention to find she's nowhere near him. *I guess she's somewhere else in the library…*

Lucas glances around and realises he's alone in the entire library, and it causes him to feel worried. *I guess she'll be back soon enough.*

He glances back at the newspaper clippings, and after a few moments of contemplation, he gathers them up in a stack, and quickly puts them all back in the envelope, which he puts back into his bag. He holds the bag for a moment, then places it on the floor beside his chair so it would be less easy for someone to grab hold of it, and Lucas shrugs at the irony of how paranoid his actions might appear to others.

* * *

Lucas glances at the remaining books still available to read, then after a moment of thinking over which book to read next and a moment later he pulls the middle book from the pile of five books he hasn't yet looked at yet. The book is about Norfolk and a more historic book than any of the others, but immediately he notes the many dog ears someone had created throughout the book, making it important in another way. Curiosity gets the better of him, so he looks at the pages where these dog ears are located.

Each entry related to something that had happened in Norfolk with a connection to Mellowstone Greene. It become apparent how much information there was about the village, though among many books. *No information on the wiki but plenty in books,* Lucas thinks, *and I guess Lou will get annoyed when she realises this…*

Because he's only looking at the dog-eared pages, Lucas gets through the thick book rather quickly. The book mentions the name Priory Mansion several times. Mostly in things that had happened earlier in the nineteenth century. But it ever mentioned no family names for any owners to show who had owned Priory Mansion, which strikes as *odd* to Lucas. He glances at the cover one more time and finally checks the back pages. Lynn's sudden return startles him.

* * *

"If anyone tells you they abandoned the house decades ago, don't listen to them. I may *not* have lived there for over three decades, but I remember the stories my mother told me about Priory Mansion."

"How old is the house?" Lucas asks as he rises to his feet to relieve Lynn of more than half of the stack of books and papers she'd arrived with a minute earlier. He places the stack on the table and she copies with the rest of the stack.

"They built the house something like two hundred years ago," Lynn answers. "Around 1830 I'd say—ever since they constructed it, it has endured mystery and bad luck, at least according to my mother."

"And the village?"

"They founded it supposedly in the first years of the nineteenth century," Lynn answers. "There are suggestions that the daughter of Lord George Seaward was directly involved in the activities to give it its later increased economic status. She was just twenty-six. She never married and there were so many whispers about a scandal for many decades afterwards, claiming she had an illegitimate son who was born just six years before she died. And then there's the scandal of the woman who had disappeared after applying for a job as a maid at the house, which had happened in 1897. My mother had always claimed it was the illegitimate son who handled her disappearance, but they never explicitly identified him and no one was ever certain that he actually existed…"

"That would make him early twenties if he handled the disappearance," Lucas comments, "and the woman? The one who'd disappeared. Who was she?"

"Her granddaughter, who is—errr—four times removed, and she still lives in the village. The woman who had gone for a job at Priory Mansion had got married a year earlier, and she had a baby at home. That's what makes all this even more tragic."

"Oh—so *who* is the relative?"

"Have you met Leigh Governor yet?"

"No, sorry—but Gylda mentioned her name to me."

"She's a woman in her mid-fifties. Based on what you've told me about which cottage you've bought there, if you turned left and then walked for three miles, and then turned left again, she lives in an old stonemason's house there—it's the first building on your right. You can't miss it if you ever walk that way… I used to live at the other end of the street, and she and I had often played together as kids."

"I'll remember it, and I'll look at the house when I have a chance."

"I suggest you don't put too much value in the name Lord George Seaward. He's the fourth son of an impoverished lord, so he only had the name to go by to give himself some amount of value. His daughter Karina is the more interesting one. She gained a lot of wealth for herself, and when her father went bankrupt, she purchased Priory Manor from him, and that was three years before the birth of *that* son—She had the child, and never mentioned who the father was, or why she kept the boy with her even though it would have diminished her status. Having a child as a single woman would do that back then."

"Is there any information about the son's name anywhere?"

"Not that I know of. This here is the information that was known back then about the woman's disappearance. It says *here* that her name was 'Nelly Sibbett,' and 'Sibbett' was her married name. The article lists here the person who investigated as Charles Fairey… although the locals in Mellowstone Greene will tell you with certainty that he was never the best investigator to be in charge. Apparently, he botched up, more than once, in investigating things there, so he has left a long paper trail behind of many grave mistakes… some of which never got solved even when people later took on the work of going through those cold cases. I believe that's what they call 'unsolved crimes' on the television programmes."

"Yes, that's right."

Lynn being called away once more interrupts their conversation. For a while she busies with normal librarian tasks. She's back twenty minutes later, carrying over even more papers and books. Lucas stares at the woman, surprised, then studies the stack of books.

"I'm uncertain, but there was a recent article about Mellowstone Greene. Haven't you seen it?" Lynn asks as she arrives back at the table where Lucas sits reading.

"You mean the article in the science magazine?"

"Yes, that one. The local council leaders had asked for the village name to be omitted from the article, but when I had read it, I knew it was about the village and the mansion."

"Is what they said in the article true?" Lucas asks. "I've noticed a reluctance to talk about the history of the village whenever I asked questions."

Lynn nods. "I think I know who in the village may have told the story. She wants justice for her ancestor, that Charles Fairey's behaviour and lack of ability didn't afford her." Lucas raises an eyebrow at how harsh the woman's voice now sounds. "You may not know this, but your neighbour, Peg Whitwell, is Leigh Governor's great aunt."

"I didn't know it until Gylda had mentioned it. Mrs Whitwell doesn't really talk much about anything. Now I think about it more precisely."

"I think she's angry at poor Leigh for telling her part of the story. She'd rather wants the past to stay buried because of everything else that went on."

"And Leigh doesn't?"

"No, she says she's had enough of the story, making its rounds every time someone comes to check out the house. By rights, she should live there, but something is going on inside the house that makes it impossible. I wouldn't say that it's actually haunted, but in the way people there talk about it, it might as well be haunted."

"I see—I guess you've never visited it?"

"No, I won't go near it even if you offered me the winning lottery ticket that would set me up for life. There's something about the house that is… odd… yes, that's the word I'd use."

"Odd? In what way?" Lucas was now feeling really curious about the mansion and whatever had happened there.

They're interrupted again when a group of girls walk into the library, telling Lynn—or Miss Lynn, as they'd refer to her—that they had a school project to do, and Lynn helped them find the books needed. Lucas sat watching them for a short while, realising that Lynn is a motherly figure, and that it's obvious that she loves children.

"Now where were we…?" she says as she walked back to the table where Lucas was sitting.

"You were telling me about Leigh and her relationship with Mrs Whitwell."

"Ahh, yes. Right—she is Leigh's great aunt, but there's never been much love between them. Leigh said once that she felt shunned by Peg—I'm not entirely certain *why* Peg might be that way, but everyone in the village has noticed it."

"Has Peg got children of her own?"

"No, she has *never* married, and from what I've heard, she isn't even interested in men. If you get *what* I mean. But it's a rumour, and with *all* the other rumours going on in Mellowstone Greene, that's *one* more rumour tainting the village."

"To me, she seems lonely. She keeps leaving me food. "

Lucas smirks for a moment, and Lynn grins before she suggests, "I guess it's not something you appreciate."

"At first I didn't, but I must admit that she makes good food. But I have a girl—friend… well, a female friend whom I'd like to come live there with me, and if she keeps it up with that attention after Louellen comes to visit I'm afraid it might put Louellen *off* the idea of moving in."

"I see… so this girlfriend or lady friend of yours wouldn't enjoy living in the village. What's she called?"

"Her name is Louellen Herbert," Lucas says as he feels himself blushing. "I think I love her." He feels shy suddenly and isn't sure why.

"How do you know she doesn't love you?"

"Errr—she and I had an argument. She said 'no' when I asked her if she'd even consider visiting me in Mellowstone Greene."

"Just because a girl might say no doesn't mean they'll always feel that way. What you need to *do* is find something that you two have in common. Then you might use that to *win* her over."

"I'll try that," Lucas whispers.

Lucas reads through a book that Lynn dropped on the table in passing him. He picks it up to find that it was about the prominent families of the latter part of the nineteenth century. Lynn taps quickly on the cover at a name. Lucas glances up and asks, "So, Lord Seaward had close connections with the people in the Palace of Westminster?"

"It's claimed that he was friends with the Prime Minister in the second half of the nineteenth century, but others say he was just a fantasist—and this notion comes mostly from the fact that he was from an impoverished family. His title—Lord—was only used to intimidate the local farmers in paying for the upkeep of Priory Mansion. His daughter Karina Seaward was who tried to fix those wrongs after he died—"

"And she had an illegitimate son, right?"

"Yes—*Her* father never accepted him. After she died, her son disappeared, and no one knows what became of him."

"It sounds so sad, really."

"That was the way it was back then. If you had a child out of wedlock, you'd ended up being ousted out of the respectable circles of society. Like what had happened to poor Karina. She had died in 1880, and she was still relatively young. But she had no friends, and none to care about her. It's claimed by some people in Mellowstone Greene that she and Nelly Sibbett *were* friends, and that her son had something to do with Nelly's disappearance, but as no one knew where he was or even who he was, this theory remains unproven and just one of the many rumours that do their rounds whenever the people there have a meeting in the hall—"

Lucas nods and makes a mental note to accept the invitation to the next one of such meetings: if only to hear the rumours first hand.

"She was wealthy, right?"

"Yes, and that was what was so unusual. You'd think that a woman, ousted from society, for having a child like she did, would have *no* chance, but she'd purchased Priory Mansion three years before her father had died. What's even more strange now is that no one knows a darn thing about *who* she had left her wealth to in her will. Leigh Governor got some money from it, but she or her family can't call themselves well off. People wonder *why* Karina Seaward had left money to the family of a servant—that's what Nelly was, but someone must own Priory Mansion, because every time someone arrives in the village asking if they can buy the house, the solicitor who deals with the situation, always has to tell them they have to decline their offer, and they always get the rejection of the offer by letter."

"So, not even the solicitor knows." Lucas smirks for a moment.

"No, he doesn't—and the last person to come *ask* about buying the place was some sort of American business owner, who'd wanted to make the field behind the mansion into a golf course, claiming it would be good for the village. His suggestion of what is good for the village got laughed off."

Lucas laughs for a bit, then he makes a comment on something he'd read in the article as well and had rolled his eyes at. "I presume there's no mention anywhere who the business person might have been…"

"No, because they'd made the offer via an obscure American lawyer, and the lawyer said they were 'acting on behalf of Mr Joe Doe who wanted to remain anonymous," Lynn explains. "There are some individuals in the village who have been trying to claim that it could be the descendants of the illegitimate son trying to make a claim on the house, but others say that any family of his might live somewhere here in Britain…"

"I doubt she would have named *her* son with the last name Seaward." Lucas stares in front of him, thinking over the information he was being told. He was finding the story intriguing and wanted to understand it better. "But what I don't understand is how he relates to Nelly Sibbett. Why do people say *he* caused her to disappear?"

"That's something I cannot answer. I'm clueless myself. All I know is what my mother and grandmother have told me, and what's commonly said in the village. That, one day, she had gone to work at Priory Mansion after a rare day off… where she was a servant and that she simply had left, and a gardener, back then, had claimed to have seen her running in a panic through the adjoining forest. Nelly would go for walks in the forest according to her family, especially in the autumn, but that day—at least according to the gardener—she had seemed different, almost scared, almost like she'd seen something, or perhaps someone, she shouldn't have."

"Hmm, that could be a crucial clue."

"It had happened seventeen years after Karina had passed away. Karina's son—if *he* was still around at the house at the time—would have been something like twenty-five or twenty-seven. Nelly was thirty if I remember things correctly, and *she* had a husband and a child." Lynn thinks for a moment. "Yes, there was only one child…" Lynn says. "Maybe that was fortunately…"

"Do individuals in Mellowstone Greene claim she might have been having an affair with Karina's son? If she was thirty when she disappeared. It might mean there was a sixteen-year age gap between Karina and Nelly."

"Yes, and that's the *other* thing people there wonder about. When Karina had died, Nelly was only thirteen, and even to someone as liberal as me, it strikes as *odd* that a woman in her forties would be friends with a girl in her early teens… and by then they'd been friends for almost five years."

CHAPTER THIRTEEN

LUCAS AND LYNN STARE AT one another for several minutes, silently contemplating their shared realisation they'd never know some answers they were seeking. Both of them look again at the last book that Lucas had been reading.

"I see—and that also could mean the son was around the *same* age," Lynn says. "Maybe there's truth in all this. Let's just say, for argument's sake, that Nelly *knew* Karina's son."

"Know him how?" Lucas mumbles, though he doesn't direct the question at Lynn, and she doesn't immediately respond but then frowns and speaks after a minute.

"If that was the case, and then she'd fallen in love with *him*, and while she was married, she'd been having an affair with this other man," she says. "Maybe someone found out about it, and threatened her, and told her then that he or she was going to tell her husband."

"Like it's any different these days," Lucas grunts, "and that's a comment about someone I used to work with, and I'd better not get into details or I'll be here for the next three days."

"Right," Lynn says. "Maybe in the future you can tell me…"

"If I understand *how* things were back then well enough, she wouldn't only have lost her job as a servant, but also her husband and her child as well. Weren't those—errr… what did they would call them - workhouses - still around, and if I remember correctly from what I saw in a programme about British history, she would have ended up there with no money, no job, nothing."

"Yes, that's right, but some people claim that she still ended up there after running off like she did." Lynn says.

"I'm actually feeling sorry for Nelly because if someone had threatened her for what or who she knew back then, and she ran away in a panic, and had to go into one of them workhouses voluntarily, and not even be able to tell anyone there who she was or why she was there… She wouldn't have had a good life at all." Lucas says.

"That's true…" Lynn says. "However, we should wait to make

assumptions like someone like Peg would do…"

"Errr—she had a child, right?" Lucas asks.

"Yes, and Leigh Governor is descended from her," Lynn answers. "Peg Whitwell is another part of the *same* family, and the two parts of the family don't get on because of what had happened… *each* blaming the other about whatever had happened to Nelly. I think her husband remarried about five years after the disappearance, and had more children with the new wife."

"How does Charles Fairey fit into all this again…?"

"He apparently came to investigate *her* disappearance, but from what I know or have read, he didn't do a good job," Lynn answers. "Then the case was closed shortly after he had died, and it's one of those cases that nowadays is called a cold case, I could say."

Lucas frowns because now the whole situation with the mansion has gone from it *just* being some sort of mysterious house to a place where someone might have committed some sort of crime.

No wonder they want to hush it up in Mellowstone Greene…

* * *

Another thirty minutes had passed when Lucas looks up and stares for a moment at the magazine that Lynn is holding out to him, after she'd spoke with him again for a while then had walked off and returned holding a magazine that appears to be old. "I found something more here about Charles Fairey…"

"When did he write the article?" Lucas asks.

"That's thing," Lynn quips. "It's a magazine from the turn of the century. Let's see… It says 'September 1903' on the front."

"It looks like a magazine that certain groups of women would have been reading," Lucas comments.

"Yes, yes, certain was one of those," Lynn quips.

"This information doesn't explain why there would be an article about Charles Fairey in such a magazine," Lucas comments, "and it seems almost like he was a celebrity…" Lucas frowns but he also feels bemused at the idea of what he'd regarded as a 'snotty-little-nobody-of-an-investigator' being given a status, like he was a film star or similar.

"It might have something to do with people's perceptions back then about the role of investigating a crime. Scotland Yard had only existed a little over seventy-something years by that time, and a year before they had written this article they had published 'The Hound of the Baskervilles,' so people probably had an idea that any person doing investigations would be like Sherlock Holmes."

"I've read the stories about Sherlock Holmes. Always have loved them. I love the stories of Miss Marple as well."

"I see… Well, if you get bored with reading all these newspapers, then we have the crime fiction books located just there." Lynn points to a location behind Lucas's left shoulder, and he glances in that direction.

"I'll have a look there in then to see if there's any book I'd like to read." He smiles at Lynn at her suggestion, and she smiles back at him.

"You're welcome to visit here when you want to get more information, but you may also want to send your girlfriend to come talk with me, because I could tell her everything I've learnt about her great-grandfather. Though being honest, until I met you, I didn't think it was someone I'd bother about. To me, he was just a reporter, but now I've met you he's more real to me, and from the sounds of it, both her family and that of her friend Anna—whom you had mentioned earlier… also have suffered because of this damned scandal that just doesn't want to go away, although I'm certain you'll find out why soon enough. But if you do, be careful. There are things that some individuals just want to keep hidden because it's in their interest that no one knows the truth."

Lucas nods.

The more that Lynn was warning him about the people involved the more it was feeling like he was in the middle of something that easily could be a plot for a Miss Marple story—or if it involved the Palace of Westminster of the late nineteenth century or later even almost a James Bond story or similar…

Lucas now wanted the truth known as much as Lynn wanted it, and from her information it would also likely interest Leigh Governor, who was an actual victim in all this. But then so were both Louellen and Anna, and neither had known about any of this stuff until he'd told Louellen some information. He was certain that Louellen would have told Anna precisely five minutes after he'd told her…

Charles Fairey had seemed to be like a real-life version of Sherlock Holmes, complete with his connections directly to the then-Prime Minister, but all information was pointing at a fall from grace for him when he hadn't quite done his job properly. The events had taken place around a time when the stories of Sherlock Holmes first got printed, so Lucas wonders if this man had tried to model himself on a fictional character. Lucas cursed then under his breath, realising that up to this moment he was almost doing the *same* thing, but had been using Miss Marple, from his beloved Agatha Christie books, instead.

If I'm going to do this right, I need to be as methodical as I had to be for my job. It means fact-checking, being very organised, not draw conclusions too early, and making sure that I don't cause any issues for people.

"Lynn," he calls towards the librarian who'd returned to her desk. She looks up, then gets up and walks over, and teasingly does a "Shush" at him, but grins when she does it.

"Okay, okay, I know *not* to be loud in libraries. My mother had worked in one until five years ago, so I actually hung out in them as a kid quite a lot. But, I want to know if Scotland Yard could have information about Charles Fairey if it connected him with the Prime Minister?"

"Perhaps, though most of the investigative work of *before* they got founded, is rather shoddy in how they stored it. I can check for you."

"Please do."

Lynn walks back to her desk and types on her keyboard. Lucas watches her as she busies herself, then sees her face go from a neutral expression to visible disbelief, and then she stares at him for a moment, still with the same disbelief still showing on her face. She glances back at her screen, then she reaches to her left for something she'd printed off. She gets up and rejoins Lucas at the table.

"This is a transcript of a conversation, recorded between the Prime Minister and someone named 'Richard Weymond,' who they apparently had appointed as the liaison between Scotland Yard and the Palace of Westminster in the first few years of its existence," Lynn says. "I suggest you read all of it thoroughly, and I've known none of *this* information myself until this moment, and this information makes me think that the case is about so much more than just about Nelly."

Lucas takes the printout, and reads the part that Lynn is pointing at, carefully.

Lucas glances up at Lynn, and he has as much disbelief as she shows him by shaking her head in dismay. "I can guess *who* the reporter that is mentioned is, but what extended family?" he asks.

"That's something new to me, too." Lynn sits down and is pale from apparent shock.

"Are you okay?"

"Yes, yes, I am—I just never thought that it would be an even bigger case than what I'd researched so far. It always fascinated me, ever since I was a child when my mother and grandmother told me the stories, but I thought it was something to do with the illegitimate son, and that he might be responsible for—To be honest, up to now I thought that perhaps he'd murdered her or something like it, but it seems someone else outside the village wanted *her* to disappear."

"It seems so to me, too."

"Help *me* find out what really happened. I think they did grave injustice back then. First, poor Karina ends up with a child, and the boy's father apparently had rejected him. And then the girl goes missing. All that after *she* had to deal with her drunkard father of hers—at least my grandmother had said so. There's not much information about that time, but what's known they wrote in that book you've taken an interest in, and if you promise to bring it back, I'll let you take that with you to read thoroughly."

"Are you sure?"

"Yes, I'm sure."

Lucas stares for a moment at the woman, then he nods before he picks the book up and is about to put it in his bag, but she stops him in mid-action. "I need to check the book out. Give it here. I'll do it in my name." Lucas hands the book back to Lynn, and watches her as she walks to the desk and swipes it over the top of the desk, then walks back with it and hands it to him. He puts it in his bag.

"How long can I keep it?" he asks.

"As a librarian I can borrow for an entire month, but if you finish it sooner, that could be helpful."

"I'll bring it back as soon as I can."

"I want *you* to read all of it, and in particular the parts that are about the village. It has some information in it about the origins of the village and the house too."

"Okay, I'm going to visit London again in two weeks' time, anyway, to collect the last of my paperwork from my old job so I can bring it back on that day."

He spends the rest of the afternoon with Lynn discussing various topics, ranging from what sort of work he had done when he still had his job to him pouring his heart out about his father having abandoned him a decade earlier. When Lynn told him that *her* father left to go to war, and never came back with her mother discovering he'd gone to live with someone else, it put into perspective for Lucas that he wasn't alone with his feelings.

Lucas told Lynn about Louellen's mother. She assured him it was common for people to find other individuals experiencing similar circumstances. She said the same had happened to Leigh too, and suddenly, the anger that Lucas had felt for so many years evaporated. He hoped then that Lynn was right, but deep down he realised that what she said was true.

"I need to say *sorry* to my mother—I was always so horrible to her for no reason."

"She knows it had hurt you. She'll have forgiven you because she knows it wasn't your fault."

"Lou has it worse. She can never have her mother back, but out of the two of us, she's the one who made things feel better for us both. She's a lot stronger than I…"

"She sounds like a caring person."

"She is!" Lucas says, nodding.

Lynn nods and then continues telling about herself and also tells as much as she can remember of the people in Mellowstone Greene. Her accounts of different people match what Gylda had told him. "I haven't lived there a long time, so my knowledge is mostly of how stuff was in the past…"

* * *

A few hours later, they're saying their goodbyes when it's time for the library to close for the day, and Lucas watches Lynn walk off through the street, then she crosses and vanishes from sight a few minutes later. He turns and walks towards the station where he'd emerged a half day earlier. He meanders through the crowd and is pensive over the things he'd learnt during his visit to the library. There were decisions he needed to make…

He had to discuss much of the new information with Louellen, but first he needed to find out more information beyond what he was told. He stops walking when he notices he just passed a bookstore and ponders for a few minutes whether to go inside it. Then he shrugs and walks inside.

"Excuse me, do you have historic books about specific counties?" he asks the girl who's standing at the till area. She looks young, and he guesses she's doing a temp job of some sort here.

"Yes, follow me," she replies. "Any specific place you want to know about?"

"Errr… Norfolk," he replies, "and books about the nineteenth century history of the county, please?"

They walk to the furthest back end of the store, and the girl stops at a display unit. "This is all the books we've got," she says, pointing at three shelves.

"Okay, thanks, I'll see if there's any book that helps me."

"Just come to the tills and ask us if you need extra help," the girl responds, before walking off.

Lucas looks after her for a moment before he mumbles, "I will… Thanks—"

It isn't like the girl would have heard him…

He looks over the books, and he realises that the sales assistant was correct. There were relatively few books for Norfolk; They aimed most of the books that were on the shelf at tourists, but then he spots a few books that were promising. Though still touristy in how the content was written, it had listings in them for a few useful facts - one listed various stately houses in the county, with the mention of Priory Mansion almost as a footnote. There were numbers listed under the entry, and looking at the preface section, he realised there was an extensive index of sources listed at the back of the book. There were just sixteen entries, and a quick study of the list revealed a list of newspapers and books used for reference.

I'll get this book at least, Lucas thinks as he closes the book and places it under his left arm.

The other books on display included a book about beaches, though Lucas got this book *more* to entice Louellen if she visited; a tourist book about places of entertainment, restaurants and the nightlife—also for Louellen to see. Then, two books about the region's medieval history, which is earlier than when Mellowstone Greene had existed, but it could give clues about how the region evolved over the centuries…

* * *

Lucas walks with five books to the till area. The girl from before greets him with a broad smile and walks to the till. She glances at the stack of books and says, "You found some you wanted…?"

"Yeah, though two of them will be for my girlfriend when she visits."

The girl laughs, then picks the books up and scans each bar code through the system. "Two of these books are by the same author," the girl says. "I guess they'll rake in the royalties from this. I guess it's enough for a visit to a pub for a drink…"

Lucas frowns a moment, unsure if the girl is being serious, or whether she's being sarcastic.

"Authors only ever get a bit of money whenever their book sells someone. I should know. I just wrote a book—"

"Oh—so, what's your book about?" Lucas asks. He's now curious about the girl. She walks off and comes back with a thick notepad with a story handwritten on it in tiny letters.

"I'll let you read a bit to see what you think. I've got to get it all typed in on a computer, then I'm going to get it edited, and then send it to this publisher who'd said he's interested in it."

Lucas reads the pages she holds out to him. It seems the story involves a woman who's married to a gangster, and the section he was told to read tells about her feelings about hearing he'd just committed a murder. Lucas wasn't sure if the story was about what he'd read, but the part he read sounded good.

"Sounds good," he says. "Interesting story about her background, to be honest…"

"Yeah, that's the thing I'm trying to do this way for a reason," she says, "because I don't want a typical gangster story. I want people to read about how they'd affect the women surrounding them by their actions and behaviour."

"Good luck with the publication of it," Lucas says, smiling.

"Thank you," she says, smiling back, then turns and puts the notepad back into a bag on the floor by her feet, and then completes the transaction. Lucas pays for the books with his credit card. About five minutes later, he stands on the pavement again…

He glances behind and notices the girl has gone back to writing on the notepad, and he smiles for another moment. *I must keep checking for a book about a woman who deals with what her gangster husband does, I guess*, he thinks. *Hopefully she gets the book published…*

Lucas walks again towards the station. This time, the chill in the air hastens his pace. He's at the station fifteen minutes later, then has to wait in the station for a train for thirty minutes. He glances through the book listing all places of entertainment first and raises an eyebrow when he sees a location that's just sixteen miles from the village.

I wonder how Lou will feel when she hears about the place, he thinks. *That's like twenty minutes' driving from my house.*

He shrugs at the realisation of having found a reason for Louellen to visit him, and only by accident. He puts the books back into his back, leans back, and relaxes in his seat. After a time, he shuts his eyes for a quick nap. However, he wakes up to find he's almost in Norwich. The train arrives there just a few minutes later, and he gets off the train and walks to his car. He drives home at a faster than normal pace because now the worry about the crates with newspaper clippings had returned with a vengeance, and he wants to make sure his house still stands there and that no one had broken in…

* * *

Life settled into a routine after arriving home. Lucas went to a nearby town for extensive shopping so he could stay home. He went out with Tucker only in the early morning or late at night to avoid encounters with the neighbour. He went into the village just twice and just briefly, leaving a note with Mr Howard, though rather cryptic in how it sounded, so she knew he'd visited the library, though he knew she might already know as Lynn could have called her either in the evening on the day he went there or afterwards.

More than a week had passed and Lucas felt a need to get back to sorting out his house, waiting for a call from Louellen, and doing this task for most of the days to come, even late at night and despite the late hour still doing it. This was one reason for his even later and rather unexpected trip out with the dog.

After arriving back, Lucas was staring up at the ceiling with the enormous gaping hole in it. It had been more than a week since he'd made the hole, mostly because he was curious *if* the loft space might be useful, but now it was becoming a portion of a growing mystery of events that seemed to have happened in the village.

Apprehension had increased in the days since arriving home because of all the information he'd uncovered. All this information pointed at a bizarre past for the village where a girl had disappeared and, based on the era in which she'd lived in, most people around her would have regarded her as a nobody and therefore never cared about the events or reasons it might have happened, or that she'd even gone from their midst.

Despite her apparently humble beginnings, she felt important to Lucas. Remembering the theme of the story the girl in the book store was writing, he set aside the notion that *she* was a nobody, and that her connection to the owner of the house had made her special. It seemed a strange connection, especially when he factored in the illegitimate son who was connected, as far as he could work out, with her disappearance.

But from what I've figured out so far, there's nothing that points towards a murder, Lucas thinks when he finally dropped on his bed, *and the girl had simply vanished…*

CHAPTER FOURTEEN

As he lay awake for a few hours, Lucas had been contemplating over the information he'd gleaned from the various times he'd pause beside the table in the kitchen and had concluded from this that so much more was going on. If he didn't know better, everything he'd found out so far could easily be a feature on the crime programme he'd discovered while he was channel hopping a few days earlier; a programme by the rather plain name of 'Crime Mystery Monthly' and it was a programme in which the presenters would go over several unsolved crimes, but usually crimes involving people who got killed in unusual ways…

* * *

The following morning, Lucas grabs the newspaper lying on the table and opens it to the page with the listings and places it flat on the table. With a stretched out finger, he checks through the listings for *when* the programme that he'd recalled about before sleeping would be on next.

He wanted to watch the programme to make notes about their techniques for solving crimes, then apply this information to everything he knew so far about Priory Mansion. After confirming that the programme was on TV the following Tuesday, Lucas glances towards where he'd dropped his coat on top of one of the 'yet-to-unpack' boxes, and walks over.

He retrieves his phone from the pocket of his coat, and searches it for Louellen's phone number. He dials it and waits for Louellen to answer the call. While he waited for her to answer, he listened to his surroundings imagining that all people living in Mellowstone Greene could turn up at any moment, at his doorstep, bang on his door, and demand to string him up on the nearest tall tree. He was uncertain where such a thought was coming from and it worried him somewhat that he'd think in this way at any time…

I'm letting my imagination get the better of me, Lucas thinks, *I guess I've read way too many detective stories for my own good*— But then he got distracted from the thought process of impending doom by Louellen's voice sounding breathless in his ear. "Hey Lucas… I didn't expect a call from you this late," she says. "I was downstairs watching a movie, and had heard the phone go off. I was almost afraid it had woken my dad."

"Sorry about this, but I've found out something," Lucas says, "and I've just come back from Priory Mansion."

"You've been to see it?" she squeals. "This late in the evening."

Lucas hears genuine shock in Louellen's voice.

"Errr… I was curious," he answers, "but I only ever got to the gate, and Tucker, who was with me, got spooked by something, and he literally pulled me back home."

"Wow… It makes me wonder what goes on there now," she comments. "Are you visiting it again tomorrow?"

"No, actually I was going there again *now*, but I wanted you to know that I did it."

"Why?" Louellen asks.

"I think I found something in these newspaper clippings," he answers. "Mrs Whitwell had claimed she'd never seen the clippings before today. Remember last week when I told you what Gylda had said to me?"

"What did you find?"

"It's rather extensive to tell, so have you got the time for *me* to discuss this? I've been told by *three* different people that you and I need to keep this information to ourselves."

"How can I ask dad if I have to do that?"

"Well, I suppose you *can* tell him, but tell also it's very important to keep it confidential. I think that in the wrong hands it could cause harm—Not only to Leigh, but to anyone involved with the newspaper as well."

"So Anna too?"

"Yes, *her* too… and your dad, and a bunch of other people. I'm certain this goes as far up as the Palace of Westminster… but inside version of the nineteenth century, and I don't know if it's still being covered up now."

"You really think that?" Louellen asks, and Lucas can hear genuine worry in her voice.

"I think so. There are *too* many people involved, either in the past or perhaps even now, for any of this to be dismissed as some sort of crazy village rumour."

Louellen is silent for a few minutes, and Lucas wonders if she'd become angry about what he'd said, but then she speaks again. Her voice has altered, and she'd stopped with sounding dismissive. "You said something about finding more newspaper clippings, right?"

"Yes, I've also visited my aunt in Norwich to keep them there with her… *before* tonight's visit to the house…"

"You did it because Lynn had told you to do it?" Louellen asks.

"Yes," Lucas replies, and he expects Louellen to laugh at him, but she doesn't laugh. Not even a snigger, like she might have done in response to some of his past ideas.

"If you're right about the neighbour, it's probably better."

"I'm planning to visit my aunt again to make photocopies of the papers which I'll bring back *here*," Lucas says, "so I can read them and research them."

"I'd wait with *that* until you know more. If that Mrs Whitwell knows about *two* of the clippings, she may guess you have the other clippings as well," Louellen says softly. "I haven't met her so I can't tell you with certainty, but when I read the article, you'd showed me it had stated that people *often* hide true motives with blatant lies. Has she said anything else besides not recognising the clippings that tell you she may lie, or even hide something?"

Lucas was quiet for a moment. Louellen had made a good point. He felt the temptation to remind her he wanted her living with him, but decided it's better let her come to that conclusion by herself.

"I think I need to see the house for myself, and this time not just look at it from a distance," Lucas says. "I think I've noticed something *odd* when I walked past it last week."

"What did you see?"

"It wasn't so much seeing something, but more the feeling that I was being watched."

"Watched…? By who…?" Louellen shrieks, "I thought you said they'd abandoned it completely, and that it had stood empty for many decades?"

"I don't know *why* I had the sensation, but if there's something going on, maybe someone is doing something inside the house to make it look abandoned."

"You remember the house in the street near here—the one with the boarded-up windows? It turns out that a group of junkies had used it once, and they had the police raiding it."

"When was this?"

"About two years ago now. It was in the local newspaper."

"How is it relevant to me going to see Priory Mansion?"

"I'm just saying it's maybe. It could be someone simply squatting there."

"We'll see."

"Anyway, I need to go. I got an early morning tomorrow. I guess we can chat whenever you've visited, and when I'm not almost going to bed or at work…"

"I guess that means Saturday, by the sound of it. I wish we could talk more often."

"Me too," Louellen whispers, then the phone goes dead before Lucas can reply. He stands staring at the phone in his hand for several minutes. He wonders why she'd say 'Me too' when she'd said 'No' to the suggestion of moving in with him. Lucas shrugs his shoulders and decides that it isn't an answer he would be able to get easily. Definitely not the way Lucas had wanted life to go in the recent months.

Lucas is indecisive for a while, but he said he was going back to the house, but now that he didn't have someone to justify the reason with, he feels unsure if he should do it. He sits down at the table, and looks over the notes he'd been making before going to look at the house, and realises he can't get any more answers in this way. He walks to the kitchen and glances towards the dark outline that's Mrs Whitwell's house.

"If there's one reason to get more answers, it's you," he mumbles, "and I wonder why you're so negative about anything to do with it."

He turns and walks further into the kitchen and makes another cup of tea. Lucas feels his apprehension grow as he considers his options.

One original thought had been nagging at his mind constantly. The option involved selling this house, moving back to London, and just setting the whole matter behind him as some sort of April Fool's prank someone had played on him. He hopes he wouldn't have to do that, and that one day all the stuff happening would just blow over…

So then comes the thought—the almost inevitable thought— about Louellen. He has loved her since he was fourteen and he'd told her after months of them being friends first. The feelings had grown during the summer they'd spent at the summer camp, and after that first summer they'd gone on more trips together, though in the last three years it had lessened, because they each had their own job to go to. *But now I'm financially independent—mostly. I want her to share in it so she can spend her days doing precisely what she'd trained for when she studied art…*

Lucas frowns and thinks again about what he'd said to Louellen about going to the house. It's late in the evening; he looks at his watch to see how *late* and sees it is just after ten o'clock. This makes him wonder *why* Louellen is going to bed so early. Or at least a couple of hours earlier than usual. He realises it didn't matter. It wasn't like she could stop him from going…

"I guess I've decided then—," Lucas says loudly, "and I'm going to stick it out here, and I'm finding answers about the house for the individuals who need them."

His voice wakes the dog.

Tucker runs into the kitchen, and he sits down at Lucas's feet, wagging his tail and looking up expectant at him. "Not yet, Tucker. We're going in an hour when *most* people in the village are asleep."

Lucas points at the dog's bed. Tucker walks to it, and after a moment of hesitation lies down on his bed, but lies there watching Lucas closely and raises his head every time Lucas walks from one part of the kitchen as he sets out—almost mechanical—to clear it up *more*.

After twenty minutes, Lucas walks into the living room and sits down on the sofa. Tucker jumps beside him and puts his head on Lucas's lap. Lucas absentmindedly scratches behind the dog's ears while he looks at every channel on his television for something to watch to fill the hour with something more exciting than twiddling his thumbs.

He settles on a science fiction movie, and even though it's already halfway through the movie, Lucas watches the rest of it. But he keeps checking the time, and after thirty minutes, goes first to the side window in the kitchen and glances at Mrs Whitwell's house, which seems dark—though nowadays he's never certain that it really is. Then he looks from the window in the living room along the street and scans the landscape for the lights of others in the village who might still be awake. Lucas realises that this would be accomplished easier by turning off his living room light, and once his eyes have adjusted to the dimmer night luminosity, he sees most people have turned their lights off. Lucas sits back down without bothering to turn the light back on and continues watching the movie, which is now almost at the end. After checking his watch once more, he suddenly feels the need that he should go.

If I don't do this after telling Lou I was going, she'll tease me for as long as we're still alive and in contact.

Lucas walks upstairs to his bedroom, where he'd left the flash-light earlier in the week, then he puts on a dark t-shirt and his jeans. From the wardrobe, he grabs his black bomber jacket, which had been a gift from Louellen a few years earlier. He also puts on a dark woollen cap too. He looks in the mirror, leaning against the wall.

I look like some sort of burglar. But I guess it will have to do. I don't want anyone to recognise me if I'm seen.

But as he plans for Tucker to come as well, it will be an impossibility, and he knows it. He picks up the flash-light and checks it, but then he reaches into the drawer of the bedside cabinet and pulls from it the unopened pack of batteries, and swaps out the ones that were in the flash-light for four brand new ones.

"Tucker," Lucas calls out. The dog rushes into the bedroom and jumps on the bed and stands there wagging his tail in excitement. Lucas grabs Tucker's face, and rubs the dog on both sides of his head thoroughly, and this causes the dog to wag even more. After a while Lucas stops, and Tucker lies down on the bed, and is now rubbing his own nose with his paw. Lucas laughs loud.

"I guess you deserve an adventure, *too*. Want to come with me to look at that mysterious building…?" Tucker wags his tail again with renewed enthusiasm. Over the last couple of weeks, the dog has bonded even more with me. Lucas smiles and remembers that Louellen showed a lot of fondness for the dog when he'd arrived with the dog in tow. He'd promised Lynn he'd be careful, but curiosity had grown so much since coming back from London, and even more after the way Louellen reacted towards his suggestion to visit Priory Mansion again, so he went back to the house. Lucas bends over for his trainers and sits down on the bed beside the dog and puts the trainers on. When Lucas gets up, Tucker jerks into an upright position and jumps from the bed. The dog circles around Lucas, filled now with apparent enthusiasm, which is infectious. Lucas grins at the dog.

"Yes, you deserve to come with me. Even if it's keeping *me* safe from nasty ghosts and horrible zombies in that house."

Lucas knows he's just making up stuff now, but to be honest, he doesn't know what he might find. For all he knows, he'd discover that a century or earlier that they had murdered a girl in the building; if television shows were to be believed, it would mean that he'd have to call the police to get the investigation going for any dead person. That prospect doesn't appeal to Lucas, especially not if there's some sort of link back to the Palace of Westminster. He guesses that he'd end with a couple of dozen reporters on his doorstep, and all asking the same questions…

Lucas shakes his head to dispel the thought from his mind and goes back to determining what to do about whatever he would discover.

Maybe I should call Louellen later, and at least tell her what I've found here tonight. Yes, that's what I'll do… and I should see if she suggests contacting the police. I should also tell her to go to see Lynn as well…

Lucas turns off the lights in the house. He wants it to appear that he has gone to bed. He stands in the living room, silently waiting for enough time to go by before walking to the front door. When he gets to the front door, Lucas sits down on the stairway, waiting. He sees that Tucker's eyes are reflecting the little of the moonlight that streams in through the tiny window halfway up the stairway. After his own eyes adjust, he notices the dog tilting his head in a curious posture, obviously questioning him about *why* they get ready for a walk, then don't go…

About fifteen minutes pass before Lucas gets up slowly, and quietly unlocks the front door, then takes care to open it just as quietly. He walks outside and quietly shuts the door and locks it. Lucas waits and listens for sounds from other houses or from the street, but it's like even the wind holds its breath to see what he's doing. Lucas walks. He opens the gate, and because it makes a sound as he opens it, he leaves it wide open, and let it slams shut by itself, which Lucas feels, is better than trying to spend a long time shutting it without people hearing it…

He doesn't know what he will find in the old building *yet*, but as he walks, it feels to him he's walking into a new existence of some sort. His indecisiveness slowly disappears as he walks. He slowly watches as the large gate looms ever closer…

* * *

Lucas opens the door of the old building, and the creaking sound it makes causes him to jump and stop and wait to see if anyone might have heard it. It's silent everywhere around him. But he waits for several minutes longer. Tucker whimpers a bit, and he hushes the dog. "Shush," Lucas scolds the dog; he jumps when his whisper echoes against the building.

Lucas strolls into the building, and he's momentarily curious why someone won't even bother closing the outer door, but he guesses that such a thing won't matter with a building no longer in use…

Lucas is observant of his surroundings; the little he could see in the house in the reduced ambience. The outer door had kept some original beauty, and he decides that it would have looked rich and luxurious back when the building was last used. He looks down at the floor, which seems to be constructed of reddish brown tiles minus the glaze that had worn away a long time ago but there were still traces of the original glaze. He makes a mental note of the feature.

Behind the door Lucas finds himself in a large hallway which was perhaps seven meters wide but the darkness prevents him from figuring out how long the hall is in length. Most of the hallway seems to be in a perpetual darkness that might also exist during daytime, evident by the appearance of clouds covering the moon visible through windows. Whenever the moon was visible it bathed the building in an eerie, bluish tint. He could easily imagine being on the set of a horror movies that he'd watch occasionally with Louellen.

To his left, there were five double door, of which two are propped open. The rooms beyond the doors were dark like the back of the hallway. To his right way, just before a stairway, were two further doors, both almost completely shut. He's certain the stairs were as grand as the outer door… once!

Lucas stares at the ceiling above, or at least at the part of it that's still a ceiling. It shows the remnants of a chandelier, and Lucas now gets curious about how more of the features look, so he pulls his flash-light out. He turns it on, and shines it in the ceiling's direction once more. The old chandelier glistens in the powerful light beam emanating from the flash-light, and Lucas can see tiny particles drifting around in it just as in the loft. He sees many webs covering the chandelier, and he wonders how much effort it might take to clean it.

Lucas moves the beam of light across the ceiling, then sees evidence that about five meters further along the ceiling, another similar chandelier would have been hanging from the ceiling. He turns the beam to the floor quickly and sees it lying on the floor, and it's clear that it had fallen down and shattered into pieces a long time ago.

The next part of the hallway that Lucas looks over is the grand stairway. He has seen similar structures in the book about the stately houses he'd been looking at in the library, and wonders if after all this time it's still safe to ascend. He disregards the idea for now.

Tucker, who starts growling at something, distracted his attention only he can smell or hear, but then whimpers a moment later like he's confused. "You coward," Lucas mumbles, when the dog visibly back-tracks and hides behind Lucas's legs. Lucas hears a muffled sound. His heart jumps.

"I guess you heard that," he says. "It's just another animal." Lucas checks the rooms to his right first. The idea of going up an unsteady stairway or going to the darkest parts of the house doesn't entirely appeal to him, and he agrees with the dog about that. He strolls to the door and wonders if perhaps the next moment someone might jump from behind it, or from the surrounding shadows, and cause him to piss in his pants.

Paranoia sets in, and Lucas keeps pointing the flash-light in every direction, where he hears a sound coming from. Even when there's no sound, he still feels like he's being watched, and this feeling of being watched feels just like when he'd looked at the house from the path beside its garden. He feels a chill go down his spine and shakes his head to dispel the feeling.

Lucas pushes the door open slowly and finds an empty room beyond. Well, almost empty, if you don't include the furniture that someone apparently needed to smash to pieces. The furniture looks old and could have been in use when the house was last used. Some chairs still have the thick silk fabric on them, and Lucas immediately knows that Louellen would have great interest in them because of her studies. It gives Lucas a new sense of understanding and appreciation for her interest in art and design.

I guess I have to say sorry to her for always dismissing it. It seems this mystery is now making me interested too...

Lucas shines his flash-light at the walls and sees that the wallpaper has torn away in places. It has a golden sheen to it still; with a right underlying coppery colour that might have been a lot lighter before age darkened its surface. There are rectangular areas, and Lucas is guessing now, were the places where paintings or mirrors hung once. If he factors this information into the picture forming in his mind about the dark room—and after counting how many he can see—the room reeks of old wealth long forgotten by passing time.

They had maintained the room obviously extremely well once and was luxurious in its appearance. That is one thing that doesn't escape his observant mind. He looks for other doors, and sees one at the other end of the room, which is positioned central to the room. To his right are three tall windows, each of which has remnants of curtains hanging from them; each in a worse state of degradation than the next; each caked in a thick layer of cobwebs, which is dulling its colour to a dark grey tone.

Lucas walks to the other doors he'd seen, and as he walks, he knows the floor gives way underfoot somewhat. He thinks in another decade, or more, the floors in the house would likely collapse—into the cellars below, perhaps…?

CHAPTER FIFTEEN

BEYOND THE SECOND DOOR LIES a long room with a partially collapsed table located in the centre. "I guess they ate here," Lucas mumbles. He glances at the room only, deciding to come back to look at it better when it's daytime and turns and walks back to the entrance hallway, and when he gets there, he looks up at the ceiling again to investigate it for evidence of degradation so he chances his luck and just rushes up the stairs and looks around for several minutes.

Lucas places his foot on the first tread and pushes down to measure its sturdiness. He takes hold of the handrail and tests its security. It seems to be safe enough to use it. He steps up and puts his other foot on the next tread. Slowly but steadily he climbs the stairs, but then finding that the floor of the landing has all but crumbled to dust, halts his attempt to go to the first floor of the building. Feeling despondent, Lucas walks back down—back to where the dog waits. When he'd climbed up, he'd let go of the lead, expecting the dog to follow him up, but Tucker stayed put at the bottom of the stairs instead. When Lucas returns, the dog whimpers again, and when Lucas reaches down to stroke the dog, he notes the dog is shaking with fear.

A noise comes again from somewhere in the building, and Lucas sees Tucker backing away like he's fearful of whatever unknown source is causing the sound. It makes Lucas unsettled once again…

Best I'd finish here soon, then go home.

The house fascinates Lucas despite the feelings of apprehension or misgivings he feels all the time. The feelings now weren't like the earlier feelings of just feeling a sense of discomfort, but it's very obvious a lot more now. Lucas had never felt this sort of feeling before in all his life. The constant feeling that someone watches him also doesn't diminish, and the dog's behaviour of growling softly—and doing this so softly that it's almost below his range of hearing—didn't make things any better.

I shouldn't have come during the night.

Lucas concludes the realisation from the feelings welling up in his gut.

But I didn't want anyone possibly to see me going here.
But he perseveres and go look at some more of the house before going home. He's curious how extensive the disrepair really is. He recalls one comment from Mrs Whitwell, "The house is in such a terrible state that the best thing for everyone would be for it all to be torn down, for the surrounding gardens to be dug up." At least in her opinion that it's best for houses to be built for families, and she seemed to be certain that removing all traces that it ever existed, is better for everyone…

That's not right.

Lucas remembers the conversation, and he remembers it mostly because it had sounded so odd. He'd noticed how condescending his neighbour had sounded, and Lucas had felt—at least—like a schoolboy being lectured by a teacher about forgetting to do his homework.

Now he realises how little he knows about his neighbour, the village, this house; it makes what Lynn Standage had said even more important. She'd stated that he needed to learn as much as he could from his own research and his own observations, and not to rely on claims made in the village by anyone. Lucas decided that this 'anyone' had also to include Gylda and Leigh until he'd gathered information that would eliminate *them* from the 'suspect list.' He chuckles softly when he realised how much like Miss Marple, Sherlock Holmes *or* Hercules Poirot he's emulating when making this sort of conclusion. He pulls his phone out and takes photos for Louellen to look at whenever he sees her again.

If she didn't believe him before, she will after seeing the photos. It will also offer her information about the architecture, so she can tell when the furniture and décor were last in use.

It makes her knowledge of art and interior design the *most* valuable knowledge that Lucas has access to. He can also email the photos to Lynn, so she also knows better how it looks. Lucas guesses he has to explain to both of them why he'd gone to Priory Mansion in the middle of the night…

The sounds he'd heard earlier had seized, so Lucas investigates the house a little longer. He walks first towards the end of the corridor that's shrouded in darkness, though it's becoming less now for the approaching morning. It's summer, and that actually helped make the area feel less like it's an oppressive type of darkness, but now almost feels like he'd got up in the middle of the night at home and went downstairs with all lights off.

He's about to pass the second open door when the brighter interior of this room catches his attention. Slowly, he pushes the door open. He hesitates for a few moments before deciding to go inside it.

Lucas frowns when he enters what might have been a living room for posh people in a time a hundred or more years earlier.

I wonder 'why' someone would leave all the houses so dilapidated. And then leave 'one' room, apparently in a fit state of repair. And who might have done this decorating?

The room contrasts compared to all the rest of the house. Lucas gets a sense of 'being lived in' from how the room feels and looks. The floor is clean, in good repair, and has obviously received a coat of lacquer to bring its old lustre back. When or by whom is now another puzzle. The walls look in an excellent state, and are free of almost all degrading wallpaper unlike other rooms, and a few of the windows even look almost like someone had recently painted them.

Though the fireplace is cold when Lucas moves his hand over it, there's something about how it looks too that makes him think it's in use, and not too long ago in the past. There's no evidence anywhere that anyone lived in the room, but it doesn't diminish the feeling growing inside Lucas that the chairs here are arranged and that they use the table. He keeps looking towards the door, expecting someone to walk into the room at any moment. But no one comes.

The apparent disparity between this room and the rest of the house is clear all around Lucas. It unsettles him more and more, and

Lucas wonders if anyone in the village is perhaps using the house in a way that no one else is aware of. It also highly contradicts what every person—Mrs Whitwell included—had said about the house. Someone knew this house was important and had sought it out as a place to use for something. Lucas walks around the room to take photos of what he sees. If he simply told Louellen about this, she'd certainly be laughing extremely loud in disbelief. But she couldn't do that if he showed her these photos. Lucas had to admit that the decorating or restoring that had been done is of a higher quality than he'd ever be capable of, and he can appreciate the beauty of it.

Tucker takes interest *too*—sniffing at every piece of furniture as he follows Lucas around the room. Lucas notices him take greater interest in one part of the old carpet, and guesses that it had got soiled by an animal of some sort in the past, and the smell still lingers.

The silence feels oppressing now, and Lucas wishes that at least the original periodical noises he'd heard earlier would return. He finds himself listen for them from time to time, but it's silent. "I guess it was an animal earlier," he mumbled softly. Lucas wanted to convince himself that he's right, but the evidence in this room overwhelmingly points at a human visitor or user instead. It worried him more and more, though he still feels like he needs to find out as much as he can. *It's entirely possible I can find the answers that Jeffrey Herbert was searching for. The house is enormous, and I've only seen six rooms so far, and the sounds came from some distance inside it.* Lucas decides that the next time he visits is with Louellen and in the daytime. *That means persuading her to visit.*

Lucas slumps his shoulders down when he realises how much of everything involves persuading her.

He sees one of the old chairs nearby and sits down on it, though cautiously at first in case it will collapse. Tucker sits down in front of him and looks at him with inquisitive motions, and as Lucas watches his dog, he knew the dog knows something he could neither hear nor smell. He sees Tucker sniff the air several times, then sneeze and repeat the process. His ears prick up like he's listening to an unknown sound. Lucas listens too, but his less attuned ears only hear silence. The dog's actions influence him. He feels his hairs on his neck stand up, and another chill travels down his spine.

Lucas looks at his watch. It's now about one o'clock, and he wanted to go for a drive around the area to see what the wider region looks like, and he wants to be away before Mrs Whitwell was awake. He grins remembering how he'd spotted his neighbour walking in the house like she'd only just woken up, and he'd noticed that his neighbour had become less thorough in covering her windows up when she saw it became increasingly though to look into his house from hers.

Lucas gets up and is about to walk around again when Tucker growls once again. It's a deep menacing growl that tells him that the dog is warning him about something…

* * *

When the gunshot rang out, Lucas knew he wasn't alone. Someone else is *also* in Priory Mansion. THAT person—whoever it was—didn't want him to know its truth. He bends over and grabs the dog from the floor, then rushes through the building towards the front door. Once outside the front door, he places Tucker on the doorstep. A second gunshot rings out, and it sounds closer this time. He looks at the front door over his shoulder only for a moment, then he runs away from the house. The dog is in a greater state of panic, and most of the time Lucas feels himself being pulled by the dog. Outside the massive old gate, Lucas stops a moment to catch his breath. He looks toward the front door, and though he doesn't see anyone, he feels like someone watches him. Then a moment later, the door slams shut. Although Lucas is over forty meters from the door, that simple action has him in a renewed panic.

Lucas walks fast through the dark street towards his house, then quietly enters it. After locking the front door, he looked through his curtains to make sure they hadn't followed him. He can feel his heart beat hard in his chest, he feels a cold sweat on his forehead…

Who had fired that gun earlier…?

Lucas glances from his window to look down the street and realises he can't see much. He walks from the living to the stairs, climbs up, and walks to his bedroom to look again. He sees no one in the street. No lights are on. It's almost like he imagined the gunshot.

There are no people in the street, and no other lights on. He walks through the hallway to the window with the wood covering it, and lifts the wood aside to look at Mrs Whitwell's house, and sees it's also covered in darkness. He feels like someone played a cruel joke on him.

Somewhat reluctantly he returns to the bedroom, where he sits down on his bed, and he picks up his phone, which he'd placed minutes earlier on the small cabinet beside his bed. He opens the application to look at the photos he'd taken, and though some were fuzzy, because he'd never mastered taking photos on his phone, unlike Louellen, who apparently did it often.

Lucas looks at all photos but sees no evidence in any of them that there had been someone else in the building with him. He glances at Tucker, who is lying on the floor in a sprawled out posture and still panting hard from the effort of running and walking fast; perhaps also from the apparent panic the dog had experienced when the two gunshots went off. The dog had acted like he smelled, and perhaps also heard, someone in the building. Lucas had to guess that the apparent occupier was some sort of squatter who wanted their identity to stay hidden. Squatting is illegal, and that person might think now that the unexpected visitor, Lucas, would call for the police to investigate the building.

Lucas gets up and looks carefully from his window once more, making sure that the curtain stays in place as much as possible so no one would see him if someone was observing him now. The action made Lucas realise in a way why Mrs Whitwell did similarly. Lucas wonders for a moment if she might have gone to Priory Mansion out of curiosity, and that her behaviour was from being spooked. He shakes his head. The idea of her doing that didn't fit in with what he'd been told about her…

Lucas turns from the window, and he goes to lie on the bed fully clothed. Lucas taps on the bed to let Tucker know that it's okay for the dog to come lie beside him. The dog is at first hesitant, then jumps on the bed. He lies down next to Lucas with his head on Lucas's stomach and looking at Lucas with a couple of dark brown eyes. Lucas looks at the dog a moment and notes how dilated the dog's pupils are. Lucas feels the occasional shaking that's going through the dog's body, and when it happens again, he puts his hand on the dog's head and slowly strokes it to calm the dog.

"I guess you liked it even less than I did," Lucas says softly. "I guess I have to make sure I talk to the vet about something calming for you when there are fireworks going on later in the year, and when it's New Year."

Lucas smiles when Tucker licks his hand.

"I won't take you with me next time," Lucas says. "That's better for you."

Lucas wonders if he should send a text to Louellen, but then remembers that she'd said something about having to be up early for her work. He wonders what requires her to be up so early. But then he remembers that she'd stated earlier in the year—a few months before he'd moved to Mellowstone Greene—that her gallery had won some sort of contract to hold exhibitions on behalf of several, well-known prominent London-based artists. Seeing she's the most senior person at the gallery, it's she who'd end up planning and organising them. But from what Lucas remembers, she'd always said she didn't go to the exhibitions.

Well, unless they had the book signing for that author from America there. She attended then, because she wanted a book autographed for her book collection, Lucas thinks, and he tries to remember the name of the author, but after a while has to shake his head.

I think she writes that fantasy series. But why can't I remember her name…?

Lucas knows the answer to *that* question. It's because he'd shown *no* genuine interest in the series in *all* the time he'd known Louellen. She'd been reading the series of books since the *first* one came out, when she was twelve years old. She owns every book written by the author, and he'd *never* ever bothered reading any of them…

If she comes to live here, that's going to change. I'll make sure I read them all. I guess I need to get a few extra bookcases if she keeps collecting them.

Lucas thinks again about Priory Mansion and now tries to analyse the two gunshots he'd heard. He had seen *no one* come from their own houses to check for the shots. It's possible that people just thought a car had backfired somewhere. If he'd been home at the time that it happened, and had heard the sounds, he might have mistaken them for that. It would tell if he went into the village when it's daytime. Lucas attempts to place the locations of *where* people live in his mind and realises that the closest resident would be Mr Howey. So if he goes to the newsagent's shop, and the man says *nothing* about any shots heard by him, then either he didn't hear *or* he could be lying. But Mr Howey didn't strike as the *type* of person who'd lie, so if *he* didn't show hearing anything, then it's a lot more likely that he didn't hear…

I guess that's my first stop tomorrow… and then I'm going for that drive to look around the area. If I'm going to do the investigation properly, I need to know as much as possible about the region, and try to find out things that some people just want to hide from everyone.

Lucas knows he's thinking about Mrs Whitwell and her apparent attempts to tell a little about the village. He'd learnt *more* about the village from Lynn in *one* day at the library than in all the time he'd had conversations with Mrs Whitwell.

I guess I must thank Gylda for her suggestion to go there… and attempt to talk to her more, and also become friends with Leigh as well, as Lynn had suggested. I guess Mrs Whitwell will hate me even more after this because she probably already does, judging from her reaction to the newspaper clippings.

Lucas doesn't like the idea of a conflict with his neighbour. He'd liked no form of conflict, not even when Louellen's friend Emlyn tried to bully him over his friendship with Louellen. That attempt to be nasty to him had made Louellen and him closer after that, and after that they'd regarded one another as boyfriend and girlfriend. It didn't mean they never had arguments, and it hurt him a lot when they broke up, because he suggested to her that studying for art was stupid.

But as he lifts his phone to look again at the pictures he'd taken inside Priory Mansion, he realises she is possibly the most valuable asset he now has in his pursuit to solve the mysteries surrounding the house…

That list of mysteries had grown by one more with the presence of a squatter of some sort inside the old stately home. Or two more if he counts the attempts at restoration as another mystery as well. Everything points at the house being at the centre of a long-term mystery, and from what he'd been told, it links so many people's fate to it. The effects of what went on in the house between a hundred and a hundred and fifty years ago; and from some evidence shows links to the Palace of Westminster unexpectedly…

Lucas falls asleep while he lies on his bed, thinking. Later in the morning, the sun pierces through a crack in the curtains where they don't quite meet up. It shines directly in Lucas's face and it wakes him with a start. When Lucas jerks his head up in annoyance for having sunlight on his face, he wakes the dog who'd been sleeping beside him with his head on the man's legs. Lucas grunts when he sees he fell asleep in his clothing, but then realises it made it easier to leave the house quicker. He hoists into an upright position and strokes the dog who'd crawled closer in the meantime. It seems the dog is still somewhat nervous about what had happened. With his other hand, he brushes over his head and glances towards the window, then looks at his watch. He sees that the time is a little after seven o'clock.

Too early to go to Mr Howey's shop really. Two hours to waste…

Lucas gets up and looks around. Maybe it's better to put on different clothes just in case someone had seen him, though he knows any person would know by Tucker's presence who'd been walking along the streets. Lucas takes off the top he'd been wearing and drops it on the bed, and a moment later pulls a t-shirt from a box. He pulls it on then walks to the window and looks outside once again, but now feels self-conscious doing it, and feels that circumstance is making him copy his neighbour.

He turns away, and looks at Tucker, and the dog wags at him, seemingly his old self again. "I guess you want to come with me for the walk to the shop." The dog wags even more in response.

Lucas walks downstairs, closely followed by Tucker, and once in the kitchen he first sorts out some breakfast for the dog, then sits down at the table with his own breakfast, which is a couple of slices of toast and a coffee. He looks again at his watch and sees it wasn't yet the opening time for the newsagent, but he goes, anyway. Perhaps he could just wait outside the shop and use the opportunity to judge the distance from it to Priory Mansion, knowing it's closer to the old house compared to where Mr Howey lives, which is only a few streets further.

After clearing up his plate and cup, and the dog's dinner bowl, Lucas goes to the living room, and watches the news broadcast until it's close enough to the shop's opening time, and therefore a time at which it won't look out of place for him to be walking through the village. It's just before eight o'clock when Lucas finally gets up to go. He gets ready, and after a few minutes is walking down the road. But then Lucas diverts his route to turn right into an alleyway to avoid going past Priory Mansion and walks the long way to the shop. If the person, who had shot the gunshot, was watching out for him he doesn't want to be seen by him or her.

Lucas stops in front of the door of the shop, and he feels annoyed when it states that they will shut it a little longer on that day of all days. And Lucas realises immediately that he really doesn't want to be seen by anyone living in the village…

CHAPTER SIXTEEN

LUCAS ISN'T FEELING SUSPICIOUS OF anyone—yet—but he wants to keep his suspicions about what happened the previous night from everyone as long as he can. Looking down every direction for Mr Howey to turn up also starts bothering him too. Lucas almost gives up on waiting there, when he sees the owner strolling along the road towards his store, not even increasing his pace when he sees Lucas waiting at the door for him.

"Good morning, Lucas!"

Mr Howey looks up and down to check over the younger man, like he's looking for something. Lucas notices it and frowns in annoyance at him. Mr Howey unlocks the door and slowly opens the door and holds it open for Lucas. Then, when Lucas is inside, he walks off, ignoring Lucas, who's left to close the shop door behind him.

"You want your usual newspaper, Lucas?" Mr Howey asks, and Lucas nods. While the shop owner goes to get the newspaper in question, Lucas picks up two bottles of cola, a pack of biscuits, a pack of chewing gum, and a box of dog treats, and carries these to the counter and waits for Mr Howey to return. He doesn't need to wait long.

Mr Howey is quieter today than Lucas has experienced before today. "Is something wrong?" he asks after a while, when he sees Mr Howey frown like he's in pain.

"It's nothing. I just didn't sleep so well last night. Some *idiot* needed to drive through the village like a maniac and then woke me up when their engine backfired."

"Oh… I heard nothing!" Lucas hopes he sounds convincing.

"You wouldn't hear anything on *that* side of the village. I think they were on the road that leads to the coast."

Lucas exits from the shop after paying for the goods purchased, and with *one* simple answer already in his mind.

If Mr Howey thought he heard a car backfire, then others might have assumed the same.

He strolls back home, contemplating en route what to do that day. He decides that he'd first go check out the road mentioned by Mr Howey, and work out if he'd mistaken a car backfiring for a couple of gunshots, and already knows he'd appear rather foolish if it had been that and not gunshots. He still wants to go on his trip around the area. Lucas is certain the dog will love the trip too. It would take his mind off the things that had been going on in recent weeks, and then at around one o'clock—when he thinks it's Louellen's lunchtime—he'd call her and try to persuade to visit the library and meet with Lynn Standage.

Lucas glances at the house next door as he stands at his own door unlocking it, but today he sees no evidence of Mrs Whitwell looking out of her house at either his house or being nosey about anyone else in the neighbourhood. Lucas wonders what changed to make her less willing to do this…

Lucas packs a bag with the groceries bought earlier, then makes himself a large stack of sandwiches. He puts the sandwiches in the bag. Lucas walks around the house, making sure he locked all windows and doors, and draws every curtain. He didn't want the chance of someone coming to nose around and seeing what he has in the house.

Lucas leaves the house with his bag, and the dog in tow, a few minutes later, gets in his car and drives off. He never looked to see if he's being watched…

Luke looks down at the road, which *could* be the one that Mr Howey had shown. A hill on the north-east side flanks Mellowstone Green, and the village descends in a steady slope down towards the coast, the positioning between the most northern road of the village and the coastal road is the first place *any* person could hear the backfiring of a car coming from. He looks to the southwest, where the northern side of the large, once-stately gardens surrounding Priory Mansion are located, with the house barely visible above the treetops. It could easily be as well he'd just heard *one* gunshot and that it echoed off the nearby hill to make it sound like a second shot, and anyone hearing *that* could have mistaken it for a car backfiring.

Lucas tries to convince himself that he's right. But he *also* knows that during the time he spent watching the news that morning that a single news bulletin shown proved him wrong. When the news broadcast started, he'd somewhat dozed off on the sofa, but jerked his head up a few moments later. In the news bulletin, someone fired a gun. And it sounded almost similar to the sound he'd heard in the house. It meant that Mr Howey was wrong when he tried to say he heard a car backfire. It meant also that someone might be a *lot* more violent towards him if he dared to return to Priory Mansion. He glances again towards the Priory Mansion. What's it hiding that causes an unknown person to chase off *any* visitor with a gunshot?

Or were they chasing me away?

Lucas frowns at the prospect of somehow having gained an enemy somewhere in the village.

Lucas turns and gets back in his car, then drives the narrow road down towards the coastal road. He pushes on his brake and stops the car for a few moments, when the coast becomes visible. The coast looks breathtaking from the angle at which he'd approached. Though most of the county had appeared flat to him whenever travelled to catch a train to London, this is probably one of the small gems where the coast seems to rise somewhat higher, and this leads now to the amazing view he sees now. He could see the coast disappear into the distance.

"Lou has to *see* this," Lucas mumbles. "I got to call her and tell her about this beautiful coast."

Lucas drives slowly down the slope and constantly watches the beautiful landscape come closer.

I'd never realised I was this close to the coast. I wouldn't have come here if it wasn't for Mr Howey's mention of a road over here.

At the bottom of the hill, Lucas stops again. He has two choices. Either he can follow the road north and then west, or go south. Something tells him he'd has more chance for discovering any good beaches going south first, so he turns right. Lucas decides he can always turn around and go back towards the north if he doesn't find what he wants to find in this direction. The beach seems to narrow in the southern direction, but that isn't what Lucas wants to check out. In two articles, he'd read a claim that the girl at the house must have gone south to one of the nearest coastal towns, then taken a ship to an old port that existed outside London in the nineteenth century. If that was the case, then he needs to figure out how long that journey took her; another theory suggested that she'd gone down to Norwich, and from there ended up in London, and that theory, to him, sounded more plausible. He already knows how long driving took to there; then the last theory is that she'd gone somewhere north. But Lucas had seen no information in the newspaper clippings, or the information that Lynn had in her possession that this was a valid theory.

Lucas hits the brake, when he sees a road sign for Great Yarmouth.

If the theory is the right one, it would have taken her 'weeks' to get to there. They would have found her long before that.

He sees a location for turning his car ahead of him and drives there, and after a few minutes of manoeuvring he's driving north instead. As he drives, Lucas opens the back window facing the coast to about two-thirds down. Tucker gets up and sticks his nose through the window, and from the 'dog grin' on his face, Lucas can tell the dog is enjoying the experience.

Definitely should go for drives with him regularly, Lucas thinks while glancing at the dog through the rear-view mirror.

Lucas stops a moment at the road he'd descended about an hour earlier and glances up in the direction where Priory Mansion had to be.

Those who lived there more than a hundred years ago they would have had a good view of the coast before. Especially with none of the overgrown trees.

The house is derelict now, and the gardens overgrown; and it was falling to pieces, but *still* someone had gone there to do some sort of repair and restoration to the building. Lucas pulls out his phone, and he turns the engine off, because he doesn't want to fall foul of some overzealous police officer coming by and fining him. He takes a photo of the hill, so he can study the contours of the house and surrounding estate in more detail later. Before putting his phone away, he looks at the photo he'd taken, and smirks that for once he'd taken one that seems okay. Lucas glances up one more time at the hill, then starts his engine again, and a moment later drives on.

It's perhaps half an hour later that he spots the beginning of the beach he'd seen from the top of the hill. He also spots something else that interests him. Before he'd started investigating the story of Priory Mansion, *this* might have been a place Lucas *never* would have gone, but *today* it looks appealing. On the left side of the road stands an extensive building, and it lists on the sign outside it: it's a county museum. Lucas turns his car to a sharp left and drives into the car park, hoping the museum isn't shut. He feels relief when a woman with two children walks out, so he parks up and makes sure all four windows are open just an inch.

"I don't think you can come along, Tucker," he whispers to the dog, who stands on the back seat with a wagging tail. He points at the seat and the dog lies down reluctantly and whimpers a bit.

"No, Tucker, I can't take you into this place. It says 'No Dogs' on the door." Lucas strokes the dog's head, saying gently, "I'll be back soon."

Lucas strokes the dog a few times to settle him, then he checks the windows a few more times to make sure they're sufficiently opened, then he steps from the car. He locks the car, and glances into the car once more, motioning for Tucker to lie down when the dog gets up. As he walks away, Lucas can hear Tucker whimpering in the car. He hurries to the entrance of what seems to be a museum. Lucas pulls the outer door open and steps in. The building is smaller than it appeared from the outside. He finds himself in what seems to be some sort of lobby. He looks both left and right for a moment. On his right, he sees some sort of art exhibit.

Lou would love that.

He looks at the date it's showing.

It's around for another month. I can bring her here if I can convince her to come visit.

He looks left, and this area seems to be the museum section of the building, as is listed outside.

"Can I help you?"

Lucas glances from where the voice had come from, and he sees a tall, somewhat ageing man standing at a door which is located towards the back of the lobby. "I was interested in the museum."

"It's open for visitors," the man replies, "but we *ask* for 'five pounds' donation in the container, there next to the desk."

"Okay." Lucas pulls his wallet out, and takes out the required banknote, and deposits this into the container. Lucas looks up to see an approving nod from the man, before the man walks into the room he'd heading towards. Lucas glances to his left and looks at the museum area, then he turns and walks into that part of the building. It wasn't a big museum, especially compared to the size of those he'd visited in London. He decides this whole exhibition could fit into a small room of the British Museum. But the items on display are interesting in a rugged sort of way.

A map displays the many stately homes the county has. Lucas sees Priory Mansion listed, but only as ruins. *At least it's listed, and that would mean they might know something about it here. I'm certain of that.* He looks over the map and sees that almost they list every other stately home in green letters. *They've got Priory Mansion listed in red letters.* Lucas checks at the legend beside the map, and he sees that green lettering would mean 'in use and occupied' and red would mean 'disused for a hundred years or longer' and he sees the legend also was listing some places as 'disused fewer than a hundred years; reasons unknown' - it listed these buildings in red, but only as an outline of a letter.

Lucas looks again at the map and sees a place listed in this second version of lettering. Five of such places were located quite close to the Priory Mansion. But someone also listed mostly them as 'Name Unknown.' He frowns…

"Are you interested in this map for any reason…?"

Lucas looks sideways to find the same ageing man from earlier standing next to him.

"Actually, yes, I hope so," Lucas says, "I've just moved to Mellowstone Greene, and I've been exploring the region more…"

"Ah, yes," the man replies, "A village with such a sorrowful past."

Lucas raises an eyebrow at hearing the explanation. He has only ever heard remarks that imply negativity to the mention of the village, so having a person refer to it as 'sorrowful' is something new. The man is saying it *also* with such conviction that Lucas wonders why he'd say this.

"What do you mean by 'sorrowful'?" Lucas asks, deciding to make out that he knew nothing about the village just yet.

"I guess, as a person *new* to the area, you don't know the story of how a girl had become a victim of a family feud then?" the answer comes.

"Oh… errr no, I didn't know it." Lucas's answer is quick.

"Well, then… I saw you have a dog with you if that's your car in the car park. It's my lunch break, so why don't you bring the dog here? My name is John, by the way. I know it says 'no dogs' but if we don't have it on the door, we'd have fifty dogs here every weekend because of the nearby dog training school."

"Alright, if you say it's okay."

Lucas walks back to the car and opens it, then puts a lead on Tucker, then he closes all but one window so the car will get a bit of fresh air and walks back to the entrance with a wagging Tucker beside him. He walks back into the museum and sees that the man—who'd introduced himself as John—has placed two chairs near the desk where the collection container stands. He has placed a tray with a teapot, a couple of cups and a bowl of biscuits on the desk. For the dog, there's a bowl of fresh water.

"So then, what is it you'd like to know?" John asks. "I know a *few* things about the village, and I hope it's enough to satisfy your curiosity."

"Well, I've been told something about it by a neighbour since moving to the village, but not much."

"How long have you lived there?"

"A few months," Lucas replies.

"I guess you haven't *yet* met the more colourful folk yet."

Lucas frowns briefly but decides not to ask who these 'colourful folk' might be.

"But you're here for history about the house. I guess… and not any gossip that seems to want to keep that house in the news. If you get what I mean."

"I think so."

"I presume you know already that its name is 'Priory Mansion.' It's listed there, but sometimes I wonder if it should because of the trouble it gives us."

"In what way?" Lucas asks.

"I said already there's something about a girl. It was the daughter of the last lord to live there. He had a sister, and she and her family always caused that girl trouble."

"What was the girl's name?" Lucas feels confused because this story isn't like anything that either Gylda or Lynn has said.

Lucas listens for the next forty minutes to how John explains the things he knows about 'Mellowstone Greene' and 'Priory Mansion'. Lucas feels shocked by some details. He remembers what Gylda had stated to him, so he decides not to tell John about anything he already knows. He also omits the existence of the newspaper clippings.

After John finishes with his account of information, they escort Lucas around the museum by John. He is told in great detail the history of the region. It makes Lucas feel more connected with the region, as though he'd heard yet another version of events. He knows that had Louellen been here with him now that she'd likely have some sort of gut feeling about what she's hearing; but she isn't here, and he needs to work out whether this is important all by himself.

After Tucker shows signs he needs to relieve himself, Lucas excuses himself. After a quick dash to the nearby bushes, where he lets Tucker do his business—and then, after glancing around real quick doing the same, Lucas departs and drives on his northbound route along the coast.

Lucas stops at a pub about an hour later for a quick meal. As he sits eating at a table on the terrace outside the pub—with Tucker curled up below the table. Lucas reads the book borrowed from Lynn's library. He realises that some 'stuff' told by John is correct, though the man had somewhat embellished the account of history to spin a story with; a somewhat fantastical approach to what he perceived as important to a newcomer in the region.

But to Lucas, the visit meant he has another version of what went on in the region. Though John didn't state any names, it seemed he was talking about someone else—and not the girl who'd gone missing. It adds another layer of mystery to what's growing into one of the biggest mysteries Lucas has ever encountered in his entire life. He wonders how he of all people had got right in the middle of it all: to find that a place he'd chosen as a place to retire early has links to Louellen's great-grandfather, adds to it in ways he couldn't even imagine. Lucas decides he needs to stop somewhere and give Louellen a call before it gets too late in the day. He glances at his watch and sees it is close to when she'd normally eats her lunch break.

Ten minutes later, circumstance presents an opportunity when he sees a car park next to the beach he'd admired from the hill hours earlier. He slows down, then turns into the car park. When he sees an ice cream vendor at the far end of the car park, Lucas decides that's the perfect place to park up and get out. He parks next to a bench…

Lucas gets out of the car, opens the back door and puts the lead on Tucker, then lets the dog jump from the car. He locks the car and walks to the ice cream vendor. He's greeted by a smiling girl of maybe seventeen or eighteen years old.

"What flavour of ice cream would you like?"

Lucas chooses a refreshing fruity ice cream on a stick. He pays for it, then walks to a bench to sit down. After enjoying the ice cream for several minutes, he pulls out his phone and sits, looking at it in a pensive mood.

I guess I 'should' call Lou and discuss that awkwardly hard matter again and also convince her to go see Lynn.

Lucas again answers the phone relatively fast. "Hi Lou." Lucas gulps a moment, feeling flustered and momentarily feels tongue-tied once more.

"Hey, Lucas. How's the research going?"

Lucas frowns when he detects a notable sarcasm in Louellen's voice. "My research—errr—it's going okay," Lucas replies, "but I called about *you,* actually."

"Me? What about me?"

"I called to talk to you about that," Lucas says.

"Are you calling *again* about me coming to visit?" Louellen snaps back at him over the phone.

"No, I'm *not* calling about that at all." Lucas sighs with frustration that this seems yet another phone call where they're having issues. He wants them to talk about the visit to the house without her getting snappy. He pauses a moment.

"Are you there still?" Louellen asks a moment later, now in a softer tone.

"Yes, I'm here," Lucas replies softly back.

"Okay, sorry that I'm snappy, but the morning was so hectic here." Louellen sighs deep and audibly over the phone.

"It sounds like *you* could do with time off," Lucas suggests, "and no, that wasn't another attempt to get you to visit. I think you should stay home with your dad for a few days to relax."

"I guess I could do that…"

Lucas notices that the almost dismissive tone has evaporated from Louellen's voice. She sounds tired. He decides on a fresh approach. "Remember Gylda, who I know from the village, and who I'd told you about?" he asks. "The person who'd told me to go to the library."

"I remember you telling about her."

"It's actually interesting. I wouldn't be driving around the county right now if *she* hadn't mentioned the library or the house."

"You're not home? Where are you now…?"

"On a nice bit of beach. Actually, rather nice and sandy, considering that pebbles cover most of the other beaches that I drove past."

"Okay, now I *am* jealous," Louellen

"Well, there's a solution to *that*, you know…" Lucas chuckles at the same time.

"Yeah, yeah. You've convinced me, but I still can't promise anything. I'm really busy with work lately."

"Just organise it whenever." Lucas then adds in an enticing tone. "It says right here *this* beach is best enjoyed in the summer months between early June and late August."

Lucas grins broadly when he hears an audible groan from Louellen, and he decides that the reason of why she'd moved her phone away to allow herself to curse a few times under her breath, "Shit, shit, shit, shit—"

Part Three

CHAPTER SEVENTEEN

NOW LUCAS IS HAVING FUN with Louellen and he keeps teasing her a bit more with details that would make her want to be with him at the beach front. "There's an ice-cream van parked up opposite of where I'm sitting…"

"Shut up!" Louellen snaps at him, but she sounds more annoyed than angry.

"I could go buy one to send you a photo—"

"I said—shut up," Louellen squeals quietly, but Lucas can hear the beginning of a giggle in her voice now.

"You feel better now?" Lucas asks.

"Actually, yes. Sorry for snapping at you."

"It's okay," Lucas says softly, "and before *you* have another go at me, I think you're in need of a well-deserved holiday."

"I think you're right, but I don't know when I—" Louellen says.

"Can you take off a few hours to visit a library?" Lucas interjects.

"Errr why?"

"Because I think *you* want to hear what Lynn Standage knows from her…"

"That's the librarian that Gylda sent you to, right?" Louellen asks.

"Yes, that's right."

"Why do you want me to go see her?"

"She has information that would interest you," Lucas says, then after a short pause he asks, "You want to know more about your great-grandfather, right?"

"Yes, I do," Louellen answers softly.

"I suggest you *go* there and specifically ask her for information about what kind of work your great-grandfather had been doing. It may change how you view Mellowstone Greene." Lucas squeezes his eyes shut as he waits for Louellen's response. He curses quietly for having brought up about the village again. But it had to be mentioned. He's sure that the information Lynn has to tell her will be very important for Louellen to know about, too.

"I think you must tell your dad about it too," he adds softly when Louellen stays silent.

"Is it *that* important?"

"It explains a lot about what went on back then. Both around here and with the newspaper. It also affects Anna in some ways too, as it was *her* great-grandfather who had run the newspaper, but it's up to you to decide whether you find what Lynn knows as important as I do."

"Lynn has information about him, too?" Louellen asks.

Lucas notices an edge to Louellen's voice. Not from annoyance, but genuine worry. It seems she's at least attempting to be interested. "Yes, she does. She has a book explaining the history of different newspapers that had existed over the years as a broadsheet, and it lists the earliest of these newspapers as originating from 1712. The book stated this list was recorded because of some sort of tax."

"Yes, that's right. I had learnt about the newspapers in a segment about publications of newspapers in my art degree." Louellen's voice sounds happier suddenly, because she's talking to Lucas about 'something' she knew more about than him.

"Actually, that's also one *other* reason I would love to have you here with me," Lucas says quietly, "so you can look at the photos that I took."

"What photos?"

"Of inside when I was at Priory Mansion."

"You mean to say you went *there* last night?" Louellen has apparent surprise in her voice now.

"Yes, and I took photos. It's—errr… it isn't at all how you might expect it to look, if *we* really considered that someone had abandoned the building."

"What do you mean?" Louellen's voice now sounds genuinely worried.

"Well, that's the thing I was calling about, too. Something has happened while I was there. Someone doesn't want the *truth* to be discovered. I heard a shot and ran—"

"What?" Louellen shrieks. "You mean someone shot at you?"

"No, I don't think so… but I think they meant for the shots to chase me off. I took the photos before it had happened."

"Got any idea who it was?" Louellen asks.

"No, I don't."

"Is that part of the reason you called me then?"

"Yes, I think there's a lot *more* going on than a simple story about an abandoned house. In some of the information that Lynn had showed me, I got the impression it had involved some sort of scandal, tied to the Prime Minister of the time—which he had distanced himself from as soon as he could. The involvement of your great-grandfather and Anna's great-grandfather is coincidental, because they were reporting about it all."

"So, you're definitely sure that my great-grandfather was a reporter at the newspaper, and not just someone selling the newspapers…?" Louellen asks with clear urgency in her voice now.

"That's correct, and I think you tell *that* to your dad—and maybe you should also tell Anna about it. If something had happened and there was a scandal, and it all comes out in the open—at least then she'd be prepared for the consequences."

"I guess I have to figure out *how* I'm going to tell her. She feels so very proud of her great-grandfather."

"I know that," Lucas says softly. "I recall the day when you two were telling me how and why you were such close friends."

"It seems so long ago," Louellen says softly. "I can't believe that almost eight years ago we were school kids worrying about homework and all that."

"Yeah, you're right."

Lucas smiles at the memories the conversation is evoking. It feels good to talk with Louellen about those early days because those conversations were when Lucas was at his happiest. Not the memories of whenever they'd been drifting apart, which seems what had been happening again lately. If he played his cards right, maybe all the current things going on *could* bring them together in a more permanent setting. He misses just walking down the road to go see Louellen whenever, and again the thought enters his mind about whether he'd made the right choice when he'd bought the cottage he now is living in…

"So, Lynn has been researching not just the village but *also* anything that's linked to the village," Louellen asks, "and also stuff that links the village to other places and people in other places?"

"That's correct," he answers. "She said she has a room filled with the information that she has gathered over the years. She said she'd started collecting the information after leaving Mellowstone Greene, and she'd lived there *last* some twenty years ago. I think she has contact with Gylda as a friend perhaps, or else Gylda wouldn't have mentioned twice to me to visit the library where Lynn works."

"Sounds fascinating, actually. How different people who aren't really connected can suddenly discover they're a lot more connected than they knew—I wonder," Louellen says pensively. "If you'd never bought *that* cottage, you wouldn't have found this extra information about my great-grandfather… or Anna's… and you wouldn't have the information that ties it all to the Palace of Westminster, with the link to the Prime Minister."

"I wonder still *how* it all ties together," Lucas comments, "because we know some of what went on, but not yet one crucial thing that Gylda told me."

"Which is what?" Louellen asks.

"Both Gylda and Lynn have mentioned about the scandal of the missing girl. Both said they linked Leigh Governor to it. She's the descendant of the child left behind by the girl who went missing, but I'm certain that there's a lot more going on than either of them realise."

"Hmm, so it's a conspiracy of some sort, then?" she asks.

"Yes, and I think it's something to do with the girl who had disappeared, or has to do with a lot *more*. According to what Lynn and I have found, someone was after your great-grandfather—and also Anna's great-grandfather… because of their insistence on keeping writing about this. I'm uncertain how it all fits together, but I think that you and I could find out how and what happened."

"I guess you're right… The more you're saying about it all, the more I'm getting convinced that I should at least go see Lynn," Louellen says, "but please, don't keep telling me about visiting. If I *go* there, and decide it's important enough, then I'll decide whether I want to come visit you there. Is that okay with you?"

"Yes, that's fine with me…!" Lucas attempts to hide a bit of the disappointment he feels from welling up from his voice.

"Okay, so what exactly did you discover there?"

"Well, I discovered this ice cream vendor, and this nice beach," Lucas says teasingly.

"Lucas, stop it," Louellen says in a mock-sincere chastising voice, but she bursts out in a hysterical giggle at the end.

"Okay, seriously, this region looks amazing. There are well over fifty beautiful houses to visit here in Norfolk, with something like ten of them in this part of the county, and this doesn't include Priory Mansion. It's got beaches already, and a lot of pubs and other stuff. I think it will take me a while before I've explored it all."

"I guess a visit might be okay, then. Even if it's just for visiting the beach that *you* keep pestering me about… Any chance of a photo of it?"

"Sure, one moment, then I'll send it to you." It's clear to Lucas that his grumbles to get a photo sorted for Louellen is being met by her endless barrage of giggles. He still isn't as efficient with the use of his phone as she is, especially judging by the fifty or sixty photos she'd send him every day; and that was apparently just the ones he would get. "I think I got it. Remind me again how to send a photo to you?"

Lucas listens to Louellen's explanation, which is periodically interrupted by another wave of giggle.

"You should have it now," he says after a last attempt.

"Yes, I do—and ooh wow! That beach is beautiful," she says a moment later, "I guess I'm sold… but just for a visit perhaps, and only if you take me there."

"Sure thing. Just work out when you can come visit."

"Okay," Louellen replies, and a bit more hesitant than Lucas wanted, adds, "I will…"

"So, I guess we settled that then," Lucas says softly.

"Lucas, so this Lynn is at the library. Is *she* somehow related to the village, too?" Louellen obviously wants to change the subject by the question.

"Yes, she is. She grew up there and told me that much. She'd moved away twenty years ago. I was told that *she* still has contact with Gylda."

"Ah, right? What sort of information does *she* have at the library because I heard you mention a book?"

"I didn't see it myself, and she brought down a few 'examples' down from a room upstairs," Lucas replies, "but it sounded like she has stacks and stacks of information, and has been busy with the work for some time."

"You make me more and more curious. Oh, hang on, there's a customer here—be right back." Lucas pulls the phone away when it's dropped rather unceremoniously onto Louellen's desk, it seems. He hears her fast pace away from her desk, walking to somewhere else in the gallery. A few moments later, he hears her voice, and then the voice of a man and a woman speaking in turns about something…

He hears some laughter and wonders what the conversation was about, because he can't quite hear it. He strains to listen as he hears first the two unfamiliar voices echo through the gallery, and then Louellen's. A few moments later, he hears Louellen's footsteps, followed by paper rustling, and then the footsteps walk off again. He wonders what's going on for a while, then he gets a bit bored from listening and starts staring aimlessly at the beach instead. Lucas is startled when a few moments later, he hears Louellen's voice on the phone again…

"Okay, so where were we?"
"I think I was making you curious."
"Ah yes, that's right. I was just wondering *why* Lynn would keep so much information. To me, it's almost like she's after a lot more information than just that of a missing girl. I wonder what else might have happened there."

Lucas frowns for a moment, and wonders if Louellen may be right. She's quite perceptive about things, and he wonders how she'd come to that specific conclusion. But then again, Louellen had often enough surprised him with her unexpected insight. It's one of those things he'd noticed really early on, when he had first spotted her at their school. Lucas smiles for a moment at the memory it evokes of Louellen standing in the school courtyard having a go at an older boy… because he'd apparently said something nasty to her and to Anna. He'd watched for a few minutes, then walked on as he hadn't felt comfortable staying around while they'd argued. But he didn't forget about what happened, and then their chance encounter happened when *she* was leaving the library with the books getting knocked from her arms.
"So, what theory do you have about it all?" Lucas asks.
"I don't know—exactly. There's something about it *all* that's giving me this kind of odd feeling. A feeling that something about any of it isn't correct, or something like it. I can't really explain."

"If that's the case, do you realise there's only one way to find out if those feelings are right—and maybe I need to take it all a bit more seriously? I have to admit that up to now I had treated it a little as some sort of fun, but I think that it's more serious than I realised before today."

"Yes, you're right, and I agree with treating this more seriously. I need to make sure I know enough information to make sure dad knows what happened to his grandfather. I guess it means I should visit the library as well. Can you give me the address, please…?"

Louellen glanced up at the library building. She'd been in a public library *last* when she was still in her mid-teen years, and ever since she'd been hanging out with her female friends, books had become less and less interesting to her, even though she *still* had an interest in the books that she'd started reading when she was thirteen. But *now* she felt differently. She'd been told about 'Lynn Standage' by Lucas, and he'd told her how much the woman knew of Mellowstone Greene…

And now she wanted to find out more for herself…

Louellen walks into the library and then she walks to the desk where an older woman is sitting, who looks up at her and then smiles at her. "I'm here for information…" Louellen states softly.

"What kind of information?" the librarian asks.

"I'm helping a friend of mine with his research about a village where he's living. It's called Mellowstone Greene, and—"
"Ahh, *you* must be the friend that Lucas had mentioned when he visited here. I'm Lynn Standage, and of course I'll help you."
Louellen wasn't sure why she had needed to blush when Lynn had mentioned Lucas, but the librarian seemed to ignore it. "Actually, I wanted to find out more about Charles Fairey. Lucas had mentioned him, and when I had talked about him with my father, he'd said that his grandfather had talked about *him* as someone he had known about when he was young—"
"Interesting… Sit down, please, and I'll find you all the newspaper sheets with the articles that were written about him." Lynn walks off, and Louellen looks at her disappearing figure for a while, then her phone distracts her. It buzzes loudly, and she quickly answers it.
"Hey, Anna, I can't talk at the moment… I'm at a library." Louellen frowns as she has to listen to Anna's laughter for a moment, then she gets annoyed at her friend for it. "Yes, I'm really in a library… I'm doing some research here for—well, I'm helping Lucas."
"Is he still chasing after you?" Anna laughs again. Louellen

frowns, then she turns her phone off. Now no one could reach her—not even work—but with work she could make a claim that she'd been in some place with poor reception. She turns and sees Lynn coming back, so she puts her phone quickly into her bag.

"I've found a *few* pages about Charles Fairey. Is your interest because of Lucas, or because of your father's grandfather?"

"Errr—both I think—and my father's grandfather worked as a writer for the newspaper," Louellen says as she points at the third broadsheet Lynn places on the table.

"Oh, really!" Lynn asks, "and what was his name?"

"I'm *first* daughter born in five generations. His name was Jeffrey Herbert. My grandfather was George Herbert, and my dad is called Peter Herbert."

"I see."

"I mentioned about 'Charles Fairey' to my father because, according to him, I stomped home after Lucas had visited. He said that I looked angry. I told him about Lucas, and that he'd asked me to come live with him, and I then mentioned what Lucas had said."

Lynn nods.

"Dad told me what his grandfather had told *him* when he was my age," Louellen continues, "and then when Lucas had called and said that he visited me, it had made me realise I needed to tell my father about where Lucas was living now. Then, dad told me there's a lot that isn't known about the case, because Charles Fairey was *no* good at solving any of it—That most that *is* known was apparently thanks to his grandfather's efforts. Thinking about all this has made me realise I care a lot more about Lucas than I'd wanted to admit to—when I talked with him. If there's something going on in Mellowstone Greene, like he has claimed on the phone, I want to help him as much as I can," and then, after a pause, Louellen adds, "and he told me then that he wanted to look at the mansion… again. He called me yesterday to say that he did it, and he didn't sound all too happy. That's why I came here today. I must help him if I can."

"I see… so he told me you're his friend, though I'd noticed he was hesitant, and frankly *you* should consider him as more…" Lynn looks sternly at the younger woman. "But in reality, it isn't my place to say such things, but to be honest, I think *he* loves you."

Louellen feels her face go bright red at the words, and she looks down. Lynn smiles knowingly then she speaks again, "I think I found the article that you might look for." Lynn makes it appear that she hadn't noticed Louellen's still reddened face.

"Huh, what?" Louellen flinches when she realises she's still distracted by her embarrassment, experienced moments earlier when Lynn had mentioned Lucas.

"There's an article here about Charles Fairey that you might find rather interesting," Lynn says, "and it mentions Jeffrey Herbert in it."

"Ohh!"

Louellen accepts the print-out of the broadsheet from Lynn, and she places it on the table in front of her, and glances at its content thoroughly. Then Lynn points with a finger at a column to the furthest left. So, she reads this specifically, and soon is finished as it's short. She glances up and stares puzzled at the librarian. "Why would they mention my great-grandfather in an article in that way?"

"I'm uncertain, but Lucas might be onto something. He emailed me yesterday, and he stated in the email that he'd found out something more about the village—I'm interested *too* as I come from there originally. I've been affected *too* by the scandal, or I wouldn't have moved away—"

Louellen sees Lynn's smile has faded and has been replaced soon after with a despondent look, so she asks the other woman, "Do you think it's all tied together? My great-grandfather, that investigator, whatever that had happened in the mansion…?"

"I think so… and maybe, your great-grandfather had discovered something about it all, and there were people with a lot more power who worked to shut him up, and they'd acted in such a way to make certain that Charles Fairey wasn't able to talk about it anymore. He'd screwed up, and because of this they had never been able to solve the mystery surrounding whatever happened in or near Priory Mansion."

"I think Lucas wants to solve the mystery that he'd found in his house—and I want to know *what* had happened to my great-grandfather because of it," Louellen says quietly, "and my dad will want to know about all this too. He was always told by his father whenever he'd asked that he'd abandoned *them*—but now I'm not so sure."

Lynn sits down again, and she takes hold of Louellen's hand. She studies the younger woman's face carefully, and she sees a tear-drop streaking her carefully applied make-up. She reaches up, and in a motherly gesture, she wipes the wetness away from Louellen's face, then after a pause she speaks again. "You and Lucas must be careful if you decide to investigate all of this and look out for one another. Especially if *you* find out from this research that your family is somehow involved. As a victim. With their involvement warped into a lie…"

Lynn pauses and regards the woman sitting beside her. "Someone might take offence to you looking into this and wanting to find the truth," she almost whispers. "This isn't the same as fiction, where the individuals investigating something are like some sort of super heroes or invincible, and can get out of sticky situations with a few chosen words. This *is* reality, and if there are people who'd want this to stay covered—and personally, I think that's the case—then they'll make it tough for everyone involved. I've also said all of this to Lucas. If you want to find out what had happened to Jeffrey Herbert, do it together with Lucas for both your safety…"

Louellen nods then she softly comments, "We argued when he visited me a few weeks back…"

"What about?" Lynn says, sounding concerned.

"He wants me to move in, and I'm uncertain I want it…"

"And you don't want to…?"

"I'm unsure. I'm not even sure if I don't love him," Louellen whispers. "It's been months since he'd moved to Mellowstone Greene, and I miss our get-togethers."

"You could suggest living together as friends. I may be old but I'm not someone who's old-fashioned in *that* way."

Louellen grins at the older woman. "I didn't know you were *that* old."

"I'm old enough to be your grandmother."

Lynn laughs for a few moments.

"You have *all* the time in the world still to decide whether you want to spend the rest of it with Lucas. Don't rush into decisions that you might regret, and that goes either way. You saying 'no' to him once doesn't mean his feelings for you are any less. I think *he* cares enough for you to wait until you to feel ready."

"How do you know…?"

"I've buried two husbands—each was loved dearly—and if tomorrow a handsome gentleman walked through those doors and knew how to sweep an old woman like me off her feet, I'd let him—

and you have such a man in arm's reach. His name is Lucas Cayton…"

CHAPTER EIGHTEEN

Louellen is amused at the suggestion of the older woman and she grins. "Maybe once all this is over," she says, "and I'll know if I want to be with him."

"That's the spirit. Now, would *you* like a cup of tea?"Lynn asks softly. "Then I'll go see if I can find more newspaper clippings to help you with your research."

"Yes, please. With a bit of milk in it only for me, please."

Lynn gets up and places her hand on Louellen's shoulder in a tender gesture for a moment, then she walks off to a cabinet behind where her desk is located. This time, Louellen glances after her, feeling grateful and even appreciative of the woman's words. She glances again at the broadsheet, and at what her great-grandfather had written in the article:

> "It is the belief that Charles Fairey missed many opportunities in pursuing Sibbett. She has a family who are demanding answers, but just like th involving the RMS Titanic, that again, it's the apparent class differences tha gets done. Had Karina Seaward been the individual who had disappeared left no stone unturned until they found her, but because the individual meant that they afforded only a minimal effort to the case, however muc tries to claim otherwise."

Louellen frowns for a moment with some anger, and she realises that if she hadn't known better that the text could easily have been a synopsis for some sort of television series. Because *her* ancestor had said these strong words, it wasn't a laughing matter anymore for her. She looked at the date of the broadsheet. It had mentioned the Titanic, which means Jeffrey Herbert had written it *after* those events. She moved her hand over the date.

17 July 1912

Not so long after the Titanic sank then. My dad said that Jeffrey Herbert had died in 1914. I wonder if he found out something that made someone nervous about his investigations.

Louellen glances up quickly when she hears footsteps.

"Here you go—with a bit of milk like you asked for."

Louellen smiles momentarily, then she says, "Lynn, do you have any information about *this* newspaper when Jeffrey Herbert had worked there…? Like who had owned it—"

"I believe I could find that information for you. In the meantime, maybe look at these broadsheets. It seems your great-grandfather was a reporter at the newspaper for quite some time. The earliest article I found dates from 1876. He might have worked there for over thirty years."

"That long? I never knew that, and I don't think my dad knew it either."

"Your family seems to have been affected too by the things that happened as well, it seems."

"But I'm wondering now what the connection might be between all *this* and the mansion in Mellowstone Greene." Louellen looks up with pleading eyes at Lynn, like she could suddenly give Louellen every answer to every question on her mind at that moment. Lynn can only look back at the younger woman compassionately.

The situation had now grown from a simple case of finding out what had happened to a building in Lynn's birth village to a mystery that now seemed to reach all the way to the highest acolytes of the government of the late nineteenth and early twentieth century. It was a lot more complex than she'd assured Lucas it to be…

They spent the next hour with them both sorting through the broadsheets to get a chronological logic going on for the articles, and then for them to check for *any* news that was happening at the same time. After this task was done, the two women looked at one another, and then they glanced at the two tables at the same time that now had all the papers lying on them.

"I'll get a couple of notepads and pens, then we can make notes." Lynn turns, and she walks back to her desk. From a drawer, she retrieves the notepads, the pens, and she also pulls out a large envelope. She walks back to Louellen. "When we're done, you can put all the notes in this envelope to take with you. I'll also make photocopies of the information to send to Lucas. He gave me his address so I cam send any information I've found."

Louellen nods. "What sort of things should I write?" she asks.

"I think you'd want to make two lists on these pages. On one side, you write the things you're reading that fit in with what you know about your family, and on the other side, you write anything that sounds 'odd' or 'out of place.' Maybe, also write things to help Lucas as well."

Louellen sat down at one table, while Lynn sat down at the other, then they glanced at one another for a moment, and then each opened their own notepad and gets to work. Louellen noticed fast that it felt difficult to read the broadsheets. The words used seemed odd to Louellen. In places, the text had faded, showing the printouts she was looking at, were the copies of the originals that already had showed deterioration by the time someone had duplicated them as photocopies. Awareness of her family history also had made it hard to read the condemning words that some articles were expressing about the actions of 'Jeffrey Herbert.'

From the book she had looked at, Louellen found out that the broadsheet had seized to exist during the 'Great Depression' - the date '1931' was showing—in part—that it was one of its earliest victims. At the height of its existence in the mid-1850s, it employed something like eleven thousand people. By the time of its demise some seventy-five to eighty years later, the number employed there had dwindled to just seven hundred and sixty…

Louellen finds it odd that they'd list the broadsheet as 'owned by Mr John C. Mutter' without listing its name in the book, and wonders why that may be.

Perhaps the scandal also caused its demise too—and that name. I wonder if he's the same John Mutter that Anna sometimes has mentioned. No, that would be too much of a coincidence for her great-grandfather and mine to have known one another and employer and employee.

But the mention of the man's name bugs Louellen, so she writes the name in the column to note down any 'odd' or 'out of place' details.

"Do you want another cup of tea, Louellen?" Lynn asks suddenly. "Yes, please—" Louellen replies without looking up.

Louellen was now reading an article that, apparently, her great-grandfather had written about the sinking of the Titanic, and although it had no relevance to the rest of the events or circumstances she was investigating, it was interesting to read a totally different account by a journalist writing it as someone who'd came from what in those days would have been a lower-class perspective. She wondered at how the brazen article, with such strong criticism, hadn't only made it to press but to the front page as well. They'd written it five days after the sinking had happened, and from the byline it showed that Jeffrey Herbert had been in New York around the time of events. "I didn't know he'd visited America," she mumbled. She also wrote this information down in the column for 'odd' or 'out of place' details. She was going to have to ask her dad *more* about this information…

It was close to four o'clock when Lynn was suggesting for them to finish what they were doing. "If we stop *now,* then I can go to the post office *before* they shut—and have the photocopies in the mail for Lucas tonight."

"I think I'm going home to talk to my dad," Louellen says. "There are things stated in the articles that don't add up. Some things I was told about my family are so different. I'll show him the photocopies of the broadsheets too and see what he says about what's written in them."

"Will you come to visit here again?"

"Yes, I will…" Louellen grins for a moment, "and I'm actually having fun doing this research."

"Good… I won't be here the next three days after, but come again on Saturday, and then we'll do more checking."

Louellen nods. "I will be here," she confirms.

Louellen stands waiting for the bus and, for a moment, she feels a chill creep up her spine. She glances down the road to see if the bus is arriving soon. The street feels deserted…

Maybe I should call for a taxi, she thinks, pulling her coat closer around her neck. *I should go shopping for a thick, warm coat instead of this stupid coat that doesn't do much to keep me warm.* She feels almost like giving up. Then she hears the distinct sound of an approaching bus. She feels relief a moment later when one heads her way and she stretches her arm out to signal to the driver that she wants to be on the bus, and a few minutes later, the bus comes to a gentle stop next to her and she steps inside.

"Single fair please." She places two pound coins into the slot for the ticket. A moment later, she pulls her ticket from the machine, then she walks to the middle of the bus and sits down, placing the ticket in her right pocket.

From her left pocket, she pulls out her phone and looks to see who'd sent her any text messages. "Oh fuck, I forgot to call Anna back." Louellen curses and opens up the address book on the phone. She taps the speed dial to call her friend.

"Hey Anna, sorry that I didn't call sooner."

"Hey Lou. How was your day?"

"Busy as usual."

"The girls and I are planning to go to London for a night out. Want to come?"

"I'll pass. I'm too tired."

"Oh, that's not how you are at normal times."

"I said I was busy—I had a lot to do, okay," Louellen snaps.

"No need to bite my head off," Anna snaps back.

"I'm sorry. It's just that I had a long day at work, and then went to do some research at the library."

"Errr—since when do *you* visit libraries?" Anna asks, and Louellen notices surprise in her friend's voice.

"Well, since—errr—I was there doing research because Lucas had told me something. It's something I need to tell dad about when I'm home. Also, your great-grandfather—Did *he* own a newspaper by chance?"

"Yes, he did. What's all this about…?"

"I'll tell you more tomorrow, but just to give you the quick version, Lucas has found out something about a house in the village where he went to live. Something had happened there," Louellen explains. "When he'd visited me last—that was about three weeks ago, and yes, that's the day he and I had *that* argument I had told you about… But what I didn't tell you, is that he had a magazine with him which had an article in it. They mentioned 'Mellowstone Greene' in the article, and it also had mentioned the house. It's called Priory Mansion."

"Why is it so important to you?" Anna asks with concern now

clear in her voice.

"Because Lucas went to look up information at the same library that I was just visiting. He found a connection between the house, a man called Charles Fairey—who was investigating something that had happened there—and the newspaper that your great-grandfather had owned, or more precisely he found they were listing my great-grandfather Jeffrey Herbert as the individual was reporting on the case."

"Why do you need to tell your dad about it?"

"Because Lucas thinks that something bad may have happened to my great-grandfather—and maybe also to *your* great-grandfather—which might be why he had to shut down the newspaper so suddenly."

"Oh, my god. You mean like someone might have done something like maybe murder him or something?"

"I don't know. Lucas was going to find out. I'm going to visit him next week to help him with all of it."

"You mean you *are* visiting him?" Anna shrieks with a sudden hysteric giggle and it makes Louellen suddenly feel angry.

"I know what I've said before, but now I have a reason to *go* there," Louellen snaps. "I want to see the house for myself. Lucas went to *see* Priory Mansion, and he wasn't his normal confident self when I had talked on the phone with him a few days ago when he'd called me."

"Oh, right—and so you've cancelled the plans for next week?"

"Yes," Louellen replies, "as I need to find out for myself what has really happened to my great-grandfather. The newspaper articles suggest connections between the last lord to own the house. Something about his daughter who had—errr—what did it say again… oh yeah, it said that she had 'bastard son' in one paragraph. He had connections with the Prime Minister in charge at the time who'd then distanced himself from him. There's a girl who'd disappeared. The librarian—she's from *there* originally—told me it's like what they might call a 'cold case' these days."

"Sounds terrible—and you think all that stuff had caused issues for my great-grandfather because he'd owned the newspaper?"

"I think so—I was going to tell you about it after I found out more in Mellowstone Greene, but I guess you deserved to know it sooner. I'm sorry if I snapped, but I feel really drained from all this, and I'm worried too."

"I understand… I'll tell the girls you're sick. They'll believe that as a reason."

"Thanks."

"Get in touch when you know more. You've made me curious about it too now." Anna sounded very concerned now.

"I will do." Louellen puts her phone back in her bag. She stares out of the window of the bus without really seeing any of the street outside, which is fast getting covered with the approaching dusk.

* * *

Louellen suddenly snapped back to full attention when she saw a familiar newsagent store, and she reached for the button to alert the driver to a stop at the next bus stop. A few minutes later, the bus halted, and Louellen walked to the front of the bus to get off.

"Have a pleasant evening—" the driver called after her.

"The same to you—" Louellen called back over her shoulder. She turned right and walked to the newsagent first and wanted to see if they would have a copy of the scientific magazine in which Lucas had found the article. She walked in and its Hindi store owner greeted her cheerfully. After a few minutes, she found the magazine she wanted. She also picked up a bottle of cola, some biscuits, and a pie for her dinner. She listened, without really hearing him, to the store owner talking about whatever inconsequential things were on his mind, then paid for her purchase and left the store.

Turning right, she backtracked and passed the bus stop where she'd got off at earlier, then turned right into a side street that was already bathed in a mixture of orange and bright white of alternating street lamps. She walked hastily tonight, feeling an unusual underlying discomfort that she was putting down to knowing the information she'd found. *Maybe living in a village is better than this. There are fewer houses there.* Deep down, a new feeling of acceptance welled up. One of recognition that she'd perhaps been *too* hasty in her dismissal of the suggestion from Lucas to move in with him. *Maybe he'll accept it if I said that I'll live there as a friend first.*

Louellen crosses the road a few minutes later. She turned left at the corner of the side street. It was another ten minutes of walking before she spotted a familiar white stone house on the left of the street. A few minutes later, she opened the gate, walked into the garden, and after closing the gate behind her, stood looking at the house for a few minutes. She walked to the front door, opened it, and called out. "Dad, I'm home—"

"Did you have a good day?" Her father—Peter Herbert—calls out from the kitchen. Louellen walks into the kitchen and gives her father a hug. She places her bag on the kitchen table.
"I've put the kettle on. You want a cuppa?" he asks.
"Yes, please… I bought a pie. We can have that for dinner."
"Oh right, what temperature in the oven?"
Louellen checks the packaging. "It says 190 C on the pack, dad."
"What kind is it?"
"Steak and kidney," Louellen replies.

Louellen takes her coat off and walks back through the hallway to hang it on the hook near the front door.
"Maybe we should have a bit of veg with that. Fancy carrots?"
"Sure."
"Why don't you sit down on the sofa, and I'll sort out the carrots. You look tired."
"I'm tired. It was a long day at work, then afterwards I went to the library for—errr… Dad, I may have something important to tell you about."
Peter Herbert studies his daughter's face intently, and he notes the concern she shows. "Let me fix these carrots, then I'll come sit with you on the sofa, and you tell me over a hot cup of tea, okay?"
Louellen nods, turns and walks to the living room, where she sits down on the sofa. In passing, she grabs her bag too, which she places on the floor at her feet, leaning against the sofa. Without really paying attention, she stares at the news on the television, and then when her father walks in and sits down beside her, it distracts her from what's on the television screen. "So, what is it *you* want to talk about?" he asks. He picks up the remote and switches the television off.
"I went to visit the library—" Louellen begins. "I went there because of what Lucas had told me."
"How is he?"
"He's doing good. I'm actually going to be visiting him next week."
"He lives in that village, right?"
"Yes… Mellowstone Greene it's called. He'd bought a cottage there."

"Sounds romantic," Peter says, and when he sees his daughter glancing at him, he winks at her, then he smiles inwardly when he sees her blushing.

"But that isn't what I wanted to talk about," Louellen says quickly.

"Has something happened to him?"

"Not exactly. He found out the information. He found—errr… something out about great-granddad."

"You mean Jeffrey Herbert?" Peter asks, looking surprised at the sudden turn in topic matter.

"Yes, *he* apparently reported on something that happened at a house in that village. Have you ever heard your grandfather talk about 'Priory Mansion,' dad?"

Peter stares ahead of him for a while, trying to remember all his childhood conversations with his grandfather. "I can't recall him mentioning it."

"Apparently, he wrote about the house, and then something had happened. You said great-granddad had died in 1914. Lucas thinks there's a connection between the events at the house and the people who were living there, the person who investigated it all, great-granddad, and even Anna's great-grandfather was involved in a way."

"Small world." Peter's voice is sarcastic. Louellen ignores it. She's used to that from her father.

"Lucas had told me that a girl—who was apparently a servant—had disappeared one day. The reports say there was a witness who saw her running into the woods, in what he had described, as 'an usual state of panic when other times she'd run through the woods for fun,' and there's a name for the person investigating it all. A man called 'Charles Fairey'…"

"That name I recognise. Granddad had mentioned *him* a few times. Not pleasantly either. He had told me that his father always spoke of him like the man's actions had disgusted him. My granddad was about twelve when *his* father died, so I cannot be entirely sure if he remembered stuff correctly. I guess it was important enough for him to first tell his son—my father—and to tell me, too."

Louellen listens closely as the man speaks; she'd never heard her father be so open and frank about the family history before this day…

Her father had always been protective of his daughter for most of her life, and even more so after her mother had died when she was just seven. He had brought her up, and they had a good relationship. But family matters were something he was always extremely private about—even to her.

"What did your granddad say?" she asks softly.

"I had said about it to my father. I was *there* when they'd talked—that his father had been trying to get justice for the girl to whom this had happened, but in the first two decades of the nineteenth century, if you weren't part of a 'well-to-do' family, you were a nobody."

"I guess that's what Lynn had meant when she was comparing this situation about how people were regarded to how it was on the Titanic—"

"Who is Lynn?" Peter asks.

"She's the librarian at the library that I visited earlier," Louellen explains. "She originally comes from the village."

"Ah, I see—and she *is* correct. Jeffrey Herbert was lucky to have had the education allowing him to become a reporter, but they always had regarded him as a third-class citizen. A bit like many on the Titanic, I guess. But the only one *never* to treat him in that way was John Mutter—who had owned the newspaper. He had treated Jeffrey Herbert like he was his own brother. I guess that's why he had got punished by 'high society' in those days when he had let Jeffrey Herbert keep putting the articles in the newspaper. To many in *that* high society—especially the people in the government—the case was rather controversial."

"Lucas says it's because of the connection between the person who was the lord of Priory Mansion, what happened to his daughter, and that he was supposedly friends with the Prime Minister in charge in the last part of the nineteenth century."

"You've been doing research. You know *more* than I do." Peter places a hand over Louellen's hand. "But I must *warn* you. I think there are risks involved if you go digging for answers."

"Lucas had said the sort of thing, too." Louellen looks down at her cup before she continues speaking. "He'd told me he went to look at the house, and he'd said that he found something disturbing there. He really sounded scared on the phone, dad."

Louellen glances up at her father, pleading with him with her eyes and hoping that he could somehow tell her that things were going to be okay.

"I see—and *you* plan to go see him next week, is that right?"

Louellen nods.

"Maybe there's safety in numbers. Maybe, if you work on this together—because if there *is* someone out there who still wants all this covered up… It won't be as easy for *them* to do something undesirable…"

Louellen nods again, slowly.

"… and I suggest you keep in touch with *me* daily, okay?"

"I will, dad."

CHAPTER NINETEEN

"IF ANY OF THIS LEADS to justice for the girl who had disappeared, then I think that Jeffrey Herbert can finally rest in peace, and so can *she*. Wherever she had ended up…"

"I got newspaper clippings and photocopies from books with me." Louellen reaches down for her bag.

"I think *we* can look at those later," Peter says. "Right now, I can smell the pie. I'm starving, aren't you?"

"Yes, I am," Louellen says, then she grins.

They both get up and before moving to the kitchen, Peter takes his daughter in his arms, and he gives her a hug. He lifts her chin and looks at her closely, searchingly. "I'm glad you brought me this information. At least now I can have a few answers to questions I've had about this all my life."

"Lucas said he wants to do this sort of stuff of investigating all the time—and I actually *am* intrigued too about it."

"What about your job at the art gallery?" Peter asks.

"I'll see what happens while I visit Lucas. I won't rush into anything."

"Don't promise Lucas anything you can't do."

"I won't, but I do care about him a lot, dad… and the recent weeks have shown me I care more about him than I realised."

***

Louellen sits down at the kitchen table, and she looks towards the steaming pie that her father is serving out onto two plates. He brings over the plates, which are half-covered with the pie, and on the other half with a large helping of the freshly cooked carrots. Usually, Louellen doesn't want such large portions, and she knows her father knows this, but *today* she doesn't mind it. The events of the previous few weeks—which had involved her argument with Lucas and then finding out her connection to a crime case, which was listed as a cold case—all had left her feeling drained. She's hungry, so she eats the meal given to her…

"You look tired," Peter says to his daughter after observing her for a few minutes.

"I am, dad."

"Work?" Peter asks.

"Everything."

"I guess I can listen." Louellen smiles at her father on hearing the familiar words. She feels grateful for his supportive nature, and now more than ever before.

"Please, dad, can we just relax a bit and eat our meals before I tell you what I've discovered?" Louellen asks imploringly. "I'm still trying to figure out for myself why I've ended up with knowing what I know now."

"Of course, Lou, just take your time." Peter gets up, and he walks to the fridge. "What would you like to drink?" he asks. "I don't have any cola, though."

Louellen leans sideways to look into the fridge. "The yoghurt drink on the top shelf for me, please."

Peter retrieves the drink for his daughter and grabs a can of beer from himself. Then he walks to the sink for a couple of glasses from the draining board there, then he sits down again opposite Louellen. As he sits down, he hands the yoghurt drink to Louellen, then he places one glass in front of her and he places the other glass next to his plate. He opens his can of beer and pours in the beer, while Louellen half-fills her glass with her drink…

They eat their dinner quietly. Peter glances occasionally at his daughter, wondering why she has conflicting emotions on her face. As he'd been her *only* parent since her mother had died when she was over fifteen years younger he'd forced himself to understand her facial expressions. He knew from the frowns that something angers her; the lip pout is from annoyance; her sighs are from desperation. Peter honours Louellen's wish for silence during the meal, but he keeps wondering. He wonders if she'd been arguing with Lucas again.

It seems they get on so well for a couple of years, then they drift apart because of a disagreement. It has only happened three times in all the time they've known one another, but each time it has happened, it has been a bit more volatile than before. I wonder if they've broken up for good this time. I hope not, because I've seen Louellen go from a shy, withdrawn, almost always somewhat sad girl who

Louellen wasn't aware that she's making every facial expression that might be possible. She was struggling with eating her meal. It felt to *her* that there's so much that had happened in the somewhat over two months since Lucas had moved away from London. She knew that the things she'd learnt from Lynn—and what he'd told her—totally changed her place in the world.

"Dad," she says, somewhat more hesitant than she might be realising herself. Her father had immediately noticed, but he'd said nothing of it. "Yes, darling!" Peter smiled. He hadn't referred to her in this way ever since she'd declared that she was *too* old for pet names. He's greeted by a weak smile when Louellen does realise what her father had just said to her…

"I don't know what to do about what I know."
"About the information of that girl, you mean?" Peter asks.
"Yes, that."
"It's simple, really. You need to follow your heart. Follow it to wherever it will take you, and make *right* what injustice was done! I know you much better than you might realise. I know deep down you already are thinking of a million ways to fix this."
Louellen smiles at her father. "I was thinking about that."
"Don't you think it's so much easier if you and Lucas help each other doing this?"
"I guess so too," Louellen says softly. "I just don't want him to push me so much with his questions."
"What questions?"
"He keeps asking me to visit him. He even asked me to move in." Louellen looks down, now feeling shy.
"And you don't want to…?" Peter asks.
"But, I do. Well, at least *now* I do. But I don't know how to tell him without it sounding like I'm just saying it to make him feel better."
"How about making yourself feel better?"
"What do you mean?" Louellen looks up again.
"How about *you* suggest you visit for a while as a friend and yes, I

know you're his girlfriend, but tell him that you want the visit only as a friend at first—and then you tell him you need to figure out, while there, how you feel about living there for good?" Peter says plainly. "Then, there's *no* pressure on you, and he can stop asking you. But I think he's asking you because he has found the woman that he wants in his life for the rest of his life."

"I guess you're right," Louellen says softly, and she looks down again, nervously moving the food around her plate. Or, at least the part of the food that she hadn't eaten still, and although she didn't actually see it anywhere in her mind, she registers that her plate is almost empty.

"Do you have any holiday time coming up at work?"

She nods.

"Then plan to get *that* time off, and just go visit him."

"I can't go tomorrow. I have to give at least three weeks' notice, and we're in the busiest part of the year right now."

"But you haven't had a holiday in over a year, Lou," Peter grunts somewhat. "Listen to your dad when *he* says that you must get time off, and go see Lucas. It will make it a lot easier for you. You cannot get rid of the way you're feeling unless you *do* something about it."

"I know that, dad, but I'd rather talk about other stuff now if it's okay."

"We can talk about what you were going to tell me about what Lucas told you about that girl."

Louellen nods.

"Are you finished with your meal?"

"Yes, I am. It was delicious. Oh, let me finish these carrots real quick."

Peter watches his daughter hastily eat the final four pieces of carrot, then he smiles as she takes two more bites of her pie, and smiles broader when she makes a face. "It's cold now. Yes, I guess I'm finished."

Peter picks up both their plates and places them on the worktop near the sink. "Go relax in the living room," he says. "I'll be there shortly."

"Okay. You sure you don't want help here?"

"Nope, I've got it under control."

* * *

Louellen walks to the living, swiping the bottle of yoghurt drink and her glass from the table. She sits down on the sofa and puts the television on for a bit. It shows the weather report, which shows that the next few days are going to be warm, dry and sunny. She turns the television off a moment later. She picks up her bag from the floor and opens it. From it, Louellen pulls out the photocopies she'd received from Lynn. She spreads the paperwork on the table in front of her and moves her drink to the small table next to the sofa to make extra space. Louellen glances at the photocopies, working out where to begin with the information gathering.

There's so much information here… More than any of us ever knew for Jeffrey Herbert having done…

She picks up a sheet and looks at the list of names it shows. Below the list, she sees a description assigning the names of the individuals to a court case of that time. Among the names on the list is the name 'D. Seaward' listed, but with no sign of *who* the person might have been.

I guess Lucas and I need to find this individual.

Louellen recognises *two* of the names from seeing them in a book she'd looked at with Lynn. In the book, it had listed them as two aides for the Prime Minister.

Why would two people working in the Palace of Westminster be on the same list for a court case as someone with the name Seaward? Something isn't right about all this. I need to tell Lucas this bit of information.

Louellen looks up when her father walks into the living room. "I found something here, dad, and I want *you* to look at it, too."

She holds the photocopy she'd been looking at moments before, up to her father. Peter sits down and takes the paper from his daughter. He looks closely at the list.

"I see you got more of granddad's writing, it seems. I recognise the bottom two names, besides seeing that one person has the last name Seaward."

"Who are they…?" Louellen asks. "Because the second and fifth names are also listed as aides to the Prime Minister at the end of the nineteenth century."

"Oh, really! The two listed at the bottom of the list were a few prominent individuals from what I recall from my conversations with my grandfather—and also if I remember right from what I've been researching, there were merchants who'd become very rich."

"It doesn't say *why* they were in court. It's almost like Jeffrey Herbert wanted to expose them."

"It could be."

"Why is all this suddenly happening, dad…?" Louellen throws herself backwards on the sofa. "If only Lucas hadn't gone and bought *that* cottage of all cottages I wouldn't have this constant 'I'm an idiot' dark cloud hanging over my head. My life would be so much simpler if—" She's interrupted by a cautionary cough from her father. She glances towards him.

"I think at any day *this* could have surfaced, and I have a feeling that it could be bad if it got uncovered too late," Peter states softly but firmly. "You told me that Lucas thinks that someone is trying to hide something… I'm thinking the same thing…"

"Hide it as in: *they* want something hidden that could cause enormous problems for someone?" Louellen asks. "For who?"

"I guess it's up to you and Lucas to find it out. I think there's something more. He was at the museum where he saw the Priory Mansion listed as a ruin is what you had said before… when you described all of it to me earlier, before dinner. You also said something about *him* finding places there listed as a ruin with the date of 'last use' as 'unknown.' I'm wondering if the places closest to Priory Mansion may have a connection with the house such as could they've been part of the estate? When Priory Mansion came to ruin, would they've followed suit…?"

Louellen frowns at her father's suggestion. It seems plausible, yet it also felt so wrong somehow. She had the same feeling as before, which she always got whenever something odd happened. There was something about the other houses in the area near Priory Mansion which had made them more like someone had targeted them for destruction, not for simple abandonment…

"A penny for your thoughts," Peter pulls Louellen from her pensive mood.

"I was just thinking about what you just said, dad."

"And…?"

"Well, I'm wondering really *who* may want to abandon a house and leave no trace of who'd lived there."

"I guess we're *not* talking about Priory Mansion right now."

"Errr—no—I'm thinking about what Lucas had said, actually."

"What did he say?"

"Almost what you just had said. About Priory Mansion getting abandoned, and that it means that there were other places around it that got abandoned too. But I can't figure out *why* anyone would just do it. Something tells me they didn't get simply abandoned, but someone really blatantly emptied them."

"If that's true, then remember my words of caution. It's better to do this *with* Lucas rather than alone. It goes for him, too."

"So, you think this is much bigger, then?"

"It's definitely *not* a simple case of a girl gone missing if the Palace of Westminster, almost two dozen people, your great-grandfather, Anna's great-grandfather, Lucas, and these *other* people—errr what were their names again—are all involved in this, and that's just here. The paperwork I have in my study shows that Karina Seaward also had travelled abroad, and most notably to just outside New York—and that's the information I've gathered so far."

"Definitely bigger," Louellen says absentmindedly, "and do you think we need to uncover about other stuff there too?"

"Depends on what you uncover in relation to Priory Mansion."

"I guess I should help Lucas with it," Louellen whispers.

"I think *you* need to sleep on it, have a few days to think it over, and then you decide—and talking about sleep, you look like you're about to nod off, so maybe do that, and leave this old man to read this stuff by himself."

"You're *not* old…!" Louellen grins for a moment. "But yes, I'm exhausted so I'll go to bed I guess." Louellen gets up, gives her father a quick hug, then walks up to her bedroom carrying her bag after quickly emptying it from the remaining paperwork and the books. Peter watches her go…

* * *

Louellen opens her bedroom door and switches on the light in the room. She feels a momentary urge to walk into her father's bedroom to look at the paperwork that she can see lying on his desk, then she shakes her head to dispel the idea. *No, just too tired for this.* She turns for a visit to the bathroom, and after using the toilet, brushing her teeth and washing her face, she walks into her bedroom, and shuts and locks the door behind her. Most days she'd leave her door open, but tonight she wanted to be undisturbed in her bedroom.

She gets undressed then puts on her pyjamas and switches on the bedside lamp and switches off the light, then she lies down on top of her bed covers, and a moment later she curls to her right side, and stares at her lamp with a blank expression. Her mind is racing even though she feels tired. She's trying to process all the things she'd been reading over the last few days and process in her mind what Lucas has told her…

* * *

Louellen wipes a tear away and realises that she's crying without knowing *why*. She feels lonely right now and wishes she was actually curled up in Lucas's arms. She wonders if he's asleep yet, but decides not to call him in case he was already sleeping…

She gets up, goes to her handbag that she'd dropped on the floor as she arrived in her bedroom, and pulls her phone from it. She lies back down in bed and spends a bit of time looking through all the messages left on the phone by dozens of different friends, and then after that she checks her calendar and frowns as there were scheduled two events listed on the calendar that hadn't been there earlier in the day. One event was going to be in three days, and the other one in twenty-four days. She pulls her nose up at the prospect of the massive amount of work it would mean for her. She was about to put her phone on the drawer chest beside her bed when a thought occurs to her.

Maybe I can bribe the boss to give me time off, Louellen thinks. *If I offered that I'll help at the event coming up in a few days from now, maybe he'll let me take a week off. It's worth a try…*

Louellen puts the phone down and climbs off the bed. She pulls the blanket up and steps back in her bed, pulling the blanket over her. She turns off the light a moment later.

If I can get the time off work, I'll make sure I do it as a surprise, so Lucas doesn't know I'm turning up—and then, after I've visited for a while. I can figure out what to do next about us…

* * *

A few days had passed by rather quickly, and Louellen ended up helping with the exhibition, and now she was getting time off from work. And now, as she was approaching the station, she was grinning with delight. There wasn't any reason *not* to surprise Lucas. She'd gone to work, as normal, a day after her long conversation with her father had happened. Then at about lunchtime she'd broached about getting some time off for a holiday. To her delight, her boss had accepted the suggestion, and she'd set up a holiday for eight days, which would start the day after the exhibition on the provision she'd work extra hard *that* day, and that she'd stay two hours longer to help at the exhibition when it was active…

Normally, Louellen didn't like the exhibitions because—in her opinion—they were too rowdy and always would give her headaches. But she'd agreed with no protest just so she could have her holiday, just as she'd planned days earlier.

When the exhibition was in full swing, Louellen kept herself as far from the bulk of the crowd as she had dared, without making it appear that she was trying to avoid doing her job. She'd talked to three guests who'd sounded like they'd come for a visit at the gallery all the way from America. Thirty minutes later, she was listening to a Japanese woman, and she'd nodded at the endless stream of conversation, without knowing what the woman had said most of the time. When she could finally sit down, her boss had walked over and sat down next to her.

"Tonight was a splendid success. Now that you've earned your holiday, you can go home," he had said, "and I'll see you in fourteen days. Have fun." With that, Louellen's boss had got up and walked off, and had started a renewed conversation with a guest, who'd obviously been waiting for him.

Louellen drank down the glass of water she'd been drinking from, then she'd placed the glass on the side of the stairs, then she got up and looked one more time at the crowd. She turned right and walked down the stairs to the ground floor of the gallery, and walked to her desk there, where she shut off her computer and locked the two cabinets behind it. Then she picked up her bag and walked to the front door.

A few minutes later, she was standing in the street where a somewhat cooler than normal evening wind greeted her. She fastened up her coat and walked to the bus stop to go home…

* * *

After arriving at the train station and buying her ticket and checking when the train would arrive, Louellen is sitting at the small table next to the café for something to eat and drink before she was getting on the train. It was forty minutes before the train would be leaving. She was reading the magazine that she'd purchased fifteen minutes earlier. She had found and bought the magazine that Lucas had shown her on his visit to London. She didn't know why, but she'd felt compelled to purchase it.

Maybe because it had offered the first connection with an unknown part of my family's history, Louellen was thinking as she skims through the lengthy list of articles for something remotely interesting to read. Science wasn't normally 'her thing,' but she was trying to appreciate the topic a *bit* more. Her finger stops moving over the page at about two-thirds down the page. She saw an article about art that might be interesting for her…

That's more like it, she thinks, though she knows the article would be more about the scientific side of arts rather than the more artistic flair she was usually interested in. Louellen turns the pages of the magazine until she gets to the listed page. She smiles when it's actually an article all about curating artworks, and in some ways this topic was similar to some of what she did *now* as part of her time at her job.

After spending twenty minutes reading the magazine and enjoying her food and drink, she hears an announcement, and Louellen gets up and walks to the train. She boards the train, then found a comfortable seat about halfway in the train, and sat down after hoisting her bag onto the rack above and opposite her. She stares dreamily from the window, already imagining how Lucas will react when she arrives at his door.

Dad was right, she thinks, *I had to go visit him…*

A few minutes later, she feels a jolt, and a minute later the station's vista was replaced by the sea of roofs visible from the train.

Then, a few minutes later, Louellen is in momentary darkness when the lights switched off for a few seconds at the same time of the train going into a tunnel. A few minutes more, then the tunnel ends and Louellen sees more houses, but now also several high rises. As the train speeds up more and more, the landscape outside turns more green as fields and trees replace the urbanisation of London…

CHAPTER TWENTY

LOUELLEN WATCHES THE LANDSCAPE ROLL by. She'd never visited Norfolk until now, and she'd always perceived the region there as a flat landscape, whenever it was shown on the news or in some sort of television programme. She finds that she's pleasantly surprised by the somewhat 'rolling hills' feeling of what is visible from the window of the train.

She glances for a few minutes at the window on the other side of the train to check the landscape on the other side out, too. "I guess I *could* cope here," she mumbles. "It doesn't look as bad as I thought."

She picks up the magazine, and continues turning the pages but most of the remaining content seems *too* boring to her.

I guess Lucas will like this magazine more…

Louellen looks at her watch. It would be another forty minutes before she'd be in Norwich, and then she would need to take a taxi to Mellowstone Green, to where Lucas lives.

I'll be there just before dinner. Perfect…

* * *

Louellen smiles when she sees the signs in the next train station saying Norwich, and she gets up, pulls her large bag down onto the seat, and opens the zip slightly to push the magazine inside. She glances through the window to see if she can see any taxis and sees that the town is a lot bigger than she'd imagined before her arrival here. When the train stops, she hauls her bag behind her and rushes to the exit. She walks a short distance to the door marked as the exit, then walks the length of the station to the outer door. Outside, she sees the row of taxis to her left and walks to the first one. As she approaches, the driver pulls down a window.

"Where to, luv?"

"I'm travelling to Mellowstone Greene," Louellen replies.

"It'll cost a bit more than average."

"That's okay, I got a boyfriend waiting there who'll pay for the ride if needed," Louellen says and she hopes she's right with the assessment.

"Righto. Hop inside—"

The driver waits for Louellen to be strapped in, then he turns on the meter and drives off.

"Had a long trip?" he asks a few minutes later.

"Not too long. I travelled from London."

"I got a brother who lives 'round there," he says. "You know the Woodford area?"

"Not really. I live more north-east of that with my father."

"Ahh, okay. Well, I hope you 'ave a good time with ye stay here. It's a beautiful county with plenty to see 'n do."

Louellen feels certain that the taxi driver always was saying the same thing to *every* person he might have in his taxi. She glances out of the window and she suspects the driver took it as a sign to stay quiet because he wasn't saying anything after she did that.

The journey time was lengthy enough for it to appear dusky in the east, and it drew Louellen inward until the taxi driver spoke up once more. "We'll be there in 'bout ten minutes, luv—"

"Okay, thanks—"

After the taxi driver's comment, Louellen is suddenly more alert, and she stares out of the window for the signs to show her they were approaching the village. When she saw a road sign with 'Mellowstone Greene' listed on it, and next to listed name it shows the number '4' so she sits up some more. She stares hard to get a grasp of the village from what Lucas had told her about it…

Another ten minutes pass, and then the taxi stops in front of a house that Louellen recognises from photos that Lucas had shown her during his most recent visit.

"That be thirty pounds, luv—" the driver says, "It's a bit more but I'm okay to make it even numbers for ya…" Louellen pulls three ten-pound notes from her purse, and hands it to the driver quickly.

"You need help with tha bag?"

"No, I'm fine, thanks," Louellen responds. She opens the door, leans in to pull the bag from the seat and slams the door shut, then walks to the front door.

* * *

Lucas looks up surprised when he first can hear a car stop in front of his house, then a car door slams shut, and minutes later it's his doorbell ringing, which surprises him even more. He gets up and walks to the front door. His face lights up when he opens the front door. He glances for a moment at a car that drives off a moment later.

"Lou—You surprised me. You got here by taxi…?"

"Hey Lucas, I thought I should come here for a holiday—and yes, I did. Dad had suggested that I should visit."

"Come in." Lucas smiles, though deep down he's hoping that he'd done enough DIY in the house to impress Louellen. Also, that he'd done it in a way that she would like. He sees her look around.

"It looks pretty," she comments, "but I think a woman's touch *will* help to make it even nicer."

"Do whatever you want," Lucas says, then he grins broadly.

"Errr—I'll start tomorrow. Actually, *we* can do it together."

"Sure thing. I've hung up the curtains in no permanent preference yet, except in one room. Didn't get the chance yet."

"Oh—and where *did* you hang some up that's supposed to be permanent…?" Louellen glances around.

"Let me carry your bag up. To be honest, I actually did one of the spare rooms more completely than most of the rest of the house, just in case I *could* persuade you to visit. Also, so you don't have any pressure about where to sleep, you could use *that* room if you want—"

"Yes, for now that will be okay," Louellen says softly. Lucas notes the same quiet sound of resignation in her voice as he'd heard when she'd spoken to him on the phone a few days earlier. He assumes from this that she's perhaps considering her options, but wants no pressure from him with it.

Lucas picks up Louellen's bag, which is way heavier than for visiting for a few days. The bag is very familiar to him, as she'd used it when they'd gone to the summer camp when he'd asked her to come. After that, she'd hoisted it with her as her preferred bag for clothing for pretty much every holiday they'd do together ever since.

"Is that the result of your effort to get into the loft?" Louellen's voice is filled with laughter. Lucas looks behind him at her, then glances up as he sees her looking up at the gaping hole in the ceiling.

"I'm going to remove all the ceiling from there, and put a window on the roof there."

"Oh, really?" she states. "It will make the stairs look nice and will make it bright here. That was one thing I liked very little about this stairway when you showed me the house before. It was too dark…"

"I'm going to do the same in all the bedrooms, and in the bathroom too," Lucas explains, "and the awful little window in the bathroom will be gone."

"Sounds good… Make sure you place a bath there so I can look up at the stars from the bathtub."

Lucas grins quietly then he thinks. *She's already making this her home. Even if she doesn't know it yet.*

"Here's the room," Lucas says as he opens the door of the room to the right of the stairs. "The bathroom is next to it."

Louellen glances inside the room, and sees some familiar-looking curtains hanging in front of the windows.

Then she realises Lucas has hung the curtains that she'd showed to be 'her favourite ones' in a room that he'd designated for her to use. She smiles at Lucas and says, "This room is perfect."

Lucas smiles. He'd hoped he'd done a good enough job, and Louellen's reaction proves he was right.

"I can make a cup of tea, and I have a pizza cooking in the oven if you're hungry."

"Sounds good."

"See you downstairs. I call for you when it's ready," Lucas states. "Take your time unpacking."

"Okay."

Lucas turns and walks downstairs to go check on the pizza that he'd placed in the oven about ten minutes before Louellen had arrived. He opens the oven, and pulls his head away for a moment to let the heat dissipate somewhat, then he sees the cheese was only just melting. He closes the oven again.

From the cupboard Lucas pulls two plates, and from another two cups, and from a drawer he retrieves a long sharp knife, the cutlery, and spoons for stirring the tea. Lucas puts fresh water in the kettle and he turns it on. He puts a tea bag in each cup, then puts two teaspoons of sugar in each and a dash of milk.

He hears footsteps coming down the stairs and smiles at Louellen as she walks into the kitchen. He pours water into each cup a moment later, then hands her a cup. Louellen smiles at him.

"That smells good."

She cranes her neck to look at the oven.

"It's chicken barbecue topping. Hope you don't mind. I wasn't expecting you."

"It's fine. I'm starving."

"It should be ready in about another *ten* minutes," Lucas said. "Why don't you relax and let me handle things here?"

"Okay, but are you sure?"

"Yes."

Louellen walks from the kitchen, and minutes later Lucas can hear the channel he had chosen a few hours earlier on the television being changed. A few moments after that, Louellen's giggles fill the house. Lucas smiles a happily. *I have to make sure I don't bring up whether this visit is temporary or more permanent.*

A few minutes later, he takes the pizza from the oven and cut it in half. He puts each half on the two plates. Lucas places the knives and forks on the plates too, then loops a finger through his cup and in an awkward balancing act carries *all* items into the living room where Louellen quickly gets up to help him. They settle on the sofa to eat their pizza, watching the comedy show Louellen had put on. Lucas guesses she had done this to make her feel a bit more secure. Though he normally doesn't really watch this type of programme, Lucas ends up laughing as loudly as Louellen at the humour…

When they'd emptied their cups of tea and eaten all their food, Lucas clears the plates and cups, then minutes later comes back to the living room with two glasses, a large bottle of cola and a large bag of crisps.

They settle in, watching a marathon of old science fiction movies that both of them like. Lucas enjoys having Louellen leaning against his chest with his arm around her. It had been a while when he last had felt so happy. He leans over and kisses Louellen on the top of her head. She glances up at him for a moment, grinning at him. He leans forward again and kisses her on her lips. When he moves away, she gives him a dreamy smile, then leans her head back against his chest once more. Finally, at the start of the fourth movie, it's when they talk for a bit…

"I remembered just now that I had told Leigh I'd visit her tomorrow—well, actually today now," Lucas says softly. "You want to come, Lou? You'll like her."

"Sure. What time were you going?"

"About three o'clock."

"Okay. Time for this one movie, then we go to bed."

"Okay…"

After the last movie, Lucas helps Louellen get her bed in the guest bedroom sorted. Even though he'd preferred her to be in the bed next to him. *This is better than dozens of miles away in London,* he thinks.

"What time do you want waking, Lou?"

"I want time for a bath and something to eat before we go," she replies. "So… I guess about eleven o'clock will be fine for me."

"Okay," Lucas says, "Sleep well." He smiles when Louellen blows a kiss at him in return. Her trademark way of saying 'good night' ever since they'd gone on their trip to the summer camp.

Lucas closes the door, and for a few moments, he stands staring at the door. The only thought now that's circling his mind is: *she's actually here with me.*

He walks to his own bedroom and glances at her door along the corridor one more time.

I hope Leigh and Louellen will get on…

* * *

The following afternoon, the conversation between Louellen and Leigh had already lasted for well over two hours, and the two women had been talking like they'd been friends for a long time. "She'd disappeared on *that* day and no one knows exactly what had happened, but one can only guess…" Leigh says, "Some individuals *here* in the village claim to have seen a ghost in the woods, but others have claimed it's just their imagination playing tricks on them."

"I don't think so," Lucas comments. "Someone uses the house from what I saw inside it…"

Leigh frowns.

"That's strange. Maybe it's a squatter of some sort," Leigh suggests.

"A squatter decorating the rooms with heavy, luxurious wallpaper…? Give me a break," Louellen blurts out, then she laughs. Lucas and Leigh both stare at Louellen like she was suddenly possessed.

"What do you mean?" Leigh asks.

"Didn't he tell you?" Louellen retorts, still grinning.

"Tell me what?" Leigh asks.

"I've studied art, and also interior design," Louellen explains, "and I've learnt about designers of different wallpaper."

"Oh—" Leigh says.

"Yes, and the wallpaper used in Priory Mansion would easily sell for fifty quid a roll in a high end shop in London," Louellen explains.

"I see, but I'm wondering then *why* anyone would want to go to the effort of decorating an old disused house," Leigh comments.

"In what way…?" Lucas asks.

"Because someone is in *there* trying to keep a secret from everyone over here."

"But I've noticed that everyone over *here* is trying to keep secret anything they seem to know about that the history of the house— you've got back to front."

"I'm uncertain of it myself," Louellen says, "but Lucas and I are going to help to find answers."

"I appreciate it," Leigh says. "My family has had to endure so many adverse comments over the years that I feel unwelcome in this village. There are a *few* who care—like Gylda—and the two of you too, but you two are *new* here and you don't know how it feels to be seen as different from others."

Lucas and Louellen glance at each other - *they* did know. Kids had bullied Lucas at school about a father who'd abandoned him; they had bullied her for a time for living with only a father, and for him being a single parent, which many had seen as odd.

After a long conversation, Lucas and Louellen finally had departed in the late hours of the afternoon, with maybe an hour to go until it's evening. Louellen is pensive for a while, then tells Lucas what's on her mind. "I'm worried about her," she whispers.

"So am I, Lou," Luke comments. "She's already a good friend, and so is Gylda."

"I can see *why*," Louellen comments. "Leigh is nice. Do you mind if I go to visit her tomorrow, on my own, for some—errr—girlie chat?"

"Of course not," Lucas says. "You may do things however you want..."

Louellen grins in a teasing way at Lucas, and she stops walking for a moment. He stops too.

"Don't you ever forget *that*," she says.

"What do you mean?"

"People seem to think that these days still it's okay to dictate *how* you're supposed to behave, and that's not good," Louellen explains, "I'm here, with you, because I want to be here, and because I love you... but I don't want to be told what to do ever by anyone. I read what it said about Nelly... She seemed to have run away from an unpleasant situation. I don't think I could tell Leigh *that*. But that's my theory about what had happened to her. I don't think she had run off because of a loving relationship. I don't know what had happened to her, but by the sounds of all the stuff told by Lynn, and now Leigh as well, and from what you've told me, from what you've discovered, there's more going on around here. A lot more than anyone realises."

"I guess I *should* listen to my wonderful, smart girlfriend." Lucas leans forward, and he kisses Louellen's forehead. She smiles when he does this.

"I guess we're learning to be detectives of some sort."

"Is that something you're interested in doing?" Lucas asks.

"Actually, the more I'm hearing about the house and what has happened, the more I'm interested in inspecting it to understand it all."

They continue walking home at an unrushed pace, and are each absorbed by their own thoughts about the future. When they arrive home, Mrs Whitwell is busy in her garden. "Ooh, so who's *this* pretty girl then?" she calls out when she sees Lucas and Louellen walking up the footpath towards his cottage.

The pair looks at one another, confused. "Why is *she* so nice now?" Louellen hisses at Lucas.

"Don't know," Lucas replies. "She hasn't spoken to me since I showed her the newspaper clippings."

"I guess I have to *be* friendly to her, or she might get really annoying," Louellen whispers. Then in a loud voice she calls out, "I'm a friend of Lucas by the way." Lucas frowns for a moment. Louellen's voice hadn't been friendly. But he waits until they're inside with the door shut before speaking.

"What was *that* about—?" he asks with some anger in his voice. He's met by her forefinger over his mouth.

He sees her forefinger on her other hand do a similar motion in front of her own mouth. Lucas listens. He hears a woman's voice, which is first close-by, then it trails off. It's followed soon by a door being slammed shut, and the voice is still audible for a few more minutes. Lucas glances back at Louellen, and he's met by a familiar gaze that he recognises - Louellen had said more with her facial expression in that moment than she would have been able to with any words.

"What's up with the neighbour, you think?" he asks her.

"I've noticed something about how she behaves ever since I've arrived," Louellen whispers, "and it's different from what you've told me about her."

"In what way…?"

"Wasn't she all super-friendly until you showed her the newspaper clippings?"

"Errr—yes."

"I think she's being so nice to me to make *me* believe what she says."

"What did she say…?" Lucas now sounds and his concern is evident in his voice, so much so that Louellen guesses he's feeling in this way.

"Well, I guess *she* doesn't realise that we've known each other for almost eight years," Louellen answers, "and *she* thinks I'm a new girlfriend of yours." Louellen grins broadly.

"Is that significant…?" Lucas asks.

"She's saying things about *you* I know aren't true."

Lucas and Louellen go to the dining room, and both sit down to work through more of the paperwork they'd been working on before visiting Leigh. They'd been sorting through it for the last couple of days. They both decide to put aside talking about the neighbour for a while.

✳ ✳ ✳

It's a bit later in the afternoon—after a lengthy silence—when Louellen speaks again. It's obvious to Lucas that the situation of what had happened to Leigh, what might have happened in Priory Mansion, and even the neighbour's behaviour, was leaving an impression on her. He knows Louellen to be a fighter; someone who always stood up for different causes. In school, she stood up when a bully tried to tease him about being friends with her. And later, her cause had become 'social justice' and criticism of any form of unfair politics…

But the situation with solving a mystery of someone's disappearance was new to her…

"I'm thinking constantly about the girl who disappeared," she finally says. "About might have happened to her. Also, wondering why the house was abandoned so drastically…"

"So am I," Lucas whispers solemnly. "So am I…"

"There's something about it all that doesn't feel right to me about at all," Louellen continues. "Leigh had said that she was always told all her life that the girl 'had just left.' That she'd disappeared as she was having an affair with someone. Then she'd just disappeared. But I saw here in the news article that the person who supposedly was the person she'd been having the affair with also disappeared at the same time…"

"I hope you won't suggest that somehow this other person had murdered both her and that man or something like that…"

"Actually, that's not at all what I'm saying. Sorry to bring it up, but *how* did your mother explain it when your father just upped and left for America?"

Lucas looks at Louellen with a perplexed expression. "What has *he* got anything to do with all this?" he grumbles, anger clear in his voice.

"Well, nothing really, but hear me out, please," Louellen says. "It's something that gives me a clue of what may have happened."

"Okay—I was angry. My mother was fuming. She told everyone what a loser *he* was. She told me to forget about him."

"And I think similar had happened in Leigh's family," Louellen interjects.

"Oh—errr—what do you mean?"

"I'm constantly wondering why no one—not even you—has thought about what the father did when she'd disappeared."

"You would think he would have reported her disappearing?" Lucas asks. "In a certain way…?"

"Yes," Louellen replies, "But, he made her want to leave."

"So, what are you saying exactly, Lou…?"

"I don't know, but I have a feeling that this isn't a simple case of a girl just leaving into the forest, and then never to be seen afterwards. She'd left on purpose but did this after something had happened, which had meant that she couldn't bring her baby with her. The child was then told lies by the father to cover up whatever he did to the missing girl. He did all he could to discredit her reputation. They had brought up the child in a village filled with gossip based on his lies. And the result of his behaviour has persisted every generation all the way to Leigh."

"So, I guess also by what you just said that I might need to change my mind about my father," Lucas comments, sounding bitter.

"That's up to you… You know he's out there somewhere, but it's clear that *he* doesn't want to be found and it means—" Louellen stops talking, and she stares at Lucas with her mouth open in surprise, "but as SHE doesn't want to be found," Louellen continues bluntly, "Lucas, I think I know *why* no one knows what had happened with the girl. Or, at least, part of what had happened. She'd left, and she didn't want to be found. I can't prove it until we find out where she ended up, but I think that's the proper story what happened…"

"You could be right."

CHAPTER TWENTY-ONE

IT'S LATER IN THE EVENING, after dinner, when Louellen speaks again, but this time it's rather obvious that she'd been thinking about Priory Mansion. Lucas finds it interesting how easily Louellen had slipped into the role of researching information about Priory Mansion ever since she'd arrived. She hadn't stopped in the three days since arriving so unexpectedly. She was even busier after their visit to Leigh's house, and her own assertion of what she'd perceived as the 'correct course of events.' Although he hadn't liked the brutish reminder about his father that had been put forward by her earlier in the day… But then, she'd pointed out how relevant his sentiments about how he felt about him just leaving were to the case. It had caused him to think deeper about that part of his own life, rather than the situation with Priory Mansion in the last few hours…

"Maybe we should go visit Priory Mansion right *now*."

"Now?" Lucas responds in an annoyed voice, "but I wanted to watch television…"

"Yes, but *you* said someone is using that place," she retorts. "They could be there at night."

"When I visited the house, I saw no one there. It was just well-decorated, and that was about it."

"Maybe they were hiding from you," Louellen suggests, "and you mentioned those two shots fired, too."

"Hiding from me…?" he asks, "and why did you have to mention about those shots fired? It had terrified me, you know…"

Louellen chuckles at the way Lucas is staring at her.

"I mean it, Lou. I was so damned scared when those shots went off."

"Which proves my earlier point."

"In what way…?" Lucas asks.

"Because someone is in *there* trying to keep a secret from everyone over here."

"But I've noticed that everyone over *here* is trying to keep secret anything they seem to know about that the history of the house—you've got back to front."

"No, I don't," Louellen retorts. "You said that *her* next door is a nosey neighbour. SHE is being a nosey neighbour. When I was in the garden yesterday to sunbathe, she saw me do it. She came to the fence—she definitely couldn't shut up about herself *or* this village. I turned on my phone to record what she said—do you want to listen to it?"

Lucas frowns for a moment, but then he nods when he realises Louellen has made a valid point. She gets up to retrieve her phone from the guest room that she's using, while Lucas pauses the programme they're watching.

He goes to the kitchen quickly to get a couple of cans of 7-Up for them both…

* * *

Louellen rushes up the stairs to her room and picks up her phone from the small table under the window where she'd left it. Before she goes back down, she peers from the window for a moment, looking at the deep, dusky darkness of the middle of a summer evening. To her, it feels for a moment like someone is looking up at her, but she quickly dismisses the feeling and shuts her curtains…

She walks down the stairs slowly, searching on the phone for the app which she'd used to record part of the monologue by her neighbour. "Where the fuck is it…?" she grumbles.

"Where is *what?*" Lucas asks in passing her to walk back into the living room.

"Just trying to find the app that I had used to record what Mrs Whitwell was saying," Louellen answers, "and I can't see to find it at the moment."

"Okay—I brought some 7-Up for us…"

"Okay thanks," Louellen replies, obviously somewhat absent-minded by her effort to find the app on her phone, "Ah found it."

She walks into the living room, where Lucas is now sitting on the sofa waiting for her and she states plainly as she sits down beside Lucas, "I don't know if she can hear very well, but when you hear it, you'll know what I mean."

Lucas listens carefully to the recording, asks for Louellen to repeat it, then looks at her. "Does *she* know you have recorded her…?" he asks.

"I don't think so," Louellen says before she sips from her drink.

"Based on how she'd reacted when I showed her the newspaper clippings, it's best that she never knows," Lucas says. "I think this could be an ace card for us to find out *more* about of how she really feels, and although you may not want to—you're the one who needs to befriend her for now, until we know more."

Lucas laughs loudly when Louellen wrinkles her nose in obvious disgust. "I'm *not* normally in the mood to befriend old grumpy ladies," she says, "but I have to be careful doing it, or I may risk the friendship I've struck up with Leigh. I don't want her to feel like I am playing both sides—if you know what I mean."

"I understand that," Lucas says, "and I know you don't enjoy having to take sides, and that you don't like it when others are in that position as well."

"Well, I find it important to help Leigh," Louellen says, "so I'm going to *do* everything possible to make sure we find out the truth of what goes on." Lucas puts his arms around Louellen, and in a gesture that's so familiar, he lifts her head with a finger. He looks in her eyes, and he sees some of her doubts melt away. He kisses her lips gently. Then he moves away and looks at her again…

She smiles at him, now feeling a wave of happiness wash over her. *Dad was right. I had to come here.*

* * *

Louellen leans her head against his chest and feels his arms tighten around her. Only months earlier, she would have pushed herself away from him when he'd do this, but now she wants the tenderness. It feels good to be enveloped in his arms. It's something he hadn't done for several years, mostly because she'd always pushed him away after a few minutes. Now the hug is allowing the trouble in her mind to settle…

A moment later, the house shakes from a loud noise that comes from somewhere outside. It's almost like some sort of large vehicle has crashed somewhere. It breaks the tender moment both are enjoying. Lucas and Louellen look up and then look at each other with wide eyes.

"What was that?" Louellen whispers.

"I don't know."

"That wasn't a gunshot."

"I know that."

"But if not that, then what was it?"

"I think we're getting paranoid now," Lucas says, "We're not too far from one of the A-roads and an airfield here. Though the airfield is more south. It might have been something on the motorway."

"I guess we'll find out about it tomorrow on the news," Louellen suggests.

Louellen pushes away from Lucas and looks at him a moment. "Are we going to the house tonight?" Louellen asks.

"I think *not*," Lucas replies, "but we can go after we've done more research, so we have something to confront the occupier with…"

* * *

"I've found something about Karina Seaward," Louellen yells. "I can hear you fine," Lucas calls out as he's walking from the kitchen to the living room. "What did you find?" he asks before going back to the kitchen for a moment.

"She'd visited Greenwich Village in New York *ten* years before she'd passed away. I don't think she'd stayed long. There's something interesting about the visit that I found. It says here she'd set up a fund of some sort."

Lucas back walks into the living room a moment later, carrying two mugs of coffee he'd gone back to get from there. He yawns uncontrollably. They'd stayed up several hours longer during that night, then had gone to sleep. Louellen had then decided that she preferred sleeping next to him rather than in her own room. But then, rather than getting any sleep, they'd talked more. But he can't remember exactly about what. Then, at long last, both had fallen asleep, and now—some nine hours later—they'd woken up and discovered it's a few hours after lunchtime…

Lucas places the mugs on the table, and he sits down next to Louellen, and then glances at her laptop with tired eyes. "You said you found something about Karina Seaward?" he asks.

"Yes—and I think the plot thickens because *she* had gone to visit New York. She was there only for a few days," Louellen explains softly. "Then she took the next ship back to England, but *not* before setting up this strange fund of some sort."

"Does it list where it was set up? I mean, what bank or something like it?"

"No, it doesn't. It says *who* is in the caption below this photo - they're the recipients together with *her*, the legal team, and a few other people who also were involved."

"That means that one person in the photo must be Karina Seaward."

"Yes—you're right," Louellen says. "Hang on, I'll save this photo on my hard drive, so we got it for later."

"Save the article too, if you can?"

"How…?" Louellen asks. "We got no printer."

"Errr—save it as a file to print out later," Lucas suggests. "You have PDF software on there, don't you?"

"Oh yeah—yes, I do."

Lucas watches as Louellen first saves the page they were looking at as a PDF file, then also does the same with almost thirty other pages she'd apparently opened in extra tabs. She saves each page as a bookmark before closing it.

"Okay, *now* we can find the original pages if needed, and once I get access to a printer, I'll print them off as well."

"Why don't I order a printer?" Lucas suggests.

"You sure you want to do that?"

"I'd need to know which type is best to get, and then check my finances. I know I've received a lot of money from the business deal, but I'd planned for it to last for at least the next decade—or longer."

"Yes, I understand that. If it's needed, I'll contribute to half the cost. Besides, it's not any rush. I saved these files into the cloud so they can't disappear."

"Cloud…?" Lucas asks, sounding puzzled.

"That's where you can store stuff on a hard drive that's online—kind of."

"Ah, okay."

They spend another hour searching for more information, but then both get hungry and he suggests a visit to a pub for a meal, and Louellen nods when he suggests it. She loves going to pubs, and the last time they'd done this was almost a year ago.

"I know of one that's near the coast. It's about thirty minutes' driving. I just checked their app, and it says they're open for food in just ten minutes from now, so it will be perfect for us to arrive when they have food service in full swing."

"Okay, but I want to take a quick shower before we go."

She gets up and rushes up the stairs.

"Don't use up all the hot water," Lucas calls out. "I want one too."

"I won't," she shouts back, but then Lucas grunts when he hears a wave of giggles from her.

Almost twenty minutes later, Lucas stands under a lukewarm shower and he's grumbling under his breath so loudly that occasionally it causes Louellen to call out from her room next door. "I can hear you…"

After he has showered, Lucas shaves. Once he has finished everything, he walks to his room with a towel around his waist. He quickly dresses, then he finishes drying off his hair and drops the towel on the bed. He brushes his hair, then walks from the room and is met by Louellen standing at the top of the stairs in a beautiful lilac flowing dress and a thin cardigan over it. She has her hair in a sideways plait with a small flowered pin at the top of it. She wears eye shadow, lip gloss and a hint of rouge. Lucas inhales his breath when he sees her.

"You look so beautiful," he mumbles as he approaches her.

"I wanted tonight to feel special."

"It will be," Lucas suggests softly, then he kisses her forehead in the same way as he'd done that first day when he'd told her how he felt about her.

* * *

Minutes later, they're walking to the car—and both stare towards the house next door just before getting in the car. Although it's almost the middle of the year, and therefore is light for many more hours each day, for a reason Mrs Whitwell has *all* her curtains closed. Through one window, Lucas notices bright light shining. He sees *no* shadow behind any window but is certain she's still somehow staring out from that *one* window and satisfying her misplaced curiosity.

He feels a moment of guilt for asking Louellen to take it upon herself to befriend her, and he thinks perhaps he should tell Louellen *not* to bother. But then, it's like Louellen knows what he's thinking when she speaks. "I'll still try to befriend her, but if she's the way you've described her to be, then she'll probably become annoying as hell towards me."

"It's completely up to you."

Lucas starts the car, and after one more glance towards his own house, he drives off. They had left Tucker home for *this* trip, so they can sit inside the pub at candlelight and really enjoy an uninterrupted, romantic evening. That's what was the plan at least…

They both know that they'll have a busy rest of the summer ahead *if* they got committed to solving as much as they can, and as Louellen had extended her holiday—and apparently annoyed her boss by doing so from the heated discussion that Lucas could overhear—they were on a limited time scale to get things done. However, as Lucas glances over towards Louellen occasionally, he notices she's a bit more quiet than she'd been in the previous few days. He wonders if she's thinking about how to 'handle' Mrs Whitwell as a friend. He hopes he didn't put a burden on her she can't handle…

"The area looks so pretty," Louellen suddenly says.

"I still need to show you the beach that I took a photo of as well…"

"We got *all* summer to go see it."

"Of course," Lucas replies, and he glances at Louellen quickly, smiling at her.

"Okay, I don't want to sound silly now, but—are we there *yet?*" she asks, and he can hear a teasing edge to her voice. A wave of laughter followed her question.

"Pretty soon!" Lucas grins broadly. "We turn *right* at the end of this country lane, and then it's maybe *four* miles to the village. It's just on the edge of the village. You'll love it."

"Okay."

Lucas glances towards the woman beside him again when no further conversation comes from her, and sees she's once again staring from the window at the landscape. He sees her grab her phone and take a photo a moment later, then she seems to text it to someone…

He guesses she's telling Anna about her trip…

"How's Anna?"

"How did you know I was texting her…?"

"I know you *too* well, Lou. Any time you're on that, you're chatting to Anna. Say 'Hi' to her for me…" Lucas smiles again at Louellen.

"She's good. She's getting ready for a date—apparently." Louellen looks down, and then types something. "I said 'Hi' to her…" She looks up at Lucas, smiling back.

"How about you pay attention to *me* now?" Lucas winks at her. "Such as—what am I looking at right now…?"

Louellen follows his gaze. She feels the car slow, and then completely stop, and after a moment she realises what Lucas is pointing out at her, and what she'd almost missed because she was texting. "Ooh—is that a doe with her two Bambi…?"

"It is," Lucas says gently. "If you're quiet with opening the window, you can take a photo of *that*."

Louellen slowly lowers her window, then holds up her phone and quickly takes several pictures. When she's finished, she turns to Lucas, and he sees a broad smile on her face and her face is glowing. He also sees her eyes glaze over.

"I think I was wrong to say I'd get bored here," she whispers. "This is possibly the nicest thing I've seen ever."

"There are *many* places here where it's really peaceful, and that despite the nearby roads," he says as he reaches up and strokes Louellen's cheek softly. He looks up past her a moment later. "They're going now," he adds quietly.

Louellen glances back at the doe and her two young fawns. When the three animals have disappeared, Lucas turns on the car engine again, then slowly drives off, and slowly speeds up.

"We'll be at the pub soon."

"Okay," Louellen says absentmindedly, and when Lucas looks, she appears to be texting again. He glimpses one photo she'd taken, and she has a dreamy smile on her face now…

A few minutes later, he turns into the car park next to the pub. When he comes to a stop, Louellen looks up and smiles. "Looks pretty," she says, and a moment later her phone is in her bag.

"Shall we go in?"

She nods.

They get out of the car, but stand looking at the landscape that's visible beyond the boundary of the village.

Louellen leans her head against Lucas' chest. "It's so pretty," she comments, "and *that* sunset. I don't think I've seen it so bright pink in London."

"When I visited Mellowstone Greene to look at the house, it was afternoon, and it was a late spring so still got dark pretty early. I had the appointment to look at the cottage at two o'clock. By the time I was almost done, the sun was setting. I saw the sunset from my bedroom window. That was what sold it for me. "

Louellen looks up at Lucas and smiles. "I guess I can see why you like it," she says, "and I'm liking it too."

Lucas smiles back.

"Lets go inside. I'm starving…" Louellen says after a few more minutes of watching the pink of the evening sky turn an almost deep violet.

"Okay."

They walk into the pub, and the barman, who obviously seems to recognise Lucas, greets them both. Lucas greets him back, then introduces Louellen. "This is my girlfriend Louellen—and this is Jake."

Lucas leans towards Louellen and whispers conspiratorially, "Okay, you're safe around him. He's more into the guys."

"You mean he's gay?" Louellen hisses back.

"Uh-uh—" Lucas says. "He and *his* sister Angela run this pub. *Her* husband, Gregory, is the one who's making the delicious meals here."

"Oh, I see," Louellen says, "How *did* you find this place?"

"Lynn told me about it. When she comes to the region, she comes to eat here. Gregory is a distant cousin of hers."

"Ah, right," Louellen says.

"Yep, it's a small world," Jake comments in response. "He'd mentioned Auntie Lynn, and the rest is history… He's come to eat 'ere at least twice a week for over a month now. When I'd asked him *why* he's always alone, he said he has a girlfriend but that he's trying to persuade her to visit or something. I guess you're her…"

Louellen and Lucas both blush for entirely different reasons, but Jake just seems to ignore it.

"Anyway, ya two love-birds go take a seat somewhere, and I'll bring over a pitcher of our trademark fruit cocktail," Jake continues.

Lucas and Louellen walk to a table in the corner, as far away from the bar and entrance of the pub as they can manage. Lucas decides on the angle of showing off he can be a perfect gentleman. As he holds the chair out for Louellen to sit down, he feels almost like Jake is observing him. But then when he sits down and looks again, he sees the bar is empty of people. He decides he probably is paranoid for a moment, especially after all the months of Mrs Whitwell's nosiness and scrutiny of him.

A few minutes later, Jake walks over with a large pitcher, containing a pink-and-orange-coloured liquid, and it has an assortment of fresh fruits floating in it—all apparently crushed partially to allow their flavours to spread. Jake places two very large, tall glasses on the table and puts the pitcher down on the table closest to the wall. From under his arm, he retrieves a couple of menus that he hands to them, first to Louellen, who receives another mischievous wink from him, which causes her to blush again, and then he hands the second one to Lucas. Both men exchange a knowing grin when they hear an audible grumbling about blushing so much coming from Louellen. Jake turns around and walks off.

Lucas and Louellen spend about five minutes deciding their choices of meal. They settle on small toasts with a spicy cheese as a starter, opting for the larger portion that can be shared. Lucas goes for a rump steak with vegetables in red wine sauce, and Louellen chooses chicken pie with grilled vegetables.

A few minutes after they've placed the menus down, Jake walks over; he quickly takes their choices for a meal, then walked off to a door which Louellen presumes to be the door leading to the kitchen. To her, it seems unusual for someone gay to even run a pub and to declare so openly to be gay. She's aware of people in her own circle of friends who'd 'come out,' but she didn't know any of them personally. And this 'Jake' seemed nice enough.
"Is he a friend of yours, because you turn up so often?" she asks.
"Yes, I consider him as a friend—and both Angela and her husband Gregory as well," Lucas says. "If you glance over your left shoulder, and look for a woman on the other side of the room with red hair and a dark purple top sitting at a table, that's them."

Louellen looks and sees the persons Lucas had pointed out.

"I guess she dyes her hair," Louellen says, when she turns back to Lucas. "No one can have hair that's that shade of red… but it's a pretty shade… and she has an excellent taste in clothing."

Lucas laughs. "I guess I can't take the shopaholic out of you."

"What's wrong with wanting to shop for clothing?" Louellen asks, grinning broadly.

"Nothing, except you can stop being a shopaholic when we're trying to have a romantic night out."

"I'm enjoying this a lot and—" Louellen says, but she stops speaking when Jake then turns up with their starter. She waits until he's gone and until she'd tasted the food, before continuing to speak. "—and I have really thought a lot about all of this… I love it here. I love you. But—" She stops speaking and looks down. Lucas, who was in the middle of placing a toast to his mouth, stops in the middle of the motion. He eyes her with some concern. He notes her hesitation from her posture and he waits for her to speak, and he feels the tension growing again, like he'd noticed each previous time when they'd been arguing.

CHAPTER TWENTY-TWO

THEY HADN'T ARGUED AND LUCAS wonders why for a moment. *Why is she so tense...?* he thinks. He lowers his head and slumps his shoulders in the expected feeling of defeat that would soon come.

What is she trying to tell me...?

* * *

Only a few minutes had passed before Louellen speaks again, but in a different tone than he'd expected. "I'm actually reconsidering *some* stuff," she whispers. Lucas looks up with a jolt. Louellen always has had the most unexpected timings to drop a bombshell, and he's immediately worried that she's going to say that she's going home. "I'm going home," she continues a moment later.

Oh, no! She doesn't want to be with me, Lucas thinks, and suddenly feels deflated and hopeless.

"But *not* to stay *there*," she says a moment later, again after another moment of hesitation. Lucas stares at Louellen with his mouth open, feeling disbelief. "Where are you going then?" he asks finally.

"Errr—here," she says then giggles, "and I've decided I want to live here with *you*, silly."

"Really?" Lucas shrieks.

"Yes—but," she says.

"But...?" he asks.

"If it's okay with you, I'd like to keep using the spare room that I'm using right now, and live here as a friend for a while." She glances down, and obviously she was feeling worried now about how Lucas would react to this idea.

"I would love it. That's better than living a train journey away from you—" Lucas says diplomatically.

"Then it's settled… I have to find a 'reason' to tell dad about all this when I visit him," Louellen says as she smiles at Lucas, "and don't worry about him, thinking he's going to persuade me against this. Actually, it's what *he* said—and perhaps also something Lynn has said—before I came here, which I've been thinking about in the last few days. It's what persuaded me I'm making the right choice coming here."

Lucas grins broadly at Louellen but decides *not* to ask for the details of what it may have been that her father had said…

* * *

Only a few hours later, when it's morning, it finally dawns on Lucas what a massive change is happening in his life. The decisive conversation at the restaurant turns life from uncertainty to knowing that he'd spend it, in the foreseeable future, with Louellen. They sit in the dining room talking about what arrangements have to be made for everything to become a reality, and also planning more of what they need to do to discover the fate of Priory Mansion, when the doorbell rings and whoever is on the doorstep seems eager to get their attention, because the doorbell rings again. Lucas and Louellen glance at each other with questioning looks.

"I wonder who'd come visit us this early in the day on a Saturday morning."

"Not sure," Lucas says. "I'm not expecting anyone."

Lucas walks to the front door—wondering who's visiting him—and feels some surprise to find Leigh Governor standing on his doorstep. He notices she stands as close as she can to the front door in what seems to be an attempt not to be seen.

"Hey Leigh, what brings you here?" he asks, stepping aside to let her into the house.

"Can I tell you when I'm inside…?" she whispers. "I don't want that *bitch* next door to hear this."

Lucas quickly closes—and then locks—the front door. He's surprised because he'd never heard Leigh swear, ever. But he smirks at the idea of anyone calling Mrs Whitwell a 'bitch.'

Louellen walks from the dining room, and she sees then who the visitor is. "Hiya, Leigh," she says, then walks up to the woman and gives her a warm hug. "Hi Lou—"

"Want a cup of tea, Leigh?" Lucas asks. "Or something cold to drink?"

"Something cold, please," Leigh says.

"You go sit with her, Lucas," Louellen says, "and I'll get something from the kitchen…" She turns and has disappeared to the kitchen before Lucas could respond. He motions towards the living room. Leigh walks there, then she looks towards the window a moment before she sits down.

"I'm glad you've got those extra curtains up," she says. "It means she cannot look at what you do here. She's an interfering bitch."

Leigh drops herself on the sofa. "I guess there's so much *you* still don't know yet," Leigh says when Louellen walks into the room carrying a pack of orange juice, a bottle of sparkling water and a bottle of 7-Up, which she'd gone to buy earlier in the day at Mr Howey's shop.

"Has something happened?" Lucas asks.

"Someone's trying to *do* something with Priory Mansion. But, each time, another 'someone' tries to block it…" Leigh throws her arms up in the air in desperation. "I guess I'm not making much sense."

"It's okay," Louellen states. "I've also felt a massive amount of confusion about this."

"If things had gone differently," Leigh says, staring at Louellen, "then your great-grandfather would never have been in the situation he found himself in."

"I guess so, but dad always says that things that have happened can't be changed so *not* to dwell on them."

"But that's the thing, Lou," Leigh says. "Something is happening *now*, and it's because of the things from the past…" Leigh pulls an envelope from her handbag. She takes out a letter and hands it to Lucas. He looks at it with a puzzled expression, then hands it to Louellen, who frowns when she sees the content of the letter.

"What is the letter about?" Lucas asks.

"I received that yesterday afternoon by special delivery—and I honestly don't know," Leigh says.

"Why does it say this *thing* about the 'collective request' being denied again, and what request…?" Lucas asks, "Who made that request?"

"I don't know," Leigh says as she bursts out in tears, which prompts both Lucas and Louellen to sit beside the woman and comfort her. They look at each other with expressions that match. "What the hell is going on?"

They wait until Leigh's sobbing has subsided, then Louellen speaks again. "We can go check Priory Mansion to see if we can find anything *there* that might tell us who sent this letter, and why."

"It would be nice if you could," Leigh says as she looks at each individual imploringly, first at Louellen, then at Lucas.

"We can go in a little while," he says, though he still has reservations about going again, but now that a second person has asked for the actions, he has no option to go. He's uncertain what he and Louellen might find in the house if they investigated it more thoroughly than he'd done on that fateful night. The hairs on his neck are standing up and he's thinking about it. "Can I see the letter once more?" he asks.

Louellen hands him the letter and he studies it. "They it sent from London," he says. "Lou, do you recognise this law firm?" He hands the letter back to Louellen, who looks at the name at the top of the letter now.

"Errr—no, I don't," she says after some hesitation, and frowns more because she strains her mind to recall having ever seen the name, "but I can call Sarah from my work, and ask her if *she* knows the name. She's the legal person at the gallery."

"Okay—" Lucas says.

Louellen gets up and quickly walks upstairs with the letter in her hand. Both Lucas and Leigh strain to listen to her talking on her phone. The call doesn't take long, and a few minutes later, she arrives back in the living room. "Sorry, no luck there, but she's going to ask around on Monday if any of the people at the law firm where she temps might know this company," Louellen explains. "She thinks I'm asking about it for dad."

"Does she know your dad…?" Lucas asks, feeling concerned that a person he doesn't know could end up calling Louellen's father.

"Nope—I told her that dad had received a letter relating to the ownership of *his* house, and had wanted to know if the letter was genuine. Oh, and these *two* letters here show that it's a firm that deals with property acquisitions. Sarah could tell me that much."

Lucas sees Leigh is frowning on hearing the explanation, and a moment later he, too, is frowning.

"Wasn't there a rumour going around in the village about an American who'd wanted to buy the house to redevelop it as some sort of golf course?" Louellen asks.

"There is... and I hope you don't believe *that*," Leigh snaps angrily, then she visibly sighs before speaking again. "I'm sorry... I didn't mean to snap at you. I'm tiring of all the rumours."

"I can understand that," Lucas says, then he glances at Louellen, who gives him a knowing glance. They know what it feels like to be at the receiving end of a rumour, which had started the moment they'd arrived back from the summer camp. It was being spread by Emlyn, who'd become *their* nemesis. Even more when she'd discovered they'd started a relationship. But the rumour-mongering had made their relationship stronger, and it had allowed both of them to grow from two shy people to strong, confident people they would become...

Now they faced a similar situation, and it was affecting a person who both had grown to care about—and especially Louellen, who'd found a new good friend when she went back for another chat with Leigh.

"If something *is* going on, then the best thing to *do* now is to find more information," Lucas says, "and Lou, can you get your phone and try a search for something for me?"

Louellen nods and rushes off to get her phone. When she comes back, she stares at Lucas sternly. "It's easier with a laptop, you know," she says in a mock-accusatory voice.

"Okay, okay—I'll get one soon," Lucas says.

"Finally he agrees!" Louellen smirks for a moment, then rolling her eyes for good measure.

Leigh is confused momentarily about what's going on between her two friends, then realises she's in the middle of some sort of disagreement Lucas and Louellen have been having. But as neither looks angry, it's their normal banter to tease one another.

"What do you want me to find?" Louellen asks.

"That term that's listed in this letter—property acquisitions—" Lucas replies. "Anything you can find that tells us *more* of what it entails, *who* can do it, *why* they might do it—and if you can, find out if any law firms in this part of Norfolk also can do such a thing..."

"That's a lot of stuff. It will take me a while," Louellen states and makes herself more comfortable on the chair she's sitting in, and curls up her legs. "Okay," she says after five minutes searching, "There are several versions… There's land acquisition, the acquisition of houses, the acquisition of assets-related legal paperwork acquisition, finance acquisition, also rights acquisition. Though I cannot figure out what the latter may be."

She stares at Lucas for *any* clues where to go next in her search. He stares for a few moments at the mysterious letter. "Look for legal paperwork acquisition," he says finally.

Louellen glances back at her phone again. "If I understand this jargon well enough, it means that someone is curating a deed for a property," Louellen says. "Hang on, I'll call Sarah again and ask her if she can explain about the legal stuff to do with property acquisition." She dials Sarah's number, then waits for the phone to get answered and it gets answered after about five rings. "Hey Sarah, it's Lou again," Louellen says. "I have another question that dad wants to know about. In the letter that I'd mentioned earlier… I'd another look at it, and it mentions property acquisition. Can you explain what that is exactly…?"

Leigh and Lucas glance at each other, perplexed when they hear Louellen is spinning a story to make a person at work *think* that she's talking about her father. Lucas hopes Louellen won't get in trouble at work for what she's saying. Deep down he wonders *why* she's saying this stuff, but he can't ask with Leigh in their house…

* * *

The conversation between Louellen and Sarah lasted well over fifteen minutes, and it was clear that Louellen was getting an extensive explanation. From the few yawns that Louellen suppresses, it's clear that the subject is boring to her. She lifts her free hand and makes a gesture of talking with it, tapping the tips of her stretched out fingers against her thumb.

When apparently Sarah has satisfied her need of telling Louellen everything she would know about the topic, Louellen ends the call and she stares at Lucas and Leigh. "This is getting more and more complex by the minute. The story of someone trying to buy the house to make it into a golf course… *Who* had started the rumour, Leigh?"

"I don't know," Leigh answers. "It's been doing its rounds for at least thirty or forty years now, but if you ask anyone, they'll all tell you they had heard it from 'someone.' If you ask who that someone is, they'll all tell you they don't know."

"Hmm, that's odd—but Sarah said that the only way they could sell Priory Mansion is if there's a property acquisition order in place and if all the people, signatory to order, are to agree to it. I had read out the letter to her—well, part of it, as you heard earlier perhaps—and she thinks it proves that someone is saying 'No' to the order."

"So, we find that person, I guess?" Lucas asks.

"Yep," Louellen replies.

"So, you believe me when I'm saying that this is bad…?" Leigh looks frantically from person to person.

"We do," Lucas replies, "but it's best we don't say too much yet about what we're planning."

After a moment of contemplation over the new information they'd uncovered, they all get up and all walk to the dining room where they got working on potential people who might have a hand in the cover-up…

Louellen is sitting at the table and is searching for more information when she calls out, "I think I've found something." Lucas walks to her end of the table, followed closely by Leigh, who looks at Louellen with curiosity and obvious fondness of the other woman. Since Louellen's arrival to the village, they'd talked more and Louellen had come for visits at Leigh's house and in that time they had regarded one another as friends.

"Yes, there's a name here for a person who'd attempted to buy the house," Louellen says, glancing up and staring a moment at Lucas and Leigh.

"What name?"

"Corey Bath," Louellen answers quickly.

"What is *his* connection in all this?" Leigh asks.

"I'd say several things, and it's rather odd," Louellen explains, "and I've been re-reading the information for the last half hour, and it just sounds like an odd account of how *he* got to America." Lucas and Leigh sit down at the table next to her, and both stare at her, expecting her to explain more. "Okay, and I guess I got designated into the role of explaining this stuff like Miss Marple might do, I guess," Louellen says and Lucas laughs before he says, "Okay then, Miss Marple, explain it to us…”

"He'd arrived in America in '1900' with his parents. The woman was calling herself Marybeth, and they had listed his father as John Corey," Louellen says, looking at her laptop once more.

"Okay, so what's odd, then?" Lucas asks.

"Because whatever I do, I cannot find *any* information about the parents," Louellen says. "It's like neither of them ever existed before 1900."

"When was this Corey Bath born? I wonder why his name differs from his parents," Leigh comments, "It strikes me as odd that a parent would give a child a 'first name' that's his own 'last name,' and then pluck some name from the air as a last name."

"That's what I find odd, too," Louellen says. "Then this 'Corey Bath' turned up in southern America as a business owner about thirty years later, and they claimed it he was one of the few weathering the 'Great Depression.' According to this other information that I found, he made his first offer for Priory Mansion a few years before the Second World War had started. It says here that he'd died when he was seventy—that would have been in the late 1950s. It says he has a son… it doesn't list the name of the son, but says he was born at the end of the war. If he's still alive now, he'd be in his seventies *now*— they give no information of any children for his son."

The newly found information opens the situation up completely. Lucas places a hand on Louellen's shoulder when he notices her endless muttering under her breath about how stupid she was and that she should have figured it all out sooner…

* * *

After he has steadied Louellen's emotions, he speaks again. "Right," Lucas says. "Can you tell more about those parents? Marybeth and John. Does it give any information about them?"

"Only a little," Louellen says. "It gives more information about John Corey than about Marybeth."

"Like what?" Leigh asks.

"It says he was in his thirties when he'd arrived in America. Corey Bath was about twelve years," Louellen answers. "It doesn't give any information about Marybeth from before they'd arrived, and it only gives this information because they were being processed as immigrants in America."

"So, if we want to find out who Corey Bath was, we need to find out more about his father," Lucas says. "For example, where was he from…?"

"It says he was born in Somerset, but doesn't say exactly where," Louellen replies.

"Errr—it does," Leigh interjects.

"Oh—where then?" Lucas asks.

"In Bath," Leigh explains. "I don't know why, but I am certain that's where John Corey was from."

"Okay, so if he was from there, then we could assume that Marybeth is from there too," Lucas suggests.

"However, this doesn't explain why the son of a person—who'd lived in Somerset before he was going to America—was ever going to be interested in a house in a small village in the northern part of Norfolk," Louellen says. "They were living on the other side of the country if we assume they lived there before going to America, and how would a person who had gone to America when he was twelve, know even to ask to buy it when he was over twenty years older? And that's what I find odd."

"I agree—that's odd," Leigh says.

All three of them sit silently contemplating the information, then Leigh speaks. "So, this Corey Bath might have been my family."

She leans back, and tears flow freely down her cheeks.

"Yes, and *if* the squatter is Corey Bath's son, it could be him who's trying to buy the house," Louellen says.

"But, how?" Leigh says. "The last person to own the house is Karina Seaward. No one knows who owns it now."

"I'm uncertain, but maybe *she* had other family who had grabbed the house from the rightful inheritors when she had died," Lucas explains. "Maybe it's related to the inheritance. People thought of Karina as someone who'd lost her status in high society, but everything shows she was a savvy businesswoman, and that she was very rich. She was who'd bought the house from her father when *he* went bankrupt. But I'm personally curious why she would have been friends with Nelly Sibbett. I wonder how Nelly had coped with her life after Karina had died."

"You're certain that there's a link between all *this* and her disappearance…?" Louellen asks.

"I am," Lucas nods as he answers the question.

"In what way…?" Leigh asks.

"Let's assume she'd gone somewhere, after they'd seen her running through the woods—seen, for example, by that gardener," Lucas explains. "Everyone seems to think that she'd ended up in a workhouse. I thought so too until now… But I think I got it wrong."

"She didn't?" Louellen asks.

"No! Her disappearance seems to have happened when Marybeth appears," he says, "and I wonder if Marybeth, in fact, is Nelly."

"How did you get to that?" Louellen asks.

"I think she had help to get her *first* to Somerset, and once there she got married and they had a child. Then, she went with her new husband to America," Lucas continues, "If you look at it all, she was married to a husband and a child when she had disappeared. Sorry Leigh, but I have to say all this. Nelly Sibbett *may* have left because things weren't in a good way at home. The gardener said she looked panicked, almost delirious, when he saw her rush into the woodland. They claimed *she* had an affair with Karina's son. But what if all that was rumours planted in people's minds by her husband to discredit her? What if she made herself disappear to escape a terrible life with him—and had been helped in making it possible? Maybe both Karina *and* her son had a hand in it."

Leigh and Louellen look at one another in disbelief, then look at Lucas again, expecting him to continue speaking. After a moment, he does this, but not before he has gathered his thoughts…

"If I recall, the story was that it was around 1897 that Karina's son had disappeared, right?" Lucas asks.

Leigh nods.

"What if 'John Corey,' in fact, was Karina's son…?" Lucas asks, "because she'd *never* publicly named her son, and was very secretive about him all her life. Her son would have inherited everything that Karina Seaward had owned when she died in 1880."

"You think he'd left for America with Nelly, and they both assumed these new identities…?" Leigh asks.

"Corey Bath was twelve at the turn of the century. It puts his date of birth in 1888, but what if they'd deliberately altered the date of birth when he travelled to America?" Lucas continues. "What if they didn't go to America in 1900 but three years earlier and in the *same* year that Nelly Sibbett had disappeared? It would make Corey Bath at least three years older. If you take this timeline, then John Corey could have been born in 1860, and that timeline would make him the right age to be Karina's son who you said was born when she was twenty-six."

"If John Corey was her son, he would have inherited Priory Mansion when she had died," Leigh says.

"Hang on," Louellen interjects. "If he, in fact, married Nelly Sibbett and Corey Bath is their son, then *who* is the squatter there now, and might he be who's sending the notes of refusal to sell via that solicitor?"

"It could be," Lucas says, and he nods again.

"Then, who's trying to claim that Priory Mansion is theirs…?" Louellen asks, "Who else has an invested interest in possibly owning the house…?"

All three of them glance perplexed at each other—each with a puzzled expression on their faces. None of them have an answer to that question.

"I guess that's a mystery to solve still," Lucas finally says.

CHAPTER TWENTY-THREE

LEIGH IS THE FIRST TO speak up. "I guess I'm descended from the child that Nelly left behind," Leigh says matter of fact.

"I think so… You'd said that your grandfather had told you that *his* grandfather lost his wife from cholera when a pandemic was going on across the world. Perhaps his grandfather had lied to cover up that his wife had left him," Lucas explains. "So yes, it can *be* that Corey Bath is a distant relation of yours. I don't think as an uncle. More like a cousin, so many times removed. I guess I need to read a decent book on genealogy to figure out how you'd be family if you are."

"But what I'm curious about is who else might want to have a claim on Priory Mansion," Louellen interjects, after a time of pensive thought. "Because whatever I do, I cannot find any siblings for Karina. There are a few uncles and an aunt for her, but they're all in wealthier family lines, and then I'd discovered that her father had a much older sister."

"I didn't know any of that," Leigh says. "Everyone in the village thinks *he* was some drunk geezer with an unfortunate daughter."

"It claims here the sister was married off to some 'local man,' because this 'Jackson Seaward'—listed as George Seaward's father—is in fact Karina's grandfather," Louellen explains, "and couldn't afford a dowry for her, but it doesn't list who she'd married, or what had happened after that. It's like she seized to exist after the wedding."

"Seems to me almost like a tug of war between a mysterious American man who lays claim on the house and another mysterious person who's more local," Lucas says, "—and sees it also as *their* right to own the house."

"And in both cases it seems we don't know who it might be," Leigh says, "but I can be certain it isn't me, and none of my family has ever claimed any connection to the house."

"But you have a connection. If you, in fact, descended from 'Nelly Sibbett,' someone is trying to make sure that the *right* person inherits the house next," Louellen says, "To me, the local individual is just some sort of money grabbing idiot who wants all the money for themselves without sharing it with the others who are also entitled to the inheritance."

"Add the rumours about Nelly Sibbett that have persisted since the 1930s, and that's when they'd attempted to buy the house—or lay claim to it," Lucas says.

"That's over eight decades ago," Louellen says, "It would mean we have to work out for every person in the village, if they might have had a family of the right age group to allow the rumour to go from generation to generation."

"Whoever is behind it is right now in their late fifties or even early sixties—and that means *half* the village population is therefore guilty, me included," Leigh says softly.

"But we can find out how many men got married in the nineteenth century," Lucas says. "There must be a record of that, at least."

"Ah yes, and from that we can at least create a list of potential families, who might have relations to Karina's aunt," Louellen says, then she types in the village name and clicks the search button. "It looks like they've recorded all the records in Norwich and it got done by the church here," she says after a few minutes, "and it would mean going to there for information. I can go there tomorrow."

"Want to have me drive you there?" Lucas asks.

"No, I think I'll take the bus," Louellen says.

Lucas glances at her, and wonders for a moment why she looks so pensive suddenly. He assumes she's just trying to figure out more of the mystery of the house in her mind.

"Maybe I should go home now," Leigh says. "Would the two of you like to come over for a meal this weekend?"

"Yeah, that sounds good," Lucas says, "Louellen…?"

"I'm up for it," Louellen says.

"Okay then, it's at about seven, but you can be there a bit earlier. I've also invited Gylda and her husband over, so it should be a fun evening for all of us," Leigh says.

"We'll be there," Lucas states to confirm the plans.

Leigh gets up, and Lucas gets her coat from the coat hook in the hall, and helps her into her coat.

"Don't lose this one, Lou," Leigh quips, then she winks at Louellen. "He's a true gentleman."

Louellen blushes, and both Leigh and Lucas suppress the urge to smile. Leigh walks to the front door, followed by Lucas. There she stops. "I have to thank you for all the hard work you've put into finding out so much stuff that I didn't even know about—Let me know if you find anything else useful."

"I'll make sure I let you know," Lucas says as he opens the door and Leigh walks outside. He sees her stare to her left for several minutes, and he realises that Mrs Whitwell was the likely culprit. He's aware that his neighbour doesn't like Leigh. It had become more and more apparent as the months had passed. Even more so since he'd started taking an interest in the whole mysterious situation that seems to permeate in the village…

* * *

After watching Leigh Governor walk away at a fast pace, Lucas shuts the door quickly before his neighbour might call out to him. In some ways, he was now getting an idea what both Leigh and Gylda meant about the curiosity being displayed by his neighbour, being more than that of some just being nosey. *Definitely not Miss Marple*, he thinks, remembering his earlier assumptions about her. *More like that, she'd be a person who Miss Marple might catch out and uncover as the culprit of a crime.* Lucas wasn't sure *why* he thought of this name in this way, but something had altered his perception of his neighbour. Ever since he'd confronted *her* with the newspaper clippings, she had seemed less than friendly towards him. She'd stopped placing food on his doorstep literally a day *after* he confronted her, and now never even greet him.

I wonder if that's why the previous owner had moved out from here. Because of her—

Lucas recalls some research efforts of the afternoon. "How many is that now?" Leigh had asked.

"Twenty three, including Leigh's family."

"That's going to be a lot of information to go through," Leigh had said.

"I guess so."

"I guess you're going to need help with this." Louellen had grinned broadly at Lucas.

"We can find out who the squatter is by simply asking him. Though I don't know if he'd want to talk."

"We can at least try," Louellen said. "Let do that first before we even go through all this list."

"Okay."

Louellen had frowned, but it had seemed that she kept quiet for reasons only she knew about. It had seemed that she'd guessed from Lucas' expression that he would discuss none of what's on his mind until Leigh left. They'd talked about inconsequential things after that for the next few hours. Until Leigh had stated that it was time to go home. Lucas and Louellen had watched after her from behind the curtains of the living room until she turned a corner, then had gone back into the dining room, and that was after Lucas had closed the front door...

Immediately, when the door was shut, Louellen had spoken. "What are you planning, Lucas?" she'd asked, and then was frowning when she saw him try his torch.

"Okay, I guess this flash light works."

"Torch! It's torch. How many times am I going to tell you *that?*"

"Torch—okay?" Lucas says, then he smirks at Louellen.

"So?" Louellen asks.

"I'm going to the house *now.*"

"Now?" Louellen asks.

"Yes, now. Something connects the house with the person who had sent that letter with whoever had shot twice that night. I need to confront that person."

"You're not going alone."

"I wasn't planning to go alone. You're coming with me. You got dark clothes to wear?"

"I got dark trousers but *no* dark top."

"You can borrow one of my sweaters—and we'll go without the dog, so no one recognises *us* from his presence."

"Okay."

They both go upstairs and each go to their own bedroom. Louellen opens her door when Lucas knocks on the door. Louellen opens it, and he sticks an arm inside, holding a dark navy blue sweater. She takes the clothing, then she thanks for him for it, and closes the door. She takes her own top off, puts on a dark purple t-shirt, then puts on the sweater given to her by Lucas.

Lucas smiles nervously at Louellen as they're approaching Priory

Mansion, then he holds out his hand. They check the street first to make sure there isn't anyone around who might watch them go inside the house. When they only see an empty street, they step quickly into the garden and they walk fast to the house. Then, a few moments later, they hear a sound coming from somewhere ahead of them. They stop and look at each other a moment.

"What was that?" Louellen hisses.
"Maybe it's some sort of squatter… Maybe I thought there was someone from the village here, but what if it's actually a squatter?" Lucas hisses back.
"We need to check it out."
"Are you mad? He had a gun last time."
"I know, but he probably won't use it if he or she sees you're not alone."
"Okay, but let's be careful."
They walk on, then they see someone dashing through the bushes, then decide simultaneously to rush quickly into the house after the person to confront him.
"That could be the squatter who they often have seen in the village," Louellen whispers.
"I've seen him around, too."
"I wonder why he uses the house for squatting."
"I don't know," Lucas says. "Maybe we need to find from him why he's there."
Louellen nods, then she says. "We need to confront him…"

Lucas feels just as nervous as Louellen appears to be as they walk single file over the unkempt path towards the mansion. At the front door, they stop and glance at each other for a moment, each searching for reassurance from the other person. Lucas opens the door quietly. This is the *first* time since that night two months ago that he was back here. He wonders if the house is like he'd seen it before.

"Who goes there?"

Lucas and Louellen freeze. They heard a man's voice—croaky from ageing—but strong and determined and not sounding friendly. They glance at one another…

"We're here for whoever lives here," Lucas calls out.

"I live here. Now go. Leave me alone," the voice replies.

"We need to speak to you. We have information," Lucas calls out.

"What information? Are you one of them villagers who likes to spread rumours about my grandmother and great-grandmother?" the voice replies.

Lucas and Louellen glance at one another once more, and Lucas sees Louellen are mouthing a few specific words at one another: "Grandmother—Great-grandmother."

Lucas nods to show that he'd heard comment, too. "We know about them—and *no*, we're not here about any rumours, but about the truth."

Silence.

"Hello," Lucas calls out in a nervous voice after a few minutes. "I'm Corey Bath's son. Mitchell is my name."

Lucas and Louellen swing around, doing a one eighty, and are now facing the man that they'd assumed always as a squatter.

"You are?" Lucas feels stupid for asking.

"Yes, I came back to England on the insistence of my mother when she was dying," Mitchell explains. "She said I needed to protect my family from the people who would want to harm *them*."

"Harm who?" Louellen asks softly.

"My father had often told my mother that *his* mother had left another child behind, but not by choice. Before he'd died, he'd asked her to promise to tell me the truth about it all, before it was too late to tell the truth. When she was dying, my mother had told me everything my father always had said about my grandmother and great-grandmother," Mitchell says, "but come, let's sit to talk…"

Mitchell Bath motions to a sofa in the room behind him. He walks to a seat, pulls it closer, then sits down.

"So, you know your mother had left a child behind when she'd disappeared…?" Lucas asks.

"Yes," Mitchell replies, "and so you know about what had happened exactly? She'd died when she was sixty-five. My father was fifteen when they had gone to America. He had tried to buy *this* place about forty years later when he'd discovered that some sort of trust was its caretaker. When he'd died, I've been trying ever since. But someone always was telling the solicitor the same answer as 'No' in each attempt."

"How old was your father when *you* were born?" Louellen asks, "If I may ask that…"

"My father married *late* in life—after the war. He was over sixty when he'd married a woman named Lynn. They'd got divorced ten years after I was born. I was born about five years after they got married," Mitchell says softly. "Apparently, she had remarried at least once more."

Louellen and Lucas look at one another.

"I know my mother had a daughter after she'd divorced my father," Mitchell continues. "The daughter is called Evelyn. My mother was twenty-five years old when she'd married my father. Everyone had frowned upon the idea that she'd be with a man so much older than she was. If I remember correct, Evelyn was born about five years after mother had divorced my father. She would be almost fifty now—"

Lucas realises that he'd been almost correct about the age of the squatter—who was claiming to be a descendant of Corey Bath and was even claiming that his mother was Karina's daughter. "Do you know where *she* might be?" he asks.

"You mean Evelyn. No, I don't, sorry," Mitchell says.

"I guess *we* could try to find her for you." Louellen says softly.

"I've been trying to find her for at least the last twenty years, but she just doesn't want to be found," Mitchell says. "And my health isn't the best anymore, so I don't really have the energy to do anything of the kind…"

Louellen places her hand on Lucas' arm and looks at him in a certain, familiar way. He sees her eyes tell him what she doesn't say.

"We could *try* to locate her, but I can't promise anything." Lucas says.

"If you find her, I'd appreciate that," Mitchell says.

"Maybe tell us as much as you can about what you know."

"I can tell you everything that I remember from being told by my parents, especially about what my father said before he died," Mitchell says. "It's important—if two people *not* even involved—are asking questions about all this."

"We're asking about it, because we found out connections between *this* and something else." Lucas glances at Louellen, considering whether to tell *who* she is, then decides it's only fair. "Louellen's great-grandfather is the reporter who'd tried to tell about the disappearance of Nelly Sibbett, and it seems someone didn't like what he wrote, and caused him to be discredited. When the owner of the newspaper, John C. Mutter—that's actually the great-grandfather of a friend of Louellen—was adamant that they'd publish the articles, and on the front cover even, the whole newspaper lost credibility. We've found evidence that the pressure to discredit came from within the Palace of Westminster. Whoever it was, also let the investigator do a botched job, and allowed the mystery of Nelly's disappearance to grow into rumour."

"I see," Mitchell says. "This correlates with something my father had told me."
"What did he tell you about the situation…?" Lucas asks.

"I'm *aware* of the rumour that still seems to persist around here about my grandmother. That she supposedly ran off and left her child behind. But I have the medical reports from when doctors had done a medical examination—when she'd arrived in London all bruised and blue," Mitchell explains. "In those reports, it shows someone badly beat her up… and it was actually Karina's son who had paid for *all* her medical bills, or she would have ended up for real in a workhouse. What people don't realise around here is that Corey Bath had adopted the child that was born… Nelly, or as she had called herself later, Marybeth, was pregnant, and her loser husband thought she was having an affair with the neighbour."
Lucas and Louellen look wide-eyed at one another. This was an unexpected twist to the events. It meant that in reality Mitchell Bath and Leigh Governor were closer related than either might have realised right now. *Their* great-grandparents were, in fact, brothers, and that would make Leigh and Mitchell a niece and nephew once removed. It also meant that Karina Seaward's son was actually a generous benefactor by adopting a child that wasn't of his blood.
Nothing in the information they now knew explained why they'd changed their names when they had moved to America…

"Why did your grandmother change her name?" Louellen asks. "Wasn't Karina's son actually called John Corey from birth?"

"Yes, my grandfather had told me that Karina called *her* son John Corey. She'd used the father's name, but neither of my parents has ever known *who* the father might have been," Mitchell answers. "In that respect, it's a fact rather than a rumour."

"So, I guess the first thing to do would be to look for a 'Corey'…" Louellen says.

"No… You got it back to front," Mitchell retorts. "John is the father's name—Karina had plucked the *last* name from the air, just to have a last name for the child, as she couldn't call him 'Seaward.' *Her* father had called John Corey a bastard child, and he'd apparently always refused to acknowledge him."

Louellen looks deflated for when she hears the information about the name, then she smiles…

"We've at least solved *part* of the mystery," she says triumphantly. "We've figured out who *you* are."

"Please, don't tell anyone in the village this information," Mitchell says. "I'd rather be dead and buried before it's made public—"

"We won't but *if* your grandfather is the brother of Nelly's other child, I think there's ONE person in this village who'd want to know about it," Lucas interjects, "and I'm certain she wouldn't tell anyone else."

"Who?" Mitchell asks, and Lucas notes curiosity in the man's voice now.

"Nelly's child grew up, and a few generations later Leigh Governor was born," Lucas said, "and from what I know about her and her background, she has suffered a lot from the persistent rumours about who or what Nelly represents to most people in this region…"

"I've met her," Mitchell says, "but I never knew who she was."

"Maybe I can get her *here* on the pretence I've found something," Lucas suggests, "then we can introduce you to her…"

"I don't mind that," Mitchell says, "but *only* if she's willing. If she says 'No' to your idea, then the secret of *who* I am dies with me, and you two tell no one ever—okay?"

Lucas and Louellen nod.

"We need to visit Leigh as soon as we can," Louellen says. "She deserves to know."

"You can bring her here if she says yes… and I'll leave the side door open, so you can come inside that way," Mitchell says. "You can make out you found it open by chance. I think that finding out about me will be shock enough for her. Let's not make the state of the inside of this house another shock." Mitchell sweeps him around to show to Lucas and Louellen what he means…

After a pause, Lucas speaks again. "By my calculation, your grandmother was around thirty when your father was born," he says.

"That's right… She'd died just after the war," Mitchell says. "They buried her in the town where we were living in. After she'd died, my parents and I moved to New York, and we lived just outside the city for the rest of the lives of my parents. I came back *here* when my mother passed away, essentially to protect the inheritance from the people who'd mean harm."

"And you don't know *who* it is?" Louellen asks.

"Unfortunately, no," Mitchell says. "I know my grandmother left a child behind—I already said that, and you confirmed it to *be* Leigh Governor. Karina Seaward was a lot smarter than everyone credits her because she'd set up the trust that maintains this house many years before she had died. As long as the trust exists, no one person can lay claim on their own to this house. My plan was to do a claim for the house *with* whatever family my grandmother had left here, because my father had left a document behind. Karina Seaward had signed this document, and in it she had legally recognised my grandmother's *first* child as family."

"Leigh Governor will find that comforting to know," Lucas says.

"I've had the document checked both by lawyers in America and at the High Court with a barrister here in Britain. I had the case heard in the both places with *me* listed as 'John Doe' to protect me from intrusions into my private life. The 'Queen's Bench Division' heard the case because it involved contractual matters. They had ruled in my favour but because no one knows the identity of the individual refusing to accept the sale of *this* house, by the trust to its rightful heirs, I'm basically stuck… and so is Leigh Governor, once she knows about this too," Mitchell explains. "This isn't a simple case of disputes about inheritance. This is a dispute where the lawyers who'd brought the case to court had identified that someone is deliberately keeping an inheritance *away* from people. I'm getting old. I have no children, but Leigh has children. If I'm right, she also has a few grandchildren. They all would benefit from this mystery being solved. Also, there's my half-sister Evelyn, who might also have children and grandchildren—" Mitchell stops talking abruptly, and he stares out of the windows absentmindedly, and both Lucas and Louellen stay silent to let the old man alone with his thoughts for a while…

"My half-sister is five years younger. She might have children in their thirties, and her grandchildren would be five to ten years old," Mitchell continues. "My half-sister would be about the *same* age as Leigh is. I know from watching what goes on in the village that Leigh has at least *one* daughter who now lives in Scotland, but I don't know really if there are any grandchildren. But I hope so…"

"If this legal case gets solved, who would get this house?" Louellen asks.

"It would remain in the hands of the trust, but *they* could then actually do something commercially with the building, and the best option open is to set it up as a luxury hotel," Mitchell replies. "For a decent enough income, so all involved would benefit well financially…"

"I guess *that* proves another rumour true," Lucas comments.

"What rumour?" Mitchell asks.

Part Four

CHAPTER TWENTY-FOUR

After considering his words carefully, Lucas cautiously gives an answer. "Several people in the village are talking of an 'American investor,' who wants to make this house into a hotel with a golf course…"

"The part about the hotel is the *only* genuine part of the rumour, I have to guess," Mitchell states. "The ruling in London means that the beauty of the landscape must be preserved—"

"Not entirely," Louellen interjects. "You are American, so the part about an 'American' wanting this house as a hotel is true, and yes, the landscape is too beautiful to spoil with a golf course."

Mitchell laughs. "I guess you're right there!" Mitchell concedes defeat in the argument.

They're all silent again for a while, then Lucas speaks. "This weekend, we're visiting Leigh for a meal. Gylda and Roger will be there too," he says softly. "We, Louellen and I, could delay our departure at the end of the meal. When Gylda and Roger have left, we can tell Leigh about visiting here, and come with her on Sunday. If that's okay with you…?"

"Yeah, yeah, I think you'll find the best way to prepare her for the shock of a lifetime," Mitchell says, then he smirks before adding in a sarcastic tone, "Just as long as you don't give her *too* much of a shock."

"We won't."

"Anyway, it's getting late. If you're seen leaving from *here* this late in the day, it will cause a few curious people to pry into what doesn't concern them," Mitchell says then he gets up, and Lucas and Louellen treat it as a 'cue,' to get up too.

The three of them walk to the side door that Mitchell had mentioned earlier in the conversation. They walk through three rooms—each of which are in various stages of decoration. They pass a room that's familiar to Lucas, who glances around it for a moment. "I'm sorry for scaring you with staging this room in this way. To make it appear like this house is being used for some sort of occult purposes," Mitchell says when he sees the younger man glance into the room. "It was scary to see it." Lucas says and then grins for a moment. Louellen, who hadn't believed the story when Lucas told it to her, now looks in the room too, just to make sense of what Mitchell Bath might have done.

"So, he *did* really scare you then," she says finally, looking up at Lucas. "It did," he replies, nodding.

"I promise *not* to scare Leigh. But there are people in this village who I'd gladly scare to their graves for how they still talk of my grandmother and great-grandmother," Mitchell says, now sounding as harsh as he'd done when they'd arrived at the house earlier in the day.

* * *

Lucas and Louellen glance over each of their shoulders, and listen as they hear the door being shut with several locks, and look towards one another. They'd come to the house to find answers, perhaps to confront a nobody of a squatter for illegally occupying the house. They hadn't expected to be confronted with the consequences of *things* that had happened in this house and in the village almost one and a half century earlier…

Lucas takes Louellen's hand, and rather than leaving through the old grand gate at the *front* of the garden, they walk the small path that Mitchell Bath had pointed out to them moments earlier. After about fifteen minutes, they arrive at a gate, which creaks loudly when Lucas pushes it open. He feels recognition when he sees where they're standing moments later.

Their walk back to their own home is a subdued discussion about what to do *next*, and Louellen says she wants to visit her dad to talk with him about some 'things'…

* * *

A few days later, Lucas sleepily walks into the kitchen in a somewhat absent-minded mood, and almost bumps into Louellen, who stares at him questioningly. He yawns, and instinctively glances through the window toward next door, but he stops in mid-stretch and frowns…

"Her again…?" she asks, nodding sideways towards where Mrs Whitwell's house is. He nods as an answer.

"She's even less friendly with me now," Louellen says softly. "I guess we can't be friends with 'everyone' the more secrets we discover."

"I guess you're right."

Louellen leans herself against his chest - something she'd started doing more lately.

"Are you sure you'll be okay going to Norwich alone tomorrow?" Lucas asks softly.

He feels her nod a moment later, faster than he'd expected her answer to come.

He slowly puts his arms around Louellen, and rather than pulling away from him, she stays leaning against his chest, letting him comfort her. Lucas guesses that she's emotionally drained from all the things she'd learnt so far. "Why don't you sit down and relax on the sofa, and I'll cook us some dinner," Lucas says softly. Louellen pulls away and looks up at him, grinning. "Since when have you learnt to cook…?" she asks.

"I *may* have had a few mishaps, but I've been trying to learn," Lucas says. "It won't be anything fancy, if that's okay…" She nods and walks to the living room. Lucas watches her go and wonders again why she's so subdued. He has to assume that it's all the things that have happened in the month since arriving to visit. Initially, she'd planned only to stay a week, then she'd visited London for a day. When she got back, Louellen had told him she'd handed in her notice at work…

Lucas knows that quitting the job must have been hard for Louellen as she'd loved it, but slowly, as she settles into the routine of helping with the investigation, it made her come alive, and she seemed to enjoy her new life. He wonders for a moment whether she's reconsidering things yet again, then shrugs this idea off as ridiculous…

* * *

But now she was going for a visit to see her father, and although Lucas normally didn't ask her about her plans, he felt the urge to ask this time. But when Louellen walks again into the kitchen—seemingly, to fetch a can of Fanta from the fridge—and it was more apparent from the glances towards him busying himself with food preparations that she was doing this to satisfy her curiosity. He can see Louellen crane her neck as she'd walked in, and then again as she'd walked from the kitchen, followed by some giggles.

Lucas takes the lid from the pan to stir the meal. He hadn't really worked out exactly *what* to make and instead he had grabbed ingredients that seemed to be 'okay' together. But when he tastes from the meal, he decides it only needs an extra bit of salt to be okay.

"Lucas—" Louellen calls out from the living room. He walks to the living room, and he sees her busying herself on the laptop once more. "I'm downloading this game," she says. "Have you got a cable to plug in for power anywhere near?"

"What game…?"

"Oh, it's a game about monsters, demons and people fighting in a long war. Seems fun enough," she says, "Now that I can set my own hours of when to work, I've got *more* time for this game. The brother of one of Anna's cousins plays it, and he says it's fun—"

"Hmm, I don't think it's for me," Lucas replies, "but okay, if you want to play it, then go ahead…"

"Aww, I was hoping we could team up for this," Louellen says as she pouts her lips.

"I'll think about it, okay," Lucas says diplomatically.

He turns and goes to the dining room, and retrieves the power cable for Louellen. He walks back into the living room where he plugs it in near when she sits. She plugs it into the back of the laptop. "That's better… and *that* smells good, by the way. How long before we eat?"

"Another ten minutes," Lucas says.

"Okay—oh, and I've booked a ticket for the day after tomorrow to go to London to see dad," she adds a moment later. "A return ticket, in case you wanted to know what type of ticket it is…" Louellen grins at Lucas. He feels happiness wash over him, realising that his fear is unfounded.

I guess I'll feel this way for a while until she's settled in, he thinks while walking back to the kitchen.

Once in the kitchen, Lucas gets a couple of plates ready then he grabs the cutlery, an extra bottle of sparkling water and a half-filled pack of juice, and brings these to the living room where Louellen clears off part of the coffee table to make space. Once she'd finished with clearing the table, she picks the laptop up again, and a moment later is frantically tapping keys on it. Lucas figures out that she's actually playing the game she'd mentioned…

"What sort of things happen in the game?" he asks.

"Oh, so you are interested, then?"

"I'm still thinking about it," he replies.

"Well, it's a game of two groups of people of different races who fight each other for control but I don't think that either side is winning… so far. Anyway, this old dude runs one group, but they got people called night elves, too. I made one of them, a hunter," Louellen explains, "and this undead elf ran the other group according to Anna's cousin. He reckons they're the most fun to play, but I'm enjoying this 'night elf' a lot already. Some of them came from other planet as well. All of them fight monsters, though I've not seen any of them yet."

"Hmm, I guess I can look at it," Lucas says. "But I won't make a promise that I'll play it."

"That's okay," Louellen says. "It's a game you play with many other people. According to Anna's cousin, I can find people in the game to play with… or that's the idea, though I've spent the past several minutes entirely on my own in this forest. Though then someone came and I had this 'mage' help me with killing a few of these beasts here."

"Ah, right, so you've been playing like what—five minutes—and you've already made friends?" Lucas chuckles.

"I didn't say it was a friend. He didn't even say 'Hi' when I said 'hello' to him, and when I had thanked him, he just did something and vanished away," Louellen says. "I guess people aren't that talkative in this game and just play it because there are others also playing this game around them."

"Ah, right, and that's why you want me playing, I guess?"

"I guess so," Louellen says, "but it's up to you. If you decide you don't want to, I can manage on my own."

Lucas walks back to the kitchen to check on the meal. Now, he has a bit of perspective on why Louellen might want to play the game. It will give her a hobby—something she never really had time for while she worked at the gallery. Now she could concentrate on her artwork, work with him on solving this massive mystery they'd uncovered—which seems to involve so many people in so many ways that it almost sounded like he'd entered some sort of parallel world, and is acting out a fictional story.

But as he stands serving out dinner, Lucas reminds himself that now finally he has a life *with* Louellen. They were living together, and the plan was for her to collect more of her clothing and few other things in her massive 'trusty bag,' and then they had a vague plan already that they'd drive into London with a van to collect the rest of her heavier stuff later.

Lucas walks with the two plates of food to the living room, which comprises pieces of chicken that he'd fried first, then had added them to a large saucepan with a bag of frozen vegetables, a can of baked beans, and some pepper and salt. He'd tried a mouthful before he'd carried the food through to the living room to make sure it tasted okay still. As he approaches the coffee table, Louellen places the laptop on the floor. She looks at the food quizzically, then picks up her fork and tastes from the food.

Lucas observes her, feeling somewhat nervous, but then when her face lights up and she smiles broadly he sighs relief.
"This tastes good."
"Thanks," Lucas replies. "I tried to do an okay meal."
"You definitely managed it… to do it, that is…"
Lucas turns the television on, and after channel hopping a bit, he leaves the channel on a science programme that even Louellen pays close attention to - when in the past she would have protested.
"I need to learn *more* of this stuff," she says after a few more mouthfuls.
"Why?"
"Because I need to know as much as possible if I'm going to do this investigating with you… and you need to learn more, too."
"I guess you're right," Lucas replies.

They're both mostly silent while they eat, each concentrating on the programme on the television. Lucas glances occasionally at

Louellen. He sees that, from time to time, Louellen shows an annoyed stare on her face. He guesses that this is because of her not knowing as much as he does about science. If she had questions he'd let her come to him with such questions, let her ask the question in her way, and then he would explain more of it in small portions. He could then explain it in such a way so she could understand…

After dinner, they went out. Louellen had said she wanted to see the specific beach that he'd photographed as a way to convince *her* to come to the village for a visit—saying that she needs to see if for herself if she was going to convince Anna to come visit. "It's easier to convince *her* if she knows what to expect."

They drove to the beach, which Louellen had only seen as a somewhat blurry image. When Lucas got to the hill from where he'd seen the beach for the first time himself, and then stopped, he heard an audible: "Ooooooh wow—" from her, and then is rewarded with an impromptu hug. He kisses Louellen on her lips in response and has a willing recipient.

Soon after, Louellen is eager for them to get to the beach, so she pulls back. "Please, drive on," Louellen says, grinning.

Lucas switches the car engine back on and drives on. About thirty minutes later, he's parking up next to the same bench where he'd been sitting when he'd made the call to Louellen. He's feeling happy when he sees that the ice cream vendor is open, and they go to get an ice cream each, then sit down on the bench.
"It's definitely pretty here," Louellen says between her licking from her massive ice cream in a cone. "I want to come here on a nice sunny day for sunbathing. I'm sure I *can* convince Anna to visit, even it's just for this."
"And *which* room will she use?" Lucas asks, looking purposely innocent when Louellen jerks her head in his direction. But he knows he'd made a good point. With three bedrooms, and the one next to his bedroom, already being turned into a studio for Louellen, there's no place for Anna to sleep in the house.
"But I've been busy with something that I hadn't told you about *yet*," Lucas continues. "I contacted an architect about a month after I'd moved in to build me something."
"Build what?"

"Well, what I had planned to get built was a studio for you. A big one, with two floors, plenty of windows, and plenty of space," Lucas explains as he looks at Louellen to see her reaction. Louellen's smile grows as he keeps describing the building. "I received the paperwork a couple of mornings ago in the mail—they had approved the ideas—" Lucas can't say anything more, because he has Louellen's arms around his neck and her lips on his. He takes hold of her tightly and enjoys the kiss. After about five minutes, they move apart. Louellen looks at Lucas with glazed eyes and a radiant smile.

"You do that for *me*?" she asks. "You were doing it despite me saying 'No' all the time…?"

"That's right," Lucas answers. "I wanted to have something there at the house to make you feel you belong there… It's your house, too."

"I love you so much," Louellen says, now reaching up to wipe away a tear trickling down her cheek.

"I love you, too," Lucas says as he reaches up to her cheek and caresses it in an all too familiar way. Louellen leans against Lucas's shoulder, and Lucas leans his head on her head. He grins. He glances sideways to see a happy, dreamy smile on Louellen's face.

Our life together starts now. I hope we'll be happy here together. I really do…

Unknown to Lucas, a similar thought goes around Louellen's mind in circles over and over. *I'm going to be happy here with Lucas. This is going to be so much fun. Well, maybe not grumpy Mrs Whitwell, but who cares?*

They sit, side by side, until a chill in the wind drives them to the car. After the beach gets absorbed by the onset of the night, Lucas turns on the engine. At a relaxed pace, he drives them back home.

Once they're home, they spend the next thirty minutes first emptying Louellen's large bag, then re-packing it with a few small things to have with her while visiting her father.

After a movie, which neither of them pays much attention to as they're discussing all their plans instead, they go upstairs, and after one final passionate kiss, each departs to their own bedroom to sleep…

* * *

"Dad, are you home?" Louellen calls out while she puts her bag on the bottom of the stairway. She hears her father's voice call out from the back of the house. "I wasn't expecting you here. I'm in my study…" Louellen walks through the long corridor and turns left into the study just in front of the kitchen doorway. She walks to her father, and she hugs him. He gives her a kiss on her forehead.

Louellen sits down on the old sofa next to her father's desk, which is covered with piles of paper.

"Are you here for a visit, or have you come home?"

"Actually—a visit—I think," Louellen says softly, and Peter notes hesitation in her voice immediately.

"You remember what I've said. If you have to decide, do what's best and don't deceive Lucas, or yourself," Peter says in a stern, fatherly voice.

"I haven't and I've only come here to visit. I've found out a lot more while I was in Mellowstone Greene. Some of it vindicates Jeffrey Herbert's efforts."

"That sounds fascinating," Peter says, "and I've been doing my bit of research. Most of this paperwork is from that research."

Louellen leans forward and looks closer at the paperwork. "What is all that?" she asks.

"I had contacted Richard, and between him and me, we've been trying to gather as many of the notes as we could find—both from Jeffrey Herbert *and* John Mutter…"

"Does Anna know about this?"

"She'd suggested for Richard to get in touch with me," Peter says. "She got worried after what you had apparently said to her on the phone, and when—and I'm using her words *here*—you 'had just upped and left' and so she asked her father questions about everything, too. Between Lucas and you, you've turned the lives of *many* people upside down."

"That applies to Mellowstone Greene as well, I guess." Louellen says, grinning broadly, "and that's one thing I had wanted to talk to you about."

"What has happened there?"

"Everything—errr—and it's actually rather fascinating," Louellen replies. "It's almost feels similar to the tip of the iceberg—especially, judging by all *this* paperwork. Is all that the notes from Jeffrey Herbert?"

"Pretty much… At least, it's all the stuff *we* could find."

"There's one *other* person who might find even more."

"Who?"

"Lynn Standage, and she's a librarian who'd come originally from Mellowstone Greene. She also seems to be interested in solving all the mysteries in the village," Louellen explains. "She even said that this *thing* with Priory Mansion isn't the only mystery there, as there's so much unknown about the origins of the family that had owned the house."

Peter leans back in his chair and contemplates over what his daughter had just told him. "Did you find anything that was unusual?" he asks after a few minutes of thinking.

"There's one bit that Lucas is now looking into," Louellen says. "He's in Norwich today. He'd said he was going to find out *who* the sister of Karina's father was. If we can find this information, we can also sort out this other thing with the inheritance."

"What inheritance?"

"Oh, I didn't tell you that part yet… We've found the grandson of the woman who had disappeared," Louellen explains. "I've seen his paperwork. He owns a photo of his grandmother when she was around twelve. The photo has the name 'K. Seaward' handwritten on it with the date 1879, so they took the photo of her a year *before* Karina had passed away. Another, earlier photo, shows her running through the woods near the mansion. Another photo shows Nelly doing the same thing. Karina and Nelly had apparently regarded one another as friends, and there's evidence that Karina even had named Nelly as a sister."

"I've found a similar account of such information in Jeffrey Herbert's writings. According to him, Karina had owned a camera that she'd purchased in Birmingham from the newly established a European branch of 'Scovill,' who was an American camera inventor. She'd owned one of the *first* Scovill cameras to exist. Jeffrey said in his notes that the camera had cost over forty dollars in America and even more here in England, though I'm uncertain the information for the cost is correct without checking… For *that* period of history, even forty dollars was a hell of a lot of money. It's as much as a good digital camera might cost sometimes."

CHAPTER TWENTY-FIVE

Louellen feels fascinated by the information her father conveys to her. She wants to know more. "So, the two photos were done with one of those cameras, then?"

"If you say that you saw *two* photos—one of Karina, and the other of Nelly—it not only means that Karina had the skill to use the camera, but that she also had taught the skill to Nelly."

"That explains something then," Louellen says. "Mitchell Bath—that's the person at Priory Mansion. In fact, Nelly's grandson had said *his* mother had become a prominent photographer at several newspapers in America. He doesn't know which ones, because she'd sold her photos under an assumed 'man's name,' according to his father. Besides inheriting a considerable amount of cash from Karina Seaward—which Nelly got after she'd left Mellowstone Greene—they had listed *her*, and all her descendants, permanently as beneficiaries in the trust that I mentioned. Most of the additional wealth that Mitchell's father had had come from the income that Nelly—or Marybeth, she'd called herself when she went to America—had been left to her family…"

Later, when Mitchell's father had checked through her belongings, he'd found literally tens of thousands of photos that she'd never sold. He sold those photos to museums and newspapers before he'd died and then had stashed the money away for his sister and for the descendants of Nelly.

* * *

Louellen and her father continue their conversation in the living room, and after Peter has sorted out some food and drink for them, he continues with the conversation like there had been no pause. "So, you say that Nelly has *other* descendants, right?"

"Yes, what we thought was a rumour about her leaving a child behind is true, but not the reasons or circumstances that people assume in the village," Louellen continues. "Apparently, her husband had abused her. He had been hitting her often. From what I've been reading, that was rather common back then."

"It was—I guess the people, back then, didn't know differently; and women didn't have any rights like they have got now."

"According to what Mitchell had said, she'd fled from her husband after one such terrible beating. Karina's son John Corey took pity, and had helped her after that," Louellen says softly, then she adds. "The reason for *his* name being different is a long story. In the village, they'd claimed that she'd had an affair with John Corey, but Mitchell had said that Nelly was already pregnant with her second child. She and John Corey had ended up in Bath, where she'd changed her name to Marybeth before they'd left for America… She'd named *her* son as Corey Bath, hence why Mitchell would later be called Mitchell Bath."

"I see… I think Jeffrey had discovered some of this information but then *someone* had wanted to shut him up," Peter states. "You said, last time that we had talked, that Karina was ousted from high society, and think you mentioned her father had a sister."
"Yep." Louellen says hastily before she takes a large mouthful of her juice.
"I've been reading Jeffrey's notes, and I have a theory of my own," Peter says, "and if *that* theory turns out the be correct, then it could also solve the puzzle with the inheritance."

"What theory?"

"You said George Seaward had a sister, but they'd never mentioned *her* by name anywhere, not even in the thorough notes by Jeffrey. But what if her family is behind this whole blocking the execution of the will?"
"You mean to say we're looking at a hundred-and-forty-year-old dispute over a will…?" Louellen shrieks out.
"Yes, you'd mentioned that Karina Seaward became extremely wealthy in her own right," Peter answers. "She bought the mansion from *her* father, but—"
"But?" Louellen echoes.
"But what if the family of *her* father's sister is behind the rumours?

What if they're who started this whole 'bastard child' thing," Peter explains, "They'd have an invested interest in taking over *all* the wealth that Karina had owned, especially if they were as impoverished or even more impoverished than her father and her grandfather had both been…"

"So, they wouldn't want some sort of *trust* to exist to give the mansion, and any potential wealth that still exists, to two people who essentially aren't even family."

"I've found in the paperwork a document from the birth registrations. There may actually be something odd going on. Maybe there's more going on than you even think. Jeffrey was getting too close to it all, and they'd silenced him for it," Peter says, "and if it can happen to *your* great-grandfather, it can happen to me—or to you. So, be careful while you investigate all this, okay?"

"I will—" Louellen swallows hard, realising there was a deeper warning in the words her father had just spoken.

For a while, both are eating silently, then Louellen speaks again. "That birth registration. Could I see it, please…?" she asks.

"Certainly… I've put it in the safe for safekeeping. I'll go get it—" Peter gets up, and he walks hastily to his study. Louellen hears the distinct sound of the safe being opened, then being shut again. A moment later, her father is back in the room, and sits down before he hands Louellen a delicate piece of paper. She looks down at it, then looks up at her father with a puzzled expression.

"This is Nelly's birth record…?"

"It is," Peter says.

"But *why* does it list Karina as the mother?" Louellen asks.

"You're the investigator. YOU will need to work it out." Peter winks at his daughter when he sees her puzzled expression become even more puzzled.

"Ermm, does *this* mean that John Corey is, in fact, Nelly's younger brother?" she asks.

"I think it means that," Peter replies, "and look at the facts that you know about. In the information you've told me so far, you've stated that Nelly was living as Marybeth in America. *She* was Corey Bath's mother. He's the son of that abusive husband she'd left behind. John Corey went with her, and he'd adopted Corey Bath as a son. But—"

Another wink from Peter towards his daughter for good measure to tease her now.

"God dammit, Dad, you and your but-but-but…"

Louellen punches her father's upper arm in annoyance.

"But—never did *you* mention any marriage for them," Peter explains, "As sister and brother, they couldn't do such a thing… They had been living together as parents for Corey Bath. He'd probably thought that they were married, but there's no evidence for it."

Louellen stares at her father, who rubs his arm where his daughter had just punched him. Much harder than he'd expected, which told him she got frustrated with what he was saying.

"You mean to say that *both* Nelly Sibbett and John Corey are Karina Seaward's illegitimate children?" she asks.

"It's Jeffrey Herbert who'd suggested it."

"Sooo—if they're brother and sister, then it means that *any* children of Nelly were all legitimate heirs to the mansion."

"Yes, and it was highly likely that the sister of Karina's father knew this, and because she'd been dealt such a bad blow of bad luck by being married off below her status, she'd probably fostered a jealousy which she'd probably conveyed to her child. They would have done the *same* to the next generation. According to Jeffrey, the sister had supposedly an only child," Peter explains, "and at almost two decades older than George Seaward, the child was in the same age group as Karina. Whereas Karina went from an almost a poverty-stricken life as the daughter of an impoverished lord, the child of the sister had lived in a perpetual impoverished environment. Jeffrey mentioned there was a grandchild too, but beyond that, the trail goes cold as Jeffrey had died at the start of the Great War."

"So, there could be a great-grandchild of the sister living in the village right now who—" Louellen says, but she pauses abruptly then she adds, "and—errr—I think the list of names that Lucas and I had created to short-list possible culprits of being behind the refusal to accept the trust *could* also include the name of whoever is the great-grandchild."

"That means you *both* need to be even more careful. Remember when I had said earlier that Jeffrey Herbert's life ended in mysterious circumstances—if you get what I mean?"

Louellen nods, then swallows hard again. A part of her mind doesn't want to accept the meaning of her father's words. The situation was just growing to a massive case of 'whodunits' and 'mysteries' and a 'hidden family history,' and then, as the cherry on top, there seemed to be someone out there out for revenge for whatever 'bad luck' that happened to *their* ancestor, who had turned out to be the sister of Karina Seaward's father…

Louellen feels nervous now, especially as she was visiting to tell her father that she wants to live with Lucas for the foreseeable future. She glances at her father, wondering if he knows that this is the reason she'd come for a visit. She remembers how he'd reacted when she'd suggested she was, in fact, staying with Lucas longer. Life seems different now…

She needs to find the *right* time to tell her father what she plans to do. When she'd told Lucas she had said it still had been possible certainty but also a maybe… But despite her father's warning now, she felt certain even more than before. She doesn't notice that her father quietly is observing her and is drawing conclusions from it. He knows his daughter well enough to know that she doesn't do things for no reason. He concludes her visit has a reason…

"Louellen?"

She looks up at him.
"I can tell that something is on your mind."
"There is, dad, it is—errr—" she says.

"Take your time."

Deep down, Peter knows already what she's here for.
"I'm actually—errr—I want… Dad, I love Lucas," Louellen finally blurts out.
"I know—I've known that the two of you *love* each other ever since you brought him home for the first time."
"How?" Louellen shrieks.
"Well—unlike *you* might want to believe I had a relationship, once, with your mother. She and I fell in love, we married, we had a daughter."
"I get your point," Louellen says softly, "but I don't feel ready for kids."
"I was thirty when you were born, and remember that your

mother was twenty-seven when she got pregnant with you. You have a few years to enjoy before settling down for kids if you want them eventually—and it's a joint decision. You'd need to find out if Lucas would want kids."

"Yes, I know," Louellen says softly, looking down at her hands in her lap.

"I think you two should just take things slow, and just take it a day at a time."

"I think *we* will."

They're both pensive for a time, each absorbed by their own thoughts.

"When are you planning to do these plans…?" Peter asks after a time.

"I've already partially moved there. I might as well pack up my old camping bag with as much as I can carry and come back later for my furniture and larger stuff."

"I can help you pack," Peter suggests.

"Errr—no—I need to do this on my own. And more for myself."

"Okay—If you want help, just ask."

"I will."

Dinner that evening feels more subdued. They talk about everything other than the impending departure.

"You need to visit Anna tomorrow," Peter suggests.

"I don't think I can tell her I'm leaving."

"You must tell her, eventually."

"I know," Louellen replies, whispering.

* * *

Louellen and Anna had been friends since childhood, and she was also a friend of Lucas. Louellen had reacted with shock when Lucas had just upped and left to go live in Mellowstone Greene.

"I hope you don't plan on following him there," Anna had said.

Louellen had made a claim at the time that living in a village would be *too* boring. But now that's different. When she went to stay with Lucas, she found a vibrant village, filled with almost five hundred people. There had been several festivals and get-togethers in the two months since arriving there, and many people living in Mellowstone

Greene were older—either retired already or close to retirement age—but there were also younger people living there.

One among the residents of the village had become a friend of hers—Leigh Governor—and even *more* after finding out some woman's background…

"I'll visit Anna tomorrow," Louellen says softly, hoping now that the visit will go smooth.

* * *

"Lou—I wasn't expecting you," Anna shrieks loudly when she sees who's standing on her doorstep so unexpectedly, "and there I thought that you'd forgotten all about me…"
"Of course not."
"How's things with Lucas?" Anna asks.
"Lucas is doing well."
"I don't mean it *that* way," Anna counters sarcastically. "I mean, between you and him?" Anna doesn't need any confirmation when Louellen blushes. "Ahh, right…" she says.
"What you mean by that?"
"I guess *you* still blush every time that someone asks you how the two of you are doing…."
"Shut up!"

Anna grins broadly at teasing her friend. She knows Louellen wasn't furious in reality. But she wanted to have a bit more fun in teasing her friend. "So then—when's the wedding?" she asks.
To that question, she gets a punch on her upper arm, but she notices that Louellen now is staring back at her somewhat looking despondent. "What's wrong, Lou…?" she asks. "I didn't mean to tease you—Did you break up with him or something?"
Louellen shakes her head and looks down.
"Lou…?" Anna says softly, "What's wrong?"
"Can we go inside…? I'm cold."
"Of course," Anna says, and she side-steps to let Louellen pass by her into the house. She closes the door and looks over her shoulder at her friend with concern all over her face. Louellen walks to the tiny living room adjoining the hallway without even taking her coat off, and drops onto the over-sized sofa there and then she slumps back,

exhaling loudly and not noticing that she did this. She looks up at her friend when Anna sits down opposite of her.

"I have something to tell you…"

"What…?" Anna asks, and now visibly looks worried. "Is something wrong with your dad?"

"No, he's fine—It's me." Although Louellen normally easily can talk with her friend of so many years, today she's struggling with what to say. In one of their last conversations, before she went to visit Lucas in Mellowstone Greene, Anna had asserted that the village he's living in was a useless pile of crap: that's how she'd stated it. Louellen, who saw her friendship with Anna as valuable as her long relationship with Lucas, had struggled to defend *his* choice and *her* opinion. It got in the way now when she was trying to tell her friend of her decision to move in with Lucas.

"I'm going to live with him," Louellen blurts out.

"What?" Anna shrieks.

"I am—really," Louellen says defensively.

"Is that why you're here?"

"Kind of—" Louellen says, "I'm going in a day or so."

"Aww—I'm going to miss you."

"It's not like I'm moving to another country of stuff like that," Louellen says, "I'll live a train trip away. You'd just travel to Norwich and tell me you're there. Lucas can drive me to the station to come and pick you up there."

"And be surrounded by all that boring countryside—No thank you."

Anna chuckles when she sees Louellen's disappointed face.

"Of course, I'll come visit you, but *only* as long as you promise to come see *me* once in a while," Anna declares.

"I will—"

"So—are you going to have your own room there, or—?" Anna asks hesitantly.

"I said to Lucas that I wanted to take it slow—"

"How did he react?"

"He seems okay with it…"

"I know he has liked you since school but really, Lou, you *need* to commit actually proper at some point…!" Anna can't help but laugh loudly when she sees Louellen blush crimson. "Admit it," Anna continues. "YOU love him." Louellen looks down, biting her lip, and for a while says nothing. She looks up at Anna, and admits: "Yes, I love him.”

“So, what about your job here…?”

“Errr—I quit—”

“When?” Anna shrieks.

“A month ago—because—errr,” Louellen stutters.

“Because of what?” Anna asks. “Lou, don’t tell me you’re pregnant.”

“Of course not.”

“What then?” Anna asks.

“Lucas has discovered something rather interesting about an old mansion in the village. It’s over two hundred years old,” Louellen explains, “and about a hundred and fifty years ago a girl went missing there.”

“Someone killed her?”

“No, she ran off to America with—errr—someone,” Louellen answers.

“Oh, really? And there I thought *that* sort of thing happened only nowadays—tell me more.”

“Well, Lucas was who’d discovered it first, and remember when you’d told my dad about what I’d said to *you*?”

“Yeah, I was so worried then.”

“It’s a lot more complex. It not only involves *your* great-granddad and mine but also it seems there was perhaps someone else involved, too—ooh, you don’t know…” Louellen explains, “but Lucas and I have met an individual when we went *back* to Priory Mansion for another visit. He’s the great-grandson of the woman who’d gone to America and he—errr—”

“Are you saying there’s a spy involved, and this is some sort of James Bond thing?” Anna asks.

“No silly—Okay, let me explain again. There was a woman called Karina Seaward. She was the daughter of the lord there… He was Lord George Seaward. Is seems she had two children, and until recently Lucas and I didn’t know about the second child. But her father had a sister—and that’s the other person involved.”

“Oh, right—”

“Okay, not exactly that, but we’ve found information which shows us *she* had a child but only just as World War Two had started, and then the rest of the family line goes missing. However, the man who’d we met—someone called Mitchell Bath—thinks it may be this person who was descended from the sister of Lord George Seaward, who might block him, his half-sister and a niece of his, who also lives in the village, from claiming the inheritance. Karina Seaward had left the house to them in a sort of trust. If they can sort this out, he wants to turn the building into a fancy hotel with beautiful gardens—I hope he succeeds and if he does, you and I are going to have a girlie weekend there."

"I'm always up for a girlie weekend, you know that," Anna says, "and I didn't realise you were interested in detective stuff."

"I guess Lucas got me interested when he told me about the newspaper clippings."

"To be honest, I'm also interested because of them," Anna says. "It involves my great-grandfather, and by the way, I've discovered he died broke. I want to clear his name because he got a lot of criticism over the scandal. I think it broke him, but I think he did what he did because *he* was friends with your great-grandfather, and that meant more."

"I guess loyal friendships run in our blood," Louellen suggests, "because you and I are loyal friends."

"That's true."

"We're going to *help* Mitchell Bath with his whole situation. We've discovered that the rumours spread in the village are partially true though, because he's from America and he's a businessperson," Louellen continues. "He'd inherited his wealth from Karina Seaward but only because, in reality, she had *two* illegitimate children, not just one, like people assume. But Lucas thinks that whoever is behind the rumours, and the refusal to accept the ruling of the High Court, is linked to the sister of Karina Seaward's father."

"Did your great-grandfather, and mine too, find out and know about it?"

"I think so… Dad thinks so too now."

"Isn't it dangerous to get involved with it, then?"

"We're already involved because of our great-grandparents. We both would still think of *them* as some sort of losers now if Lucas hadn't found those newspaper clippings."

"Does he know who had owned the house before him?" Anna asks..

"Apparently, it had stood empty for two decades," Louellen replies. "They had the owner listed as 'Elizabeth Michaels'—and from what Gylda has told me is that she was the older sister of Dorrie Michaels, who's *her* grandmother. Elizabeth Michaels never married, and she'd left the house to Gylda, who had sold it to a business that deals in property management. They're who then put it up for sale, and it was their advert that Lucas had responded to."

"It sounds like Dorrie is quite old."

"She is…" Louellen says. "She's in a retirement home. Gylda had then placed an advert about her dog in the newsagent's window, which Lucas saw, and that's essentially how they met."

* * *

They pause their conversation when the doorbell rings, and someone had arrived to deliver a box for Anna, who showed off her new purchases to Louellen, which comprised a few pieces of clothing and items for the house. But then she sat down, putting a can of cola down in front of Louellen, and opened her own can before asking her next question…

"Who there knows about all this?" Anna asks.

"If you mean about *who* has direct knowledge, only Mitchell, Gylda, Leigh, Lucas and I—"

"And have the rumours stopped since then…?"

"Actually, no—because before I had come to London, I went to see Leigh. She said she'd received a call from the solicitors managing the trust who told her they'd received something that they perceived as a threat."

"A threat?" Anna asks sharply.

"It was in a letter. They thought the sender had sent it from Nottingham, based on the postmark," Louellen replies. "They've sent it off for fingerprints and other analysis to Scotland Yard, apparently. That's what Leigh had told me."

"Sounds serious… Be really careful, Lou, because maybe someone doesn't want the *truth* be known," Anna says softly. "Maybe it's a past that, in reality, should better stay buried and undiscovered—"

"I know what you're saying," Louellen responds, "but I *want* to clear great-grandfather's name in all this. He died for nothing. Someone had it in for him when he was alive. I think they could have murdered him, but that's just my theory, and neither Dad nor Lucas shares *that* theory."

CHAPTER TWENTY-SIX

"WELL, I DO BECAUSE OF how he'd died so soon after he wrote all those articles," Anna interjects. "My great-grandfather didn't simply go out of business because of the Great Depression—and it happened in the 1920s. Someone used the way the economy was back then, in a deliberate way, so to put him out of business. What I've discovered is that, in the 1850s, the newspaper was employing over thirty thousand people at the time his grandfather had been running it. It went down to ten thousand but, according to the papers I've found since all this investigation began, that was mostly because they'd started using mechanised printers more and more. That was at around the turn of the century. It looks *odd* to me that a company can go from 'ten thousand' employed to just 'five hundred' in just one decade, and that had happened between 1905 and 1910, so no can even blame the Great War for it. The company had shut down seven years later with my great-grandfather broke, his reputation in ruins and his best friend dead."

Louellen stares at Anna. Some information her friend had just conveyed was new to her, but she was even more worried about how desperate her friend sounded. And she's crying uncontrollably too…

Louellen gets up, and she sits down next to Anna and puts her arms around her shoulders. "We'll figure out what's going on," Louellen says softly. "I'll make sure of it." Louellen pulls away from Anna, and stares at intently at her. "Dad said it was *also* the government who may have been involved," she says. "According to what he has found, since you'd told him about this, is that Lord George Seaward—that was Karina Seaward's father—was a liability… because of the illegitimate pregnancies of *his* daughter. The Prime Minister in the 1850s distanced himself from him because of this scandal when he became aware of it. That's when Lord George Seaward began calling the children of Karina 'her bastard children.' It was a bad thing to be a woman and become pregnant without being married, back then."

"What happened to the children?" Anna asks softly, still sobbing a bit from her own upset.

"Mitchell Bath is actually the interesting part in the answer to your question," Louellen answers. "You know the case about the girl who'd gone missing, which was what my great-grandfather had investigated?"

Anna nods.

"It turns out she didn't disappear because of being murdered, or anything like it. She'd disappeared because she ran away from an abusive husband," Louellen says. "In part, Jeffrey Herbert had got the story right. But *not* the part of why, and what had happened to her next. It was her abusive husband who'd started the rumour of her having an affair with Karina Seaward's son. That's John Corey, but—"

"But?" Anna asks.

"But he was the *other* illegitimate child of Karina."

"Other?" Anna asked, "In what way…?"

"The other child was the girl who'd disappeared. She was *his* older sister. He'd helped her escape from her abusive husband."

"So, that means that the child she'd left is Karina's grandchild…?" Anna asks hesitantly.

"Yes, and when she left, she was already pregnant with Corey Bath, who was Mitchell Bath's father."

"Pregnant by who?" Anna asks.

"The father was apparently the abusive husband."

"So, she left, and where did she go?" Anna asks.

"She took on a new name—Marybeth—and John Corey had agreed to pose as her husband. They'd migrated to America at around the turn of the century, and had never come back here. Karina Seaward knew who they really were, and she took the secret to her grave, but while she was alive she'd made provisions for them, and for any descendants, and she'd included also the child that got left behind," Louellen explains. "According to Mitchell, it was the abusive husband who'd refused to let Nelly Sibbett take the child with her. On the day that the gardener saw her running, he'd beaten her up so hard that, when she'd finally arrived in London, she'd ended up in hospital for more than a year. Her baby was born there. It was John Corey who'd visited her, who'd paid her bills, who'd claimed he was the child's father, and had stopped her from going into a workhouse. So, the part of the story of her running off and ending up in a workhouse, and dying there, wasn't true. Her abusive husband had started this story…"

"It all sounds so fascinating…"

"The name 'Bath' was because she and John Corey had ended up *there* for a while before they went to America," Louellen continues, "and Karina had always helped them financially, but she couldn't do anything about Nelly's other child because of the husband. He'd remarried, and if she'd helped the other child, he would have discovered that Nelly was still alive. So, she'd made provisions to make sure that any offspring of the child got helped instead. Corey Bath had his own children, and he was only told the truth after Nelly had died, so he couldn't become angry at her."

"So, if I understand correctly, Mitchell Bath is *here* to make sure the original will of Karina Seaward gets honoured, right?"

"Yes, that's right. Lucas and I are going to help Mitchell with it."

"Okay then, if that's the case—well, you've mentioned a sister of Karina's father earlier. Where does *she* fit in all this?" Anna asks hesitantly.

"Her father had married her off below her status. Mitchell had theorised that it might be one of *her* descendants, who is maybe blocking the execution of the will, because he or she got spoon-fed generation after generation to hate Karina and her bastard children who all 'had it so well.' Karina was an excellent businesswoman while she was alive. She'd actually accumulated so much wealth throughout her life that it makes Lucas, with his windfall, look like a pauper," Louellen explains. "It's my great-grandfather who'd also discovered this, and he'd written to Corey Bath to warn *him* about what was going on here in England. That's the real reason someone had shut him up. He got too close to whatever someone was doing to steal all the rightful inheritance that's being managed by the trust, which is supposed to go to Nelly and John's descendants."

"And no one knows *who* maybe's still doing this stuff, like spreading the rumours even now, and blocking the will?" Anna asks, frowning with an expression of disgust on her face.

"No," Louellen says, "and Mitchell had stated that whoever it is would be in their late fifties or early sixties. Lucas and I have done a partial list of culprits, but we're a long way from finding out who to cross off the list."

"And that's people in the right age group?"

"Yes, though to be honest, I have my theory of who it could be," Louellen says, "but until I know more, I'd rather keep the theory to myself."

* * *

Louellen and Anna walk into a nearby pizza takeaway that had been used by them before, always previously visited whenever they'd had their 'girlie nights' in the past. Tonight the reason is to have *one* final full-blown girlie night to say farewell to Louellen, though both knows that either individual could simply hop on a train and visit the other person easily, and that it would only take a few hours for such a journey…

"Hey, Lou—Haven't seen you around for a while," a man calls out from behind the counter.

"Hey there, Stew, how's things?" Louellen responds.

"Louellen is moving to live with Lucas," Anna blurts out.

Stew, the owner of the pizza takeaway, looks somewhat surprised at the two women at hearing the news.

"About time…!" he calls out, then he laughs on seeing Louellen blush visibly.

God dammit, Louellen thinks, w*hen will I stop going red every time someone mentions Lucas and me…*

Anna nudges Louellen. "What pizza do you want?" she asks. "My treat—and make it a large pan pizza."

"Errr—let me see," Louellen says, though she's still distracted somewhat by the embarrassment she had felt moments earlier.

"Actually, if *this* is for saying goodbye to Lou, then consider it my treat," Stew says. "Any pizza you want, and it's 'on the house,' as they would say in the posh bars."

Anna's face lights up, and her gaze goes from Louellen towards the list of the more expensive pan pizzas on offer, and back again. It's clear to both Louellen and Stew that she's after the pizza called 'Full House Deluxe' that normally would be considered too expensive by her friend, but that she hopes that with Stew's offer, Louellen would select it. Louellen sees her friend's glances, and chances her luck.

"What about *that* one?" she asks, pointing at the Full House

Deluxe option. Stew glances towards where she points, and Louellen's eyes fly open in surprise when he simply says. "Sure—be right back."

Louellen and Anna gape amazed at one another for a moment, then burst out in a girlish giggle. "So, I guess it's going to be a feast tonight," Anna says, then giggles more.

"I hope he won't regret it," Louellen says softly, while she glances over the counter towards where the kitchen area of the takeaway is located. "I can see him grumbling over there."

Anna looks too. She nods.

"I guess he's just annoyed that he needs to make *that* pizza, and then just give it to us," she says.

"Remember when we came here the first time?" Louellen whispers back.

"You mean that day when it hailed so hard?" Anna asks. "Yeah, I remember."

"I guess *we* really teased him that day," Louellen whispers back. "He'd only just started this place, and he'd got a right bollocking from the franchise manager, who was inspecting the store on that day."

"I can't believe we've visited here that long," Anna says, then she smiles wistfully.

"Whenever I visit you in the future, we should always come here for a pizza," Louellen suggests, "and yes, I'll select the Full House Deluxe every time, okay?"

"Good—and make sure you find somewhere decent near Mellowstone Greene where we can do the *same* whenever I visit you there, okay…?"

"I can ask Lucas," Louellen said. "He's a lot more familiar already with the region than I am. It isn't like I've gone anywhere else other than hanging out at his house so far. For the most part…"

"How far is it from the beach?"

"According to Lucas, not that far," Louellen replies. "He has already suggested for him and me to go to the beach this summer."

"Okay then, if you're going then I'll travel there to *go* too," Anna quips, "but I have to make sure I can go as I have to give like two months' notice for any holiday at my job."

"Try to organise something for the end of July or beginning of August," Louellen suggests. "There's a huge beach festival on from mid-July to mid-August, and according to Leigh and Gylda *they* go there every year because it's so much fun."

"It seems to me they're friends…"

"Yes, they *are*, and you'd like them too. They're really nice…"

Anna smiles.

"Here's your pizza," Stew says, "and in this bag are two colas, a mud cake pie, and a pot of ice cream… and in this bag I've put a bag of chips and a pack of fried shrimps. All… on the house."

When he sees the shock on both Anna's and Louellen's faces, he laughs loudly. "I guess that's payback for when you'd tricked *me* when I first opened the store—and don't expect *this* sort of feast in the future. This is a one-off deal. Only available for today and for celebrating you finally making a correct decision about Lucas…" He winks mischievously at the two young women, who scramble to grab their feast and rush quickly from the store.

Each individual curses under their breath when they can *still* hear Stew laugh loudly as they're pacing quickly along the street back toward Anna's house.

* * *

Louellen and Anna sit opposite each other with the feast between them, and for a while each individual is indecisive about what item among the choices in the meal to start with. Anna pours them each a glass of cola after she hastily retrieves two glasses from the kitchen. They each pick up a large triangle of hot pizza and bite off a piece before they put them down. They don't bother with cutlery or any plates for this feast.

"Besides this sleuthing, are you planning to do *other* stuff, work and such?" Anna asks.

"I suggested doing something with my art skills."

"And how did Lucas react to that…?" Anna asks plainly, knowing from Louellen how he'd reacted years earlier when she'd suggested studying art.

"Actually—he was rather enthusiastic. He has been talking about renovating the cottage—making it bigger and such—and he said he's going to build *me* a proper studio to work in."

"Be careful," Anna says. "His idea of a studio could easily be a room one third the size of my kitchen."

Anna laughs loudly.

"No, no, no… I've seen the plans already. He'd had some drawn up but went back to the architect who was doing them, and asked him to *add* to it," Louellen says defensively. "He had the space on the plot already planned but apparently had said to the architect that it wasn't big enough. It's clearly marked as 'Lou's Studio' on the plans—"

"How big is it, then?" Anna asks.

"You remember the loft at dad's house?"

"Yeah."

"It's bigger than that."

Anna's eyes fly open. She sits gaping at her friend for a moment, silent for several minutes and then glancing around her small living room to get sense of how big it would be compared to her rather small flat.

"That—big?" she asks finally. "Take photos when it's built. I want to see it for myself that it's true."

"Lucas has said that the building work would start in August, after we've come back from going to the festival. The company he's using can build the whole extension in under three months. By mid-October I'll have a studio that I can use… I'll have a website sorted by then, too."

"A website?" Anna asks. "Who's doing that for you?"

"I am," Louellen replies, "and I'm learning how—"

"Good luck. I've never figured it out ever," Anna says. "You can do mine when you've sorted yours."

"Yours?" Louellen asks while reaching for her third large triangle of pizza.

"Yes, I want to have one for my business."

"How's it going?" Louellen asks.

"It's growing… I have a booth at an upcoming dog show…."

Then Anna explains extensively for the next ten minutes that having a website would make things easier, concluding the explanation with, "I want a website where I can sell my products."

"I'm not that good at doing websites."

"Oh, I'm not after that for the website," Anna counters. "I want a few pages with dog photos and information about my business done…"

"I could try to do that."

"Do your website first," Anna says. "Mine can wait until after the dog show."

"When is the dog show?"

"At the end of November," Anna said. "Why do you ask?"

"Are people allowed to bring dogs with them to it?"

"Errr—I'd need to check. Be right back… I got the brochure upstairs." Anna walks off, and while she's gone Louellen quickly eats a few more of the fried shrimps—smiling knowingly at the realisation that Anna would get annoyed once she realises her friend has had more of the shrimps than she did. Only moments later, Anna walks back into the room with a small brochure in her hand. She sits down and leaves through it, then she reads through the content on a specific page. "Yes, visitors can bring one dog—and why do you ask…?"

"Because Lucas has adopted a dog who is called Tucker," Louellen answers, "and I'm sure that Lucas would *go* if he knew the dog can go, too."
Louellen grins.
"You had mentioned the dog before…"
"Yes, that's the dog that he adopted from Dorrie—that's Gylda's grandmother."
"I'd love to *meet* the dog," Anna says. "You know how I feel about dogs."
"I do," Louellen says. "That's why I asked about that show."
"And you're certain that you can persuade Lucas to *go?*" Anna asks. "Every other time, for as long as I've been attending the show, each time you'd asked him to come he would have said 'No'—"
"I think owning Tucker has changed him," Louellen says. "He really adores the dog… and I him, too."

*** *

Anna grins at a sudden memory of when they were younger that the comment conjures up of Louellen always playing with her dog whenever she'd come to her childhood home. It was Louellen who'd encouraged her to pursue a career involving the care of dogs…

The thousand quid that she'd borrowed from her friend had helped Anna buy her *first* professional grooming kit. Slowly, between the age of sixteen years old and just *one* year ago, she'd expanded from going on foot to people's houses; from doing the grooming of people's dogs on top of a piece of plastic that she'd lay down on the ground in front of her house initially, to being able to rent a small shop she was using these days. Now business was really picking up, and *one* reason for going to the dog show is to see if she could persuade a few boys and girls who might attend there to help her as volunteers, to come train to end up as staff and then work in her new larger store that she'd just opened four months earlier…

Anna still feels grateful for Louellen's generosity for lending the money that had made it all possible…

* * *

They both look at one another when the doorbell rings. "Who could that be?" Anna asks.

"You're not expecting anyone?"

"No," Anna replies, then she gets up and walks to the front door.

"Kayla!" Anna shrieks when she sees the new guest. Louellen looks up in surprise, but smiles broadly when she hears the name.

"Hey, Lou," Kayla says as she enters the living room, "Your Dad called *me* saying that you're leaving to live with Lucas, and had said that I'd find you here. I can't stay too long because Thomas is working a night shift later, and that means I need to be home *before* he goes, so the baby isn't alone."

Louellen gets up, and she hugs Kayla, then she sits back down, and Kayla sits down beside her, asking, "Can I have some of that pizza?" She nods at the half-eaten pizza.

"Sure."

Anna and Louellen glance at each other, and both giggle when they realise they'd answered Kayla's question at the same time.

"Who paid for this?" Kayla asks, looking at them both.

"We didn't," Anna says, grinning broadly. "Stew gave it 'on the house' for reasons only he understands…"

"How the hell did you persuade him to give you this pizza?" Kayla asks.

"He had offered," Anna answers. "Lou was so obliging to ask for *this* as her choice."

Kayla stares at Louellen for a moment. "I guess she *can* be persuasive when she wants to—" Kayla receives a punch in the upper arm from Louellen in return. "Ouch—Watch it." Kayla squeals.

"Or what?" Louellen says, smiling—and using a teasing voice.

"Or I'll smear *that* mud cake pie all over your face," Kayla answers, grinning.

Suddenly, they all are laughing. It feels then for all of them like they're suddenly a half decade younger, and that this was their *first* girlie night organised in the summer after their exams had been over.

"How's your dad coping with you leaving?" Kayla asks. "He sounded sad to me."

"He doesn't like it but says I *have* to live my own life," Louellen says softly.

"She should get married to Lucas—and then you and me can be *her* bridesmaids," Anna says bluntly.

"I already said that it's *too* early for that, Anna," Louellen protests.

"I don't think so," Anna says. "You two have been together since—like you *both* were fourteen or something like that…"

"Yep, I remember I was talking to Lou—Lucas was sitting next to her," Kayla says, "and then that *bitch* Emlyn, and her sister, and you, had then turned up. Emlyn tried to make you choose between your best friend and her. She didn't like it when you were more loyal to Lou—"

"I heard she and Sylv don't get on much now either," Anna says. "Something about Em trying to steal Sylv's boyfriend… but I can't remember now how many boyfriends she's had by now…"

"I didn't know about that," Kayla says.

"Yeah, and apparently Sylv got so angry that she moved away," Anna says, "and then told everyone she doesn't want *them* to know where she lives now—"

"Errr—Anna—Do you realise something there…?" Louellen says pensively after she has listened to the explanations.

"Realise what?" Anna asks.

"How similar the story of Sylv is to that of Nelly Sibbett really," Louellen says.

"I guess so, except in Sylv's case she ran *off* to get away from her horrid sister who seems bossy as hell…" Anna says softly, "and she's still trying to make everyone else's lives miserable…"

"I wonder where *she* is," Louellen says. "Maybe I could find her, and at least make amends with her."

"Why?" Anna shrieks.

"Because, if this story about Nelly Sibbett and John Corey and their mother, and all that other stuff teaches me something, is *not* to keep holding grudges against people who wrong you," Louellen says. "Lucas said something the other day. That now makes me realise how right *he* is. I had mentioned about Emlyn while we were still at school by accident. I was almost expecting him to go into a rage about it, and that he'd tell me he was still hating her for bullying him so much. Instead, he'd said that he felt sorry for her, and that she'd lost out on having another good friend. I don't want to make this sort of mistake with Sylvia. If she and I can be friends, I'd want that…"

"Sounds fair," Anna says. "It's your choice—"

"You need to do the same, Anna," Louellen says.

"Why?" Anna asks.

"Because of what I had said about *that* sister of Karina's father," Louellen answers. "She'd never forgiven her family, and look at what it had led to."

"Okay, but I make *no* promises," Anna says.

"I do the *same* if possible, but I didn't know her much back then," Kayla says.

They're all in a pensive mood for a while, then Louellen changes the topic. "So, how's Thomas…?" she asks, smiling at her younger niece.

"Oh, I didn't tell you yet… He got a promotion," Kayla says. "It means that he's working an hour *less* per day but getting a bit more money each month."

"Sounds good," Louellen says.

"Trish is growing up fast," Kayla continues.

"I'll come for a visit with you this weekend to see her," Anna says.

"Sure," Kayla says after a few more morsels of the meal, smiling broadly.

CHAPTER TWENTY-SEVEN

KAYLA THINKS FOR A MOMENT then she adds, "—but we're out on Saturday morning, and we're taking Trish to *his* parents for them to spend some time with her, and that's on Sunday for most of the day… You could visit on Saturday in the afternoon."

"I'll be there," Anna comments.

"Talking babies, I wonder *how* the baby that Nelly had to leave behind had ever coped with her loser father after the mother had disappeared, Lou," Anna says, "because I just can't get it out of my mind at how nasty it all sounds… and if I didn't know better, it's almost like it was the plot belonging to some sort of mystery novel…"

"Is this a way for you to tell me to go home to be with *my* baby, Anna?" Kayla interjects defensively.

"Nooo, before you arrived just now we were talking about someone else… about someone called Nelly," Anna explains, "and it's just an intriguing story…"

"Okay, I get it… You were talking about someone called Nelly Sibbett, but are you going to tell me ever *who* she even is…?" Kayla asks bluntly, "and what's this other stuff of you going on about a baby being left behind…? By who and why…?"

***

Early in the morning, Peter holds his daughter tightly for several minutes with them both silently contemplating the impending departure, and each person is feeling the sense of loss it was causing them both. "I hope you'll be happy in Mellowstone Greene with Lucas," Peter says quietly to his daughter. "I think I will, dad," she replies, "and I think I've found a purpose to be there…"

"Remember what I said about your feelings for Lucas," Peter says. "If you cannot feel honest about them, it's no point pretending around him. It will hurt him, and ultimately it will hurt you."

Louellen picks up her very heavy bag and stares again at her father for a few moments. She can feel something like a lump in her throat, and sees her father was fighting similar emotions. It would be the first time that considerable distance of travel was going to separate them; ever since her mother had died, and for a moment Louellen feels indecisive and lost, and part of her doesn't want to leave her father, but she realised it had to be done…

"Lucas and I will come back here with a van to collect all my other belongings."

Peter nods, then he says, "I'm going to miss having you here."

"I'm going to miss you too, but like I said to Lucas, this is just a temporary trial thing," Louellen says, "and I want to be sure of my feelings first."

"I can understand that…" Peter responds, "and if it doesn't work out, remember that my door is always open for you." Louellen smiles at her father when she hears the words. It makes her feel more secure about her decision to move in with Lucas. Peter hugs his daughter tightly, then kisses her on her forehead. Then he pushes her away and looks at her for a few moments.

"Don't leave that taxi waiting for you," he finally says. Louellen nods, turns, and walks to the waiting taxi.

She puts the bag inside on the seat first and pushes it to the other side of the seat. She turns and waves at her father once more, then gets into the taxi and shuts the door.

Louellen leans forward to speak to the taxi driver through the open front window. "Victoria Station, please," she says. A nod from the driver shows he'd heard her. As the taxi sets off, Louellen waves frantically at her father, until the taxi turns a corner and her father is out of sight.

Peter stands in the street for a few more moments, shuffling from place to place rather indecisively on the pavement, then he turns and goes back into his house. Once inside, he sighs and listens to the silence in the house, realising suddenly how empty the house will be without Louellen there…

He knows she has her own life to lead. He glances at a piece of paper that she'd left on the table near the front door.

Perhaps I should go meet this Lynn Standage. According to Louellen, she'd been married twice before, and she'd ended up as a widow in each case. I wonder how old she is. Maybe she'll accept an invitation to go out for a meal. Perhaps…

* * *

Louellen wonders about her father as the taxi speeds through the busy traffic of London. Her reason to go to Victoria Station is two-fold. She first wants to stop at Anna's house to say a temporary goodbye to her friend and to ask her friend one more time to come visit her, then she'd go to the station and take a train directly to Norwich. Louellen looks at her watch. The train she wants to take would be leaving in two hours. She diverts the driver towards Anna's house, and he obliges. After ten minutes, Louellen feels the taxi come to a stop and Louellen realises she's outside Anna's house. She sees Anna standing at her door…

"I'm only going to be a few minutes. Can you wait, please?" Louellen says to the taxi driver.
"The meter will continue running, sweetheart."
"I know that. I won't be long…"
She climbs out of the taxi, and Anna rushes to her when she realises who the taxi has brought to her doorstep. They hug.
"I hope you're making the right decision," Anna says.
"I think I *am*. I love him, and the work we've started doing together is rather interesting."
"Keep in touch. Call me every day."
"I will."
Louellen and Anna look at one another.
"Come visit *me*," Louellen says hastily. "I know that you've said you don't enjoy boring villages, but I'm going to be *there*, and together we could make the place into a party."
"I'll visit you later in the summer when the weather is warm—I promise."

Louellen and Anna hug one more time, then Louellen walks back to the taxi and climbs inside it. For a second time, she waves as the taxi drives off…

* * *

Forty-five minutes later, after an uneventful journey, Louellen stands at the entrance of Victoria Station. She looks up at the massive building and wonders for a moment where she'd find the entrance. There's a stream of people walking through a doorway to the left of her. She walks through the door, and finds herself in a large open space, and can hear the sounds of trains, and the entire building is awash with the sounds of people walking; people talking; people's phones going off; music being played in the small shops in the station. She sees an employee and heads to the man.

"Excuse me, where do I buy tickets…?" she asks.

"Where ya going, luv?" the man asks.

"To Norwich."

"Righto, ya want to go over there? Ya can see where I'm pointing at. Ya see tha shop with tha flag on its roof… Just on the other side is where ya can get ya tickets bought."

"Thanks."

"Pleasant trip."

Louellen walks to where the man had pointed and finds the ticket booth—with a queue in front of it. She sighs, looks at her watch, and decides there's time to wait in the queue. If she's lucky enough, she'd be in Norwich in about three and a half hours…

* * *

Lucas was making a similar determination about the timing as he got the house ready for Louellen's arrival. He'd cleaned up the living room, then the kitchen. He'd mowed the grass, ignoring Mrs Whitwell's disapproving looks at him as he moved through his garden shirtless.

I might as well plant a few trees along that side of the garden during this summer. That way, she won't be able to spy on what I do in or around my house anymore. Maybe even sooner than that… If Louellen comes to live here permanently, maybe I can persuade her to help me with doing it.

He looks around the house, and makes sure it's as tidied up as he can get it before Louellen was going to arrive, and then he could also visit Mr Howey's shop for some food. *Maybe buy a few magazines and a couple of newspapers too, so she got something to read. Well, she can always entertain herself with the computer game that she had found online. I wonder if I should try it out too. But I guess it would mean I need my laptop then…*

Lucas grins at the idea of what sort 'couple' they would seem to everyone around them. *So, we'll be two sleuths solving crimes of hundreds of years ago, and as our hobby in our spare time, we'll be killing demons, orcs and ogres…*

Lucas suddenly finds the idea so funny he can't help but laugh loudly. His laughter catches the attention of the dog, who stands beside him a moment later, wagging his tail, and Lucas bends over to scratch the dog behind his ears. "I don't think there's space in the car when Lou comes home," he said softly, "and I guess you'll need to stay home for once." The dog whimpers as if he understood the words spoken by Lucas. "I won't be long," Lucas says gently to the dog. Tucker wags his tail vigorously in response.

Lucas straightens and looks around again. These days, he kept the house a lot more organised than he'd done while living the bachelor's life in London. He wonders if now he cared more about how he presented himself: he wants to be seen as a *good* neighbour in Mellowstone Greene.

Lucas walks to the seat where his coat was lying and picks it up. He looks over at Louellen's laptop sitting on the table corner.

Maybe I need to just check out the game before I go get her and also order a laptop for myself. That will be a delightful surprise for her. Then perhaps next week when she's settled in, we can have a bit of fun together with that game…

He sits down at the table and pulls the laptop towards him. He opens it and pushes the button to turn it on, then clicks on the button to open a browser, then tries to remember the name of the game Louellen had been playing for a few minutes.

Something—warcraft. Hang on, I can check in the list of programs installed…

Moments later, he sits reading a website, then clicks on a button and watches a video showing a man on some sort of flying ship being attacked by some the demons he'd seen Louellen fight in the game. He frowns for a moment, then he has to smile at his own realisation.

Lucas knows from the many times listening to Louellen cursing loudly that it's probably a more tough game than he realises. He clicks the button where it said he can buy the game and is taken aback for when the website asked him to create an account.

Alright then, I can do that…

After about ten minutes, he has created the account and bought the game. Now he goes to the website where he'd purchased the laptop that Louellen is using. Another fifteen minutes later, and he has a laptop coming by delivery, and has also purchased a printer at the same time as well for making it easier to print things found on the internet.

He smiles and feels satisfied. Lucas turns off the laptop and pushes to the back of the table. He gets up, readjusts his coat, then he goes to the hallway and shuts the door so the only places available for Tucker to run around in would be the hallway, stairs and the landing and a small portion of the kitchen. Lucas opens the front door. Tucker whimpers when he seems to realise there was no lead being put on him.

Lucas points to inside the house. "Lie down," he says firmly.

* * *

For a moment, the dog seems confused, then he lies down on his bed in the hallway, places his head on his front paws, and whimpers loudly again. Lucas shuts the door, then hears the dog whimpering even louder, and he cringes for a moment. He was already imagining hearing sirens and police men arresting him in his mind… because Mrs Whitwell had called them, telling them he was—somehow— doing animal brutality…

Lucas looks at the house to his left, at the windows. They were purposely looking more mysterious right now; even though it was still a bright day, and it would be for a few more hours before evening descended over the village. He smirks toward her house with a purposeful intent to cause additional annoyance to his neighbour, who'd gradually turned from this nice old lady that he'd once equated to Miss Marple to possibly the nastiest female villain that Agatha Christie could have dreamt up in her lifetime.

He walks in a slow, deliberate pace over the path to the gate, then really slowly opens it, so it makes its annoyingly creaking noise that *she* had so fervently complained about a month ago. Then he steps into the street and repeats the action; all the time staring at the next-door house and grinning in an as annoying way as he could make himself do.

Lucas is about to walk to his car when he stops and glances back at the house. *Tucker is coming with me anyway*, he thinks.

So, he repeats the actions in the reverse to make out that he was letting Tucker come with him in the car as a last moment decision. He turns and walks with the dog in tow to his parked car that was parked opposite his house. He decides that Tucker could sit in the front with him. He starts the engine, and then speeds up hard, so he drives off by causing as much loud noise as possible, echoing in the street.

The drive to the station gives Lucas time to reflect on all the things that he'd experienced in the last several months—half of the time with Louellen with him—and Lucas realises that he'd done more and experienced more than possibly the whole of the previous two years while he was at the job still.

That job was so boring—I'm glad we did this stuff together. Just hope we can earn an income from it.

He remembers Louellen had stated that she could do art in her spare time, and she'd said she was going to sell the paintings online on a website. When he'd asked how she'd get a website, she'd suggested they'd both learn how to do it. Though he didn't like the idea of computers much, but because he'd gone and purchased the extra laptop he'd now committed himself to the cause by his actions before leaving the house…

There were some road works, and Lucas sat cursing for twenty minutes, wondering why. Suddenly, the road works were gone, and Lucas had put his foot down to make up for lost time. He drove into

Norwich, and then had parked at the usual spot that he'd usually use and exited the car, checked that the boot was sorted so the bag, that Louellen had planned to bring, would fit in there. He shuts the boot and locks the car.

He turns and almost feels his heart stop when he sees a face that seems familiar. He squints for a moment, then he stares hard at the woman, who seems oblivious of everything around her. Including the car that had come to a hard stop because she'd just crossed the road without looking. Lucas is certain that he's correct in who he just saw across the road. He waits until she's further away, before he walks on towards the station. He stops a moment to consider the woman's presence once more. If he was more sure about certain things, he could have sworn that he'd just seen Sylvia—the younger sister of Louellen's former nemesis, Emlyn—walking away from the station. He stops to watch for a moment more and then he sees the woman get into a car and drive off at a much too fast speed.

What's she doing here, of all places? I have to tell Louellen later if I remember it...

He walks into the station, and sees the familiar cashier at the ticket booth look up and then lean forward, expecting to see Tucker with him. Then she appears deflated when she doesn't see the dog with him.
"I've left him just outside the train station entrance," he says to her, "and I'm here to collect Lou from the station."
"Oh, right," she replies. "Is she here for another visit...?"
"No, she's moving in with me today."
"Nice," comes her genuinely happy-sounding reply, "and maybe let the dog greet her, too. I know that, normally, the rule is for dogs *not* to be on the platform, but I'll make an exception for *you*." Lucas nods and walks back out of the train station, scoops up Tucker in his arms and un-clips the lead. He carries the dog past the station attendant with him and she grins broadly on seeing the dog. She makes cooing sounds as he walks by, causing Tucker to wag wildly. Lucas walks quickly through the second doorway, and looks up at the display.

The train carrying Louellen should arrive soon...

Lucas had felt a momentary wave of anxiety as he'd walked onto the platform to wait for the train that was apparently carrying Louellen. If the doors open of train, and she wasn't there, he'd know then that she'd decided about him, and that he just has to live a life without her…

* * *

Too much had happened in the last three months for either of them to ignore their feelings for one another. He'd blurted out over the phone the previous evening when they spoke before bedtime and before she'd come to Mellowstone Greene, to say that he loved her, and for a while she'd been silent. Lucas had felt scared that she'd just hung up the phone, and that it would be the last he'd ever heard from her.

"We'll see how it goes… I'll move in but as a friend for now," Louellen had finally said softly, "and I'll be a tenant for now…"

He'd agreed to the compromise just to have her with him.

* * *

Lucas feels even more anxious as the train closes in. Tucker seemed to recognise that something important was going on and got up, and instinctively smelled the air for the now-familiar scent of the *other* human he'd grown to appreciate; the newest member of his dog pack. Lucas looks down at the dog for a moment when he'd sensed him getting restless. Suddenly, he feels Tucker's tail flapping hard against his leg just after the train had come to a full stop. He looks up and sees Louellen standing on the platform close to the other end. He lets go of the lead, and immediately Tucker rushes towards her. She kneels down, and grinning widely, she lets the dog lick her chin and hands while she rubs him over his back and chest and tickles behind his ears…

Lucas approaches her slowly to allow her to have enough time to greet the dog as a friend, and he also smiles on seeing the dog's reaction, then Louellen straightens and she looks up at him directly. "Just as friends," she reminds him softly.

"Just as friends," he repeats but then she surprised him a moment later when she rushes to him and lets his arms envelop her. She lets him embrace her for a lengthy time without speaking or moving. They stand a while on the platform as it empties of other people.

The train comes into motion beside them, and moments later, the train station is almost devoid of sound once more. The silence almost feels peaceful to Lucas. He waits for a few minutes then he pushes her from him.

They move apart slowly, and after staring at one another for a moment more Lucas picks up Louellen's heavy bag and then scoops up the dog in his other arm. The walks side by side towards the exit, and Louellen occasionally reaches out to the dog to caress him. A slap of a wagging tale amuses Lucas inwardly…

She brought a heavy bag of belongings with her despite already having many of her clothing at his house. It seemed that she'd packed up everything else she owned to bring with her, or at least what could have managed to carry with her on a journey via taxi, a short time on foot and on the train afterwards. The bag was heavy and Lucas felt the muscles in his arm strain under the weight but purposefully kept silent and walked on.

He also was contemplating in that moment as to *where* to rent a van from as they still also had a trip planned to visit her father's house to collect all the rest of her belongings, which consisted mostly of furniture except for her bed, and her trusty old wardrobe she'd bought from a flea market five years earlier and had restored meticulously. He realises suddenly it was as old as his cottage…

Probably was mostly fluke that she had bought the wardrobe, he thinks as he glances at the woman walking by his side, *but maybe it was karma telling us both for the first time and certainly not the last time that this day might come… Somehow…*

He wonders how Louellen's father is feeling about the situation, because he knows they're very close, always had been close. So decided that he'd let her tell him about her father once she has settled in…

* * *

They walk at an unhurried pace to his car, and Lucas puts the bag on the back seat, then they get in the car with the dog occupying the floor in front of Louellen. She smiles at Lucas when she fastens her seatbelt.

"I guess this is it—" she says resolutely.

"Yep—to *our* home," Lucas says, nodding once. He was going to let Louellen regard it as *home*, even if she wanted to live there just as a friend, as she'd stated.

Louellen places her hand over his for a moment, and she looks at him, smiling. Lucas looks back at her with an equally radiant smile. However, he can see some hesitation, and she acts like she wants to say something, but then she looks away… but her hand stays. He interprets it as hesitation about her feelings for him.

Remembering what he'd read in an article, that had started everything three months earlier, he decides on a new angle with his approach to the current situation. "Louellen, you don't need to tell me right now or any time soon about what you're feeling. I *know* already know how you feel about me," he says softly, "and I love you, and you've known *that* for a long time. But if you need time, I'll wait as long as you need for you to figure out these feelings…" He pauses to weigh up the rest of his words even more careful to make sure he said the right thing…

CHAPTER TWENTY-EIGHT

AFTER LESS THAN A MINUTE, Lucas speaks again. "—and WE can do this together, and if you decide later that your feelings aren't the same as mine are for you then you can either tell me or not, and if you can't, that's okay and I'll accept the answer without protest…"

Louellen looks back at Lucas and he sees that his comment had caused for her eyes to glaze over, like she's about to cry.

"I think I love you *too*," she whispers. "However… let's do all this *first* as friends for a while, okay?"

Lucas nods curtly but he smiles nonetheless, and realises that for the first time since they'd began their relationship eight years earlier that he's okay with them being friends *first*. He speaks further about his feelings after another minute of pausing, and whilst also now struggling against the lump in his throat that had welled up as she'd said her last few words. He wasn't able to say anything for a few more moments then he adds a few crucial words to his comment of moments before, speaking softly, "WE have all the time in the world," he says finally. "Unlike Karina Seaward, who had *her* love thwarted, and unlike Nelly Sibbett, who had found that the man that she had loved first didn't love her back and therefore looked for it in other places… We'll do all this slowly, and I'll be here whenever you decide you're ready…"

Louellen smiles and now feels her heart beating faster. "Maybe we can teach the other people in the village a thing or two about trust and friendship," she says. "About loving especially. About not giving up on another person. About trust… You taught me all that before and I guess I forgot about it for a while, and had to find those feelings again. My dad reminded to remember all of that stuff…"

"Okay, well, maybe not grumpy old Mrs Whitwell."

"Maybe not *her*."

Both of them laugh suddenly without any reservation.

"Anyway, if you move your hand off mine, maybe *we* can actually go home," Lucas says, grinning broadly.

* * *

Realising then what she'd been doing ever since they'd got in the car she glances down quickly then back at Lucas, and grins broadly back at him, then she moves her hand away, but not back to her lap. She reaches up and caresses over his cheek with the back of her hand first before she lowers it slowly to her lap. He smiles at her, then turns to concentrate on turning on the car engine. After that, he concentrates on pulling the car out of the parking spot.

Initially, both are silent while he drives home towards Mellowstone Greene, but then gradually Louellen is asking him questions, mostly it seemed to learn more about the region she'd be living in for the foreseeable future.

"So, when you're doing your food shopping, where do you go for it?" is her first question.

"In the town on the north coast is where I get my shopping which is twenty minutes away by car," he answers. "There's a shop there that actually sells rather decent food, and they also offer deliveries which I've taken advantage of a few times…"

"Are there pubs?" she asks. "Well, besides the pub we had used, that is…"

"Actually, we aren't too far from a nightclub right now," Lucas answers with a slight chuckle as he was reminding her of her assertion of the countryside being a boring a place.

"What? You mean there's a nightclub, right here, in the middle of—" Louellen says, then she stops speaking, and is realising then what she's about to say. She clasps a hand over her mouth to stop herself from uncontrolled giggle.

"—right *here* in the middle of nowhere," Lucas finishes the sentence for her in a mock-teasing tone. When Louellen glances at him, she was expecting for him to look annoyed at her despite the tone in his voice but she's met with a big, mischievous grin. Her initial annoyance evaporates, and moments later she's giggling loudly.

"I guess it's no longer the middle of nowhere," she says. "It's my home now."

"It's *our* home," Lucas says, smiling warmly at her, then he raises his hand and brushes it over her cheek like she'd done earlier whilst they'd sat in the station car park. The gesture makes Louellen grin more and then she says, "You always used to do *that* when we first got together… I didn't know that you remembered that I like it so much…"

"I can do it more if you want it…" Lucas says softly. "Just as much as you need it…"

"I would like that," she whispers.

After a minute of looking at Lucas, she smiles one more time at him, then she turns her head to look at the landscape they're passing by. As she glances out of the window she spots a curious-looking building a few hundred meters from the road that immediately interests her so much that she cranes her neck to keep looking at it as it gets behind them instead, then she turns to Lucas. "That building that we just have passed," she says. "It seems like there was a fire there once…"

"I've never even noticed this building before today, until you just mentioned it to me," he comments after glancing quickly over his shoulder before he continues looking at where to drive. "Want to go look at it…?"

"Maybe another time. I'm so tired from the train journey… I'd like to go home," she says softly she's glancing again out of the window. Lucas had said nothing, but a smile had flashed on his face when he had heard her say the word… 'home.'

It's her home too now, he thinks, and for the first time in many months, a warm feeling of happiness washes over him. He glances at Louellen and grins when he notices she has shut her eyes.

"Lou," he whispers gently, smiling momentarily.

No reply comes.

Lucas pushes his foot down just a small amount so to go a little faster, because a warm bed will be a *better* option than leaning against a cold car window for sleeping. He also feels tired suddenly, then he decides he needs to be careful instead, and decelerates again significantly. The journey home was giving him ample time to think about how things will be from the next day onward. Having Louellen *actually* living with him would mean he had to change how he did certain things, such as when he'd sleep and when to do certain other things…

* * *

An hour later, he sees the outline of a now-familiar building, their home, in the distance. "Lou," he says, then he repeats the name in a louder voice. "Lou—wake up. We're almost home…"

"Huh what?" Louellen mumbles in a sleepy voice, not quite registering where she was for several minutes and glancing around confused.
"We're home," Lucas repeats gently as he turns off the engine.
"We are…?" Louellen asks.
"We are…" he replies, smiling and caressing her over her cheek for a moment. She leans in for a moment then she looks at the white stone building that she'd lived in for the last several months, while also helping Lucas with his research about the old stately house called Priory Mansion. She glances back at Lucas and she smiles warmly at him. "Yes, I'm home," she says softly. "I *feel* home now."

Both of them get out of the car, and they pull her heavy bag from the boot, then walk companionably to the front door. The sound of rushing feet tells Lucas that Tucker is happy to leave the car and is now getting excited about being home with *both* of them…

* * *

Lucas opens the front door, and he pushes it open fully, and a flurry of 'happy dog' that surrounds them in the next moment as the dog enters the house first, then turns and rushes back towards Louellen excitedly. She kneels down and lets Tucker rush at her and lick her face. She rubs the dog all over, and she's grinning broadly at the dog's antics. The dog rushes from person to person, then rushes inside, then runs back out into the garden in his next dash back. It's so he can pull a leg up and pee on the grass, then a moment after gets back to licking Louellen's face…

Normally Lucas gets annoyed about whenever the dog is peeing on the lawn, but today he doesn't any annoyance in the slightest and just grins. He's happy, because he has the woman he loves with him, and they have a happy dog who loves both of them to keep them company.

They both momentarily glance intently toward Mrs Whitwell's house, and a glance a moment later at one another confirms that both are certain that the shadow behind the curtain on the first floor had been the old woman spying on *them*. But today it doesn't matter. They both know from Gylda and from Leigh that there's something *odd* about their neighbour that they'd be able to discover as to why she's in this way with enough of their research. Lucas and Louellen look at each other for a couple of minutes then look back at Mrs Whitwell's house at the same time, then back at each other and grin at one another conspiratorially…

They walk inside, and they have to wait for a moment more with closing the front door when the dog does another pee on the lawn, and then Lucas grimaces when the dog does a 'number two' on the flower bed but it would mean that he doesn't need to go for a walk with the dog that evening.

"I guess that needs cleaning up tomorrow," he mumbles.

"He hates her too," Louellen whispers maliciously. "He did it real close to her favourite flowers. She's going to get the stink of it whenever she gets on with gardening tomorrow…"

Lucas chuckles softly and realises that things that bothered him before do so less with Louellen here now with him. Not even such a thing as the dog soiling the garden…

Not really, Lucas thinks. *I was never bothered about the dog. It was always Mrs Whitwell who annoyed me…*

Once the dog is inside, Lucas shuts the door. "Don't use the switch at the top of the stairs," Lucas states plainly, nodding at the stairs beside them.

"Why not…?"

"Remember 'the repairs' made to fix the switch," he explains. "Well, I guess I need to get another electrician in to look it over, because the one I had used wasn't too good."

"Oh, right—Okay?"

"You want something to eat?" Lucas asks. "Some cola or a cup of tea, perhaps?"

"Yes, something to eat, but not too much, and cola please," Louellen replies.

"I'll sort something out while you settle in—Want me to carry the bag up for you?"

"I can manage," Louellen answers, "but thanks for offering."

Lucas stands for a few minutes watching her walk upstairs. She'd sounded tired to him, but her voice did sound happy at the same time. Happier than it had done for the past few months it seems. He hopes it was true…

* * *

Lucas walks to the kitchen, and he first retrieves a bottle of cola from the fridge and glasses from the cupboard, then he walks into the living room and puts the bottle and glasses on the table. He looks around a moment, and then he realises that the curtains are still open. He shuts them quickly and turns on the light before he walks back to the kitchen.

Once back in the kitchen, he opens the fridge again and looks for something to make as a light meal. He sees the carton of soup that he'd purchased the previous day and opts for heating that up, and serving it in two bowls with a few slices of freshly toasted bread beside it.

I hope Louellen will approve of my choice of meal…

* * *

Louellen arrives at the top of the stairs and she listens for a moment to the sounds of Lucas being busy in the kitchen downstairs. She turns right and walks to the room that she'd be using for a while already. It wasn't the biggest room, but she guesses it would be big enough for all the belongings she planned to bring over from her dad's house the following week.

My room at dad's house is so much smaller than this one…

She stands at the bedroom door for a moment and holds the door handle in her hand as she glances to her left at the window there, which has an unobstructed view of Mrs Whitwell's house. She shrugs off the feeling of 'being watched.' "I should ask Lucas if he mind if I want a blind put up there," she mumbles. "That way she can't see me going to the bathroom every time I need to go…"

The bathroom is behind the door to her left and she glances towards it for a moment, weighing up using it.

Louellen glances for a moment to her right, and for a moment she feels tempted to ignore her *own* assertion that she'd live in the house under the banner of friendship only and nothing more than that. She almost feels tempted to go to what she knows is his room which is at the other end of the long corridor. She shrugs her shoulders to dismiss the idea and walks into 'her room' but she leaves the door open…

Louellen looks around the room as she places her over sized heavy bag down, which she'd hauled up the stairs moments earlier despite being tired and despite really having wanted Lucas to do it for her. She'd finally agreed to the suggestion of moving in with Lucas. But *only* because the history of the village was so intriguing. It's her conversation with Lynn Standage—while she'd visited the library where the woman works—that had convinced her of the choices to make. The room she'd chosen as 'her room' was a compromise. Right now, she'd moved in as a friend, or perhaps even as a tenant of Lucas. She still felt uncertain of her feelings for him, even if she had told him she loves him too…

But if the life he has chosen is anything to go by, I'm in for a few rather interesting few years ahead, she thinks pensively, *and I know that he likely meant it when he had told me in the car that he loves me…*

* * *

"I'm going to call you 'Mr Marple,' from now on, after all the stuff you've done recently." They'd both laughed at the idea of Lucas being some sort of sleuth.

"If *you* think I'm a sleuth, then I guess I best get on with finding a more mysteries in this village to solve," Lucas had said, "and I guess that if I'm Mr Marple, then you're going to be Miss Watson." They'd been laughing even more at that idea.

"So—we're going to operate from this house, in secret, as the 'Marple & Watson Detective Agency' then?" she'd asked.

"We could *do* that… but we 'only' can do it if you move in forever," Lucas had said, and he'd looked at Louellen more seriously, suddenly, or as she'd interpreted it, in a 'pleading' way.

And then she had moved in. By her own choice no less…

They'd set up a business as a detective agency, but quickly had changed the name to 'L&L Investigates,' which had seemed more fitting for them. Louellen had grinned as she'd watched Lucas sign the papers they had to file in Norwich in person, and even more when she thought over what all *her* female friends, in the big city, might think of her new life, both of her actually moving in—finally, at long last—with Lucas, and then to do this detective stuff with him…

* * *

"Lou," Lucas calls up the stairs then he walks back to the kitchen.

"Yes, I'll be there shortly," Louellen calls out then listens to the man's footsteps moving around in the kitchen. She changes her top, brushes her hair, and nips into the bathroom, and quickly splashes water on her face and dries her face off.

A few minutes later, she's downstairs in the kitchen where she finds Lucas reading a newspaper, but judging by the colour, it's quite old though she's uncertain how old really.

"I found this in the cellar just now, and until now I hadn't actually ever used the cellar. Priory Mansion isn't the only mystery that this village hides," he says as she walks into the kitchen glancing up at her. "I think stuff went on that was just the tip of the iceberg…"

"Oh well, when will we get started solving *that* mystery then?"

"It mentions here it's about a village about three miles from here. We passed it just after you mentioned the odd house by the way… This article is about a house which had burned down to a crisp with all seven residents inside it. And no one seems to know why it happened back when it had happened, or why the people in the house didn't leave the house when their lives were endangered by a fire," Lucas explains, pointing at the newspaper.

"Do you think something bad happened, and the fire was to cover it up?" Louellen asks. "Might it *be* the building I saw…?"

"Yes, I think so, and this happened a hundred and twenty years ago. About thirty years after what happened in Priory Mansion."

"Sounds like we're going places," Louellen says, smiling, and in response Louellen places her hand gently over his hand. "I guess I was *wrong*. I'll enjoy living here with you, and it seems we're also investigating another cold case from the information listed here…"

Lucas smiles warmly at Louellen.

"I cannot promise anything about my feelings for *you*, so, for now, we'll do *this* as friends, and perhaps later," Louellen adds quickly. "If you don't mind…"

"Perhaps later," Lucas repeats, while nodding and smiling, but he thinks, *That's better than the never' answer, like it was before—*

They both read the newspaper clip again, then Louellen goes to get her newly-bought laptop, and they search for more information about the village listed in the article. They find a page on the internet listing the village as 'having 211 people' living in it in 1995.'

"Tomorrow we'll drive there for a visit," Lucas had suggested. "If you want to…"

Louellen had nodded eagerly. "Tomorrow we'll start doing things like real detectives—" she says softly.

the end

Here's how to keep in touch with me!

My website is nathaliemlromer.com with all the information you may need to know about my books, social media links and information about how to order my books.

I'm **@nathaliemlromer** on every social media resource.

Find my books in all stores across the world because I'm published with Draft2Digital, KDP, Ingram Book Group and many other places.

ABOUT THE AUTHOR

Nathalie M.L. Römer was born in the Netherlands, lived there during childhood before she moved to Curaçao as a teenager. From there, she then moved to Britain to live there for twenty-five years, before moving to Sweden where she now lives with her partner Anders.

In her childhood years and beyond, Nathalie has always loved to read novels. In her local library as a child, she would often borrow "adult audience" science fiction and fantasy novels, and as the bookworm, that she was (and still is), would read them all in a few days... and go back for more, often. The genres that interest Nathalie the most are science fiction, fantasy and historical novels. Her favourite authors include various science fiction, fantasy and historic authors that include (but are not limited to) Isaac Asimov, Richard A. Knaak, Jean M. Auel, and Christie Golden.

Besides reading novels, the other interests she pursues include needlework and crafts, archaeology, various science topics, home cooking, photography, web design, and playing MMO games.